THE INFINITE MILES

THE INFINITE MILES

HANNAH FERGESEN

Published in 2023 by Blackstone Publishing
Cover and book design by Luis Alejandro Cruz Castillo

Printed in the United States of America

First edition: 2023
ISBN 979-8-200-85008-2
Fiction / Science Fiction / Time Travel

Version 1

Blackstone Publishing
31 Mistletoe Rd.
Ashland, OR 97520

www.BlackstonePublishing.com

For Dad

I love you. I miss you.

Come back! Even as a shadow, even as a dream.

—Euripides, translated by Anne Carson

AUTHOR'S NOTE

Before you dive in to *The Infinite Miles*, there are two things I want you to know:

The first is that the world of this story is not our world. It's an alternate universe, a separate timeline. I've traded the classic Western TV show *Gunsmoke* for a series called *Gunpowder*, and while David Bowie sadly never made it to the stage in this alternate world, an androgynous rockstar named Miles Moonraker did. And though *Doctor Who* doesn't exist in this universe, what *does* exist is a beloved TV show about an alien named the Argonaut who traverses space-time in his Tesseract Engine, Argo.

My hope is that, in imagining an alternate version of our world, I have given you permission as an observer of an exotic dimension to imagine *other* differences too. To see yourself there, in spaces you perhaps have been denied entry to here. This world is your oyster, as much as it's Harper Starling's, or Miles's, or even mine. If you want to believe it, you are encouraged to do so, as emphatically as Peggy believes in the Argonaut, and as ardently as Harper believes in the stars.

Which brings me to the second thing I'd like you to know going in: Through characters like Miles, Harper, and even the Incarnate, this book celebrates people in all their imperfect forms. The ones making terrible choices, for both selfish and unselfish reasons. The ones seeking and exploring their truth, no matter how many times that truth might change throughout their lifetimes. The ones who give in to the darkness, and the ones who refuse to be subsumed.

If you have lost someone, or if you have lost yourself and returned from the brink, you will understand. And even if you haven't, I hope this message is still clear.

Hate is a parasite. Starve it out.

EPISODE ONE
THE BIG BANG

This week on Infinite Odyssey*:*

The Argonaut is in trouble as he makes for Sintoh, the Kixorians hot on his trail. He has something they want, and they'll stop at nothing to get their mechanized hands on it. The sanctuary planet is in sight—can he make it? Or will he be waylaid in the past, as Argo's time crystal seems to be on the fritz? Find out this week on Infinite Odyssey*!*

BEFORE

It happened on the glittering black sand beach of a distant, alien world. If you'd told Peggy a year ago that she was going to die so very far from home, light-years and light-years away, she would have said you were one crayon short of a full pack. She'd always assumed she could slip right back into her life whenever she was ready, that everything would be waiting for her, exactly as she'd left it. Her life, frozen in amber.

It was arrogant, when you think about it. Did she really think her friends had no lives of their own? That her family members were automatons who powered down whenever she left the house and rebooted when she graced them all with her presence again? But in a way, that's exactly what she thought.

Now here she was, basking in the light of a different sun innumerable miles from Earth, sunbathing in her two-piece on a lush world uncharted by anyone, human or alien alike, as though it were any old Tuesday at the local pool.

The dying didn't start right away, of course. She and Miles splashed around for hours in that virgin, ballerina-pink water, laughing with abandon. The water had a strange iron tang, and the air smelled like heated metal, but they could ignore that when everything else was so beautiful.

Their adventures were so often like this. She'd wake up to find him in her driveway, listening to old Miles Moonraker songs in the driver's seat of his 1972 Dodge Charger. She would climb in and tease him for the music—"Ego, much?"—and he would ask her where, or when, she wanted to go. The car, of course, was not a car—she was a spaceship, a time ship, and she could look like anything, but with Miles at the helm, she always looked like this. Her name was Argo. She could take them anywhere, anywhen, and she loved zipping across the universe just as much as they did. They were a team, the three of them. Bonded by their travels, their laughter. By days like this.

Peggy had watched *Infinite Odyssey* for years before she met Miles. She'd watched its main character, the Argonaut, zip around the universe with Argo, his Tesseract Engine, saving people, having adventures across time and space. When she met the real Argonaut herself at Rockwood Music Hall on a warm night in autumn, she'd understood right away just who she'd met. It was easy to say yes to the adventure that was offered; it was all she'd ever dreamed about.

Though on Earth Argo's preferred form was usually a vintage muscle car, today the ship had taken on the shape of a common planet hopper, artificial rust gathering around her faux nuts and bolts, just in case they were spotted, and though the tangled forest where the ship hid loomed behind her, Peggy could feel Argo's comforting presence just through the trees, like a mother watching her children splash around from her beach blanket. In the calm, rosy water, Miles floated on his back, pale face slathered in zinc sunscreen at Peggy's behest. Once, she might have said there was one thing that could sweeten this deal. But it had been a long time since she'd felt any guilt about not including Harper in her extracurricular time-and-space travel. This, this was paradise. Just the three of them on a far-off world.

She felt the change in Argo's energy even from the water, the distress that crashed over the ship's former calm. Then, Miles was trundling them both out of the water, trying to pull Peggy out faster than she could swim. She swallowed a gulp of water and tasted iron, and before she could gather her beach bag or towel, they were back inside Argo, zooming back to Earth.

Miles told her to call him if she started to feel strange after he dropped her off, but she didn't understand why he would say that, and he refused to elaborate. She spent the rest of the night furious with him, a foreign feeling, for hiding whatever had happened from her. They were supposed to be partners, a team. She knew Miles had lived a life, many lifetimes, that he'd lost people before Peggy came into the picture, but that didn't mean he had the right to pull away when something scared him.

She was so angry with him that when she did start to feel strange later that night—a dull ache blooming at the place where her spine met her skull—she didn't call him. She gritted her teeth and bore the pain out of pure spite. She got a text from Harper at ten o'clock, something trivial about InfiniCon being in Boston that year, and would Peggy want to go with her? Could they just talk about what happened, please?

And in that moment, blinking down at the harsh light of her phone screen, she forgot who Harper was. Harper Starling, who had, once upon a time, been her best friend, the girl with whom she'd done everything, anything, before Miles came into Peggy's life and everything changed. She read the name in her phone over and over, trying to conjure the memory, any memory at all, of Harper Starling. Of why she might love her.

It happened very quickly after that. Other memories blinked out of existence, small things at first, like her favorite color or candy bar, followed by bigger things—her days as number-one on the varsity track team, homecoming dances and childhood sleepovers and InfiniCons with Harper, matching their sequined dresses and hairstyles, telling each other scary stories from their sleeping bags, cosplaying together as the Argonaut and his various first mates. The way her father's avgolemono never tasted like her mother's, no matter hard he tried, probably because he was just too damn Irish. The day she met Miles, back when he wasn't Miles, but Flora, tall and beautiful and auburn-haired, and Peggy had been swept off her feet and into the stars.

In a flash, all of it was gone, and the world went dark for Peggy Mara.

She would have moments of awareness, after. Tiny insignificant moments she hoarded like precious gems in the starlit prison of her mind. She'd awake for seconds and find herself on a desolate moon or a bustling space station, wondering just how the hell she got there. Something else was in her body, driving it around, and she had no control at all. Then she was underwater again, lost in the tangle of the labyrinth that had been built in her own mind. She didn't remember what life was like before this. She didn't remember her own name. She didn't remember that she had once traveled across space and time with a man named Miles. She found refuge in the broken booth of a crumbling diner, the remnant of one memory that had burrowed deep enough to remain. And there she waited, praying that someone, anyone at all, might find her there.

I.

NEW YORK CITY
SUMMER, 2023

On the third anniversary of Peggy Mara's mysterious disappearance, Harper was watching old episodes of *Infinite Odyssey*. She lay in the tangled sheets of her small bed, the laptop perched on her chest, blue light flashing against the walls of the otherwise dark room. It was late, a few minutes past midnight, and she was winding down from a long, chaotic day waitressing at the Starlight Diner with discounted wine and an episode from one of the later seasons.

It was the one where the Argonaut's estranged wife, a human with whom he'd fallen in love despite a contentious introduction many years before, sacrificed herself to save the inhabitants of a planet on the verge of collapse. The loss of his partner would haunt him for the rest of the series, and when their son joined the Argonaut on his jaunt across the galaxies, sometimes the older alien would look into the boy's eyes and tell him, with such heaviness, that he saw his mother there.

Harper always cried with the Argonaut after his wife drew her final breaths. Even now, the episode not even halfway over, she felt the threat of tears just behind her eyes, though she'd argue it was for very different reasons now. Thank god her roommate was spending the night at the apartment of her current situationship.

Peggy had never made fun of Harper for her emotion. They'd watched it together a million times, the lines and actions of each character chiseled into their memories, recited with perfect execution around mouthfuls of popcorn. This was the episode she'd been watching three years ago, tangled in these same pilling sheets in this very same room, trying to soothe the fresh ache of a friendship ruined only days prior, when her cell phone rang. And like a spiteful asshole, she had looked at the name on the screen and decided not to answer.

When Harper had finally plucked up the courage to listen to the voicemail days later, long after she heard the news and got on a plane back to Denver for the memorial service, she was dismayed to find it was garbled and staticky, as if Peggy were trying to call from inside an elevator, and revealed nothing more about what happened that night than what Harper would later come to know.

These days she only watched the show once a year. She'd buy herself a bottle of something cheap and dry and red, acidic enough to chap her mouth after a few glasses, and pull the show up on whatever streaming service owned it that year. She would watch that episode once, twice, maybe even three times, every detail burned into her memory like the fine lines of a laser-cut image. The next morning her hangover would rage as she shuffled blearily onto the 1 train and shuttled herself to Riverdale for work, scrolling through the newest images from the James Webb Space Telescope until the train stuttered into the station.

It was an act of penitence more than anything—an invitation for the universe to rewrite history, if the universe were so inclined. They never had found a body, after all. Or perhaps it was a faith in something else, Harper's true religion—a kind of scientific method, an arranging of circumstances so that they resembled the original event, an experiment to see if she could replicate, and then change, what happened next.

But no one else had seen the text message Peggy sent Harper after their fight in the diner, the last one Harper would ever receive from her, mere months before her disappearance. She couldn't bear to show it to Greg Mara, who was content to believe his daughter had been in an innocent accident, kayaking or maybe rock climbing alone, something reckless but forgivable, as she was wont to do. But if anyone knew that Peggy was not coming back, that the universe would not be performing any miracles, that science would not be replicating the experiment of Peggy's last moments on Earth, it was Harper.

> I'm sorry that everything got so fucked up. And I'm saying it now because I'm blocking your number so there won't be another chance. Don't look for me, Harper. I'm never coming home.

The episode ended and she clicked the Start Over icon. While the opening credits rolled and the jaunty theme music warbled out of her shitty laptop speakers, she got up and poured herself another glass of wine in the cluttered kitchen. She stopped in the bedroom doorway upon returning, her instinct to go back to the bed, to nestle down into the covers and never come out, warring with a new thought, one she hadn't had in three years.

There was a box of Peggy's things stashed in the back of her tiny closet, taking up precious real estate in the only bit of storage space Harper possessed. Greg Mara mailed it once Harper was back in New York after the funeral, apparently assuming she would be excited to torture herself with the memories inside. Instead, she'd hidden it away, incapable of even looking at the words scrawled on the top in Greg's atrocious handwriting (*Peggy's Things for Harper*) without her heart kicking into a gallop. Apparently, opening the box was a matter of flight or fight, and she chose flight every time.

But not tonight. Tonight the wine was making her bold, bolder than she'd been in three years. Maybe grief was like that; maybe it changed and bent around the edges and transformed into something new when you weren't looking. What would year four look like, she wondered, and five and six? How long could this possibly go on?

She tossed her dusty shoes and fallen clothing out of the way and yanked the box from the hidden depths of the closet. She wiped at the thick layer of dust that had accumulated, but it seemed to like the old grooves of the cardboard, so she finally gave up and pulled at the packing tape that sealed the box shut. She gulped a healthy swish of wine and opened the box.

It wasn't as full as she'd expected it to be, but it was full enough. Peggy's father had gathered every photo the pair of them had ever taken and bothered to print—Peggy was a lover of disposable cameras—and now both young faces grinned up at Harper from the dark depths of the box. Grainy photos of the pair of them sweaty and sunburned at summer camp, Harper's curls rising in the heat, while Peggy's dark waterfall remained long and smooth; or speeding across the roller rink, light glinting off of their braces; or posing together at homecoming in their ill-fitting dresses and overly styled hair. There were photos Harper had taken of Peggy racing across the track during track meets, pulling easily ahead of her competition. Pictures of Peggy pointing with pride at Harper's first-place science fair projects while Harper blushed off to the side.

Aside from the piles of photos, he had also sent Harper every piece of *Infinite Odyssey* and InfiniCon merch Peggy ever spent money on: two T-shirts, one with an illustration of Argo and a starry sky with the words *The Chariot* underneath, the other a more generic photo of the Argonaut in his trench coat from the pilot; a red bandanna like the one the Argonaut wore for at least two seasons to hide his third eye; a scarf akin to the one he'd worn during his more collegiate phase; and a handful of knickknacks that would never be worth a dime—key chains, figurines, cheap little toys that could have come out of any old Happy Meal.

The last thing Harper pulled out of the box was the one thing that didn't seem to belong, and she wondered if Greg had dropped it in by accident. It was a cheap little harmonica, the kind you might pick up for ten tickets at the arcade, its grill somewhat dented, the metal face tarnished and smudgy black. Harper almost tossed it aside, when something caught her eye: Peggy's name carved into the tin plate screwed to the face of the instrument. She'd probably used the little penknife she used to keep in a pencil cup on her desk. She'd always been fidgety, carving her name into chairs and trees and bathroom walls just to have something to do with her hands.

It wasn't like Harper had memorized the inventory of Peggy's childhood bedroom. But the sight of this busted little instrument awoke something bitter in her, as though this toy represented another secret, another piece of Peggy she'd hidden from Harper, one of the many she'd locked away and refused to share toward the end.

She put the grubby grill to her lips and blew, expecting that classic harmonica sound to interrupt the adventurous orchestral movement happening a few feet away on Harper's laptop, signaling that the Argonaut and his wife had just tripped the alarm and were running for their lives. But instead, a sad deflating-balloon sound emitted from the instrument, just ridiculous enough that she laughed out loud, tension uncurling just a little. The bitterness ebbed. What was the point, after all, in harboring so many unresolved emotions toward Peggy? They'd grown apart, yes. And they'd fought, true. But whatever happened to Peggy, Harper knew that blaming herself was an exercise in futility. It was what her therapist had been trying to get her to understand for years.

And so Harper reached the moment in her annual ritual when the wine conspired with sleep and lulled her into a state of fraught dreaming, right there on the floor next to the box, which she'd apparently tipped over, Peggy's things flowering out of it like a cornucopia. She gripped the harmonica tight as she crashed into sleep, a strange kind of security blanket.

She dreamed about Peggy, surprise, surprise.

The last time Harper saw Peggy Mara, Harper had just finished her final exam for the semester, her first grueling year at Columbia now done. She'd forgone most of the parties and campus events in favor of top-loading her schedule with required courses, studying hard, and acing every class. Why did she need to make fleeting friendships with tipsy college freshmen or put herself in the path of strange young men insisting she drink from their red plastic cups? Why did she need to join the a cappella club or the Bird Watcher's Union? She had her coursework, and she had Peggy.

By winter, though, it seemed her relationship with Peggy was the one that was fleeting. Peggy, who had agreed to go to school in New York so she and Harper could stay close. Peggy, who had always made sure their friendship endured, even when it seemed like their interests might pull them in different directions. Best friends since they could make baby chatter at one another, they had something very important in common: their love of the stars. Harper might have been the only one pursuing them physically, but Peggy adored them with an ardor that matched Harper's in different ways. It was why they both loved *Infinite Odyssey* so deeply, why they watched every episode on repeat, so obsessed with the Argonaut and his space-and-time-traveling ship, Argo, that they could spend hours playacting the titular character and any of his myriad first mates.

Harper didn't understand it. From what she could gather—and this was, admittedly, dependent on Peggy's own accounting, which was sparse and vague at best—Peggy had not made friends at City College, which was unusual for someone who seemed to make friends everywhere she went. And yet, two months into the semester, her phone was out of service constantly, text messages were left unread or ignored, calls were left to ring and ring, and her voicemail was disabled. If she wasn't partying with new friends, then where the hell was she?

It came to a head that night. The year was over, their dorm rooms forfeit, their tickets back to Denver for the summer booked. While Harper had loved her first year at school, she was looking forward to being home with Peggy for a little while, a chance for a reset. They needed to sort out what was breaking in their friendship and patch it before it was too late. Harper took for granted that Peggy wanted this too.

She learned something very different when they met at the diner. Peggy had been missing classes. Peggy had been gallivanting around the city with some guy named Paul French. Peggy was not going back to Denver, and she wasn't going back to school. She—

But Harper had become skilled at avoiding the subject of that particular night. It was too painful to relive, which she did many times after Peggy went missing, racking her brain for hints that she should have seen it coming, clues that Peggy might have dropped, one final test.

No, she preferred to remember herself and Peggy as they were before, when they first arrived in New York and spent the week before orientation sightseeing and eating their way through the city. On their last day before their respective schools filled up with students, Peggy surprised Harper with a sojourn north, even farther north than Harlem, where Harper now lived in a dorm she would share with a girl who had not yet arrived. It was another forty-five minutes on the train, of which they were quickly becoming expert navigators, and by the time they emerged from the subway station, blinking like newborns into the sun, Harper, utterly lost, had abandoned all guesses as to what Peggy planned to show her. Her heart swelled when they arrived at their destination, and she understood.

They stood in front of an unassuming diner in the middle of Riverdale, a wealthy Bronx exurb, its neon pink sign naming it the Starlight. It had served as a recurring set for an Earth-based diner for three seasons on *Infinite Odyssey* before the Kixorians destroyed it while chasing the Argonaut and that year's first mate, Lucinda Freely. The Starlight had been in business at least two decades before its cameo, but it was already perfect for the show. Cherry-red booths, a jukebox playing the latest hits through brassy speakers, and menus covered in '70s-style shooting stars and flying saucers set the perfect backdrop for the Argonaut and his first mate as they made their weekly plan of exploration. Harper and Peggy did the same, mapping out the rest of their quest while they ate pancakes and fries and greasy hamburgers, full and happy, before hopping the train a few stops south to the Cloisters, where they spent the rest of their day, daydreaming and wandering.

"I knew you'd like it," Peggy had said as they parted ways that night.

"Best pancakes ever," Harper said, and given the context, it was entirely true.

This is what Harper liked to dream about, if she could help it. The two of them in that red booth, sharing a milkshake in a new city, laughing with their whole bodies at some nonsense joke only they would ever know.

When she woke up, she was cramped into the fetal position on the hard, dirty floor. The apartment was dark; her show had ended, no ecstatic music permeating the silence. A siren outside shocked her fully awake, but it was just a fire truck barreling down the avenue.

She knew she was still alone in the apartment because there would be a perpetual drumbeat emanating from Emily's room if she had returned. A new text from her roommate stating that she had no plans to come home tonight and that Harper shouldn't wait up confirmed it.

But . . . she didn't feel alone.

She stood up, stretched her stiff limbs, and though she couldn't have explained why just then, she put the harmonica in her pocket. She was grabbing socks from the dresser when she heard it, so quiet she might have missed it had she not already been on alert: the gentle click of the front-door dead bolt retreating into the century-old lock.

2.

NEW YORK
SUMMER, 2023

“Emily?” Harper’s voice trembled. “That you?”

There was no answer.

Then: *Whump. Smash. Crash.*

She should have turned back around and retrieved her phone from the floor. She should have called the police. But something cracked open like an egg inside her, and the underdeveloped wing of a feeling that had long been dormant nudged its way out. She imagined Peggy on the other side of the door, finally coming back to Harper, finally coming home. It was ridiculous. Just a silly, stupid hope, a far-flung dream.

Harper tiptoed down the dark hall toward the living room. From here, she could hear the frantic jostle of the lock as someone attempted to open the door. She didn’t call her roommate’s name again because Emily never struggled with the lock. It was Harper who was always misplacing her keys or forgetting which direction to turn the bolt. Whoever fiddled with her front door now clearly did not have the legal means of opening it.

She was still in the hall, shaded by the darkness there, when the door swung triumphantly open and the intruder entered the apartment.

Harper held her breath, caught between running back to her room for her phone and staying perfectly still in the hope that she might remain unseen.

But then, the intruder stepped into the hazy nighttime New York light that filtered in through the living room windows, and Harper forgot all about her indecisive fear. Neurons misfired. Promising mental calculations condensed and fell apart. Harper stared, slack-jawed, all survival instinct obliterated. She knew that posture, that gait. If not for those, she never would have recognized the girl before her.

"My god." Adrenaline turned her words to mush. "Peggy?"

Better it had been a stranger. Better it had been someone trying to rob her, to steal all of her meager worldly possessions, because this Peggy was not her Peggy at all. Her friend's eyes were a shiny beetle-shell black, a strange oil-slick iridescence swirling on the surface when they caught the light. Her long, straight hair had been shorn away, and what remained could barely be called peach fuzz. Her once smooth, tanned skin bore myriad new scars, shiny pink rivulets that told the story of a fighter, not varsity track star Peggy Mara. Stranger still, she wore a sleek, high-tech outfit one might observe on an agent in an outlandish spy movie.

Peggy took a step forward. "You recognize this face," she said. Harper nodded, unable to speak. "It recognizes you."

She found her voice. "What the hell happened to you?"

"It is beyond your comprehension."

"Beyond . . . Peggy, I'm your best friend. I know . . . I know we fought, but leaving like that? We all thought you were dead!"

"Tell us where the instrument is. We know you have it."

It was Peggy, and Peggy's voice, and yet it sounded nothing like her. She used her voice differently, emphasized words differently, structured sentences differently. Years of linguistic patterns and habits, gone. It was like talking to a version of Peggy made by someone who knew nothing about her. This was not the friend Harper had lost. Wherever she'd gone three years earlier, she'd left herself there. It was her shell walking around this apartment. Her shell talking to Harper now.

Harper wanted to be unafraid, like that blissful moment seconds before, but a new terror clawed its way into her nervous system, and it was dazzling. She had never felt anything like it.

"I don't play an instrument," she whispered. "You know I don't."

Peggy took a step forward. Her eyes were two dark marbles in her eye sockets. "Tell us where to find it or we will mine it from your dreams. Though truthfully," she said with a small smile, "we will mine them anyway."

"Peggy, talk to me. Tell me what happened. We'll get you help, we'll—"

Peggy was across the room in a flash, and Harper was on the floor, cheek stinging and red, before she could even process that Peggy had backhanded her.

"That is not our name," Peggy said.

Harper couldn't help it. She started crying. "Do you . . . do you really remember nothing?" Did you really forget me?

What kind of drug could do that?

Not-Peggy frowned. "Remember?"

"You went missing. For three years. They looked for you everywhere. Everyone thought you'd gotten yourself into an accident but I . . . I knew you left. I knew you left and that maybe you'd hurt yourself. And I'm sorry for the things I said. I didn't think . . . but you were just gone. Nowhere."

"I am nowhere," Peggy said thoughtfully, tasting the words. "That is accurate."

And there it was: a spark. *I am nowhere.* A line from the pilot of *Infinite Odyssey*, dialogue embedded in Harper's memory like the lines in her palms. They had recited that line back and forth for years and years, at first in recognition that they'd found a show they both loved, then as an inside joke, and finally, when it had burrowed so deep into their psyches there was no undoing it, as a way of saying things unsaid. Confessions, heartbreak, deepest wishes of the soul.

Where are you right now?

I am nowhere.

But when this Peggy said it, the words felt cold and wrong and empty.

Despair settled in. "Why are you doing this?" she asked, exhausted.

"Peggy is no longer here. She is part of something bigger than herself. We are older than you can imagine. We are everywhere. We heard the call and knew what it meant. It will be better for you if you comply."

"What call?" Harper asked.

"This is becoming tiresome. We will take the information if you do not give it willingly." Peggy leaned over her, hand outstretched, something tarry black and glittering beneath her fingernails.

"Wait!" Harper shrieked, leaning away from Peggy's hand. "If you'd just tell me what it looks like, I could help you look for it, you know?"

Peggy cocked her head, as if listening for a frequency Harper couldn't hear. "You would call it a harmonica. It is long and rectangular. Sound emits from the long, narrow side."

Harper's next words stuck in her throat. For the first time, she noticed the sharp pain of the harmonica's edge digging into her pelvis, gouging a hole through the thin fabric of her pocket to the skin.

She could give Peggy the instrument and end this whole bizarre charade right now if she wanted to. But if she did that, she would never know just what was so special about a crappy harmonica that one note blown into its rusted grill could bring someone back from the dead. She would never get answers about where Peggy had been for three years while everyone mourned and grieved her, convinced she was never coming back. She would never be able to help bring her friend back from whatever ledge this was, whether it was drug-fueled delusion or some kind of psychotic break. She knew that the moment she gave Not-Peggy the harmonica, what was left of her friend would walk out the front door and disappear for real. For good.

"Hmm," she said. "I'm not sure I can picture it. What's so special about it?"

"It calls a man," Peggy replied.

Harper almost laughed at the ridiculousness of it. "A man?"

"It sends a signal across the stars and beckons him."

Now *that* was strange. It reminded her of something else from *Infinite Odyssey*, a special whistle the Argonaut crafted for his first mates so they might be able to call to him wherever he was in the universe. If Peggy *was* delusional, maybe she had invented a new reality for herself, one where the Argonaut existed.

Peggy knelt and leaned in close. Harper, still on the floor in the hallway, had nowhere to go. From this closeness, she could detect the tang of ash and something metallic on Peggy's ruined skin. Her friend didn't smell at all like the unisex cologne she used to favor, woodsy and sharp.

"Enough questions."

She raised an arm and Harper flinched, expecting a blow, but Peggy rested her palm against the back of Harper's neck, her touch gentle and scalding. Now that she was so close, Harper could see the feverish perspiration beading at her hairline, her nose, and her chin. She was pale, eyes ringed in sickly dark circles. Harper was sent back in time, back into remembering, when Peggy was healthy and whole, and the two of them would sit in their red vinyl booth at the Starlight Diner and eat their weight in fluffy pancakes, and Harper would steal as many glances as she could when she thought Peggy wasn't watching.

Something sharp pricked her, ripping her from her reverie, then gouged into the skin on the back of her neck. Peggy's nails, working through layers of skin toward vulnerable muscle. The pain stole the breath right out of Harper's lungs. A scream lodged in her throat, unable to escape.

And then, the room stuttered. Like a corrupted video, the darkness around her spasmed and warped. Images began to blink in and out of existence around her as if on a projector screen, replacing her view of the room for brief bursts, then disappearing again. Peggy as herself, laughing. The bedroom again. A young man with auburn hair at her side. Not-Peggy's eyes on hers. A classic muscle car inexplicably drifting through the cosmic glitter of the Milky Way. But that . . . that was impossible. The dark room, spinning. A harmonica passed from his hands to Peggy's. But he was just a character, just someone made up by a TV writer named Anthony Detweiler in the '70s. A significant look between the two of them. No, no, no. The images stuttered, and Harper slumped against the wall as Not-Peggy's nails ripped from her skin. The room was still turning nauseously. There were black specks at the edge of her vision, the promise of a migraine.

"What," she gasped, willing herself not to vomit, "the fuck was that?"

"That was transference."

"That was . . . How did you do . . . And that man . . . But it can't be . . ."

"He uses many names," Peggy said. "According to the memories stored in this body, you will likely know him as 'the Argonaut.'"

Impossible. All of it. Not-Peggy, the harmonica, the man, the psychedelic visions. It was a dream. A fucked-up, clock-melting, world-dissolving, bad-trip kind of dream. Peggy must have dosed her with something, a hallucinogen delivered straight into a vein in the back of her neck—probably the same shit that had hollowed Peggy out. Panic gripped her lungs tight; her breath came in shorter and shorter bursts.

"Peggy, the Argonaut—he's not coming." She forced herself to her feet despite the tremor in her legs. "You've been drugged or something, brainwashed somehow. And what you did to me was . . . a trick. An illusion." She licked her lips. Maybe there was hope, a way to reach Peggy's subconscious, to spark the dry fuse of her memory. "But your name is Peggy Mara. You're from Denver. You love cherry pie, and Hanson is your guilty pleasure, and you were going to be a famous runner, and we used to watch *Infinite Odyssey* together, and we always said one day we'd get to the stars, just like the Argonaut. But he was just a character, Peggy; he was just make-believe. I'm real," she managed to scrape out, "and I know you're in there somewhere, I know it—"

Without warning, Peggy released Harper from her viselike grip and stumbled backward. Anguish exploded across Peggy's face, just for a moment. Recognition, maybe, or something unimaginably sad. When she looked at Harper again, her eyes were glassy and bright. Pearlescent black ooze dribbled from Peggy's nose.

"I . . . I can't . . . Please . . . don't . . ."

And then she slapped her hands to her head, assaulted by a spike of neural pain, and screamed.

For a moment, Harper didn't move. Maybe Peggy was having a breakthrough, her real self swimming out of the hallucinatory haze. Then Peggy looked up, and her dark eyes flashed with anger.

Harper sprinted through the front door and ran for her miserable life.

Adrenaline rocketed her through the shadowed hall and down the emergency stairs two steps at a time. She abandoned all thought for pure, unadulterated flight mode, and it sent her careening around the banister at the bottom of the stairs, across the slick hardwood, past the communal mailboxes, and through the heavy security door. Humid summer air enveloped her as soon as she was through.

A black car idled on the street across from her building—the orange headlights cut a strange path through the sweltering night. It looked like an old Dodge from where Harper stood, its exterior incredibly well-maintained for a car from another time. The man inside, illuminated by his own overhead lights inside the car, was headbanging to a song she couldn't hear.

The concrete was uncomfortably hot beneath her feet, but she barely noticed as she crossed the sidewalk. She knocked on the window of the car, startling the man inside. His hair was shot through with gray, and he possessed a face that might have been handsome once, but he'd had too many hard nights, perhaps even a few close calls—the scar through his eyebrow told a story she didn't want to know.

He looked around, bewildered, as if he had not realized he was parked on a residential street in Harlem, blasting music which could not, oddly, be heard from the exterior of the car; it was only once he rolled the window down that Miles Moonraker's tinny voice spilled out, crooning about being lost in the stars. "Galaxy Man," 1978. Harper knew it well because she and Peggy had both unironically loved Miles Moonraker, even though kids at school thought it was "old-people music." The speakers weren't bad, but they didn't do the song justice.

As if the car had heard her thoughts, the music brightened, expanded. Before, it sounded tinny; now, the melody was clear as a bell.

"Excuse me," Harper said breathlessly. "Please—you need to call the police. I left my phone inside the building, and someone in there—she wants to kill me."

Instead of pulling out his phone to call the police as most Good Samaritans would have done, the man's expression darkened. He said,

"I don't help anymore." Then he turned the ignition, the car roaring to life, and he sped away, driving entirely too fast down the street, nearly hitting a cab as he careened away in the direction of downtown and disappeared.

3.

NEW YORK
SUMMER, 2023

Harper teetered on the edge of the sidewalk and stared into the darkness he'd left behind, feeling suddenly that this might be the end of her short life. Her heartbeat calmed. Maybe that was all right. She couldn't have explained why, except that nothing had felt entirely correct in her life since Peggy's disappearance. Everything she'd done and felt and thought swirled around the edge of the drain, making laps but never quite reaching that deep, lightless place. Quitting university, getting a thankless job at the Starlight, performing her annual ritual with *Infinite Odyssey* and alcohol. Better to go through the motions and pretend everything was fine. Not great and not terrible. Squarely in the middle, where the grief couldn't reach.

Peggy Mara, superspy, was pushing through the security door when Harper finally turned back to face the building. Peggy took her sweet time, like those big cats Harper had often watched on the Discovery Channel while stoned, the ones that made a game out of hunting down vulnerable prey.

"You should not have attempted to run," Peggy said. "But I knew you would." She spoke softly, but her voice carried in the night.

There were so many things Harper wanted to say she now never would. Entire conversations the friends would never have. *I'm angry with you for leaving. For growing distant. For fighting with me. For letting me chase you away. I'm angry with myself too. For not noticing what was going on. For not answering my phone that night. For not looking harder when I got your text. For not saving you.*

"I know," Harper said. "It was dumb. You're still wicked fast."

"I am not mad," Peggy replied. "Only determined."

"But there's no Argonaut, Peggy. He doesn't exist. He never did. And you . . . you're clearly sick."

The black sludge had dribbled from Peggy's nose down her neck, untended. Smeared across her face.

Then: Harper heard the roar of an old engine. Felt a rush of air as the muscle car pulled up behind her, the steady putter of its motor a lifeline in the frigid night. The man was back; perhaps his conscience had gotten the better of him and he'd decided to help her after all, and now here he was, like an idiot. He should have stayed gone; now Peggy would kill him too.

There was sudden pressure on Harper's brain, like an incoming headache. A thought came to her unbidden.

Back up to the car. Do not break eye contact. Go now.

The thought both felt as though it belonged to her and didn't belong to her, but there was no time to question it. Harper started to back away from Peggy.

"He has come. He heard the call, just as we did. And to think," Peggy said with a growing grin, "we nearly believed you."

Harper backed away slowly, bare feet scraping against the rough concrete. She felt something like a breath on her neck, the whisper of a presence, but she dared not turn. She bumped up against the car.

Peggy's expression hardened. She slowed, as if she could sense that something had changed, something was different. The car behind Harper, the lifeline. Perhaps more dangerous than she knew.

Go to the car, Harper Starling.

She knew, somehow, that getting into this stranger's car, which arguably should have been just as dangerous as staying put, was going to make the difference between her life and her death.

"I love you, you know," Harper said. It wasn't even obvious if Peggy heard it. She was impassive, still as a mountain. "And whoever did this to you, I'll make sure they pay for it."

Get in the car, Harper Starling. NOW.

The passenger door swung open, and Harper scrambled around the front of the car and dove inside, slamming the door shut just as Peggy launched into motion, her hand on the door almost as soon as Harper had closed it—and was thrown high and back, as if yanked by some invisible rope. She rolled across the road and was still.

Harper screamed and made to open the door.

"If you want to live you will stay where you are."

She turned to the stranger in the driver's seat, incredulous. He spoke in an accent she couldn't place. She guessed it was Scandinavian, or maybe a gentle Irish brogue, for all Harper knew about the Irish. And brogues.

"That's my friend," Harper told him, "and she's hurt."

"Yes, because she tried to get into my car without an invitation. Don't worry, she's not dead—just stunned."

And as Harper watched, Peggy twitched back into consciousness, pushed herself to all fours, and then unsteadily to her full height. A cab honked and swerved around her, but she paid it no mind. Even through the glass, Harper could hear her voice, breathless from the impact.

"We will never stop coming," Peggy said. "There is no distance you can run that we will not gain. No planet remote enough that we will not someday find."

"Oh, here we go," the man muttered.

"We are too vast to be escaped, too intent on our mission."

"Blah, blah, blah," he said with an eye roll. "Fucking chatty is what you are."

"Shut up!" Harper hissed. She knew it was dangerous, telling a strange man to shut up in his own car, but she couldn't help it. He was goading someone who clearly wanted him dead.

Peggy had not heard him. "We will get what we want, even if we must pry it from his rigid corpse."

"Colorful," the man said. Harper resisted the urge to shush him again. She'd only known him two minutes and was ready to kill him.

"And if you are with him, Harper Starling, your fate will be the same. See you soon."

As if the whole event was not enough to make Harper feel certifiably insane, Peggy's whole body shimmered for a moment, pearlescent light engulfing her, and then she was gone.

Harper blinked and then blinked again. That was all it was—a blink. A trick of the adrenaline, of the heat, of the night. It had to be that. There was no other explanation.

She stared at the space where Peggy used to be, nearly forgetting about the man in the car with her. She jumped in surprise when she turned and found him watching her.

"She's gone," he said grimly. "Probably back to the Adama system to regroup. Now she's seen me, she'll be back. I have to go." He rolled his eyes and glared at the console. "I'm telling her!" He turned back to Harper. "Don't mind Argo. She's a fucking nag sometimes. But she's right, much as I hate to admit it. You can't stay here. They'll be back, and when they come, you won't survive it this time. And I won't be here to save your ass."

"Save my ass? You're kidding me, right? You drove away! You didn't even get out of the car! What, exactly, did you save—"

Harper's jaw snapped shut. Because she hadn't noticed it at first, the name he said. But now that his words had penetrated her traumatized mind, she heard it. Argo.

The name of the ship on *Infinite Odyssey*. The ship the Argonaut was named for.

It was too much. When Harper Starling finally realized what was going on, when she finally understood that she had seen her best friend's body dematerialize, that whatever had happened to her in the apartment was not simply a drug-induced nightmare, and that she was sitting in an honest-to-god spaceship disguised as a muscle car next to its honest-to-god space-and-time-traveling pilot, she did the only sensible thing she'd done all day: she lost consciousness.

———

For the first time in three years, Harper Starling dreams. If you can call it dreaming. Really, it's more like a slideshow, images clicking into place like the scenes in Not-Peggy's psychedelic mind movie, one after another, some too distorted or scarred to see properly. Sometimes it's Peggy, surrounded by impossible landscapes—violet trees, emerald oceans, ice as far as the eye can see, deserts coated in volcanic basalt and glittering pyrite, the way Harper has always imagined Venus must look, coated in a layer of gently falling galena snow. Impossible, impossible. But easier to grasp than the rest—images of people she has never met, of the Argonaut's trademark muscle car capable of traveling through time and space, of whole planets coated in something oozing and oil-slick iridescent, dying beneath the choke of that strange, exotic substance.

And in between each slide, the front seat of the strange man's car. His faraway voice nattering on to someone, maybe even her. Fingertips against the back of her inflamed neck. Something cool against the wound there, leeching heat and inflammation from the site where Peggy's nails punctured her skin. More slides. More worlds. More dreams.

———

There was a breeze. A steady stream of air cooling her dream-flushed cheeks. The breeze, coupled with the hypnotic rush of air in her ears, stirred her awake. Reminded her of being half-asleep in Peggy's passenger seat, wrapped in a blanket while the cool air of spring circulated through the car, the two of them driving and driving into the dark of the quiet mountains, unsure where they were going or when they might return.

Harper opened her eyes, expecting, for a moment, to be back in that old Jeep, Peggy at her side, hands fiddling with the CD player. Her memory was jumbled, her mind still clawing out of a dense fog. But she was not seventeen; not anymore. She was a college dropout with a double shift starting at the diner in three hours. Peggy was dead. Gone.

No. She was something else.

Harper gasped as memory well and truly woke her.

She sat, awkwardly slumped, in the sunken leather passenger seat of an old muscle car, the windows down even though the car was going ninety along some empty highway. Her ears rang, a strange, high frequency piercing through the last remnants of unconsciousness. The sky was just beginning to purple with new light over a flat, scraggly desert reaching to the horizon; they had clearly been driving all night, the Harlem streets long behind them.

"You okay?" the driver asked. "That scratch was quite nasty."

She wasn't ready to look at him just yet, to face where she was, so she mumbled a small, disoriented, "Yes." Panic seemed to be the next logical course of action, but Harper found that she was actually quite calm. That same feeling she'd had before on the sidewalk, with Peggy—of something pressing on her brain—was there. *You're safe,* she knew, deep in her soul.

She mentally cataloged everything that had happened the night before. Peggy in her apartment. The harmonica, which seemed to no longer be in her possession. Had she dropped it back at the apartment? The car, which resembled the vintage muscle car her favorite character drove in her favorite TV show. The driver, who looked like he could use a good night's sleep and a warm meal. The dreams, which ricocheted around her mind even now. Here, wherever here was.

"Mojave Desert," the driver replied, as if reading her mind. "Figured it was far enough that we could relax, but not so far we might ripple causality."

"Desert," she muttered. "Causality." Sure. That made perfect sense.

Finally, she looked to her left. Pain shot through her neck as she turned it, protesting the movement. Yep, same man as before. Wiry thin, a little haggard, a bruising sleeplessness betraying his relatively young age. Thirty-five, maybe. Forty, more likely. He was wearing a Miles Moonraker T-shirt she hadn't noticed before. It was tattered and thin, worn to destruction.

Kidnapper, she had time to think, before the pressing calm took over again. It felt artificial, not hers, as if someone else were reaching into her mind and soothing her from the outside in. Like Argo used to do on *Infinite Odyssey*. In the show, the ship itself was telepathic. She intuited the needs of her passengers and often helped in other regards as well. In the show, Argo had always been a boundary pusher. Was it possible . . . ?

The car shivered, sending a strange vibration through her body. The man looked over.

"What were you thinking just now?"

"None of your business."

"Well, whatever it was, Argo liked it." Harper stared. The man rolled his eyes. "Come on, don't let's act like you think last night was a hallucination and you have no idea who I am. I know you watch that ridiculous TV show. We're way past that."

"Are we?" Her voice sounded high, tight. And just like that, any residual grogginess, the artificial calm, was zapped away by a kick of adrenaline to her system and the flood of questions for which she had no answers. The high frequency pulsed in her ears. "Are we, really? Because I'm in the car of a strange man, having just seen my best friend for the first time in three years, and she's been MKUltra'd or something, thank you very much, and I have no idea where you're taking me, or what your name is, or what you plan to do with me—"

"Don't be ridiculous. I saved your life. She tried to infect you, by the way, but we got it all out, you're welcome—"

"—or where she went, or what she did to me, or what that stuff coming out of her nose was, or if my parents are safe, or if they think I'm dead, or if this car is really a spaceship, or if I'm crazy for even entertaining the possibility, or what's going to happen, or . . . or . . ."

"Breathe."

"Do not tell me to breathe!" She breathed. "How the hell do you expect me to breathe at a time like this?"

"God, it's a lot of questions, isn't it?" He pinched between his eyes. "First, I didn't even want to take you with me. I'm done helping, I've said so many times."

"So then why did you?"

"Because Argo's a pushy little shit and maintains a much more holier-than-thou attitude than I do."

The car vibrated, more aggressively this time.

Harper, very near the end of her rope, turned away from the man and watched the desert roll by. It was easier to do than attempt to parse what was happening. She tried very hard not to scream.

"What now?" she asked the window. A tumbleweed rolled through the scrubby desert.

"Now, I take you somewhere safe."

"Home?"

"I said *safe*, do you listen?"

"Then where? With you?" Her heart skipped a beat. If this man was . . . who her heart seemed to want to think he was, did that mean they were going to . . . going to . . . travel time and space?

No. The thought was so ridiculous she almost burst out laughing.

"Of course not," he said. "It'll be safer for both of us if we find somewhere to put you until this is all over."

"Find somewhere to put me. Like I'm a piece of furniture or something."

"Listen," the man said, exasperation edging in. "I know it's a lot. Most people aren't cut out for this."

"Cut out for what?"

He huffed. "You're really going to make me say it, aren't you?"

"Yes."

"Can you believe I used to love this part?" He sighed. "Most people, Harper, aren't cut out for time-and-space travel."

He said it. He really said it.

She shook her head. This was— "Impossible."

"You asked."

"But it's *impossible*. This is a fucking car. You would have to have a vessel that could (a) get you out of Earth's orbit and then (b) reach speeds so insane that you travel *faster* than light, which simply can't be done. Not to mention that the sophisticated engines and the fuel required are nowhere near—"

"All of that is true if you're a human trying to build a time machine in the year 2023. But that's not what I am, and you know it. Frankly, your willful disbelief is tiring and I'm far too sober for this."

"Or you're a kidnapping maniac and you're trying to trick me into thinking something impossible so you can, I don't know, make me trust you."

If she were as smart as she once prided herself on being, she would have shut her mouth. Screaming at someone who might be her kidnapper would likely just find her digging her own shallow grave in this very desert. But she felt oddly outside of herself, outside of everything, and felt no remorse for her tone, no need to pay attention to that small inner voice telling her to shut the hell up if she wanted to live.

"And Peggy?" the man asked. Had she told him her friend's name? The last hour was a blur of fear and hallucinations. "How do you explain that?"

Harper turned toward the dashboard and the long, endless highway, crossing her arms as if to quell the rapid beating of her heart. "Drugs. Or mind control."

"I see. And the teleporting?"

"A hallucination. Thanks to whatever she injected me with." She felt the back of her neck instinctively, but a bandage had been taped over the wound.

"What she injected . . . ? Good god, you're a nightmare. Most people love finding out this shit is real, but you?"

Harper turned to face him again. "I can't just take the word of a creepy stranger!"

"Creepy? Excuse you."

"I— I need proof. Evidence."

"Proof? Is this not proof enough?" He gestured at the endless beige desert.

She crossed her arms. "This can't be Argo. In the show, Argo was purple."

His responding laugh was not kind. "Purple! Good lord. All right. I'll give you proof. Though you're going to want your seat belt."

He pushed a button on the dashboard. For a moment, nothing happened. Then, a strange kind of centrifugal force started to build, her body growing heavier and heavier, her breath crushed out of her lungs until it felt like she was on that popular county fair ride, the Gravitron, pinned to the wall of the ride as it spun so fast its occupants were rendered completely immobile. A high-pitched frequency built deep in her ears and became almost unbearably loud, and her head felt pinched, as though trapped in a barbaric vise, the pressure of which caused black spots to pop like fireworks in her vision.

And then, the world blinked out. No thrust, no rockets, no dramatic liftoff. It was only a moment, a blip in time, a hot second of pitch-black before gravity released her and she slumped in her seat, gasping for breath.

She looked out the window, shocked and somehow not shocked to see that the entire landscape outside the vintage car had changed. Gone was the desert, the thirsty shrubs and parched, cracking earth. Gone was the purple smear of the rising desert sun. Now, the car was driving through residential streets lined with teetering old row houses and the leafless trees of early winter, the desert sunrise that had blinded her moments before now the crisp orange of a late-afternoon sun. It was nothing like the bone-dry landscape of the Mojave; rather, it was a place Harper knew like the back of her hand.

"Holy shit," she breathed, "you brought me back to fucking Riverdale."

EPISODE TWO
CLOSED TIME-LIKE CURVES

This week on Infinite Odyssey:

First Mate Maxfield Crawford is lost in time, with no sight of the Argonaut! Little does he know that Argo's captain has been captured by a Kixorian cult on planet Roz, and if he doesn't find a way home, the Argonaut may not make it out alive!

4.

RIVERDALE
FALL, YEAR UNKNOWN

She was a little disappointed, actually, that it wasn't Europa or something. What would have been more convincing than the icy surface of a moon four hundred and eighty-five million miles from the sun? But even though it wasn't as magical or even as miraculous as Jupiter's moon might have been, as they drove through the affluent suburb of Riverdale, snow pelting the dashboard, Harper was grudgingly convinced. The Mojave to Riverdale in three seconds flat was just as impossible as a quick jaunt to the limits of the solar system. There was no getting around it: she was seated next to the honest-to-god Argonaut in his honest-to-god ship, Argo, and they were running from Peggy Mara, who had been honest-to-god memory wiped, just like First Mate Alyra in episode three, season two.

And for his last trick, the Argonaut pulled up in front of the Starlight Diner.

"I'm starving," he said. "I could use a burger."

As a matter of fact, she was hungry, her stomach trying desperately to get her attention with progressively louder rumbles. And ordering a familiar meal at a restaurant she knew well seemed easier than sorting out just what the fuck was going on. But how had he known about her connection to the Starlight? Or was this simply a coincidence, the presence of a diner in and of itself the lure for someone who was craving some warm food and crappy coffee on a cold afternoon?

"I don't even know what to call you," she said, staring at the hot-pink neon Starlight sign above them. "The Argonaut?"

"Absolutely *not.* That stupid show gets just enough right to be irritating, and enough wrong to be extremely irritating."

"So, the guy who created the show, Anthony Detweiler . . . he traveled with you?"

"He absolutely did not. I don't know who squealed to him, but I should obviously be having people sign some kind of nondisclosure when they're with me." He unbuckled his seat belt. "You can call me Miles."

Harper glanced at his tattered shirt. "Like Miles Moonraker?"

Miles scowled again. "I never remember to just give a fake name. No one would ever know. Come on, I'm going to need food if we're doing the whole thing."

"The whole thing?"

"You know, the part where you ask a million questions about the universe, and I buy you a stack of pancakes and a side of bacon because traveling across space and time is hungry work."

How had he known Harper's usual Starlight order? Another thing she'd mumbled in the fog of the last hours, like Peggy's name?

"Fine," she said. She made to open the door, but the glove box fell open. Inside sat a bulky leather bomber jacket and white Keds like the ones her grandmother used to wear. They had probably been here for decades, left behind by some other person the Argonaut had whisked off to the stars.

"What is this, the lost and found?"

"It's cold and you're barefoot," Miles admonished. "Put them on."

He disappeared into the diner, leaving her alone in the parking lot.

She slipped the stiff shoes on, hating how they squished her toes. The bomber was stiff too, but blessedly warm.

The diner smelled like fresh pancakes, stale coffee, and cigarettes. A few truckers were tucked away in the dimmer corners of the restaurant, puffing away on their cigarettes in the smoking section. She couldn't recall there ever being a smoking section at the Starlight. She wondered if Cindy or Sheryl were working tonight so she could ask, but she didn't see them.

She slid into the empty side of the corner booth Miles had chosen, her jeans catching on the long, frayed cracks in the cherry-red vinyl she knew so well. The rest of the diner bore the same faded '50s aesthetic: bright-red stools and booths, black-and-white linoleum tile, menus with blue piping and spacey '50s typeface. It clashed horribly with the oddly uniform aesthetic of tonight's customers: muted oranges and mustard yellows, pale-blue or rusty-brown slacks, sweaters in every manner of garish check imaginable.

"The Starlight?" Harper said to Miles. The stiff tongue of her new shoes dug into the tops of her feet, and she lamented the loss of her more-forgiving sneakers back at her apartment. "Really?"

Miles looked up and put down the menu he was perusing. "Peggy had fond memories of this place."

"And how would you know?"

He passed her a menu. "You hungry? Most people are after their first spin in Argo. Excuse me," he said to a passing waitress. "Two coffees, please."

The way he said it. Like he'd done this a thousand times, with a thousand different people. How many had been lost? And how the hell was Peggy involved?

Miles cleared his throat. "So."

Harper crossed her arms. "So."

Harper's questions, so abundant moments before, were suddenly nowhere to be found. It was as if starting the conversation meant admitting they were truly in the shit now, that something was beginning and neither was equipped to deal with it. In any normal circumstance, Harper would be creating a mental list. Things she knew and things she didn't know. Variables that might come into play, constants she knew she could count on. This was what science had taught her.

But this was different. This was the entirety of the universe, a beloved TV show that was, apparently, more like a manual for how to explore it. It was her friend back from the dead, memoryless and mercenary. It was Miles the Argonaut, sitting in the tattered booth across from her. Where the hell was she supposed to start?

"You don't look like him," Harper said. "On the show he has a third eye that he hides with this psychic glamour thing he has. Or a really stupid-looking bandanna, if it's season two and three."

She opened her menu. It looked a little different, more retro, the design subtly changed. Typical Marty. Her manager was always doing that. Changing little things, just to see if anyone was paying attention. She applied for a job at the diner after that first visit with Peggy, and Marty had been all too pleased to have a shiny new waitress. Oh, how quickly that shine could wear off of things.

"A third eye?" Miles asked. "What for?"

"It helps him communicate with Argo and, like, guess the bad guy's motives. Things like that."

"If he's psychic, why does he have to guess?"

Two steaming coffees appeared in front of them. Harper took a sip and immediately regretted it; the liquid was just as scalding and tasted exactly as bad as it always had.

"Well, he's not a mind reader." She blew on the steaming liquid. "It just helps him connect to other psychic frequencies. That's how he uses his clairvoyant key and all his psychic tools."

"You don't need a third eye to connect with other quantum telepathic signals. You just need to unlock parts of your brain that humans simply haven't yet. You can't believe everything you watch on television."

"That why you go by Miles and not the Argonaut?"

"Miles is my name. For the moment." He glanced at her over the menu. "I could use a burger right about now. How about you? Pancakes? Bacon extra crispy?"

"So you *are* psychic."

"Hmm?"

"You keep saying my order. As if . . . Oh."

All at once, the shining facade of the Argonaut and his felicitous arrival cracked and fell away, leaving only the truth.

She couldn't believe she hadn't seen it before, actually. The harmonica should have been her first clue, followed by the fact that Miles knew Peggy's name, knew that she loved the Starlight, knew about Harper. And what about all the days Peggy had disappeared, phone out of service, utterly unreachable? The way she had cared less and less for school, for New York, for Harper. And of course—

"You're the boyfriend she was going to ditch school and travel with. Paul French. You're the reason she disappeared."

If Miles was surprised she'd finally figured it out, he didn't show it. Just sipped his coffee and read his menu. "Technically," he muttered, "the Incarnate is the reason she disappeared."

Harper made to stand. She had no idea where she would go, but her legs wanted to carry her out of that place and far, far away from this man who had ruined everything. The scorching desert would have been preferable to sitting here with this smug, bitter motherfucker, this man who was nothing like the beloved TV character who was based on him. How silly of her to believe it could have been so easy—her best friend, returned! The Argonaut, manifested! She'd been right to question it, all of it. It *was* too good to be true.

Her desire to know everything warred with her desire to know nothing, to get out, to get away, to never look back and never think on any of this again. Peggy had not been MKUltra'd by some shady government operation. Her mind, her memories, had been scooped out by an alien force while traveling across the universe with Miles.

She considered asking how they met. What they did together, how far they'd gone. After eighteen years of friendship, much of it bonding over *Infinite Odyssey*, Peggy had met the flesh-and-blood Argonaut, and rather than tell Harper, rather than bring her into the adventure they both craved, she'd decided to keep it for herself. She supposed if Peggy had fallen in love with Miles—though looking at him right now, she couldn't see how that was possible—she could understand why Peggy had wanted to keep it for herself. And it explained Peggy's response that night, that last night at the Starlight, when Harper had said what she'd said, and Peggy had said nothing at all.

So she would not ask Miles how they met. She would not ask about his adventures with Peggy. She would not pry into a life that Peggy had obviously not intended to divulge to Harper. She would keep it to the facts. And the fact was, Peggy needed help. Peggy needed to be saved.

"Okay," Harper said, settling back in to the booth. "Fine. You can buy me dinner. Or breakfast. Or whatever this is. And then we're going to make a plan."

"A plan?"

"Yes, a plan. For how to save Peggy."

Miles stiffened. "What on earth are you talking about?"

"Well, we can't just leave her with that . . . that Incarnate or whatever you called it. We have to save her."

Miles laughed. It was not a nice sound. "I'll forgive you for your ignorance because you've been a time traveler for all of two hours, but there is no going up against the Incarnate. Besides the fact that they can spread like an illness and communicate across great distances via their hive mind, they are simply too vast and too brutal to be beaten."

"But why Peggy? It doesn't make any sense."

"Because Peggy is a time traveler—it made her valuable to them. And because they have been trying so desperately to get to me." He sipped his coffee. "I'm sorry. Peggy is gone."

She put her menu down. "I don't accept that."

Miles did not look up. "You don't have to. It's just the way it is. Therefore, there will be no plan, and when enough time has passed, you're going home. Back to your studies. You can become the astronaut you always dreamed of, and we're going to forget this ever happened."

The coffee soured on Harper's tongue. "I quit school."

"You quit?" He did look at her then.

"When Peggy disappeared. I've been deferring for three years. You know why?"

"I—"

"Because I couldn't do it. Without Peggy, I just couldn't fucking do it. And then I kept not doing it. So here I am, straight-A student, brightest future you could imagine, and I work here, at the Starlight fucking Diner, day in and day out because Peggy is gone. And now there's a chance I could bring her home, and you're acting like it doesn't matter to you in the slightest. Like it's not all your fault."

Miles pursed his lips. "I think I'll have a milkshake." He turned his attention back to his menu. His way, apparently, of ending the conversation.

The waitress she didn't recognize came by. She refilled their coffee; Miles ordered a milkshake and a plate of pancakes, eggs, and bacon. Harper ordered a burger just to be spiteful and shifted her attention to the window. Argo was out there, pretending to be an ordinary old car. Just as they were pretending to be ordinary people. But she wasn't ordinary, not anymore. Never would be again.

The sounds of the diner filled their tense silence: plates clanking, the low chatter of the truckers and the waitresses, the hum of "(They Long to Be) Close to You" by the Carpenters on the jukebox, tinny and warped, lacking the clarity afforded by a real music system on which they could have played popular radio stations or CDs. Harper had been on Marty to splurge on one for years, though he insisted the jukebox brought a retro quality to the already-retro establishment. She noticed that several of the waitresses sported feathered hairstyles, fluffy and brassy. Had she missed a memo while she was gone? Would she come back to work and be forced to shape her hair this way to satisfy Marty's continually evolving vintage obsession? But as Harper took a second look around the place, Miles's words clicked.

You've been a time traveler for all of two hours.

"What year is this?"

Miles choked on his coffee a little. "Ah, well. You see. Hmm."

"What fucking year is it?"

Miles whispered, as if he could compensate for her volume with a lack of it. "It's November 1971."

"Excuse me, it's what?"

"Well, you can thank Argo for the year; it's certainly not the one I would have chosen. I told her to pick a time without the internet. It was safer than your present era. You're welcome."

Her stomach dropped and kept dropping. *Cold,* he'd said. *It's cold and you're barefoot.* When they left Riverdale, it had been a balmy eighty-five degrees and late summer. She hadn't even put it together. And worse than November, it was *nineteen-freaking-seventy-one.* The diner that had, moments before, felt like a bastion of comfort after the events she'd been through now looked as foreign as Peggy's hardened gaze.

She tried to remember what she even knew of the year. So much of her knowledge was based around science history or the 1972 debut of *Infinite Odyssey.* One thing she knew for certain: the '70s were an era of protest. The race riots that followed Martin Luther King Jr.'s assassination in 1968 and the Stonewall riots in 1969 were just a few events that precipitated liberation movements that formed in the '70s and continued well into Harper's century. Until historians stopped recording the sanitized versions of history, omitting entire perspectives altogether, humanity seemed bound to repeat the worst parts of it until entropy tore the universe apart.

She certainly didn't want to have to live through it.

"You realize this makes you a hypocrite, don't you? Barring the fact that it doesn't even make sense, you can't just drive into the past. It breaks so many rules—"

"What?"

"Turning me into a time traveler!" Her stomach rolled as she said it. A time traveler. She was a time traveler now. Just like Peggy—the thing he'd said made her valuable to the alien entity called the Incarnate, worth having in their hive. Worth coring Peggy out and using her shell to go after the Argonaut.

Miles's expression darkened. "Argo and I also removed that Incarnate goo Peggy injected you with before it could turn you into another vessel for their destruction, but, by all means, continue with your indignation."

"No wonder you lost Peggy!" she snapped. "No fucking wonder!"

"Now that's not—"

"I grew up watching a show about an alien who could be anything and who inspired the humans he brought along to feel they could do the same. But you . . . you're nothing like him. The one you let Peggy believe was real. Maybe at one time you were. Maybe that's why Anthony Detweiler made an entire show about you. But maybe it was all just a really good guess. You and him, similar but nowhere near the same. Nowhere fucking near it." Several patrons in the surrounding booths grumbled reproachfully, as if they'd never heard a woman angrily cursing at a male companion before. Well, if she was making a scene, she was too angry to care.

It was clear from the way Miles lowered his voice that he *did* care. "You're right. I have made terrible decisions, and she is just one of several who paid dearly for them. And I keep doing it. Repeating my mistakes." He laughed mirthlessly. "What do you want me to say? I'm a wreck. I'm nothing like the man from that TV show. I never was. I don't know where this Detweiler fellow got his information, but he's done you a disservice. I let Peggy think it was all true, and now she's . . ." he trailed off, his pinched face showing the first signs of real shame.

"Listen," she said slowly. "I'm sitting in the diner where I work, only I'm sitting in it fifty years before I ever worked my first shift, and I may look calm but I'm freaking the fuck out. So, I'm going to need you to focus and explain to me why the hell we are here."

"Is 2023 a year anyone wants to be in right now?" The look she gave him must have been less than amused because he cleared his throat and continued. "Your time is volatile, Starling. There are cameras on every corner, every building. There's facial recognition software in every cell phone, on every computer, at every airport. You carry a tracking device with you everywhere you go, and the systems that carry this information are extremely fallible. As if all that weren't enough, you've been half-heartedly battling a handful of viruses that will just keep mutating until half the world is dead. In a way, I've done you a favor."

"Oh, really?" Harper said through gritted teeth. "A favor."

"Besides, if the Incarnate has been to Earth, there's a good chance there are people in your time who are part of the hive now. Like Peggy tried to make you. Better to regroup in a time when our every step isn't being recorded. Besides, I lived here for a time; it isn't as bad as you think."

The waitress lugged a tray with all their various plates and shake to the side of their table and began depositing everything. Harper didn't know what she'd expected—did 1971 taste different? Smell different? Not so far. Her burger smelled like a burger. Her fries were crunchy and oily like any diner's fries. There were the aesthetic differences, of course, but otherwise, the Starlight Diner was exactly the same as the one where she served the burgers. Maybe a little cleaner, but probably not.

Miles tucked into the milkshake first, sipping the straw speared through a tower of whipped cream, a quintessential cherry resting atop its pillowy surface.

Harper stared at Argo through the window, the late-afternoon sun refracting off of the hood and blinding her. "This isn't fair."

"I don't care about fair, Starling. I'm not getting you involved."

"I'm already involved—"

"I would never forgive myself—"

"Well, cry me a fucking river!"

A few truckers turned to stare at her outburst. Miles grimaced at them as if to say, *Women, am I right?*

She took a calming breath. "Peggy's been brainwashed. Used like a battering ram by some gross alien species, and it's your fault. So what are we going to do about it?"

Miles leaned over the table. "We are not going to do anything. You are going to finish your burger. And then I am going to take you home, and you'll never see me again."

She pushed her plate away, appetite utterly gone. "And what about Peggy?"

"Peggy's lost, Starling. Best to mourn her and move on."

"I can't do that."

"And I can't help you."

"No." She crossed her arms. "I guess you're really sticking to your guns on that one."

She shoved out of the booth and stalked through the smoking section to the restroom. Another waitress was reapplying her lipstick in the mirror.

"I like your hair," she said to Harper, who thanked her automatically, despite knowing her hair was a curly nest on top of her head, and then holed up in one of the stalls.

Mourn Peggy? Get over it? Just go home, pretend like none of this had ever happened? There was no way. She couldn't go back to her apartment and drink her wine and work at the diner and pretend like her life had not just been irrevocably altered, mentally and physically. There was no going back. Miles had made sure of it.

And now, Peggy needed saving. Harper was blazing with purpose now. She would not take his pathetic, whiny no for an answer.

Reinvigorated, she left the bathroom.

Miles was not at the table when she sat back down. Probably he'd gone to the bathroom too. If his species even required it.

But she'd only been sitting for a moment before a weird feeling took hold, a suspicion that seized her heart. When the waitress came by to clear the plates, she handed Harper an envelope and told her that the man had asked the waitress to give this to the girl sitting with him in the booth, paid up, and left. The waitress told her everything with a look that said she wasn't amused by the drama, but Harper suspected he'd given her a generous tip.

She took the envelope and went outside, her insides contracting, and sure enough, Argo was gone. Miles had said he would take her home, and she'd made it clear that wasn't an option. So he left her at the Starlight Diner in 1971. No quantum whistle, no harmonica of her own to call him back. Just—she opened the envelope to see what he'd left her—a wad of cash; a fake New York ID that named her as Susan Feldman, a name she recognized but didn't know why (had Argo always been able to create false ID's?); and a hastily scribbled note.

I'm sorry.

And just like that, her state of shock was abruptly over, and she bent over where she stood and wept. She wept until it hurt, until she felt emptied out and ragged, and even then, it seemed like the tears might never stop. The wound on her neck was sore beneath the bandage. Her head pounded from sorrow and exhaustion.

Everything, everything had been a lie.

5.

NEW YORK CITY
FALL, 1971

Harper Starling spent her first night in the year 1971 holed up in a seedy hotel several blocks from Penn Station. The events of her most recent waking hours seemed both viscerally real and like an utter dream. She had no idea how much time had truly lapsed between her encounter with Peggy, her mind meld with Argo, or her half-finished meal with Miles at the Starlight Diner, but it felt like a century. Surrounded by the red vinyl booths, the wad of cash crumpled in her tight fist, she'd been hit with a kind of fervor. She needed to see it for herself. Needed to know if she'd been taken for a ride and deposited at the Starlight by a total nutcase who got his kicks out of fucking with people.

She'd hopped on a bus from Riverdale into the city, the lack of MetroCard apparatus her first post-Miles clue that things were different, and was deposited at the newly constructed underground Penn Station, right at the edge of New York's busy core. She emerged from the labyrinth with her heart in her throat, gasping audibly at her first glimpse of the city as the windows and spires of its towering buildings caught and dispersed the final rays of an absurdly gorgeous sunset. It was impossible. Insane. Impossible again. Her heart did an odd kind of jig, skipping around like it had every intention of dancing straight out of her chest. Someone catcalled her and it felt like hearing a foreign language, even though she understood perfectly well what he was proposing to stick where.

New York City in 1971 was exactly and nothing like the city Harper knew. The historic churches and their cemeteries, the building facades claiming the advanced workmanship of another century, Central Park and its twisting paths, aged fountains, and horse-drawn carriages were all familiar sights. The lights of Times Square, the screech and steam of the subway through the sidewalk grates, the narrow streets clogged with yellow taxis. But this New York had not yet fully seen the ruthless and racist urban scrubbing that began in the latter half of the twentieth century, nor the "well-meaning" laws passed by white lawmakers in the '80s and '90s that had inadvertently created such astronomic climbs in rent prices that anyone who had been around to see what it looked like before was forced out or into homelessness.

This New York was loud and odorous in a way that Harper's New York was not, which was a surprise because twenty-first-century New York was quite loud and quite odorous. But the air here was thick with diesel and cigarette smoke, clouds of cloying, powdery perfume and rotting garbage that crowded the sidewalks. Times Square, marquees bright enough to limn passersby with hazy, sunlit halos, was littered with theaters devoted to live pornographic displays, set conspicuously and inconspicuously amongst the old movie houses and Broadway theaters. Ads for brands and products Harper had never seen in her life towered over the busy Midtown streets: Castro's cars, Yashica cameras, Kent cigarettes.

There truly was no denying where and when she was. Despite all her study, and all the studying she still intended to do, human time travel was a thing she had not, in her wildest dreaming, assumed might actually be possible. Individual atomic particles within the huge barrel of a monolithic particle accelerator? Maybe. But Argo, the Tesseract Engine from her favorite TV show come to life? The would-be scientist in her knew better. And yet, here she was. She had to allow that Miles was right; there were rules in the universe that humans would not come even close to understanding in her lifetime. That Peggy was not dead but held captive by an alien unlike any she had seen in sci-fi movies. That her life as she knew it was gone, over, just like that.

But this line of thinking made her heart hurt and her depth perception vertiginous. So instead, she stumbled aimlessly from avenue to avenue, up to the edge of Central Park—Central Park! The very same and yet wildly different Central Park!—and back down again. She passed cafés with names in retro fonts. Unfamiliar restaurants spilling over with boisterous crowds. Greasy bodegas where the smell of bacon and cheese nearly lured her in. Everything the same and yet intensely new.

As the shock died and blisters reared their ugly heads inside her stiff Keds, she found herself back at Penn Station, asking for directions to the nearest hotel.

The room her scant cash bought was dark, and the dingy lamp did little to change that. She stood in the doorway and took in the evidence of the era all around her, from the ridiculously boxy little television set and gangly antennae to the rotary telephone on the nightstand and the dated colors splashed about the room. She lay down on the hard bed and listened to the sounds of a city that had not existed, at least to Harper Starling, for over fifty years. To the taxis honking outside, the laughter of women and men on the street, and the couple in the room next door, thrusting out their own frustrations in what sounded like an entirely unpleasant sexual encounter.

She did not want to think about Peggy and her scarred face, her sharp nails on the back of Harper's neck. She did not want to think about Miles and his cold, tired eyes, his incredible cowardice.

But she couldn't help it.

Her mind whirled through a running replay of the night's events—Peggy in her apartment, Peggy changed, Peggy chasing her through the Harlem night. Miles in his space-and-time-traveling ship named Argo, the impossible Tesseract Engine. The way he looked at her, the things he said. The adventures he and Peggy had. She tried so hard to convince herself it was all just a nightmare, a terrible, terrible dream. But then she would look at her surroundings, the crappy hotel room decorated in '70s-style wood paneling, and the delusion fell apart.

Bleary-eyed at six a.m. the next morning and hungrier than she'd ever been in her life, she stumbled out of the hotel in the same clothes she'd worn the day before and into the restaurant around the corner. It was a mixed crowd: businessmen sitting down for a morning coffee and newspaper across from men and women still rolling from whatever they'd taken the night before, reeking of pot and sweat. Harper tried not to stare at the scene laid out around her, like something out of a historical film, as she ordered a coffee (resolving to drink it this time), a plate of eggs, home fries, and toast. The waitress commented on Harper's appetite and something about watching her figure, the audacity of which astounded Harper so much she didn't even bother being offended. She had plenty of time for the misogyny of the era to grind her down. She didn't have to start today.

She got everything for a dollar twenty-five and handed over the cash gladly, then joined the increasingly chaotic Midtown foot traffic with a bloated but happier stomach.

Now that she was properly fed, the French fries of last night's abandonment veering into the territory of a bad dream, she could see her situation more clearly. It was time to gather the facts and begin arranging them into usable action items. She decided a reasonable first order of business would be to search for Miles in this time. He'd mentioned he had lived here; perhaps she could find his past self and appeal to his better nature. And threaten him, if it came down to it.

She searched several name variations in the white pages, and after thirty fruitless minutes of flipping through the book several times, she remembered the alias he had used with Peggy. Paul. Paul French. So simple, so obvious, the pseudonym itself had been a clue this entire time because it was someone else's pseudonym first: Isaac Asimov's first literary alias, to be precise, which she knew because she loved Isaac Asimov. And sure enough, she saw it the moment she turned the page to the *F*s: several Paul Frenches, but only one Paul M. French.

She managed to nab a taxi despite the protest mounting alongside Fifth

Avenue, people toting signs with phrases like War is Over and Bring Them Home and 45,000 Isn't Enough. It was an eerily familiar scene, just dressed differently. She'd been to her share of rallies in recent years as things in America became more dire and the national hope frayed. But these people had been protesting this same war for years, demanding Johnson and then Nixon bring home loved ones serving in a chaotic guerrilla war against their will. Just over a year ago the Kent State massacre saw thirteen university students brutalized for protesting the United States' involvement in Vietnam. Four of them died. Harper was glad she didn't have to be the one to tell them it would take two more years for America to finally pull out of the war.

The taxi zipped past the protest and jerked its way down toward Greenwich Village while she marveled at the retro stiffness of the cab's interior, the squeaky, torn seats, the plastic divider, the faint cheese smell. She was careful not to flaunt her wad of cash as she pulled a couple dollars from the stack, passed them up to the driver, and got out of the car, greeted by trees still shedding their autumnal leaves and the faintly colonial row houses of the Village still lined by narrow stone streets.

Paul M. French lived in one of these town houses, a beautiful place with a wrought iron balcony barely visible beneath the blanket of lush, greedy ivy. She stood outside that apartment for hours, waiting for someone to enter through the front door, for the lights to go on, for telltale movement inside. But everything was dark as a moonless sky, and though Harper camped out in front of his building—melding with the shadows was becoming remarkably easy—for the better part of the day and into the afternoon, the apartment was cloaked in shadow, utterly silent. When she finally had the courage to knock on the door, a neighbor from the building next door poked her head out.

"Paul French?" Harper asked her. "Does he live here?"

"You must mean Miles—he never went by Paul."

"Yes, that's who I mean. Have you seen him?"

The neighbor's eyes went somber. "Oh, such a sad story, that. Lived here for years but he hasn't returned in months. Not since . . . well, not since his partner died, you know?"

Well, that was a revelation. The person Miles had lost before Peggy was not another assistant or friend—it was a human person with whom he had shared a life, a home. She hadn't known the selfish prick she met the day before was even capable of falling in love, at least with someone other than himself.

She wandered down Miles's street, marveling at how familiar it all was. The statuesque row houses with their ubiquitous red brick and bay windows, the towering trees breaking through cement and concrete to breathe a little better, the people sitting on their stoops with a cigarette or chatting with a neighbor. It didn't matter that their hair was longer and styled in ways no one attempted anymore, or that their jeans were starched and stiff, or that their sunglasses were more Coke-bottle than couture. People changed, but the city never did.

She wandered onto Bleecker Street and went east, ignoring the whistles and calls from the bell-bottomed men as she passed businesses and restaurants she had never seen and would never see again because she was going to find Miles and make him fix this. She was too tired to properly appreciate where and when she was, too frustrated. Everything would be normal again, very, very soon, because it had to be.

She was hungry again by the time she reached MacDougal Street, so she went into a crowded café there and ordered a sandwich and a coffee. She sat under the striped awning outside and found herself surrounded by people chattering animatedly at one another. A cool breeze blew through, reminding her that it was November, not the muggy August she left behind, and she wondered what the significance of November 1971 was. Miles said he'd spent time in New York in the 1970s, but apparently that wasn't entirely true. And if Argo had chosen this year, this month, what reason could she have had?

A shadow fell over her table.

"Excuse me, miss?"

Harper looked up at the man, his sideburns razor-sharp, his afro impeccable. "Yes?"

"Someone left this for you." He handed her an envelope.

Miles had left her an envelope too. Not twenty-four hours before, when he abandoned her. Could this be his work?

"Who left it?"

The man shook his head. "Don't remember. Someone left it a while ago, said to give it to the girl named Harper who ordered the macchiato. That's you, right?"

Her heart beat erratically. If he'd been here a while ago to drop off something for her, then he'd known she would be here.

"That's me," she replied. She took the envelope, managed an approximation of a thankful smile, and ripped it open as he walked away.

It was, indeed, a letter. But the handwriting was not the same scrawl she'd found on Miles's note at the Starlight; it was much neater, straighter lines and scooping curves.

Go to the Sky Theater at the planetarium.

And that was all it said. No signature, nothing. Not even her name written on the envelope.

She didn't have to be told twice. She scarfed the rest of her sandwich then hailed another taxi and directed the driver to the museum. The planetarium had always been her destination on a trying day; whoever sent her the letter clearly knew this. But who?

So, the cab made its way up Sixth, past all the things that were different and the same, and Harper trained her mind on the dark of the space theater, letting it crowd out all the other thoughts squirming at the edges, the terror, the shock, the excitement, the bitter, bitter anger.

6.

NEW YORK CITY
FALL, 1971

At first, she wasn't sure she was in the right place. It was West Eighty-First, all right, and there was the museum. But the monolithic glass box that housed the spherical theater in the twenty-first century was nowhere to be found. Instead, there was a simple, somewhat art-deco brick structure with long, thin windows and a copper dome where the roof should have been. Any second, she expected to see it light up with electricity, like a colossal plasma globe.

This was the original Hayden Planetarium, and the dome had the green patina of a structure that had been weathering the elements for decades. She'd seen photos of it in the office of her Intro to Astronomy professor. Somehow, she'd assumed it was demolished long ago, but then, she supposed, she was now living in the long ago. And so, her own beloved planetarium, the place she'd spent many hours during school and even more after she deferred, would not exist yet for several more decades, and she was stuck with a relic. So much for the constants.

Still, it was here, and inside she would find exhibits on the stars and the solar system and space exploration. Plaques with information, soothing scientific facts. Things she could count on in the face of everything that had happened and didn't make sense. For a moment, she forgot that she'd been lured here. Still, she would have ended up here sooner or later, regardless; she needed a familiar space, a place to regroup and rebuild her mental list of next steps from the ground up. She wasn't like Peggy; she hadn't spent three years traveling the universe with an Argonaut who was electric and dedicated. She'd spent one day with a jaded, bitter, waste of a man, for whom nursing his own trauma apparently trumped what he then inflicted on Harper. And he was fucking cheap to boot—there was no way the cash he'd left would last her more than a week.

Ah, but the promise of stars! Walking into the planetarium, even the version she didn't know, soothed her frayed nerves. It was time to start seeing the half-full of the situation: Had she been left in an era she didn't know by a sad drunk in a time-traveling muscle car? Yes. Was she lucky he didn't leave her with the ancient Egyptians or the dinosaurs or, god forbid, in the Dark Ages? Also yes. There were worse places she could be. And besides, amazing things were happening right now, things she'd only read about in history books and would now see the effects of firsthand. This month, *Mariner 9* would be the first spacecraft to successfully enter Mars's orbit; in another month, the Soviet Union's *Mars 3* probe would actually land on the surface of Mars, the first craft to ever do so. As Harper paid the admission, too happy inside these walls to worry about being so cavalier with what little cash she had, scientist Vera Rubin was, maybe at that very moment, sitting in the astronomy lab at Carnegie, discovering the rotation curves of various galaxies and solidifying the earth-shattering evidence for dark matter in the universe. It was an amazing year for astronomy, and while she was stranded here against her will, she could at least appreciate how astounding it was to be here all the same.

A cluster of children on a field trip ran past her, chattering excitedly about the gravity well display in another wing. Just ahead, she spotted the telltale darkness of the famous *Black Light Murals*, an installation that had remained until the planetarium was demolished in the '90s and now only existed in photographs and that Woody Allen movie everyone loved so much. Of course, the planetarium was soon rebuilt, the giant glass cube that Harper would have recognized in her own time a serious departure from the brutalist design of the original.

She drifted toward them, the pull of the glowing stars and planets in the dark room too insistent to be ignored. Along the walls, renderings of the beautiful, gaseous Milky Way guided her tour through the exhibit. Celestial debris cluttering up the cold vacuum of space. Cast-off light from stars hundreds of years apart from one another illuminating the clouds and dust so everything glowed with the dull luster of paper lanterns. Nebulae in a rainbow swirl of colors. A pitch-black solar eclipse. The craterous lunar landscape.

A prickle on the back of her neck made her turn, but there was no one behind her. The lack of light and her isolation in the room began to make her feel observed, so she walked through the exhibit and finally found herself at the entrance to an orrery, which was thrilling because she had never seen one in person. The room was circular but possessed a flat ceiling, where curved tracks carried models of the planets and sun, the whole apparatus mechanically spinning according to their corresponding rotations in the actual sky. On the walls, constellations had been painted, and the plush theater seating all seemed to be oriented around the large Aztec mural at the center of the room. Here and there a few people lazed in the chairs while they waited for the show to begin, so Harper followed their lead and sat.

Exhaustion crushed her the moment her body hit the plush seat. She could feel the newness of it against every curve, coaxing her into relaxation. She had barely slept in two nights and wasn't sure that timeline was even accurate. It could have been longer, for all she knew; the five-decade time change was terribly disorienting. Either way, she was dangerously close to falling asleep. But then, there was that feeling again, that tickle on her neck, pulling her neck hairs taut, jolting her back to awareness. When she looked around, she saw no one overtly observing her. No one watching from the shadows.

A few moments later, twelve projection screens slid down over the painted walls. For the next fifteen minutes, the small audience in the orrery was treated to a slideshow journeying from Earth to Pluto with accompanying narration about each of their unique conditions. The narrator sounded somewhat bored, but the information was fascinating. She lost herself in the monotonous drone of the show, taking advantage of the first genuine calm she'd experienced in days.

When the slideshow was over, an attendant directed the group up a set of stairs to the second floor, where a plaque on the wall told her she would find the Sky Theater the note had mentioned. She paused, wondering if she should consider this plan more carefully before subjecting herself to whatever waited. She knew nothing about the Incarnate—were they intelligent enough to leave such a casual note? Or were they more like Peggy had been, blasting through doors and making threats?

What did it really matter, in the end? She had no other leads. That handwriting didn't belong to Miles, but that didn't mean he hadn't sent her the note. Maybe it was a different Miles, from a different future where he'd improved his penmanship, rectifying the mistakes of his past self.

She entered the theater through a pair of double doors, found a seat, and tilted herself back to stare at the familiar domed screen. She was stuck in 1971, but some things didn't change—or didn't change entirely—and though that went for both the negatives and the positives, there was something profound in it.

The lights dimmed and the screen filled with stars. She felt the prick of that uneasy, being-watched feeling again but was soon immersed in the images overhead. The black expanse filled with the explosions of cosmic gas and dust that instantly ignited the birth of the universe. She watched stars spark into existence, the image roving through the brand-new solar system until it found purchase on an infant planet convulsed with volcanic eruptions, followed by centuries of torrential rain.

For the next thirty minutes, she was treated to the biography of Earth, from start to dismal projected end, the solemn voice of the narrator warning of early destruction due to cataclysmic global warming, before cheerfully surmising that we would be on our way to new planets before the effects could be felt by humans.

If only they knew that December of 1972 would see the last astronauts leave the surface of the moon until . . . well, not yet in Harper's lifetime.

When the film was done, the lights brightened to a dim, and the handful of other viewers filed out of the theater. No one approached her, and no one dropped any new notes in her lap. Maybe whoever she was supposed to look for was outside the door, waiting for her to exit with the small crowd. But Harper couldn't bring herself to leave. The moment she got up and went through those doors, she would be back where she started. Alone, unmoored in a time she didn't know, her best friend lost to the vacuum of space-time and the whims of a parasitic alien species. Miles the Argonaut in the wind, and not coming back.

Besides, no one was asking her to go. When she looked around the theater, it was still empty, save for the projectionist, doors shut. Normally a new audience would be filtering in by now, the planetarium on a steady rotation of screenings. But she was alone and remained alone for another five minutes. For some reason, it didn't make her nervous. The silence of the theater was simply too soothing.

And then, the strangest thing: the light above dimmed again. No one new had entered, but the lights from the massive projector in the floor beneath the dome brightened, and an image was cast onto the screen above. Assuming it was just a slow day for the planetarium, Harper leaned back once again, happy to enjoy the somewhat ominous show a second time.

But it was not the big bang that appeared on the screen. It was not the Milky Way or an infant Earth pelted with monsoon rains. It was something impossible because it would not exist for another year—not until 1972.

It was the first-ever episode of *Infinite Odyssey.*

She watched the pilot without moving a muscle, too dumbfounded to speak. Above her the Argonaut's first human friend, Betty Fisk, a first-year college student, walked across an unnamed New York campus, a map in hand. She was utterly lost. A man in a beige hat, trench coat, and dark sunglasses approached her, offering to assist.

"Oh, that's nice. And who are you?" she asked.

"The question is not who, but where. And I am nowhere."

Harper's heart jumped into her throat and made it hard to breathe. She heard the words in Not-Peggy's Incarnate voice. *I am nowhere. That is accurate.*

Nowhere reached for Betty, whose expression indicated that she was starting to understand she was in deep shit, when he was interrupted by the blare of a car radio and the squeal of old brakes against the curb. Betty turned and there was the world's first-ever glimpse of the Argonaut, sitting behind the wheel of a purple Dodge Charger. Harper knew this show by heart and could have recited each beat without looking at the screen. This was it. The real thing.

"Don't trust him, miss!" the driver of the car shouted.

"Oh, and I should trust you?" Betty replied. But before she could extricate herself from an increasingly hostile situation, the stranger in the trench yanked her to him.

"Don't come any closer, Argonaut!" the stranger hissed. "Or she dies!"

"What is happening?" Betty wailed.

"You wouldn't believe me if I told you," the Argonaut replied as he jumped out of the driver's seat, clutching what looked like a modern calculator. He punched several buttons, and a high-pitched keening emitted from the prop, causing the stranger to release Betty and slam his hands dramatically over his ears.

The Argonaut held out a hand. "Okay, Betty," he said, "it's time to run!"

Harper twisted in her seat, scanning the theater for the person responsible for this impromptu screening. Was Miles here after all? Had he come back for her? Was he taunting her? Was Peggy?

But she found neither of their shapes in the seating nor along the unilluminated wall. Only the bank of blocky computers—where the huge glass lenses and multicolored lights on the massive projector were controlled—interrupted the clean lines of the domed room. Behind those computers, obscured in dim shadow, sat the same bored projectionist she'd seen upon entering. In fact, he was worse than bored—he was sleeping.

"Excuse me," she said, maintaining her composure as best she could. When he didn't wake, she stood up, cleared her throat, and shouted. "Excuse me!"

The projectionist sat up quickly, gaze swiveling blearily around the theater for the source of the call. He slumped when he saw her. "You scared me."

"No, *you're* scaring *me*. What is this?" She gestured at the screen, where the pilot episode continued uninterrupted, the Argonaut chatting to a stunned Betty in the passenger seat as the city whipped past them.

The projectionist eyed her warily. "What do you mean? You're Susan, aren't you? Susan Feldman? You rented this place out. You paid me to put this on."

"Me? How? I—"

"Lady, if this is some kind of joke—"

Harper did laugh, then, because if this was a joke, it was on her. But . . . he'd called her Susan Feldman, the name on the ID Miles left her. He was playing the pilot episode of a TV show that didn't yet exist. Could her future self really have orchestrated all of this?

"A Kixorian!" the Argonaut shouted at Betty. "Nasty pieces of work."

"And what are you?" Betty asked.

"I'm not sure what I am," the Argonaut replied. "It's why I'm traveling the universe: to find out. I woke up in this ship one day with no memory of who I am or where I came from. Her name is Argo, by the way. She's what we call a Tesseract Engine."

"A Tesseract Engine? What does that mean?"

"It refers to the crystal that allows us to traverse both space and time. A tesseract is a four-dimensional hypercube, impossible to observe with the human eye. The crystal itself comes from what I can only guess is my home planet. That is what I'm trying to find out."

Slowly, Harper sat back down.

She watched the Argonaut of her memory and Betty drive upstate. She watched them park at a diner along the highway, the flickering neon sign boasting the name Moondust Café. She knew that the real sign for the real establishment, the Starlight Diner she knew so well, sat just out of frame next to the prop sign. Her stomach twisted tighter and tighter as the pair sat down in a booth Harper had bussed a hundred times, and the Argonaut said as he passed Betty a menu, "A lot to take in, isn't it? You hungry? Most people are after their first spin in Argo. Excuse me," he said to a passing waitress. "Two coffees, please."

It was exactly what Miles had said to her the afternoon before.

From there, the show progressed as she remembered. They left the diner, and the Argonaut, assuming Betty was safe now and that the Kixorians had gone, took Betty home—only to find that the Kixorian was waiting for her. "What is it about you that's so special, Betty?" the Argonaut wondered. They would spend the next four episodes trying to figure that out. Betty would see the stars, the Old West, and an alien planet. And by the end of it, the Argonaut would determine why the Kixorians were after Betty and decide that it was safer for her to stick with him. Traveling the universe in his space-and-time-traversing ship disguised as a purple Dodge Charger named Argo.

Now that Harper was watching through the lens of her recent experience, the similarities couldn't be missed. The alien ambush? The Argonaut rolling up in his muscle car and taking her to the diner? Their exact exchange about taking Argo for a spin? The Moondust Café, really? It was too on the nose to be a coincidence. Almost as if someone had used *Infinite Odyssey* to send a message . . . to her.

"How do you do it, Argonaut?" Betty asked as they neared the end of the episode. "How can you try to reason with the Kixorians when they so clearly want you dead?"

"Sometimes, Betty, you must lead with compassion. It's easy enough to let hate take over your heart. It is much harder to lead with love. Sometimes, you must even try to love what you hate. It's the only way to continue in this universe as long as I have."

The credits rolled, and for the first time in her life, she read them as they scrolled across the curved screen. Now, she noticed that Anthony Detweiler was not the only writer credited. Several lines down from his, in smaller letters, were the words *Story by: Susan Feldman.*

The name Miles had given to her, just before abandoning her in 1971.

The projectionist's voice punctured her shock. "Time's up," he said. "I have to do another show now."

Wearily, Harper stood. She had hoped to find Miles here, waiting with Argo and effusive apologies. Instead, she'd only found more questions. Mysterious notes at a Greenwich café in the past. Her future self renting out a planetarium theater to make sure she saw . . . what? Her fake name in the credits of her favorite TV show? How could she be sure it wasn't another Susan Feldman? Harper didn't know the first thing about writing for television.

But that was wishful thinking. She hadn't noticed in all the excitement of running from a changed Peggy and time traveling in the actual Argo, but now that she considered the events of yesterday, the pilot bore too much of a resemblance to the last forty-eight hours to be a coincidence. And it was her future self who had rented this planetarium to send Harper a message here, now. Maybe her future self thought this would help ease her mind—the promise of a plan, a path. *Look, Harper, there's hope!* But it only deepened her despair. How the hell was she supposed to get her name into those credits? Assuming, of course, that it was even her future self who had orchestrated this event. What if this was the Incarnate's work? What if they got to her in the future, and this was the hive itself, endeavoring to lure her into their grasp?

Maybe it would be better to do nothing. To avoid pulling this thread at all, to refuse this calling and make sure *Infinite Odyssey* never existed.

Oh, that was a strange feeling. To consider what might have happened if she had never seen *Infinite Odyssey*, if she and Peggy had never spent Saturday afternoons arm to arm on a pile of blankets puddled on the floor, popcorn scattered everywhere while they watched and rewatched episodes of their favorite vintage television show. If Peggy had never met Miles the Argonaut and known what he was.

Would Harper be back in 2023? Would Peggy be there too?

Would they even be friends?

"The next group is coming through," the projectionist said, an edge of warning in his young voice.

"Did she—I—leave a note or anything?" she asked hopefully as she approached the door.

The projectionist just shrugged. A quick glance at his desk didn't catch on any paper or envelopes—just a panel of controls and what looked like a travel pillow. No more notes, then. No more clues at all.

So, this was it. The end of her one and only encounter with travel through space and time. Alone in tumultuous 1970s New York with a handful of crumpled bills and no one to explain what she was supposed to do next.

Harper did not go back to that tiny hotel room near Penn Station. Instead, she got on the train to Riverdale and walked into the Starlight Diner, the only anchor she had left, and sat down in the booth she had shared with Miles not twenty-four hours prior.

Whatever her future self, or the Incarnate, or whoever it was wanted her to know, she didn't care. She didn't care that her fake name was in those credits—she had no plans to be here long enough to put it there. There was certainly no way that Miles, troubled and bitter as he might be, would not come to his senses and return for her. She just had to stay in one place. To be there when he arrived.

She ordered a coffee, and another, and another. She sat in the booth for hours, stubbornly watching the sun move across the black-and-white tile. She thought about Peggy and her web of scars. She thought about Miles and his haunted, drunk stare, and the last thing he said to her before disappearing: *I can't help you. I can't help you.* She drank cold coffee until night descended and the waitstaff turned over. They muttered about her in the corner, watching, waiting for her to move, to do something. Anything.

But she didn't.

By the time she'd spent most of her cash on diner food and a handful of nights at the nearby motel, she was badly in need of new clothes and had given up hope that Miles would realize his mistake and come back for her. Long hours spent in the same booth had done little more than give her leg cramps and a heavy stone of hopelessness in her gut. She considered going back to the planetarium and demanding more information from the young projectionist, begging for another clue that might point her in the right direction, or at least toward a job. But she knew he wouldn't have anything more than he had that afternoon, if he even remembered her at all.

It was one of the waitresses on the morning shift who finally sat down across from Harper, taking Miles's empty place, and folded Harper's hands into her own, pulling her out of her days-long reverie and back into the world.

"Honey," she said, traces of a native New York accent tinging her words, "whoever he is, he ain't worth it."

Harper almost didn't realize that the woman was speaking to her. She dragged her gaze from the window, where she'd been imagining all the ways Argo might appear, just an old muscle car in a half-empty parking lot, ready to take her away.

"What did you say?"

"That man you were with. The one who left. Don't wait up for him."

"You saw me? With him?"

"I'm the one who gave you the note he left behind. Remember?" Harper shook her head and the woman sighed, full of a motherly pity Harper didn't want. Like she was just some lovesick girl abandoned by her no-good boyfriend. If only it were so simple.

"Looked like he'd been living a little too hard, if you know what I mean. Now you got that look too. And it's a damn shame."

"Tell me something—" Harper looked down at the plastic name tag pinned to the waitress's dress, "—Angie. If you had just found out the best friend you thought was dead was not, in fact, dead, and the one guy who could tell you where to find her had left you here without a goodbye and barely enough cash to last the week, what would you do?"

Angie's eyes went soft. "I'd say fuck him," she said, "and find my friend by myself." She stood. "And then I'd thank the nice waitress for comping my meal."

Harper chewed her cheek, the reality of her situation crashing down all over again. Though she wanted Miles to see the error of his ways, and to understand how the hell she factored into the creation of *Infinite Odyssey*, she couldn't deny that cash flow seemed to be her most immediate problem, or that the nice waitress was, in fact, very nice.

"Thank you, Angie," Harper said. "I appreciate it."

"Don't mention it." Angie started to go.

"Wait. Are you hiring?"

Angie smiled and brought her an application.

EPISODE THREE
COSMIC INFLATION

This week on Infinite Odyssey:

The Argonaut is lured to the edges of the universe by his estranged wife, who is working for a shady band of smugglers. Will she betray him again, or can the Argonaut convince her to side with him and dismantle the band before they steal something they can't put back?

7.

RIVERDALE
1971

Harper, of course, got the job. Or rather, Susan Feldman did. It was easy enough to convince Joseph, this era's manager, once it became clear she would not have to be trained much. She'd wowed them with her uncanny knowledge of the diner's layout, her comprehension of the special diner language the Starlight used to relay orders to the kitchen, and her agility with a tray filled with dishes. Considering how often the register was busted in her time, using the antiquated machine in this one was a breeze.

The uniform, too, had barely changed in fifty years. Still a bright robin's-egg blue that did nothing for Harper's complexion, made of a thick, starched cotton that did her body no favors. The only differences seemed to be the slightly boxier cut and the mandatory nylons. Even the kitchen looked the same—everything a little newer, though not by much. She was right back where she had spent the last three years, avoiding school and facing the reality of Peggy's disappearance. What did it say about Harper and her life that she always found herself at a dead fucking end? Even a time machine and fifty years couldn't get her away from the Starlight Diner.

And a month later, here she was. Clearing off tables caked in syrup and soggy French fries. Singing along with 1971's Billboard Hot 100, Donny Osmond to the Doors, which played on repeat all day and all night. Going home each evening with aching feet and a sore back. Avoiding thoughts of Miles and Peggy and the planetarium all together.

She'd moved out of the motel and into the apartment of another Starlight waitress named Dottie, whose second room had been miraculously vacated by a former hostess the month before. Dottie didn't seem to be fazed by much of anything. With no cell phone to consult, no computer or lightning-fast Wi-Fi or search engines to draw up handy answers, Harper was always asking what felt like stupid questions. But Dottie didn't mind when Harper inquired about pop culture she should have known or asked for clarification about current events. She was gentle with Harper when she came back from the store with the wrong food items. She must have had a doddering old grandmother somewhere, for whom Dottie was forced to answer a similar constant stream of inquiries. Otherwise, maybe she assumed Harper was just dim or from a town so small it was practically off-the-grid, and honestly, Harper could live with that.

Each day that passed was a new exercise in helplessness. She counted them against that first night. Ten, fifteen, twenty, twenty-five. Twenty-five turned into thirty turned into forty, until almost two months had passed, the time gone in a long, slow blink. She lay awake at night, avoiding the sleep that awaited, tainted as it seemed to be these days with dreams of alien landscapes and Peggy's face painted with scars; otherwise, she would wake in a cold sweat, a scream dying on her lips for no obvious reason, Dottie in her doorway, annoyed.

To distract from the agonizing questions and the lack of electronics that had always kept her occupied in times of boredom, she began to read. There was a library in Riverdale with a decent enough selection of nonfiction and a hefty newspaper archive of which she availed herself for the better part of two weeks. It was helpful to know exactly what to expect from this time period. But it soon became obvious that the historical editorializing was egregious, the omissions many. Women's

Liberation was regarded through a racist and patronizing lens. There were Op-Eds in the crinkled newspapers denouncing the idea of reparations for formerly interned Japanese Americans. Articles about Martin Luther King Jr.'s assassination speculated about his apparent ties to unsavory revolutionary groups. Science journals excluded major contributing scientists from announcements of incredible discoveries from past decades, apparently deeming them less important than the white men on their teams. The reporting on Vietnam was all over the map. After weeks of studying, Harper was ready to get out of 1971 for good.

But after two months, there was no sign of Paul M. French or her best-friend-turned-galactic assassin. No further clues as to what she should do. And with no further appearances from the Incarnate, she was starting to think that maybe it really was her future self who had sent her that message. Or maybe, a small voice sometimes countered, it *was* the Incarnate, baiting her into preserving a timeline that should have been destroyed.

Somehow, though, she didn't think so. The Incarnate didn't seem the type to goad and lure with mysterious notes and private screenings. It seemed the type to bash, take, and steal what it wanted. And the more she considered the note and planetarium, the more she felt compelled to make it all happen. To get her name into the credits of that TV show, somehow, some way.

And so, bleary-eyed from reading and frustrated with her lack of progress, she gave in. If she was going to be stuck in the '70s for the foreseeable future, if she was going to find a way to involve herself with *Infinite Odyssey*, she was going to start living like she belonged there. She joined a weekly girls' night with Angie and some of the other early shifters at a bar down the road, where the pours were generous and the drinks cheap. They'd do their hair and laugh about their day and withstand stares from thirsty men who had even less decorum now than they did in the twenty-first century, all in the name of getting out of the diner, of doing something, anything fun.

It did help. She'd resisted leaving that place for weeks before accepting the invitation, just in case Miles ever showed up, but she was beginning to understand that giving herself a break now and then was important too. Letting Angie entertain them with her wild stories—she had a tendency to get herself in trouble, with men and with the law—was the perfect distraction from the hopelessness that had plagued her.

Tonight was one of those nights. Harper clocked out and followed the girls to the bar. It was housed in an old building a few blocks away, accessible via the alley, and, as far as Harper could tell, nameless.

For the first time, Harper let Angie order for her. She was apparently tired of watching Harper nurse her unfussy gin and soda every week, which she tended to suck down slowly, carefully, as if afraid to miss any clues the universe might choose to drop at the exact wrong moment. She'd been coming out with the other waitresses for weeks now—wasn't it time, Angie said, that Harper finally have a little fun?

The drink was something overly sweet and fruity, spiked generously with caustic rum, and came in a fishbowl glass as big as her head, much to Angie's delight. When it arrived, Harper nearly sent it back, fearful in a way she had never stopped to interrogate. She looked at the women around her, laughing with one another, allowing themselves a good time, and that fear loosened, just a little. Did she really think Miles was going to saunter through that blacked-out dive-bar door looking for her?

The truth was, Miles was not coming back for her. Not tonight and not ever. He could have found her anywhere, if he really wanted to, the same way her future self had. If she hadn't seen him or heard from him by now, then she was never going to. Peggy was gone. Her family was gone. Harper lived in 1971 now. This was her new home. Best make the most of it.

So she finished off the fishbowl drink and ordered another while Dottie slipped a quarter into the jukebox, punched a button, and grinned as Tina Turner wailed through the speakers. Harper got up with the other waitresses and finally allowed herself to dance. At one point, Angie grabbed her hand and the two of them swayed and spun until they were breathless with laughter and exertion, before sitting back down at the table to rest their sore feet. She was still wearing those stupid, stiff Keds.

"Honey. You adjusting okay?" Angie popped a cigarette between her lips. "You seem like you're doing better."

Harper nodded. The world tilted oddly around her. "Yeah. I'm okay."

"Dottie a good roommate?" She took a practiced drag then let the cigarette dangle between her manicured fingers. Harper got the distinct impression that Angie was a woman who was used to getting her way.

"The best," Harper said honestly. "She's so patient."

She sipped from the fishbowl, amazed that it seemed to become more drinkable with every sip.

"Not still thinking about that scumbag boyfriend of yours, are you?"

"Definitely not," Harper lied.

"Good. Cause—"

"Angie Marie Detweiler, is that you?"

Both women turned, and Angie's face lit up. She launched herself out of the booth and hugged the person who had said her name, a newcomer, decidedly not a Starlight waitress. She took him by the hand and sat him down across from Harper. He wore his hair slicked back and a once-crisp tweed suit. You might have called him attractive, more when he smiled, but there was a prominent crease between his thick brows despite his youth that said he spent much of his time worrying.

"Harper," Angie said through her grin, "this is my brother, Nathan. Nathan, I can't believe you're here. When did you get home?"

Nathan checked his watch. "About three hours ago."

Angie swatted his arm playfully. "Three hours in New York and you're already hanging out at Ricky's. Typical."

"Mom said you'd be here. I'm just paying my beloved baby sister a visit."

"You're a good man. I bet all the ladies in LA just love you."

"I wish," he said, that lopsided smile making a welcome appearance. He glanced at Harper. "Who's your friend?"

"Oh gosh, I'm the worst. Nathan, Harper. Harper, Nathan."

"Nice to meet you, Harper," Nathan replied. He put out a hand to shake and she took it, desperately wishing in that moment that she'd stayed as sober as she usually did. It was always the moment you'd had enough alcohol to spin the room that the attractive man walked through the door.

"You too."

"Don't mind me," Angie said. "I'm going to get another drink. Nate?"

"The usual for me, Ange. Thanks a million."

Angie flounced away from the table, leaving Harper alone with her decidedly better-dressed and probably better-employed brother.

"So let me guess," he said. "Girls' night?"

"Something like that." She pushed the fishbowl away, no longer wanting to be associated with it. "I work at the Starlight. With Angie."

"Yeah, I figured that one out."

"I go to school for astrophysics, though. I'm just here until I can sort a few things out." What on earth had made her tell him that? Embarrassment? Shame? She certainly didn't have any of the paperwork to prove it.

But Nathan lit up. "Astrophysics, really? That's a big subject for such a small girl."

"Jesus. Ever heard of Vera Rubin, who's probably at Carnegie right now proving the existence of dark matter? How about Hedy Lamarr, code-breaker and inventor of the internet?"

"The inter-what?"

That merited a deep drink from the unwanted fishbowl. She sipped, unable to decide what would be worse—sobering up so she could at least lie properly or getting just drunk enough that she might not have to remember this conversation. "Forget it."

"You one of those feminists? Rah-rahing for Women's Lib and all that?"

She almost choked on her drink. She wanted to tell him where he could stick his rah-rah, but she was pretty sure she knew the right answer for 1971.

"No," she muttered. "Definitely not one of those bra burners. I just know if you took a second to look at women who're doing amazing things in science, you wouldn't be so flip."

Nathan's laughed. "I guess it was a pretty dumb thing to say."

"I guess so."

"I promise I wasn't trying to downplay your studies. In fact, I think it's real impressive."

"Well, it's not meant to be impressive. It was meant to get me into NASA. It was supposed to make me an astronaut like Sally freaking Ride."

Nathan whistled. "I'm afraid to ask who that is."

Harper realized her mistake and waved a hand dismissively. "Don't bother, she hasn't done anything yet." She glanced over at the bar; Angie was talking animatedly with the bartender, her friend and brother forgotten. Great.

Nathan's voice brought her back. Why was he so determined to talk to someone who'd just spent the last five minutes dressing him down? Peggy was better at this kind of thing. Flirting. Being flirted with.

He asked, "So what brought you to the Starlight, then?"

"My friend died," she said, cursing herself again. "And my life sort of just fell apart."

"Oh. Wow. I'm sorry to hear that."

"Yeah." The fruity drink made a gurgling sound as she sucked the dregs of it through her straw.

"For what it's worth, you seem incredibly well-adjusted."

She glanced up quickly, surprised. But he was smiling again, proud of his own sarcasm.

She looked at him properly. He was quite good-looking, now that she thought about it. A soft, square jaw. Thick brows. A smile that tugged left first, before evening out. She thought about kissing him.

"What about you?" she asked. "What do you do?"

"I'm a writer. On a TV show."

She sat up straight. He said it like he'd just admitted to being the garbage man, but Harper was really wishing he'd led with that.

"Oh, wow," she said casually, despite the quickening beat of her heart. "What show?"

"*Gunpowder*. It's silly. There's a million of us on staff and I've written less than an hour of television in my own right. I'll probably never have my own show."

"*Gunpowder*."

A twinge of recognition. A memory crawling out of a murky place. The television on late at night. Old reruns. *Star Trek* and *Bonanza*,

Infinite Odyssey and . . . and *Gunpowder*. When he didn't want to think too hard, her father pulled out his DVD box sets and let the familiar plots of his childhood lull him to sleep on the couch. The shows all had something in common, though it wouldn't have been obvious to just anyone. But her father always paid attention to these things because he loved a good story, and he insisted on appreciating those who were responsible for the ones he loved best.

The twinge became more insistent.

"I love that show," she said. She heard the terror and excitement in her own voice and hoped he could not.

Nathan stared in surprise. "You do?"

"Well, sure," she lied. "Who doesn't love a good western?"

"Well, I'll be damned. Most girls wouldn't be caught dead watching a bunch of cowboys shoot at each other."

"Oh?" she said. "You've spoken with most girls, then?"

Nathan smiled, caught. "No, I suppose I can't claim that after all, can I?"

"I think most girls would surprise you," Harper said, "if you gave them half a chance."

"You know what? I like you."

She leaned over the table and threaded her hands together. Rested her chin demurely against them. "That'll keep me warm at night."

He raised an eyebrow. "You want someone to keep you warm at night?"

"I want—"

The sentence dangled there, unfinished. What *did* she want? For three years it had been easier to convince herself that no one had what she was looking for, that no one was worth her time, than to bother with the question of what she really wanted.

Still, she had basic needs, just like anybody.

He was close enough to kiss, so she did. Gently, just a taste. A question. She pulled back just enough to look into his eyes.

"You're pretty forward for a lady," he said.

"Does that bother you?"

He shook his head.

"Good. Then I'm going to powder my nose." She tried to make it sound like an invitation. Nathan's smile told her he was glad to RSVP.

She stood and made for the dark restrooms on the other side of the bar, doing her best not to catch Angie's attention as she slipped past. She left the door to the dingy, single-person bathroom unlocked, and a moment later, Nathan poked his head in.

"You weren't really gonna powder your nose, were you?"

Harper laughed and shook her head. "Not unless that's a really strange euphemism for the other thing I want."

He stepped in and locked the door. "And what's that?"

She put a hand on his chest and looked up. "Is it really not obvious?"

He didn't waste any more breath answering the question.

Though making out in a grungy bathroom that was in desperate need of a scrub would not, on any given night, be her first choice, she was pleasantly surprised to find that Nathan was a generous kisser. There was something earnest about the way their lips met, the way his hands fumbled around the buttons on her dress, the thick strap of her uncomfortable '70s bra. For all their banter, it was clear they both had pent-up desires that made them less than suave. Maybe he was just a guy she was trying to get close to for less-than-honest reasons, but he was also gentle and a good kisser, and what else did a person need to be, really?

After a moment, Nathan pulled back and just looked at her. She stared back, waiting. Was he about to drop a bombshell on her? No condom on hand? Some kind of STD?

"Gotta admit, Harper. I like you."

Ah, yes. That kind of bombshell.

She swallowed, calculating. "And I like you too."

"Yeah?"

"Yeah." She pressed close again. "And hey, maybe you could show me around set sometime. I'd love to see where you work."

"Well, that's going to be hard. Because I just quit."

And that blooming hope died on the vine.

"You quit."

"Well, I'm going to. I already split my time between LA and New

York, so I'm home for the holidays and then I'm just . . . not going to go back."

Panic. Panic rising, hot and vile in her throat. She hadn't chosen yet, but she still wanted the ability to do so on her own terms.

"You can't do that."

"What do you care?"

The dim bathroom tilted around her, the pulse of the music outside bending along with it. The edges of a panic attack inched toward her heart, her lungs.

"Nothing." She licked her suddenly dry lips. *Be the girl in the bar. Smile and touch his arm and pretend.* "Only I don't think you should give up on the stuff you love to do."

"Well, it's happening. Whether you like that or not."

She tried to smile, like she was just being supportive. "You should really reconsider."

Nathan's expression turned bitter. "I see. I'm only interesting if I'm working in television. Is that it?" He unlocked and opened the door.

"No, that's not—"

"Listen, it was real nice to meet you. Tell my sister I'll see her later."

He brushed off his wool suit jacket and took long strides away from the bathroom, through the bar, and out the front door, taking all of Harper's hopes with him.

She went back to the booth and stared forlornly at the fishbowl.

When Angie finally sat down, Harper drank the scotch Nathan had ordered in two gulps.

"What the hell happened?" Angie asked. "I thought you two were hitting it off."

"I messed up," Harper said. Simple as that.

"Well, Anthony's a sensitive soul, you know," Angie replied, sipping at her own florid cocktail. "He'll come around."

Harper stilled. "You called him Nathan before."

"Oh, we call him Nathan at home. But he's always liked his middle name better, so he's been going by Anthony professionally. Like you, with Harper instead of Susan. Sometimes I slip up."

She had never heard Angie's last name before. She'd never bothered to ask. Angie had always just been Angie. But now, Harper went back to that moment, Nathan calling his sister's name across the crowded bar. Angie Marie Detweiler.

And Anthony Detweiler, creator of the show Harper loved, the show that had launched all of her troubles but might solve them too, was about to quit television for good.

8.

RIVERDALE
WINTER, 1971

It was New Year's Eve 1971, and Harper had no idea what to wear. Before Peggy disappeared, she'd borrowed Harper's clothes all the time. It was easier to take a dress in than it was to let one out, so the lending only ever worked one way. Anyway, Peggy always looked better in Harper's things than Harper ever did, but Peggy insisted that she wouldn't have been inspired to borrow at all if Harper hadn't looked so good in it.

Harper wished she had someone to borrow from now.

Instead, she threw on a plain blue dress she'd worn dozens of times because it was one of only a handful of clothing items she now owned, a sweater that matched only in the dimmest lighting, and the bomber jacket Argo gave her, which was the only heavier coat she possessed. She tried not to look too hard at her haphazard ensemble before getting in a taxi and heading north to Yonkers.

Was it possible that she was in a new timeline? That something as iconic and culturally pervasive as *Infinite Odyssey* was not fixed in time but subject to the whims of a man who was feeling unappreciated at work? These were the questions Harper had pondered the rest of the week, so distracted that she continually passed plates to the wrong customers or forgot their orders entirely. Her problems were bigger than a switched sandwich or a neglected coffee. Anthony was just an average guy, a would-be writer who had grown tired of waiting for his big break. How was she supposed to convince him that if he could just hold on a little longer, he'd have it? And that perhaps she, somehow, was going to help him?

It wasn't until Angie invited Harper to her New Year's Eve party, a significant look in her eye as she casually mentioned that Anthony would be there, that Harper had her chance. She had worked through Christmas, determined not to notice the holiday drifting by while the lights Joseph had haphazardly strung across half the windows blinked and twinkled in competition with the pink neon sign out front, Frank Sinatra crooning about silver bells through the diner's tinny speakers. She'd planned to do the same with New Year's, but Indira had graciously covered her shift last minute, and Harper made her way north to Angie's home in her faded blue dress.

The cab let her out on the corner of Angie's block.

The late December chill wrapped long fingers around her as she approached Angie's apartment building. She'd forgotten, somehow, that New York winters were unforgiving. The cold and the damp had a tendency to seep under one's clothes, settle into one's skin, regardless of layers.

Still, she took a minute to admire the streets draped in tinsel, the stores blaring Christmas carols despite the fact that Christmas was over, the houses iced with red and green twinkling lights, every other one as inviting as a gingerbread house.

Peggy would have loved this. She and Harper had always been opposites, despite their common goals: Peggy adored the cool winter months, while Harper preferred the warm spring and summer. Growing up in Colorado, Peggy went skiing every year, while Harper could be found hiking the trails once everything started blooming. And though the Maras were not religious, Peggy had loved Christmastime. The colors, the songs, the snow. She imagined Peggy here with her, standing on this sidewalk in this Hudson River–adjacent suburb, dazzled by the lights draping the old Victorians along the quiet street. But her projection of Peggy quickly morphed into the version with scars, the version who had chased her into Argo and further, and the wistful imagining disappeared like the smoke from Angie's afternoon cigarette.

"Harper? Is that you?" Harper looked up—Angie was staring down at her from the third-floor row house window. Harper waved. "What are you doing on the sidewalk? Come up!"

The stairwell of the old house-turned-apartments was dingy and reeked of stale cigarettes, but once Harper had huffed up the three flights of stairs, she barely noticed the odor and instead found herself unable to tear her thoughts from the burning in her calves. Angie's door was slightly ajar; Harper had expected to hear a wild party from the hall but there was only polite laughter, the faint echo of a record player warbling out Bing Crosby Christmas carols, and the tinkling of glassware. A far cry, even in audio, from the parties she'd barely attended in college and the ones she'd imagined Angie hosting given the more raucous nature of their girls' nights.

Harper peered into the apartment. The door led straight into the cramped kitchen where comically large bottles of wine and liquor crowded Angie's small dining table for two. Beyond that was a living room with a modest couch, a record player, and a boxy television set, its antennae slightly crooked. And of course, guests—a few girls from the diner and a lot more strangers—chatting amiably and milling about the apartment with an ease that said they'd all done this together many times.

She hung her bomber jacket on the overstuffed hook by the wall, feeling somewhat liberated from the disunity of the outfit it made, and reached for a bottle of wine, hoping to remain unseen for as long as it took to fill a glass and down just enough to calm her nerves.

People she knew from the diner approached and struck up conversations. Pointless discussions about Joseph's plans for a new cash register or how he had fired Emmeline so unfairly. She nodded along while peering at the rest of the room through her peripheral vision. *Twilight Zone* reruns on the television. Guests adorned in festive green-and-red outfits, light-catching baubles, and satin hair ribbons. Angie playing hostess to a group in the corner, her body relaxed and confident as she relayed one of her many stories about the terrible men she had a habit of dating. It was not so unlike Harper's own century, really. You even got used to the Farrah hair and the turtlenecks and the discordant color combinations after a while.

She was on her second glass of wine and working up the nerve to join the party in earnest when Anthony stumbled through the door. Harper, still stationed by the liquor table, was perfectly positioned to catch him before he could nose-dive into the bottles perched there.

"Whoa!" she said quietly, not wishing to embarrass him. "You okay?"

It was, perhaps, a stupid question; he reeked of booze and cigarettes.

"Not my proudest moment," he slurred.

"You do know that Angie has plenty of alcohol here, don't you? Could have saved your money."

"Still funny, Harper."

"What happened?" she asked, shifting to face him.

"Nothing happened," he said bitterly. "Nothing ever happened. Two years of my life, nothing to show for it. That's the whole point."

"Nathan?" Angie's voice was close, quiet. Anthony was still leaning on Harper when she reached them, arms crossed. Behind her, her audience peered at them, curious, whispering. "What the hell?"

"Sorry, sis. Got carried away at the bar."

"'Carried away'? This is a gathering for polite society. I won't have you stumbling around making a mess of my party."

"I'll help him get home, Ange," Harper offered.

"Oh, of course you will," Angie replied, a little nastily. Her expression softened, immediately repentant. "Yes, please. Take him to the diner first. Get him a plate of something greasy. God knows he has nothing in his cupboards to soak up all that gin." She handed Harper a wad of cash and turned away, the pair forgotten, exiled.

Harper called the taxi service. Outside, it had begun to snow, little particles drifting blithely past the window, creating a deceptively beautiful tableau that would be brown and mucky when she tried to navigate it tomorrow morning.

But tonight those fluffy flakes drifting past, glinting red and green and blue as they floated across strings of lights in windows and trees, reminded her of her favorite holiday episode of *Infinite Odyssey*, the Christmas event from 1980 when the Argonaut loses his memory and Argo loses power, and his first mate at the time, Elton Akron, must find Argo's power source and get her recharged so he can find a hospital. And when Argo is charged up, she zings the pair through twenty different versions of Christmas as they get their bearings straight.

It was Peggy's favorite too. She could recite every line of dialogue from each episode, but this one engrossed her so much that she'd remain silent through each and every watch. And the man responsible for that was at Harper's side and in danger of never creating that episode, or any others, at all. And maybe that was all right. Maybe everything that had happened in the last few years would unspool and she would find herself in a timeline where none of this had happened, memoryless and safe.

Or maybe it would create a future even worse than the one she was living now.

The taxi pulled up ten minutes later, and she helped Anthony in.

"My head is swimming," he muttered at one point, before leaning on Harper's shoulder. He closed his eyes against the flashes of green-and-red light, strings of tiny colored bulbs along every eave, every window.

Her head was swimming too. This had seemed so much easier when she rehearsed it in her head. But Anthony was not plastered in her staged mental play, and besides, she wasn't even really sure how to broach the topic. *You can't quit now, Anthony. Why not? Well, I just have this feeling.* That should have been number one on her list of things not to do.

"Sorry to make you miss Angie's shindig," Anthony mumbled, pulling her from her thoughts.

"It's all right."

"Yeah, probably not your scene anyway."

She looked down at his head on her shoulder. His hair was unkempt, sticking up at odd angles. "What's that supposed to mean?"

"Just that you're cooler than her friends."

Harper tried not to smile at that. "You wouldn't know; you were only there for about thirty seconds."

"Listen." He sat up suddenly, swaying with the sudden motion. "I'm sorry about the other night."

"It's okay," she said, startled.

"No, it isn't. You were just trying to be nice and I acted like a turkey." He was trying to make serious eye contact with her but having a hard time with all the swaying.

"You did," she decided to agree. "But who hasn't acted like a turkey every now and then?"

"See? That's what I'm talking about. You're cool, Harper."

"Well, maybe I'm the forgiving type." She wondered how true that would be if she ever saw Miles again.

The diner was nearly empty when they walked in. Frank Sinatra serenaded them about a white Christmas. Joseph and Indira were chatting at the counter, foreheads close, voices low. Joseph nodded at the pair as they entered, and Indira, festive glitter swiped across her brown cheekbones and dark eyes, gave Harper a funny look as Harper ushered Anthony into an empty booth.

Indira pulled her notepad from her apron and approached their table. "What are you doing here?" she asked, notepad poised for their order.

"Helping this one sober up," Harper said. Anthony gave a pathetic little wave, then dropped his head to his forearms on the table. "Angie's orders. This is her brother."

"In that case, it's on the house." Indira winked.

In that moment, Harper was grateful for the Starlight. You could say a lot of things about this place, both in her time and now, but the truth was, they weren't all bad things. And one of the best qualities was that the staff took care of one another, even in small ways. That apparently didn't change, no matter the year.

"Thanks, Indira. Let's get him a coffee high and dry, water, a short stack with eggs up, and a side of bacon."

"And you?"

"You got any of your secret spiked eggnog left?"

Indira scribbled the order on her pad of paper. "Oh, and happy New Year." Indira smirked conspiratorially and sauntered off.

Outside, the snow was piling up in window corners, blanketing the nearly empty parking lot in crystalline white. The night sky had taken on an orangey hue, light pollution refracting through the falling snow. Hazy, strange, familiar. Not her sky, but still the same, somehow. Around them, Frank Sinatra's voice became the Carpenters, the crisp chime of bells echoing around the diner.

Harper nudged Anthony's arm. "Hey. Anth— Nathan."

"What?" came his muffled reply.

Jesus, the man was a pathetic drunk.

"Why are you really doing this?"

"Doing what?"

"Quitting your job. Drinking yourself silly."

He lifted his head. His eyes were red and sore. "Because nothing is ever going to happen, so what's the point?"

"Don't you think you're being a little dramatic?"

He scoffed. "Oh, you've been talking to Angie."

Indira brought out the requested hot coffee and a large glass of eggnog. Harper took a gulp as Indira walked away. The ratio of rum to eggnog was higher than anticipated, but not unwelcome.

"Angie thinks you're dramatic, all right," she said. "But you shouldn't give something up that makes you happy enough to be this sad about it."

"How would you even know?"

"Because that's what I did."

"Right." Anthony blew on his coffee. "You were going to be an astronaut."

This made her bristle in a way she truly hated. "Gosh, I know how silly that must sound coming from a woman. Well, guess what? I'm actually smart as hell when it comes to space but an idiot when it comes to living my fucking life." It dawned on her that this was actually true—just how deeply she'd let Peggy's disappearance worm its way in and rot away at her ambitions. "Take it from me, or you'll end up wishing you'd just waited it out a few more months. Weeks, even. I'll bet you they're discussing your promotion as you sit here sulking."

But Anthony wasn't biting. He just stared at his steaming beverage, as if wishing it would rise from the cup and slip down his throat of its own accord. He seemed unwilling to make any effort at all. If he knew what Harper had been through these past months, would he continue acting like the world was crumbling around him? If he knew the magnitude of what he was giving up, would he rethink his choice?

The fact was, Anthony Detweiler was as average as they came. Good-looking, sure, but that was about it. Doors would open for him because of his skin and demeanor and the appendage in his slacks. And here he was, closing a golden door in his own face, a door Harper desperately needed him to walk through. But this Anthony never would. Not without something extraordinary to bring through with him.

Not without the Argonaut.

"Look, Harper, I know you're just trying to help—"

"Actually, you don't know jack shit, Anthony." At this, he sat up a little straighter. She didn't even feel bad—the words just tumbled out. Something was happening in her mind; a realization was unspooling, hot and shining, uncontainable. "You strike me as someone who is used to being coddled, so I'm going to do us both a favor and stop. You don't want my opinion about what you should do with your life? That's fine. I'll tell you a story about mine instead." She sipped her eggnog, steeling her nerves and her pounding heart. "Once upon a time, there was a girl named Harper. She had a best friend named Peggy. The girls did everything together, and that included playing a lot of make-believe. One of their favorite games was Infinite Odyssey."

She'd assumed it would be harder to talk about Peggy like this, but instead it released a pressure valve inside her, the tight ball in her chest where she'd locked her memories of Peggy blooming open. Not just the bad memories, but the good ones too. Both of them playing in the park nearby, using the jungle gym as their Argo. Giggling madly at their own cleverness, their own secret game no one else knew how to play. That light-as-air feeling that nothing would ever have to change.

"In the girls' game," she continued, "the Argonaut was a mysterious figure who'd woken up one day without any memory of who he was or where he came from. What made him special, though, was his psychic third eye and his incredible ship, a vessel made to travel through time and space without disrupting causality. They called it a Tesseract Engine and named it Argo."

"Psychic third eye? Tesser-what? And what the hell is causality?"

"Just shut up and listen." His mouth snapped obediently shut. "The Argonaut was alone. He needed answers—about where he came from and who he was—but he needed people too. He needed them to help him understand the places he explored and the people who lived there. He needed them to be human in ways he couldn't be. And this was the game."

Anthony's attention was on her now, gears turning in his intoxicated mind, and for the first time, she saw the truth clear as the snow in his glassy eyes. Anthony Detweiler would always just be a regular guy in need of an idea, in need of direction, in need of someone to point him toward that golden door.

"They took turns playing the Argonaut every day," she continued. "The other girl would play the Argonaut's first mate. Together, they had galactic adventures. They traveled the galaxies and found planets in need of saving. They learned about the future and times long past. As long as they were together, they were unstoppable."

He asked her to describe one of their adventures, so she did. She described episode eight of the very first season, the one Harper and Peggy liked to play out the most. The first few seasons of *Infinite Odyssey* were grouped into serials, story arcs that played out over two and sometimes as many as six episodes. Episode eight was the central chapter of their favorite serial, "The Enemy of the Argonaut," where the Argonaut finally gets a clue about his past when he crash-lands on a planet he believes is uninhabited until he comes face-to-face with another man who possesses a psychic third eye—a man who claims the Argonaut is responsible for the destruction of their world and who vows to make sure he is punished for his crimes. It was one of the only times the characters Harper and Peggy played were equally powerful, equally strange and fun—neither's arc playing out in service of the other.

She had Anthony's full, slowly sobering attention now.

"And this . . . this was the friend you lost?"

Harper nodded numbly. God, she wished Peggy could be here to see this. To see what she was doing, would do. But memories of their last night stabbed through those wishes—the way Peggy had looked at her, the text she sent after. The disappearance that was not really a disappearance, not an accident, but a choosing. A leaving.

But Harper, too, had a choice. She'd spent the last three years living as though her free will had been taken, disappeared along with Peggy, but it hadn't. Here, now, she was finally, finally making a choice of her own.

"I loved her more than anything in this world," she told Anthony. "And she's gone. I gave up on my dreams when I lost her. Even though she would have wanted me to keep going. To do what she never did." She swallowed the last of her eggnog, relishing the scorch of it in her throat. "Tell me, Anthony, what is it you've lost? Besides a couple of years and maybe some pegs on your ego?"

He gripped his mug tight and stared thoughtfully into his cooling coffee.

"You're right," he said finally. "I should be fighting harder, not less." He looked up at Harper with a new fervor. "They didn't like my last screenplay, Harper. That's the reality. They told me I'm a great writer with less-than-great ideas. I thought that meant I was fucked, you know? If I have no good ideas, then how the hell am I supposed to get further in this business?" Harper opened her mouth to respond but Anthony wasn't done. "But you! I could have listened to you talk about Peggy and the Argonaut all day. I want to know about those worlds you saved, about the Tesseract Engine that took you all over space and time." And then he started laughing. Actually fucking laughing, giddy as a kid on Christmas. "Don't you see, Harper? I don't need good ideas. I need a partner." He reached for her hands and folded them into his coffee-warmed palms. "I need you."

9.

RIVERDALE
WINTER, 1971

Harper watched mutely as Anthony finished off the plate of fluffy pancakes, greasy eggs, and oily bacon. He ate like something starved, and she supposed in a way he was. Starved of validation, starved of creative fulfillment. Harper had given him neither of those things, but she'd given him a path to them. To that golden door.

And she would walk through it beside him whether he remembered this in the morning or not.

Just as easily as he had slipped into a morose, self-pitying despair, Anthony's confidence returned with a vengeance. She was starting to understand that it was probably how he commanded most decisions, including his recent choice to resign from the world of television: abrupt and with full confidence, no thought of future regrets. Even if he turned around in a month and decided he'd made a grave mistake, at least he'd had no reservations about the idea at the time. She found, horrifyingly, that despite the potential for catastrophic consequences, she admired this about him.

Especially right now. As he ate, Anthony Detweiler made plans. It was fascinating to watch. So fascinating that she barely heard him when he said, "I have a confession."

At one point, Indira had set another glass of eggnog in front of her. She drank from it now, having lost track of her sobriety.

"What's your confession?"

"You promise not to tell my sister?"

"Scout's honor."

Anthony looked puzzled but carried on. "Okay, here goes: I'm a Trekkie."

She choked on her eggnog a little. "That is not at all where I thought that was going."

"The fact is," he said, "even though NBC canceled the show years ago, Trekkies are growing in numbers. CCNTV, *Gunpowder*'s network, has taken notice. They want a show that can capitalize on the fanbase that *Star Trek* left behind. You know what that means?" He leaned back, hands clasped behind his head. He watched Harper with a smug, drunken grin.

"You're the TV writer, not me," she said, but his excitement was infectious. Her mouth gave her away; she was smiling too. "It means there's a good chance they'll want a sci-fi show to fill the void."

"Bingo. And I think that you and I should write that show, Harper. I think it should be about your Argonaut. And I think we should pitch it to the network VP when we see her at the first-ever *Trek* convention."

"We?"

"We. On the twenty-first."

"The twenty-first? Of January?"

That was three weeks from now. They'd have just that much time to put together whatever materials a writer used to pitch a show to a network. A few lines? A whole script? Was it enough?

"I know it's not much time, but it's the perfect place to do it. Sheila's got a thing about Gene Roddenberry, and she knows that CCNTV needs something flashy and new to stay relevant. And she's going to see how excited people still are about *Star Trek*, and she's going to be thinking to herself, 'Gosh, I really wish we had a show to scoop up the viewers *Star Trek* ditched,' and there you and I will be, pitch in hand." When she hesitated, he got out of the booth and knelt at her side, hands pressed together in the prayer position. "Please, Harper. I need you. I really need you."

She ignored a sudden pang of nausea in her gut. The eggnog must have been getting to her. Or, you know, the buckets of rum Indira had ladled into it. But maybe, too, it was that shard of anger that had festered there ever since Miles stashed her in the '70s like a box of unwanted clothing you'd forget about in your garage, forced to find her own solutions, her own path forward, with barely any help and barely any of the information she desperately needed. She still had no idea if this was the right path forward, if her future self had given her the idea that her name belonged in those credits, or if the Incarnate was using her to create the future it wanted.

"I don't know," she started to say. And then the world began to spin.

"Just think about it, Harper. Please."

"I'll think about it."

"Good." Anthony smiled at her and held out his hand. "Should we dance? Last chance we'll get this year." He got to his feet and took her hands, pulling her out of the booth.

She let him guide them in a slow dance across the black-and-white tile, closing her eyes against the various tilting planes of the room. He wasn't making plans anymore, just smiling and humming along with the song. Happy to be there, with Harper, in the Starlight Diner on New Year's Eve. She wanted to be happy too. She wanted his excitement to infect her. But everything had begun to move sluggishly in both her mind and her vision. It was hard to focus on any one thing. To remember.

At one point she opened her eyes again and saw that Joseph and Indira had joined them, participating in the impromptu festivities. Her field of vision was narrowing, a strange, glittery twilight crowding in. "Auld Lang Syne" played on the crackly speakers.

"It's almost midnight!" Indira said, her voice swimming to Harper through a murky fog.

The group started counting down. Her range of sight was alarmingly condensed, now just pinpricks of light. And then she heard it:

somewhere, someone was screaming. A mind-piercing scream, ragged and emptied out, as if it had been going on for hours, hours.

Harper stopped dancing. The countdown continued.

"Harper?" Anthony said. "What's wrong?"

"I'm okay," she stuttered. She didn't know why she couldn't seem to tell him that she wasn't, wasn't, wasn't.

"Three . . . two . . . one . . . Happy New Year!" chorused the handful of diners. Someone had confetti poppers; a rain of shiny red confetti sprinkled through the air around her, mimicking the snow outside.

To Harper, it looked like flecks of blood.

The last she would remember of the Starlight Diner as the year rolled over was the dying music, the gasps and panic as she crumpled in Anthony's arms, and the feeling of confetti against her skin as consciousness finally fled, featherlight and hot, like ashes.

She wakes somewhere far, far away. Her body feels strange and sluggish, almost like there's a delay, the way a transmission from space might take a moment to arrive as it bounces between relay satellites and Earth. She's in a dank, dark room, so cold she's practically paralyzed. Even the stale air seems to have an echo. There is light, but only just, and she can't see the source of it—only the way it refracts off of hundreds of thousands of black mirror faces across the walls and ceiling. No, wait; they're not mirrors—they're glinting onyx spears the size of ancient speleothems that have been left to accumulate for centuries, massive anthodite formations unlike anything she's ever seen.

And then the scene changes, and she is not only in the cavern. She is also striding through the harsh sun of a purple jungle, swimming through a vast body of water toward a sandy shore, and picking through the ashen remains of a ruined library. She is in a hundred places all at once, each one laid over the other, a thousand negatives overlapping into a single confusing image. She understands that this is how the thing inside Peggy's mind operates—it scatters itself across worlds and infects them with itself—a planet-killing psychic parasite. She knows this implicitly, somehow.

It feels like that moment back in her bedroom, when Peggy pressed her nails to Harper's neck and the clutter gave way to images of other worlds. But now she is physically in each world, physically in each separate body commandeered by this parasite, and her mind is a broken computer that simply cannot process what's happening, except a strange, deep-seated hatred. She wants to be afraid, but her heart is inexplicably steady as a drumbeat, and so any fear she might have had feels far away. There is only hate. She hates this jungle, this ocean, this library. It is too much. It is not enough. Remembers, though she's not sure how she remembers, the people who used to inhabit these places, because this parasite now inhabits those same people. It takes on their injustices, their horrible wars, and subsumes it all until everything is part of the perfect whole. Those worlds become part of something better. The people there do too, vessels to carry out the cleansing in the next world.

No. No. She can't stand this feeling, this rage. It goes too deep, fills every part of her. It's edging out so many things that matter. She wills herself back to the diner, back to the body she left there. She can see it in her mind's eye, in stuttering fits and bursts—Anthony's face hovering over hers; Indira pressing a cloth to her forehead; Joseph turning off the music. But she can't seem to get back there—her mind sucks her back to the confusing flicker of myriad other landscapes.

And then, a hundred thousand voices speak as one inside her mind.

Someone is here.

Her consciousness is vacuumed out of the bewildering array of experiences happening simultaneously and slammed back into that dank, eerie cavern. No, not a cavern; the once grand, palatial hall of a civilization fallen to the Incarnate.

But when she tries to lift her arm, she can't. Her body moves but it isn't her own mind instructing it to do so. For the first time, she realizes she's standing. One leg takes a step, then the other, until she has crossed the funereal darkness of the great hall. She catches her reflection in a black spar and realizes that it is not her face—it's Peggy's. Peggy's scarred visage, her once-warm eyes now glassy, clouded marbles inside her angular face.

Peggy smiles at her reflection.

I see you.

And then Harper is ripped painfully out of Peggy's body, out of that palace, out of that prismatic darkness, so instantaneously it is as if she was never there at all. She wakes up screaming in a bed that isn't hers.

—

Anthony stared down at Harper as she came to. He was sitting on the edge of the fluffy bed in which she found herself, face screwed up in concern.

"I took you to my place—I didn't know where you lived. Guess that eggnog was pretty strong," he said. He seemed utterly sober now. She wondered how long she'd been out.

She pulled herself into a sitting position, pain jackhammering through her head with each small movement. Images flashed behind her sore eyes—a jungle, an ocean, a library. A dim, glistening cave. A smiling reflection.

"Guess so," she muttered, voice crackling as if she had never used it. Her body felt off-kilter, wrong, limbs too tight, skin too small. She'd had the strangest dream.

No. Not a dream. Her consciousness flung across the vastness of space and time to a million places at once, a stowaway inside a million minds, all connected—including Peggy, who was somewhere dark and cold and glittering. Peggy's face in the hazy light. Peggy's voice in her mind. *I see you.*

Some part of her had wondered these last few months whether what happened to her was even real. Whether she'd ever lived in the twenty-first century, or if she had dreamed it all up. If the Argonaut, in the disappointing flesh, had truly left her in the Starlight Diner, or if her fear of wasting her life had created a compelling, sci-fi reason for her presence there. If Peggy had actually been in her bedroom, or if Harper's desire to see her again had manifested a complicated delusion.

But there could be no doubt now. Because when she felt something drip from her nose, blood in the aftermath of her lost consciousness, and she swiped a hand across her face, it came back shimmering like an oil slick.

"Holy shit, Harper," Anthony breathed. He dashed from the room and returned with a kitchen towel. "What kind of drugs are you into?"

She dabbed at the substance. Stared down at the inky smear on the towel. She trembled as she said, "Something I'll never use again."

Miles said they got rid of it. That he'd removed whatever Incarnate goo Peggy had injected her with. But he was wrong.

He had made a mistake. He thought she was safe, that he had made her safe. That he would dump her here and everyone would forget about her, like he planned to. He'd left her here with no way out, no way of escape, the tip of the hook Peggy had stuck in her still festering under the skin.

Rage was a funny thing. You could put it away for months or even years, tucked neatly inside a drawer alongside your sorrow and your childlike love for an old TV show. You could glance at it once in a while and think, *Maybe I'll wear that today*. But it was easier not to. Nothing else in the drawer matched, and besides, you grew out of it years ago.

Until one day, it fits again.

"Well then, you get some sleep." Anthony patted the blanket, tucking her in. It was unexpectedly sweet. "I'll be on the couch if you need anything."

"Thanks, Anthony."

"Good night, Harper."

He left the room. Harper lay awake in the dark. Snow drifted past the window, beautiful, unconcerned. She watched it for hours until the flakes became sparse and the sun began to peek over the trees outside.

10.

NEW YORK CITY
WINTER, 1972

The next morning, before Anthony and most of New York were awake, Harper went back to the planetarium. She was nursing the most wicked hangover she'd ever been unlucky enough to suffer and a festering, abject terror in the pit of her stomach. She had to see if her future self had left any more notes, any more clues—if she knew that Harper had a hand in creating *Infinite Odyssey*, then she must also know that Miles had not eradicated the Incarnate from her system. She would know Harper was getting in a cab and seeking answers—and if she wasn't an asshole, she would give them.

Because now, things were unraveling. Harper had the same thing inside her that had stolen her best friend. It was no longer hypothetical, an if-then scenario. If Miles didn't come back for her, Harper would succumb to the parasite in her mind, her consciousness spread thin across the cosmos. She would no longer be in control. The choice to help Anthony create her beloved TV show would no longer exist.

But there was no note, no clues, no hints of any kind from her future self. Not with the projectionist in the Sky Theater, not with the box-office attendant, not in the orrery. She resorted to wandering the exhibits, searching for slips of paper or weathered envelopes in the nooks and crannies of each display.

She meandered the museum for hours, unwilling to give up. It was nearly empty; the planetarium only closed for Thanksgiving and Christmas but was clearly not the first stop of those who normally spent New Year's Day sleeping off the party of the night before. The silence was eerie—it made her feel exposed.

Finally, she ended her full-circle search in the Astronomia exhibit, though all she found were two academics by the gravity well, deep in excited chatter about the resounding success of *Mariner 9*.

She nearly wandered off again, distracted by a promising shadow at the end of the exhibit, when she heard one of the academics, the man with red cheeks and an ill-fitting yellow blazer, say, "I'm sure Mr. French will have some ideas. He's practically a savant, that Paul."

"Yes, I noticed he was here earlier, prepping the new probe just shipped over from NASA. Been gone for months, then shows up again out of the blue? He's a strange man, that French."

The other man, a skinny fellow with a crooked bow tie, replied, "Well, the chairman will have his ear for the next twenty minutes; you know how they get."

She wandered behind them, barely pretending to look at the exhibits. Mr. French. Mr. Paul French. Could it really be him?

"Once I saw he'd returned, I'd hoped to chat with him about doing a guest lecture with my students; I know they would be thrilled to hear his thoughts on Fred Hoyle."

"Indeed, but you know how busy that man is."

They were nearly to the door, but Harper needed something she could use to tip her hypothesis closer to real fact. A confirmation.

"Excuse me," she said. They turned and gave her a look that said they would rather not stop, especially for a woman, but what can you do? "I couldn't help but overhear. I've been trying to get in touch with Mr. French for ages. I'm writing . . . a column about him."

At this, the men lit up. "The man is quite the character."

"He really is," she said.

The red-faced academic chuckled. "He's an anomaly, my dear. Ask him about the topography of Venus and he can tell you what it looks like down to the very last volcano. Try to engage him on Fermi and he has no clue what you're talking about."

That's because he's a time-and-space traveler, not an astrophysicist, she didn't say.

"Sometimes he's Mr. Peabody and others he's just Sherman," she provided, hoping she remembered the right cartoon.

"You *are* looking for French!" the thin man laughed.

"Tell me, is he here today?"

"Yes—in fact, there he is now."

Harper spun around. She could have laughed in relief. It was him. It was really him, too tall for his own good, loping down the corridor alongside a stockier man with a shiny bald patch and a prim blazer. She didn't recognize him but knew immediately that this must be the predecessor of her own time's Emmett Frost Wilson. They were arguing, though it sounded good-natured.

The closer they came, the more she realized that, while she was definitely looking at Miles the Argonaut, there was no denying that he was not *her* Miles—he was at least ten years younger, smooth-cheeked and bright-eyed, no gray to be seen in his auburn hair. In the TV show, the Argonaut could reverse his age using Argo and the tesseract crystal that powered her engine—was she looking at a Miles who had made himself young after their last meeting, or a man who had not yet met her?

She thanked the red-faced academic quickly, having all but forgotten about him, and walked with purpose toward the chairman and Miles. This was better than notes from her future self. This was the Argonaut himself, which meant Argo was nearby, and so was her ticket to getting out of here and finding Peggy.

The chairman and Miles shook hands and took off in opposite directions. Miles began the descent toward the first floor. Realizing that in her shock she was letting him get away, she dashed after him, calling his name. "Miles!"

He paused at the bottom of the stairs and turned. She wasn't sure what she expected, but he didn't seem to recognize her. Though she had used his real name rather than his silly pseudonym, his expression remained pleasantly blank, waiting for further conversation.

She cleared her throat. "Um. Sorry. I wanted to talk to you about . . . something."

Miles tilted his head. "Do I know you?" The confusion in his eyes seemed utterly sincere.

"Oh, I, um, am writing an article—"

His expression relaxed. "Sorry, I don't do interviews, Miss . . . ?"

She started down the stairs. "Starling. Harper."

"Miss Starling. I cherish my privacy. You understand."

He started walking, as if that was the end of the conversation.

"No, I'm not . . . This isn't . . . Oh, for the love of god." She picked up speed, trying to catch up with him as he sauntered with those absurdly long legs toward the lobby. "This is ridiculous. Where are you going?"

"Have a pleasant day, Miss Starling," he said over his shoulder. "I think we're done here."

More swiftly than was fair, he walked out the front doors and out of the building. Harper groaned and ran after him. A pain shot up her shins, then another. This was why she had not done track in high school, preferring instead to sit in the bleachers during meets with giant posters sporting Peggy's name, cheering her friend on from the sidelines.

"Miles, wait!"

He did not.

"Fine!" The word came out like a whipcrack. She ground to a halt, breathing hard. Central Park sprawled out to their right, an unnaturally quiet Park Avenue to their left. "Run away, Moonraker; it's what you're good at."

It was just a guess, but she couldn't ignore the clues he'd laid out for her. His obsession with Miles Moonraker, for one. His uncanny resemblance to the lanky rock star who had worn a full face of makeup or a spangled mask during every show. The musician's mysterious disappearance from the limelight thirty years after his debut. She hadn't had time to ask him before he ditched her in this year, but she could still put two and two together. Aliens must get bored too. Maybe, to pass the time, you became a famous rock star, and once that got boring, you left.

Miles did slow then. He turned, his face pale, as if his obliviousness were a balloon that she'd punctured and it was slowly deflating.

"What did you just say?" An elderly man walked his dog past and Miles smiled impatiently. He slunk toward Harper once the man was out of earshot. "No one's supposed to know about that."

But Harper just laughed bitterly.

Miles looked utterly chilled. "All right. What did I do? I don't get the sense we've slept together, though with the number of drugs I did in those days—"

"First of all, Miles Moonraker doesn't even exist yet. You're getting your years mixed up. God, why did I ever think you were a genius? Second, you got my best friend kidnapped and brainwashed by something called the Incarnate, and then you abandoned me here, in the 1970s." Her lungs squeezed uncomfortably—she would have to remember to start going to the gym when this was all over.

"The Incarnate?" Miles looked properly shocked this time. "No. I don't believe you."

"Oh, it's still out there. And it was a different you that did this. An older you. Meaner."

In that moment, Harper realized that there was an entire sordid history this version of Miles had not yet lived. For whatever reason, he was contentedly working and living in the '70s as Mr. French, museum curator, oblivious to what his future held. His neighbor had told her about the death of his partner, so why did this Miles seem utterly ignorant of the grief that had turned him into the Miles who left her here? When did this man become the one who had so callously left her at the Starlight Diner months before?

"No," Miles said, "I'm . . . Well, okay, I haven't always been entirely honest, and yes, I'm a little overly fond of scotch, and maybe I spent a long time making a lot of bad choices but they were always for the right reasons, even if the outcome . . ." he trailed off, as if his arguments weren't even convincing himself. "I've messed up plenty in my time, Miss Starling, but I've never left anyone behind. No one who didn't deserve it."

"I didn't deserve it!"

"I'm not saying you did! Though maybe I'm asking if there's any chance—"

"There's no chance I deserved to be left behind," she hissed. "And you need to get me out of here so I can save my friend."

"Oh, no." To her dismay, Miles took up his leggy walk again. Where the hell was he even going? "I can't cross my own time path, Miss Starling, nor yours—any points where they intersect are off-limits. My ship would explode. I would disintegrate. The laws of time and space might be bent around time travelers, but there are still limits to how much we can test it. However much you might wish I could help you, I would be useless to you."

She ran around him, forcing him to stop. "No. I won't accept that. You owe me, Miles."

"And from your terrifying expression, I honestly don't doubt that's true, but that doesn't change the rules of time and space."

"So, you won't even try to fix your own mistake?" she asked. "You won't try to defeat the Incarnate?"

"Defeat it? Exactly who do you think I am?" When Harper didn't answer, he sighed. "I'm not a swashbuckling space hero with Herculean courage and a heart of gold. In my wilder days, I . . . Oh, who am I kidding?" He let out a sad laugh. "In my wilder days, I fucked up with the Incarnate. I left it in the rearview thinking that was it, the end. What did I know? I was young and in way over my head. I didn't know what I was doing. If I can be honest for a second? I still don't. I make it all up as I go."

Her heart sank as she realized, "You won't do anything. You won't even try to get us both home."

The words sparked a raw nerve—they were enough to shock her *out* of her shock. She'd buried it all so deep and ignored the truth of it—because the mind protects you in trauma, you see, and because everything had moved so damn quickly.

Seeing her best friend's face in her shadowy apartment—the scars marring her skin, the cold glare of her once-warm eyes, the lack of recognition on her face, and feeling, for a fleeting instant before the fear kicked in, that her friend had returned, that Harper could have Peggy Mara back from the dead—had whipped up a boil of old hope that had somehow sustained its simmer, even over the long months that she had been alone in this century. And then: New Year's Eve. Peggy's face in the dim reflection of a nightmare, and a hundred alien vistas flashing, even now, behind her eyes.

I see you.

Could Peggy Mara ever go home, even if Harper ended this? Could Harper?

Tears sprung to her eyes, and Harper cried right there on the sidewalk next to a bewildered Argonaut.

Miles patted her back awkwardly. "There, there. Mind, if people see you crying like this, they're going to think I did something to you."

"Well, you did," Harper said savagely. Anger was good; anger was conductive. It felt better than her revived grief, better than helplessness. "And now I'm stuck here. You lost my best friend, Miles, do you understand? You were supposed to protect her. And now she's part of the Incarnate's hive and they're looking for you . . . and for me. And you—you're useless." She lost the energy to stand and teetered toward a snowy bench lining the sidewalk. "He knew. He must have known."

"He who? He me? Knew what?"

She wiped the snow from the bench and sat. "That I'd met you here, in 1971. And he knew what you'd say. He knew you wouldn't help me."

"Time is . . . different for time travelers. What's happened for me may have never happened for him."

Harper rubbed her tired eyes. It was time to try a different tactic.

"My future self sent me a letter. At least, I'm pretty sure it was my future self. And it directed me here, where a projectionist screened the first episode of *Infinite Odyssey*. Only, the show won't exist until 1972. So, my future self gave him that tape to screen for me, and then she sent me here so I would watch it. And you know what I saw?"

"I'm afraid to ask. I rue the day anyone decided to create that abominable show—"

"It was my name in the credits, Miles. I helped make that show what it is. But I've been thinking—what if I don't?"

"Don't what?"

"Make the show. What if I do nothing, and the show is never created, and Peggy never figures out who you are, and I don't lose my best friend?"

"I'm more concerned with the fact that you seem to be able to influence the timeline. Didn't I give you a shot of something when you entered Argo the first time?"

"A shot of something? Like what?"

He waved his hands vaguely. "You know, like an injection you'd get at the doctor. Like a booster shot. A time booster, if you will."

Harper sat up straight. "You're saying the Paradox Serum is real too?"

On the show, all of the Argonaut's passengers received a vaccine against the rules of time. His blood and the lifeblood of the ship mixed to create a physiology-altering serum designed to prevent time travelers from accidentally creating paradoxes or rewriting history. It turned them into quantum ghosts, never meaningfully affecting the timeline and thus never harming time with their movements.

"Oh, so you gave it a name. Well done. Very fitting. Yes, everyone who travels with me gets one so they don't set off a thousand causality bombs. If I didn't give it to you when you got into Argo the first time then I really am losing my touch. And so is Argo."

Harper tried to remember if Miles had given her a shot of some kind that night but couldn't remember ever receiving one. In all the chaos, the wound on her neck, the desperate run for their lives, had he forgotten entirely? Was she a walking causality bomb?

Could things get any worse?

"All right." Miles settled onto the bench beside her. "Forgetting, for the moment, that I hate that show with all the passion in my heart—have you ever considered that if you don't do as the note-giver asks, the situation with the Incarnate could get worse, not better? That not only would Peggy be a victim to it, but whole galaxies, one by one, until the entire universe is under its thrall?"

"I . . ."

No, actually. She hadn't considered that. Though perhaps she should have, given what she'd been subjected to the night before. It was obvious to her now that the hive was legion. Peggy was not the first person to fall victim to the Incarnate and would not be the last. The truth was this: if Harper never mobilized Peggy with *Infinite Odyssey*, then she would never mobilize herself. And god knew Miles wasn't going to try and save Peggy, if this conversation was any indication. So, if not Harper, then . . . who?

"So, I have to create the show," she said slowly, "because even if things are better, the odds are also high enough that the universe might be completely fucked if I don't."

"I feel like that about sums it up."

"Fuck me." She sniffed. "You know, I always loved this about the show, the intricacies of time and whatever, but I really fucking hate it right now."

Harper leaned back against the bench and watched the uncharacteristically light traffic on Park Avenue. Taxis zipped happily down the unencumbered holiday streets, getting their fill of the open road before the late-morning rush of hungover partygoers filed out of their homes and hotels for New Year's brunch. They had no idea that they were in danger. That the Incarnate was on this planet in the form of a parasite in Harper's own mind, and that soon it would take control. And once she was part of the hive, she would spread it far and wide—just as Peggy had done with her.

The fight went out of her. Her hangover headache blazed behind her eyes. She thought about telling him about what Peggy had done to her. About what happened last night as a result. But something stopped her. A gut instinct that crawled up her throat and clamped down on her tongue.

Miles put a hand tentatively on her shoulder and squeezed in an apparent attempt to be reassuring. She peered into his young face then. She needed to look into his eyes and see him as he was.

Seeing the version of Miles that Peggy must have been dazzled by, Harper understood. She saw shades of the Miles she'd met, lurking in fleeting frowns and furrowed brows. This man had seen more of the universe than one person—or alien—ever had or would again, and it was taking its toll.

He stood. "This is the last you'll see me in this time, Miss Starling."

She swallowed hard. "Tell Argo something for me. Please. Tell her . . . she didn't get it all out. Tell her that I'm running out of time. That if she cares she'll come, no matter what Miles says."

"I will."

He was walking away before she could think of how to say goodbye. All she saw as he strode down Park Avenue was the steady retreat of her hopes and far-flung dreams into the polluted winter morning of New York City.

She hailed a taxi on the corner and went back to Anthony's apartment. He answered the door, still rubbing his exhausted eyes, perking up when he realized it was her.

"Harper. I thought . . ."

"I took a walk," she said. "I wanted to clear my head and think about what we discussed last night. About the pitch."

His face brightened, and she was glad to see he remembered the conversation despite the copious amounts of alcohol they'd both consumed.

"And?"

"And . . . I'm in."

EPISODE FOUR
LIGHT VELOCITY

This week on Infinite Odyssey:

The Argonaut and First Mate Lucinda Freely have found themselves in another dimension, in which their doubles are mortal enemies. Can they escape before they're targeted by their doppelgängers—or maybe even set things right between them?

II.

NEW YORK CITY
WINTER, 1972

The convention was a block from Penn Station on the eighteenth floor of a stately Hilton and was filling fast with attendees.

Harper had finally scraped together enough money for a new dress and a new coat, a cause to which Angie and Dottie had also generously contributed. The wool was more constricting than the things she might have worn in the twenty-first century, but at least her new ensemble was more cohesive than her blue dress and the old bomber jacket.

Her nerves were frayed by the time the convention arrived. At times she thought she could feel the Incarnate inside her, writhing under the skin, testing receptors in her mind, feeling around for the door that would let it all the way in. She waited for another chaotic dream of distant worlds, another spy following her silently down a dark alley, a threat in the shadows of her bedroom as she lay awake at night. But there had been nothing, no one. She got the sense that they were biding their time. Letting Harper's unease build like bile, until the anticipation was high enough to tear her apart all on its own.

"I thought you said they expected six hundred people," Harper said as Anthony checked them in.

He shrugged. He looked sharp in his blue tweed, eyes alight as he observed the crowd. "Looks like they underestimated the power of *Trek*." He held out a badge and smiled. "Come on, let's go find Sheila."

She took the badge, straightened her itchy skirt, and followed Anthony into the gathering throng, shocked to realize as they waded through the groups of fans chattering excitedly that cosplay and booths loaded down with comic-book art were not recent evolutions of the twenty-first-century convention scene but had been firmly rooted in geek culture even before the full bloom of the *Star Trek* fandom. Little boys dressed as Spock watched the auditorium door impatiently, while women decked out in the siren-red uniform of Lieutenant Uhura chatted with men sporting aspirational yellow shirts in an homage to Captain Kirk. Fake weapons and lumpy wigs were abundant. It reminded Harper of the days she and Peggy used to spend at InfiniCon each summer, sweating in their lovingly crafted, seasonally inappropriate costumes.

It hadn't quite dawned on her in the moments after Anthony asked her to attend the convention with him that she would be observing something truly historic. As she and Anthony spent long days after New Year's together, cooped up in his apartment while they wrote their pilot, subsisting on cheese and crackers and scotch, her mind had been possessed by thoughts of Peggy and the Incarnate. She relived that night in the cavern over and over until it was imprinted on the dark side of her every waking moment. The look in Peggy's lightless marble eyes. The thick, ropy scars marring her skin. The thump of Harper's heart as she faced the icy stare of a girl who had shared her sour gummy worms because Harper's parents wouldn't allow candy in the house. She'd forgotten that, if this worked, she would make history.

To Anthony the project was simply that—a project. If nothing came of it, then his life went on as usual. Maybe he quit writing TV and maybe he didn't. But to Harper it was a lasso, and one wrong throw might strand her in 1972 for good. Worse, it could apparently destroy the universe. And so, despite everything she now knew about Miles, the Argonaut had to be inspiring. He had to be the kind of hero that Peggy and Harper would later watch as children and love so ardently it paved the foundation for their entire lives. So, Harper put aside everything she'd felt in the last three years, every moment of disillusionment, from Peggy's disappearance to her disastrous time with Miles, and she did her best to recall how the show itself, not Miles, made her feel once upon a time.

She told Anthony everything she knew about *Infinite Odyssey* in those weeks, framing it as a game she played with her best friend, remembering the joy she once felt while watching. In return, he spitballed ideas for future episodes, full season arcs, new characters they might introduce. Harper recognized a good number of them as story lines that had indeed come to fruition during the show's run, which felt like a sign they were on the right track—this was going to work. The proof was in the fact that it already had.

But as they wandered the crowded eighteenth floor, Harper was struck with a different kind of longing. It had been years since she was part of a community like this one. Since she'd donned her own costumes at InfiniCon and waited in line with Peggy to hear influential guests speak about their time on the show. She'd forgotten how much she missed it.

One fan, standing alone on the far side of the room, caught her eye. From this distance, it was hard to see him very well, but he was noticeable for his height—tall, lanky, with a familiar mop of unwashed auburn hair—and his apparent lack of costume, neglected in favor of . . . a Miles Moonraker T-shirt.

"You all right?"

She looked at Anthony. Her heart was beating madly in her chest, but when she searched for him out of the corner of her eye, the man was already gone. Maybe even a trick of her imagination.

She smiled at Anthony, shaky. "Of course."

"You nervous?"

"Very."

She looked into his calm face and wondered if there was something wrong with her. They had not kissed again, the incident in the bathroom at Ricky's a barrier neither seemed capable of breaking. She wasn't sure she wanted to. A crush would have been normal under these circumstances—the two of them huddled close in the dim light of his apartment for three weeks, hunched over a typewriter while they combined their creative efforts into one hand-typed document. Liquor and laughter, witnessing triumphs and failures, comforting one another through moments of doubt or sadness or anger.

Anthony, as it turned out, was a lot of fun to be around when he wasn't moping about his job.

But—though she'd caught his looks here and there, or a flush along the back of his freckled neck when she smiled at him, or the way his fingers sometimes settled against hers on the sticky keys of his typewriter—Peggy's shiny black boot stomped on any urges Harper might have nurtured in the wake of his interest, any thirst she might have wished to quench, once upon a time. Now all she could think about was the memory of that place, that semiprecious gloom, the jungle, the ocean, and the tar-like ooze dripping from her nose when she awoke.

He gave her shoulder an encouraging squeeze. "It's all right to be nervous. But listen, Sheila's a lamb. Plus, she loves me. She'll gobble this idea up. I promise you."

"You're right. Of course you're right."

"Listen. Harper." He faced her straight on and put on his pep talk face. "Whatever happens today, I want you to know, none of this was time wasted. If Sheila says no, we'll just keep trying. I'm determined to make a show out of the stuff that's in your brain."

"You just said she would gobble it up."

Anthony looked playfully pained. "Do you make it your mission in life to harass me?"

"No, that's just my hobby. It's a lot of fun, you might try it sometime."

They shoved through the crowded lobby to the Dealer's Room, a banquet hall now packed full of people and booths. This was where they might run into people from the Committee, the superfans responsible for organizing the convention after a series of successful smaller fan events gave them hope for something bigger. Well, this was bigger all right, bigger than anyone had bargained for, and a strange claustrophobia was taking hold. Not simply because the crush of people made it hard to move around, to breathe, to see, but because once she saw the man in the lobby, Harper became suspicious that she was being watched. That someone else knew she was here, and she wasn't sure who—Miles, looking out for her? Or his enemy, taunting her?

She didn't think Miles, the young one or the old one, truly gave one shit whether she was all right. Which left the other, far more chilling option—one of the hive, dressed like Miles to trick her. And now, everywhere she turned, eyes were on her. Peggy's gaze, hard and coal-black. Staring her down as if through the reflection of a nebulous mirror.

A warm hand enfolded her own and for a moment her anxiety eased. Anthony had a way of returning her to calm before her mind drifted too far on a turbulent tide. There was something rough in his palm, though, a crumpled piece of paper. He pressed it against her own palm until she was holding it, and then his hand broke away from hers. She finally looked up, expecting her companion, only to see someone else disappearing into the crowd. Tall, too skinny. The tatters of his dark band T-shirt winking at her as he vanished.

She stopped dead where she stood. Anthony was nowhere to be seen. The crowd undulated around her, that ocean pulling her deep into its current, the shore long gone.

"Anthony?" she called, but the room was so loud, hundreds of voices twining into one dull roar. "Anthony!"

"There you are," came a voice at her ear. A hand on her shoulder pulled her around, and she was facing her writing partner again, his eyebrows lifted in amusement.

"Got lost," she said breathlessly. The paper burned like a wound in the palm of her hand. But there would be no reading it just yet; Anthony was already guiding her to a small table in the corner of the room where a poised woman in a smart tweed suit, huge glasses, and graying but fashionably feathered hair waited.

"Harper, meet Sheila. Sheila, this is Susan, but she goes by Harper."

Sheila's lips lifted in some approximation of a smile, as if she'd exhausted this dance already. "A pleasure, Miss Feldman."

"The pleasure's mine," Harper replied automatically, trying to remember her manners just then, even as the weight of a million unseen eyes threatened to obliterate the facade of calm. She was grateful for the dozens of cumulative hours of *Masterpiece Theatre* still vivid in her memory.

"I can't believe how many people are here," Anthony said.

"It's certainly unexpected," Sheila agreed.

Harper could practically see the dollars tallying in Sheila's mind as she looked around the room.

"Well, they did a stupendous job." Harper immediately regretted saying the word *stupendous* out loud. "I mean, look at all these people!"

"Audiences are clearly hungry for good American science fiction. Wouldn't you say, Sheila?"

"They canceled *Trek*, Anthony," Sheila said, still staring about the room.

"And do you think that was the right call?"

Sheila smiled pointedly. She was looking for someone. One of the stars, maybe? Someone, anyone else to talk to?

Anthony continued. "What if there was a show that could capitalize on exactly this—the audience that *Star Trek* built and left dangling?"

Sheila's attention snapped back to Anthony, her eyes wide. "Anthony Detweiler, are you pitching me?"

He laughed. "I'm pitching you, Sheila."

"And what's her story?" Sheila nodded at Harper.

"Harper's the brains. The world, the characters, all hers."

Sheila shook her head, though she seemed impressed. She also looked like she might kill someone for a cigarette. "Know this is your last freebie, understand?"

"Understood."

Anthony launched into their carefully crafted pitch. Harper listened, a strange longing rippling through her as Anthony told the story of the spacefaring Argonaut. He had clearly come to love *Infinite Odyssey* too. He gave Sheila the snappy, Hollywood version, and she asked questions he answered easily, proudly. He pitched her the pilot episode they'd already written, describing word for word the story arc and scenes Harper had watched only a few months earlier on the domed screen of the Sky Theater. By the time someone shouted that Gene Roddenberry had arrived and the crowd began to sift out of the Dealer's Room, Anthony's eyes were bright.

"That's quite the pitch," Sheila said. The room was mostly empty now. "It seems you've found something truly unique, Anthony. I'm proud of you. Just last month you were pitching me more westerns."

Anthony's neck flushed to his ears, but he had the good grace to laugh it off. "I realized the value of having a partner with good ideas."

Sheila looked at Harper, appraising. "Yes. A partner can do wonders." She looked back at Anthony. "But listen, Anthony. Darling. There's a lot to like about this Argonaut character, and I do appreciate that there's family appeal, but I just don't see this on our network. Now if you'll excuse me, I'm going to see if I can still get into the auditorium for Gene. Can you believe how many people are here?"

With that, she bustled off, taking their hopes and dreams with her.

Anthony's mouth hung open. He had no idea what just happened, and neither did Harper. *Infinite Odyssey* had lived on CCNTV its first few years on the air. That was simply the truth. This should have been the easiest part.

But now, Harper questioned for the umpteenth time whether she was dealing with free will or destiny. If the past was still just as free to make new choices as the present, creating new timelines, new dimensions, with wild abandon, or if things were fixed. If the latter was true, then some way, somehow, this show made it to air. If the former . . .

"Well, I'm going to powder my nose," Harper said.

"I'll be here, nursing my wounded pride," Anthony replied balefully. He lowered his face to his arms on the table and went still.

Harper left the room. She found a dim corner away from the hubbub in the halls where she could open the note still crumpled against her palm. There were only three words.

Don't go home.

An odd prickle crawled down her back as the words settled. She could still feel someone's eyes on her, the weight of observation. She thought about searching for the Miles look-alike, telling Anthony she got lost. But something told her that whoever had passed the note her way was long gone and that this feeling of being observed came from somewhere, someone, else.

She was about to go back to the Dealer's Room and shuffle Anthony out of that godforsaken convention when she heard a familiar voice.

Though the hallway seemed to have emptied, the Trekkies now piled on top of each other in the ballroom to see Gene Roddenberry speak, Sheila and another man in a fashionable, pressed suit idled at the auditorium door. Anthony had said that Sheila had a thing for the *Star Trek* creator, but this was not him; Harper had seen pictures of Gene Roddenberry, and unlike him, this man possessed a full head of long, coiffed hair.

"You know I can't tell you about ABC's numbers, Sheila," he was saying. "They would have my head."

"I'll tell you ours," Sheila replied, a small smile on her lips.

"That would be information given of your own volition and would not entitle you to information in return," the man replied. He was smiling too. "But if you must know, we're bringing a sci-fi show on board. It's gonna be a real experiment for us."

Sheila looked at him sharply. "A sci-fi show? Really?"

"Look at this convention, Sheila. Look at how many people showed up just to let the world know they're Trekkies. You think we aren't going to try and reel in that audience?"

Sheila looked thoughtful. "Listen, Al, I think I left something back in the Dealer's Room. I'll catch you inside?"

"I'll save you a seat."

He walked away, and Sheila turned around. Harper, unable to move before Sheila spotted her, met the network executive's eyes.

Sheila slowed and crossed her arms. "I suppose you heard that."

"I did," Harper said. "Looks like Anthony was right."

"Look, Heather—"

"Harper."

"I don't know you from Adam. I know you're not a writer. This *Infinite* show sounds exceedingly expensive. And I'm not interested in giving Anthony's girlfriend unearned benefit of the doubt."

Harper almost choked. "Girlfriend? Are you serious? I'm not Anthony's girlfriend. I'm his writing partner who *happens* to have tits. That's it."

Through the walls adjacent, Harper could hear the crowd in the ballroom, their chatter rising in volume as they waited restlessly for Gene to arrive.

"A writing partner with zero experience," Sheila said.

"People have entered this industry with less."

"Yes, but those people aren't women. I'll have a lot more people to convince with your name on this thing instead of, say, Joe Smith. Do you have any idea how hard it was for me to get where I am?"

"I don't," Harper admitted. "But I can guess it took you twice as long as your coworkers and that you work twice as hard for half the recognition."

Sheila looked at Harper appraisingly. That would not have been the common answer in 1972—too Women's Lib—but it was a gamble Harper was willing to put her money on. Sheila seemed like she might respond to that sort of thing, even if she would never admit to it in public.

"And what," Sheila asked, "do you bring to the table that Anthony doesn't?"

"From the sounds of it, good ideas."

Sheila did smile at that. She crossed her arms and stared at Harper, chewing on her lip thoughtfully. Harper wondered if she was supposed to speak up during this process but decided that keeping quiet was likely her best option.

"What the hell," Sheila said. "If Al's doing it, then so should I."

"You're serious?"

"Here's the deal. We'd need a script, we would need approvals, yadda yadda. And given that production season has already started, we're running behind. But as long as the script lives up, I'm willing to put my butt on the line for this. I'll be in touch with Anthony on Monday about the contract. In the meantime, send the screenplay quick as you can. If I like it and I get my way, we'll be shooting in a month."

"Holy shit!"

"Listen." Sheila leaned closer, her voice a whisper now. "If you take this to any other networks, I swear to god you will forever wish you had never met and defied me." She straightened her skirt. "Tell Anthony: 'Don't say I never did anything for you.'"

Harper's grin was wide. "I'll deliver the message."

Sheila gave her that same approximate smile and turned in the direction Al had gone, disappearing into the ballroom.

Alone in the hotel corridor, relief split open inside her. It worked. It was happening.

And then she remembered the paper in her palm. Slipped between cupped fingers by someone she never saw, the Miles look-alike or perhaps Miles himself. No matter how many islands she found, ultimately, she was always still out to sea. Drifting along on her poorly crafted raft.

She went back to the Dealer's Room and gave Anthony the good news. He responded by scooping her up and twirling her around until she was laughing and dizzy.

12.

NEW YORK CITY
WINTER, 1972

They ended up in a cozy leather booth inside a little snug on Tenth Avenue, enjoying their victory and the warm light of the candles clustered on the table. Harper's blood was electric. A healthy dose of champagne made the world around her liquid and strange, moving too slow and too quick all at once. She knew it was stupid to tempt fate like this, but part of her didn't care. One more tick in the destiny column meant she was feeling cocky.

"I can't believe it worked," she said. She stared at the flickering flame of a lopsided candle, distracted and tipsy.

"Damn right it worked. I told you Sheila loves me."

Anthony was leaning back in the booth, comfortable and confident, like that first night at Ricky's. A cigarette dangled from his fingers, smoke pluming toward the ceiling in a spiraled dance. Harper didn't smoke, but she took the cigarette from him and breathed deep, then let the smoke unfurl from the halls of her mouth. She needed to calm her nerves. There was a jackhammer in her heart and a crumpled note in her purse and a trauma in her past and a decision to be made.

Don't go home. But which home did they mean? Home with Dottie in 1972 or home in 2023?

"Where do you go, Harper?" Anthony asked suddenly.

Her eyes refocused. "What do you mean?"

"You zone out sometimes. We'll be hammering out a plotline and your eyes will go fuzzy."

"Just thinking." She smiled. "Our lives are about to change." The bartender refilled their empty glasses. Straight scotch now, no point trifling with the extras.

"Almost too good to be true," Anthony said with a laugh, and it struck her that that was exactly it. The other thing that made her so uneasy, besides the note, besides the Miles look-alike.

No. Paranoid thinking. Harper couldn't trust her own mind right now.

Don't go home.

No home, then. She should warn Dottie, maybe. Tell her to stay away.

"What if she doesn't like the script?" Harper asked.

"Chin up, kid. We're going to shake things up, you'll see. Sheila plays it cool, but I guarantee you she was dying of excitement."

"Well, I hope not. We need her to make the show."

"Quick-witted, you are, Miss Feldman."

"Someone has to be, Mr. Detweiler."

He put a hand over his heart. "You wound me."

She laughed. "I could never. You know it's your words that make this show real. Without them I'd still just be a girl with an idea."

"Happy to oblige." His smile faltered, gave way to something else. He snared her gaze in his, and she understood.

Anthony knew her better now, but he didn't know her completely. And even if he did, even if she let him in far enough to touch the frayed nerve at the center of her being, it wouldn't have mattered. She could hide her pain so well these days. Had been doing it for years.

Don't go home, the note had said. The funniest part: she had no home. Not since Peggy.

And Anthony was looking at her with glassy green eyes and a lopsided smile. One of those looks she usually only caught in fleeting glances, in whisper-light touches, in sheepish heat on the back of his neck.

"I like you, Harper," he said. A callback to their first night in that stupid little bathroom. "You must know that I like you."

"I like you too," she told him, and it was true, dammit, it was. He wasn't perfect, but she didn't need him to be. She could lie about so many things, it seemed, but she couldn't lie about that. Maybe Peggy couldn't ruin everything, after all.

She kissed him. Whisky-tongued and wanting. He palmed her cheek and kissed her back, hard and soft, hard and soft, until they were leaving the bar, and in a cab, probably, and then walking up the steps to his place, and into the unlit apartment, where she was caught, fleetingly, with the memory of that morning after New Year's, black ooze dripping from her nose while she sat in his bed, a moment of fear, of knowing she wasn't alone. But then the memory was gone, and they were in his room, and their clothes came off in a heap, and they moved together in the dark, the action snipping something inside her taut as a guitar string, releasing her from a prison she built for herself years and years ago. And after, Harper cried in the bathroom when Anthony fell asleep, not for herself, but for Peggy. For Peggy, for Peggy, for Peggy.

Okay, fine. For herself a little too.

They stand at a busy intersection, cars whizzing by as they decide which direction to turn. The city lights are a kaleidoscope blur in the late winter rain they find themselves in now. Those lights burn their eyes, too bright for them, a creature of the void. This body, too, has begun to fail, and with that comes the failure of the senses, of the mind. Soon they will be forced to abandon it, but for now, it is getting the job done. The woman recognized this vessel. The Incarnate wants to inspire that same recognition once more. To create confusion, the potential for emotional mistakes. This is a skill they can call up as easily as the myriad abilities they harnessed in the wake of their merge with that spacefaring species of Pelegaea and their subsequent rebirth as the Incarnate. They are part of her now too. A seed left behind, almost not enough to establish a connection, but growing again. Soon enough she will be theirs. The rest will come not long after.

They have waited so long.

They close their eyes and reach across their slowly forming hivelink to her mind. The bond is still young, imprecise, but through the boisterous chaos of what they believe is a crowd of people and the haze of some toxic substance leaking into her system, they can feel her desire for something called home. *A small apartment crammed with furniture, another bedroom where someone else, someone unimportant, lives.*

They go to her apartment. They buzz the intercom and someone lets them in without asking their name or identity. They slip up the stairs, a wraith in the night. They pick the lock—it's easy with so many minds, so many varied life experiences, chained together. They enter the apartment.

And no one is home.

The call came in early. Too early. Harper's head was ringing, her eyes gummy with sleep. The raucous *brrring!* Jarred her out of a strange, muzzy dream. Bright city lights and an empty apartment. The jagged echo of a hundred thousand minds working as one in the dark.

It wasn't until Anthony answered the phone, voice hoarse with sleep and remnant alcohol, that she remembered she had not slept in her own uncomfortable bed last night. The note, and the convention, and the look-alike.

Anthony rolled over, phone to his ear, and faced Harper. "Sure, she's here. Uh-huh." He sat up abruptly. "You're not serious. Last night? Did they take anything?"

Harper sat up too. "What's going on?"

"Of course, Angie. I'll get her a cab." He looked at Harper. "Thanks. Yep. See you later. Bye." He put the phone back on the cradle and looked at Harper like he was about to try and pick up a wild animal. "Listen."

"Someone broke in," she supplied. She was already out of bed, getting dressed, suddenly self-conscious in her nudity, now that she was sober.

"Harper, take it easy—"

"Is Dottie okay?"

"Dottie's fine; she's with the police now. She called Angie to find out where you were."

"Okay. Okay. I'm, um, gonna get a cab."

"Damn," Anthony said softly, looking bemused. "Of all the days. I was going to take you for a hearty breakfast."

"If you really cared for me, you'd make it a bucket of coffee." She got on hands and knees to find her other shoe.

Anthony pulled on some briefs and came to help her, and they found it under the bed, dust bunnies clinging. She brushed them away and slipped it on, mind awhirl. The parts of yesterday that replayed over and over in her mind were not those moments with Sheila, not those seconds of *yes*, but those seconds of uncertainty, searching the crowd for the man who had placed a warning against her palm. And now this.

The full meaning of the note became clear. *Don't go home.* Not last night or any other night. That apartment was not and would never again be a safe place. Someone had known to search for her there and would almost certainly try again.

Anthony walked her downstairs, rubbing her shoulders and her neck, sympathetic. She'd done a bad thing, getting close to him like this. She should have stayed far away. But there was nothing for it now.

The force of this realization spun her to face him as a cab pulled up. "Thank you," she said, trying to mean it more than she usually did. Just in case. She kissed him, meaning that too, and left him scratching his head on the curb as the taxi drove away.

She didn't go back to Dottie's apartment. She directed the cab instead to Greenwich Village. The younger Miles had insisted she wouldn't see him again. But she couldn't keep doing this alone. If there was any chance he was still in the city after their encounter, hiding from her in the row house he probably believed was a secret, she had to know.

When she arrived, the same neighbor she'd spoken to all those weeks ago, the woman who had once been Paul M. French's neighbor, poked her head out of her front door and gestured Harper over.

"Are you Susan?" the neighbor asked. Harper paused, suspicious. The woman held an envelope out to her. "Found this in my mail slot this morning. Courier got the building wrong. It's Mr. French's address, but it's addressed to a Susan. That you?"

"That's me," Harper said. "Susan Feldman."

"Thought so. You're the only one I've seen 'round this place in ages. Go on, I haven't opened it."

"Thank you," Harper replied, grasping the envelope. Above the address, her fake name was scrawled in that familiar, careful cursive from the note at the café. The woman smiled, a little sad, and disappeared again.

Harper ripped the envelope open. There was no letter, no explanation, no paper at all. Just a small tarnished brass key. A house key.

She peered around the narrow street. A couple walked together on the other side, but they weren't looking at her. There was no one else. Miles, or someone who looked like him, had saved her from an attack last night. Was he saving her again? Was this the work of her future self? Or was his enemy cleverly guiding her into a trap, having made her feel like someone was watching out for her, that the notes and letters could be trusted?

She inserted the key into the lock of Paul French's door and turned the knob. A creak, a moan, and the door swung open to reveal a crepuscular, unswept house, utterly quiet. She closed the door behind her, her nose tickling from the dust kicked up by her entrance. She stared into the room, unable to make her feet move, to enter this untouched shrine to the human life Miles had lived with the partner he lost. It didn't make sense, that he would offer this up to her. In fact, none of this made sense. What was he doing at the planetarium that day if he had not come back here? The dust on every surface spoke of long neglect. Where had he come from? Where had he gone?

And how did the person who sent her this key—Miles or someone more sinister—know she would be here now? Was Peggy waiting for her in an empty room, having lured Harper into her web? Or was this a safe haven, a place no one would think to look for her?

Framed photos lined an undusted entry table and covered the

sun-brightened walls. Most featured the same couple, yellowing, decades-old photos of a handsome blond man and an auburn-haired woman at their wedding or in posed studio photos, their hair perfectly coiffed, their expressions radiantly happy. They complimented one another in a way that might suggest they were, quite literally, made for each other.

"Hello?" Harper called. The house swallowed her words and answered with silence.

As she walked down the line of photos, now in the belly of the apartment, the content of the pictures began to change. Photos of the couple, aging gracefully side by side, were soon replaced by photos finally containing a Miles she knew, the hale and healthy version she'd met at the planetarium, alongside that same radiant, but much older, blond man, the woman nowhere to be found. Miles could have been a son or a nephew, and probably appeared that way to unsuspecting visitors. If she didn't know better, Harper might have believed it too, but for the ease with which both men leaned into one another. She wondered where the woman had gone, if perhaps she had passed away. If Miles had come along and captured a grieving widower's broken heart, his own heart cracking when he himself became a widower years later.

She stopped exploring for a moment and listened to the house. Still no sound, no movement betraying another's presence. "If you're here," she said loudly, "you can come out. Let's talk like adults."

Still nothing.

She wandered through the kitchen and touched Miles's things, chipped cups and yellowed mail and weathered cookbooks, easing into the idea that she might be here alone. She meandered up the stairs, listening for creaks with each step, relieved when she heard none. On the second floor, she found two bedrooms, a bathroom, and an office whose furniture was barely visible beneath the chaos of clutter left behind. She checked under the beds and in the closets and behind moldering shower curtains, searching for an intruder she had stopped believing was there.

There was something oddly comforting about this place, despite how strange it felt to know that the Argonaut, the formerly fictional character she'd dreamed of for years, had once lived a human life here. She sat down on the edge of the bed in the master bedroom, clouds of dust puffing into the air, and decided that for the moment, she was safe.

Mollified, she called Dottie from a pay phone up the block and told her that she was fine, not to worry, and that everything would make sense soon enough.

13.

NEW YORK CITY
WINTER, 1972

Sheila rang on Tuesday, which Harper learned when she finally phoned Anthony after several nights spent in Paul French's empty town house. She endured a long string of anxious questioning from her cowriter. *Where are you? Why haven't I heard from you? Just come back to my place.* Harper responded to the barrage with a vague, "I'm okay."

Anthony had news: Sheila loved the pilot, she had the green light from the network to produce it, and she was taking them out to a fancy club in Midtown to celebrate.

She set the celebration for eight p.m. that night, so Harper did something she had not done since arriving: searched the house for clues. Anything off, anything alien. Anything that might give her an edge against those who hunted Miles, and now Harper. If she was going to be amongst a crowd once more, she wanted to be prepared for any surprise notes or encounters. But the house was perfectly ordinary, so much so that she could scarcely believe it ever belonged to a man who piloted a sentient space-and-time ship whose preferred shape was that of an old muscle car.

She found books about the universe and quantum mechanics in the small office upstairs, spines stiff from having never been opened, and the desk she had noted earlier scattered with coffee-stained papers, old cups from which liquids had long since evaporated, and Miles Moonraker memorabilia tossed amongst the piles, their existence in this house predating the musician's debut by a good six years.

She picked up a notebook and opened it at random, a list scrawled haphazardly down the page in what she recognized as Miles's handwriting, thanks to the note he left her in the diner.

Find out what the hell the Drake equation is

Check if dark matter has been discovered yet

Figure out how to lie better about knowing actual science

This last note was not written in Miles's barely legible scratch, but a much more elegant cursive she attributed to the older man in the photos. Something about it made her smile. The idea of him sitting downstairs, listening blithely to the record player while Miles studied up on the era's theorems.

There was nothing else here. Nothing she might recognize as alien. Not even a not-harmonica. Though, if he was hiding alien tech inside perfectly ordinary Earth instruments, then it stood to reason that half this apartment might house alien tech and Harper would never, ever know.

By the time she gave up, the sun was beginning to sink behind the other ivy-coated buildings outside, and it was time to go. She would have to use her wits to protect herself.

Since she usually went out drinking on a waitress's salary, Harper was used to "celebrating" personal victories in dive bars or dank little clubs, and even if she had been back in the apartment she shared with Dottie, she did not own a stitch of glamorous fabric. She could not wear her current outfit—she'd been in it for three days now and it was badly in need of a wash. She would have to go out and buy something or risk Sheila's disdain, again.

She knew this house had once been inhabited by two men, but she remembered the woman in the other photos and recalled noticing the satin shimmer of dresses and blouses in the primary bedroom closet, clothing the older man likely couldn't part with after his wife's death. She decided to peruse the collection there, just in case she could save herself the trouble and the money she couldn't really spare.

She was surprised to find quite a few swishy pieces in the wardrobe, perfect for a night on the town. Unfortunately, the clothes were clearly made for a taller woman with a lankier physique, but that didn't mean she couldn't browse. She sifted through the dresses like she'd stumbled into a vintage store, admiring the fabric, the cut, the care. There was something so intoxicating about touching these time capsules from another life.

A brooch on the collar of a red dress caught the light and winked, snagging her attention. It was a beautiful dress too. More carefully crafted than any single item of clothing Harper had ever owned. What could it hurt to try it on? There was no one around to judge her inability to zip the thing over her fleshy hips. And she felt a strange, inexplicable longing to see herself in that red silhouette. Or as much of it as she could before the dress gave up.

She pulled the garment from the hanger and removed her ripe wool shift, wishing suddenly that she had done so days ago. She pulled the ruby dress over her legs, her hips, and pushed her arms through the holes at the torso. She found the zipper at the side and tugged it upward, surprised to find that it gave without any resistance, despite its age. She was also surprised, as the zipper pull forced its teeth together, that the dress seemed to fit after all. She touched the brooch—had it always been a bumblebee? She seemed to remember it looking more like a peacock when she first plucked the dress from the hanger. And the color had been a much deeper crimson in the closet but was now clearly more of an orange red, like poppies. The satin shine, too, had dulled to an attractive eggshell. Had the fabric changed entirely?

Holy shit. It had. The dress had changed, was changing, before Harper's very eyes. It was making adjustments to itself, shifting the color, the length, the fit. When she first pulled it from the hanger, the dress had obviously been too small for her to wear—but it was accommodating this new, curvier body without any resistance at all. It was almost as if the dress had been made for Harper, and Harper alone. She didn't even have to test the theory; as she watched, the hem shortened to just below the knee, a more flattering length for her figure.

She racked her brain for any ideas from the show's lore and rules about shape-changing clothing but could think of none. It appeared she had finally found her alien tech—fabric that changed to fit any wearer. And part of her wondered if this garment, too, was a little bit psychic. The way it had caught her eye when she spied it in the closet felt similar to the way Argo seemed to nudge people toward certain feelings, certain conclusions. Psychic alien fabric. Go figure.

As she hurried to leave the house in her new outfit, she noticed another photo of the nameless woman, wearing the very same red dress at what appeared to be a Christmas party. It took Harper a moment to realize that the woman was not actually nameless at all—she was the Argonaut, effortlessly beautiful in each of these photos, her hair perfectly curled, makeup perfectly done. There was a caption at the bottom of the photo, written in the older man's elegant script: *Flora, 1957.*

Oh. All of a sudden, it came back to her: Harper and Peggy side by side on a shaded bench, the autumn afternoon sun warming their shoulders while they devoured hefty bodega sandwiches. School was just beginning and Harper had only gotten busier and busier with each new week. They barely found time to meet, but they'd taken advantage of this rare window on a breezy Thursday afternoon. Peggy had nodded along with Harper's anecdotes, humoring her friend as she gushed about her professors and her curriculum, but she'd seemed distracted by something. Finally, Harper asked her what was on her mind, and a secretive grin broke across Peggy's face.

"I made a new friend," she told Harper. "I went to a show at Rockwood and she bought me a drink and we ended up walking around after, just talking. I don't think I got home until two in the morning. Her name is Flora. Isn't that a great name?"

"Will you see her again?" Harper had asked, a lump in her throat. Part of her had known Peggy was interested in women, though they'd never actually talked about it. Part of her hoped.

Peggy had shrugged. "I don't know. I hope so."

She hadn't. And over the next few weeks, Peggy had become increasingly despondent, sullen. It was obvious she'd really liked Flora, had felt an instant connection. Harper was secretly glad when Flora's name never came up again.

So Flora must have met the blond man just after her epic night with Peggy. And when Peggy started disappearing, her cell incapable of pinging her wherever in the universe she'd gone, it was because Miles had returned to make amends for leaving her hanging for so long. It made sense.

At first, as she clambered into a cab, there was a spike of empathy, a kindred pain. And then Greenwich Village rolled away, and the familiar anger simmered to a boil once more, wiping out any understanding that had sparked in her. Miles lived a full life with someone he adored, privy to a love so full it transcended gender and dozens of societal boundaries and taboos. What right did he have to gamble so cavalierly with Peggy's life? To rob her of any chance to experience the same? What about her family, her friends, who would always feel the premature loss of her as deeply as a poorly healed wound, an infection of the blood?

The dress gained new meaning then. As the cab rolled and stopped and rolled its way through busy Manhattan, she felt an unbearable smugness. Something pulsed in the back of her mind, a lurid thought she couldn't help but relish. It was so small, compared. But she'd taken something that clearly had meaning to Miles, to the part of him that still cherished Flora enough to keep it, years after she was gone. Harper had altered it, claimed it as her own. She wished he could see her, just so she could see the look on his face when he understood what she'd done.

The address Harper gave the cab driver was somewhere in Midtown, near the Rockefeller. As Harper exited the taxi and saw other clubgoers shimmering in their sequins and metallic halter tops, she was glad she took the dress. At the very least, she looked presentable. The bouncer waved her through with a sage nod, and she was inside, swallowed up by the mirror-ball darkness. Music throbbed through the club, melody high and loud over the excited thrum. Couples danced, though their movements were more reserved than you might have found in the sweatier, dingier clubs of the city. No one slinking and swiveling like their lives depended on it, speed and whatever else stringing them along on a three-day high. Not yet anyway.

Still, it was too dark in here. It reminded her of another too-dark place.

"Harper!"

She turned to find Anthony parting the crowd. It should have made her feel better, to see him, a person she knew in that room full of strange music and people. But it awoke another facet of the dread that seemed to have made a permanent home in her. She liked Anthony. He might have been a little simple, but she found his company pleasant and sex with him also pleasant. He didn't deserve to get caught in the cross fire of a cosmic war, as ridiculous as that sounded in her head.

"Where have you been?" He stopped and stared at her dress. "That's new."

"Yeah, it seemed like it was time for something different," she said. "Where's Sheila?"

Anthony pointed to the balcony. "Listen, I'm gonna get something a little manlier than champagne from the bar, and then I expect you to tell me exactly what's been going on."

Harper smiled reassuringly. "Everything's fine. I'll meet you up there."

He squeezed her shoulder and stalked off through the crowd. Harper ascended the stairs to the balcony, where she was met with a velvet rope and another bouncer.

"Name?" He said gruffly. She told him.

"She's with me!" Sheila's voice cracked over the din. She was seated on a tufted couch shaped into a half-moon around a tiny table at the center. A caddy with ice and a bottle of champagne stood beside it. Sheila had donned a sparkling sequin jumpsuit, entirely unlike the stuffy pantsuit she'd worn to the *Star Trek* convention and entirely too like the mirror ball swirling above. Her eyes were slicked with thick, winged black liner, her hair long and straight. She seemed relaxed in a way Harper honestly hadn't thought her capable.

Harper squeezed past the suspicious bouncer and sat down, glad she would not be expected to dance amongst the couples below. She knew disco was still a fairly underground craze in the early '70s, but she didn't want to be tested.

"Susan Harper Feldman!" Sheila's approximate smile was gone, replaced by a full, toothy grin. "Have a drink." She poured Harper a glass of champagne and passed it her way. "On the network."

Harper took the flute and stared into it, bubbles fizzing and popping menacingly on the surface. Sheila raised her glass and clinked it against Harper's.

"Congratulations, Harper. Your pilot could end up on national television. And just last week you were some random girl I had never even heard of." She drank half the glass and poured again.

"Thanks, Sheila." Harper pressed her lips to the flute and let the barest slosh of champagne pass her teeth. She wasn't interested in losing control tonight. Not this time.

"I have to admit, I find that Argonaut fellow a bit unbelievable. But the network enjoyed it."

"Unbelievable? It's a sci-fi show."

"Of course it is. But he's so good. His whole purpose is flying around the universe, saving people? Ridiculous." She didn't know how right she was. "I've known men like him. That god complex will make a good man dangerous. But I suppose that's what makes me a good VP. I see what others don't." She cocked her head. "You don't seem terribly excited for someone who just bypassed all of the usual methods of entering this business and got the green light to make her first hour of television."

Harper looked around, distracted. The balcony was filling with other dazzling clubgoers, and the dance floor could barely be seen through the throng moving like an anemone below. She wondered what was taking Anthony so long.

Sheila cleared her throat.

"I'm excited," Harper said quickly. "I'm very excited."

Sheila looked at her like she thought Harper might be very, very thick. "Do you know how hard I had to fight to get where I am, Harper? Any idea at all?"

Harper had wondered. When Anthony first brought up Sheila's name, Harper thought she'd misheard. She'd expected *Mad Men* types, all their memos and brilliant ideas transcribed by secretaries clacking away on typewriters outside the mahogany doors of the executive offices. She knew there were women in important jobs, of course. But they were the exception, not the rule. And to be a female executive in 1970s television, Harper had to guess that the answer to Sheila's question was *extremely hard.*

Sheila continued without an answer. "My children don't get it, of course. The long hours I spend at the office. How hard I have to work just to be given half the credit, half the respect. How hard it is to want something with your entire being, something you've been told your entire life you can't have. I'm the only female VP CCNTV's ever had. I have to leave my shoes outside the restroom door when I go because there is only one on our floor, and before I came along it was a men's restroom only, Harper. Do you understand?"

"It's so they won't come in while you're in there?"

Sheila's lips pinched into that approximate smile, and Harper knew she'd missed the point. "I busted my ass for this. I still do. I always wanted to work in television, but everywhere I went they told me they weren't interested in hiring women. They wouldn't even give me a job fetching coffee. So, I wrote a letter asking to visit the set of one of the network's more popular shows as a fan. Just a fan, right? And they said yes. Women can be fans, of course. That was allowed. But when I got there, I was smart. I offered to do odd jobs. Little errands. Fetch coffee. I came back the next day, and the next. Little by little, I made myself indispensable. Before they knew it, I'd convinced them to make me their director of casting. Now I'm here. VP of an entire network.

"I think you want this too, Harper. I didn't believe so at first. But there's no way Anthony had any part in this concept. He's a sweet boy, but his talents are writing other people's ideas, not his own. You were right about that. So." She leaned back, completely in command. "Get your head on straight, drink your champagne, and for god's sake, smile like you actually want this."

It would be a lie to say Harper had ever considered writing as a potential career. But she couldn't deny that sitting side by side with Anthony while they created that first script had given her an unexpected thrill. Was it what she actually wanted, though? She couldn't say. But she understood what Sheila was saying, about sacrifice, about dreams. Harper could smile like that, for Peggy's sake.

"That's better," Sheila said.

The seat next to Harper shifted and suddenly Anthony was there, slinging an arm around her and lifting a glass of scotch when Sheila offered him champagne. Sheila raised a questioning brow at Harper. *Not a side piece, huh?*

Harper shrugged out from under Anthony's arm. "I'd like to propose a toast," she said, raising her glass. "To Sheila, who took a chance on a show about an alien and his friends traveling the universe."

"May it be more successful than *Star Trek*," Sheila supplemented. They tapped the rims of their glasses against one another and drank.

The champagne fizzed down her throat. She almost took another sip when she felt an odd tug at the center of her being, a string tied around her subconscious and pulled taut by something, someone, down below.

"I'm going to powder my nose," Harper said, unable to ignore the feeling that someone was here, someone was watching her. She pushed past the eagle-eyed bouncer, making her way through the swaying couples and the sequins and feathered shags toward the shadowy hall past the bar.

A hand on her arm yanked her attention toward a man in an absurdly tight shirt and bushy mustache.

"Sorry, lady," he said, releasing her, "but I think you dropped this." He held his other hand out to her. She saw what he held and felt a strange, bright calm wash over her. Three months. For three months she'd been trapped in the 1970s. For three months she had struggled to find a way out, a way home, a way to save herself and Peggy. Could it really be so easy? But maybe she needed to feel like there was no way out, because there *was* and always had been, and if it had been too easy to leave, there would be no *Infinite Odyssey*. Now that she had done it, now that she had accomplished what she set out to do, she was being shown the door by this random stranger in this dazzling nightclub.

Harper stared at the harmonica. "Thank you," she said numbly.

The man laughed, confused. "Well, aren't you going to take it?"

She reached for the instrument in a daze. He didn't say anything else before dancing off, and she stared down at the chintzy child's toy she was sure she'd dropped somewhere in 2023, before Miles whisked her fifty years into the past. Sure enough, carved into the tarnished metal was the name Peggy.

Harper spun on her heel and ran for the restrooms, which were blessedly empty. She couldn't bring herself to look at the harmonica still gripped tight in her shaking hand, so she looked at herself in the mirror instead. As she stared at her made-up face, incapable, suddenly, of recognizing herself, something strange happened: her dress turned blue.

She spun away from the sinks and locked herself in a stall, then examined the alien garment. Not only was it now blue, it was swiftly turning black. Not only was it swiftly turning black, it was connecting between the legs and separating into tubes, no longer a dress at all. As she watched, it morphed into something else entirely, a deep-black jumpsuit, fabric snug and inexplicably thick, like a wet suit. The brooch at her shoulder spidered out and broadened until it covered her entire chest—some kind of hard casing, almost like armor—the jeweled sheen dulling to beetle-shell black. She kicked off her pumps before they could be consumed by the fabric, which stretched over her feet until the material resembled stiff, heavy boots.

She didn't move for several long minutes, terrified any shift would cause the garment to change further or into something else entirely. How could she have been so stupid? Wearing alien technology to drinks with her new boss? A dress she had known could change, would change, because it had done so before her very eyes back at Miles's house. Did she hate Miles so much that spiting him was more important than keeping her cover intact?

When she finally looked at the outfit as a whole, her legs nearly gave out. It was not a wet suit or some kind of ridiculous alien romper. It was exactly like the high-tech suit Peggy had worn that first night in Harper's old bedroom. It was the uniform of an assassin.

The bathroom door creaked open, the music spilling in and then fading again as the door closed once more, and Harper held her breath. The last thing she wanted was to stumble out of the stall and reveal her high-tech outfit to some random clubgoer. Then again, maybe they would be too drunk to notice. Maybe they would believe her when she told them it was for a scuba-diving convention. Or maybe, if she could get out of this bathroom, she could sneak out of the club unseen by Sheila and Anthony. She could call them from a pay phone and tell them she'd fallen ill—food poisoning, what a drag—and rushed home. Then she could decide what she wanted to do with this stupid harmonica. If she even still wanted to use it at all.

She opened the stall, her new boots utterly silent against the squeaky tile floor.

"Hello," Not-Peggy said. She was leaning against the sinks. "You got yourself a new outfit."

14.

NEW YORK CITY
WINTER, 1972

Harper slammed the stall door shut.

Peggy tutted from the other side. "You cannot think this door will protect you."

She didn't. It was a gut reaction, her flight instincts shoving her as far away from Peggy as possible within the two-foot radius available.

"Who am I speaking to," Harper said, remembering the assassin's reaction to hearing Peggy's favorite things that night in Harper's apartment, "Peggy or the Incarnate?"

"What is the difference?" was Peggy's reply.

"The difference is, I know Peggy is in there."

"A scrap here and there," Peggy said. "Echoes. Nothing more."

From under the stall door, Harper watched Peggy's feet pacing the restroom.

"We must say," Peggy said, "we are impressed. How did you come to possess nanotextile bots?"

"How did you know I would be here?" Harper ignored the urge to ask what the fuck nanotextile bots even were and why they had put her in this costume. She was cornered like an animal in a bathroom stall by an agent of the Incarnate. That it wore Peggy's body didn't matter—the hive would take her without remorse.

She looked down at the harmonica.

"We tracked you," Peggy said. "We felt you."

"You're here to finish the job. To make me part of the hive."

"We like you, Harper. Your anger. Your hatred." She said the words with such euphoria that Harper was not sure she'd heard right. Anger? Hatred? These were the emotions they valued, the feelings that connected them? "We want to bring you into our family. Is that truly so terrible?"

Yes, it was bad. It was very, very bad.

"It was quite clever, the way you tricked us several nights past," Peggy continued. "We thought we had you." She played with the sink faucet. Harper heard water splash into the deep ceramic bowls, the creak of the handles, and silence again. On, then off, then on again. "But our bond is growing stronger. It will be harder for you to hide. Can you feel it?"

And even though she wanted to say no and mean it, Harper did feel it. She hadn't wanted to acknowledge the gentle, steady pulse in her brain, the nagging sense that someone was knocking on a door at the back of her mind, asking to be let in. She'd been holding it closed without realizing, but one of these days, the thing on the other side would become a battering ram. She knew this as surely as she knew that the door was splintering already, darkness snaking through the cracks, tasting her mind. Her anger. Her hate.

"Come out, Harper Starling. Come to us, and we will take you to our home. There, we will unmake you."

She leaned her head back against the wall. Tears crowded her vision and blurred the plain wall in front of her. She was running out of time.

Harper raised the harmonica as if to play but hesitated.

"All this," she said, "to get back at Miles? What did he do to you?"

Not-Peggy laughed. It sent shivers down Harper's spine. "We do not care about him. We care about what he stole."

"What he stole?"

"The impossible ship."

"Argo?"

The stall door slammed open, kicked in by a heavy black boot.

Harper jumped in surprise and dropped the harmonica, immediately grateful that Peggy didn't seem to notice the clatter as it skittered behind the toilet. She stared at Harper, at their identical suits. Her expression was brutally hard. It reminded Harper of the way Peggy had looked at her that night at the Starlight, before Harper got up and left without another word. Angry, yes. But remorseful too.

There was remorse now too. Tarry blood dripped from Peggy's nose. The host rejecting its parasite. Harper knew, somehow, that the Incarnate would take Peggy's life before it gave her up. "End of the line, Harper Starling."

"Wait. Wait. Can't you see you're killing her?"

"We all die," Peggy replied, but her voice seemed weaker suddenly. She swiped at her ear as though something were buzzing in it; her fingertips came away coated in glimmering black ooze.

"Oh my god, Peggy—"

Harper was interrupted by Peggy's prompt loss of consciousness.

For a brief, stupid moment, she was torn between kneeling at her friend's side and running for her life. Her choices warred with each other until her survival instincts took hold. If Peggy woke up, it was over.

Harper retrieved the harmonica and sprinted past Peggy's prone form, out of the bathroom, and into the rising frenzy of the club, where she took a deep breath and blew into the instrument, its off-key wail lost in the beat of "Smiling Faces Sometimes" by the Undisputed Truth. She just had to make it out of this club and let the night swallow her up, hide her from those who would carve her out of her own mind until the only thing left was hate. She didn't know how long it would take Miles and Argo to respond, if they did at all, so she just kept running, shoving through bodies damp with sweat and couples gyrating against each other.

A drunk man stumbled into her path. Another man dipped his dance partner just as Harper was shoving past the drunk. A woman dropped her drink, splashing Harper with half of the hot-pink concoction she'd been imbibing. The suit absorbed it like it was a minor irritation and not something Harper would have spent hours scrubbing out of her normal clothes. The disco ball scattered the light in the club and flung it across the room, kaleidoscope shimmers dappling the floor, the ceiling, the eyes that watched her as she snaked past.

She looked behind her. If she'd regained consciousness, Peggy would be close behind. It should have been easy to spot her in the crowd—an inky blot parting the sea of silver sequins and red minidresses and white disco jackets. For a moment, all she saw was the undulating ocean of bodies. Relieved, she started to turn away, freezing midturn when she saw Peggy glowering across the crowd like something from a horror movie, eyes wide with fury, face smeared with oil-slick blood.

"What is wrong, Harper Starling?" Peggy said, advancing on her through the crowd. "Maybe we will make you a deal." Her hand snaked out, too fast for Harper to dodge, and tightened painfully on her arm. She was abnormally strong, squeezing Harper's bicep until Harper was certain it would simply crumple, useless meat and fibrous string, pliable in Peggy's grip. "Maybe if you bring the ship to us, we will let you leave."

Harper was suddenly aware she was making an awful, inhuman kind of sound. And then, inexplicably, Peggy hissed and let go, black ooze welling up in the palm of her hand, and Harper was dismayed to realize that the ooze was not ooze at all—it was blood. When she looked at the place where Peggy's fingers had squeezed, sinister, razor-sharp spikes now protruded from the thick material of Harper's suit. Nanotextile bots to her rescue.

Harper ran. Toward the front door and the Manhattan chaos that awaited beyond it. She was nearly there. She could run as far and as fast as she needed to out there. She could lose the Incarnate in a taxi or even the subway. Forget the harmonica, forget Miles. Forget home.

Except, Peggy was already ahead of her. In the blink of an eye, smooth as you please, waiting for Harper in front of the doors as if she'd been there the whole time.

Harper slowed. "How . . . ?"

Peggy raised her arm, showing off a wristwatch with a black crystal where the face should have been, its myriad facets impossible to perceive. "You can never outrun me," she said, and Harper knew she was right.

"I'm sorry," Harper said, because she was sorry, and she'd never really had a chance to say it, and she wasn't sure when she would again. If everything was ending here, now, then it made sense to let Peggy know. "I'm sorry this happened to you. I'm sorry for the things I said that night. I'm sorry for chasing you away. I'm sorry I can't seem to fix it."

"Your apologies are pointless."

"What about me?" This question came from another familiar voice some distance behind Harper.

Peggy's eyes narrowed at the person, her mouth twisted in a snarl, the hatred steaming off of her like heat off the pavement in summer. Harper didn't dare turn despite the sudden and overwhelming urge to spin around and face the person she had started to believe was simply a wish of her dreaming mind.

All Peggy said was: "You."

"Not quite an answer to the question, but I suppose it'll do," came Miles's voice again. It was the elder Miles, the one who had left her behind, voice gruff with age.

"If you are seeking remorse from us, you will not get it. But it is assured: we will make you sorry."

Harper imagined Peggy herself, trapped deep inside her own mind, calling voicelessly to her old, time-traveling friend for help as the Incarnate used her mouth to threaten him. How Peggy, the hidden one, was going to feel when Miles disappeared once again. The way he always did. The way Harper was going to ask him to.

"I've no doubt," Miles replied. "All right, Starling?"

She gasped a laugh, shocked to hear her name spoken in that voice.

"No," she said, grinning inexplicably. "I am most definitely not all right."

"Are you ready to go?"

"Get me the fuck out of here, Miles, or I—"

"Harper? What the hell is going on?"

This time, foolishly, she did turn. Because now Anthony was standing next to Miles—and oh god, it was really Miles, that time-and-space-traveling *asshole*, hair streaked through with gray, and she had never been so happy to see someone she hated.

"Harper?" Anthony said again. "Why are you dressed like that? Who's this?" He looked Miles up and down in jealous disgust. "And who's she? And why's she wearing—"

A long arm snaked across Harper's chest and brought her close to the assassin she had turned her back on. "Cease talking." Peggy's breath was hot on Harper's ear, and for a moment Harper's body warred with itself. With love and loathing.

"Oh, for the love of paradoxes," Miles said tiredly. "Harper, I'm sorry about this."

For the first time, she noticed something in his hand. His thumb on a button—a trigger.

Bomb, she had time to think, before his thumb pressed down and a pulse rippled through the club, through her body, through her ears, and knocked everyone in a ten-foot radius off their feet.

Harper drifted in a slow, lazy arc toward the floor. Her vision blurred. A high-pitched whine took up in her ears. She felt her body hit the ground but didn't hear it.

Miles's blurry face appeared in her line of sight. She could only watch him, unable to move as he bent over her, pulled her arms up and over his shoulder, gathered her like a sack of potatoes off the ground, and carried her clumsily back toward the restrooms and down the dim hall, through the emergency exit, and onto the street, where the hazy outline of a 1972 Dodge Charger idled innocently against the curb. He opened the passenger-side door, deposited her into the familiar bucket seat, and got into the driver's side. Vaguely, Harper pondered how easy it must have been to kidnap a person in 1970s New York because she didn't hear a single person object to this strange man throwing her body into his vehicle.

She was so glad to be back inside Argo that she could have cried.

Oh. In fact, she was.

What was that? she tried to ask but couldn't hear or feel her own voice.

Sonic pulse, she thought she saw him mouth. *Are you okay?*

I don't know. Where is the harmonica? Did she say the words aloud? Or were they just ricocheting inside her keening mind?

Here, Miles told her as he started the car and drove away from the club. *Safe.* He said nothing else as they drove, and she did not try to ask any more questions. After a moment, the sounds of the city came back, the honking, the rumble of myriad taxis on the road. Even so, they were both quiet, unwilling, or perhaps simply unable, to speak.

He drove them north, through Manhattan, Harlem, Washington Heights, into the Bronx. For a moment she thought he might drive them back to Riverdale, back to the Starlight Diner, and she squirmed a little, her whole body resistant to the very notion that he might once again leave her behind. She wondered what happened to Anthony. She hoped that he was okay.

Miles did not stop at the Starlight Diner. He drove past Riverdale, took them out of the city entirely, into the starry twilight upstate, and still, everything was silent. He owed her an apology, and she certainly was not going to beg for one. If they couldn't begin there, then where the hell else were they supposed to start? Even Argo's psychic presence was noticeably reticent. So they said nothing, and the silence spoke for them.

It was only once Miles pulled off the road at a no-name motel that either of them said anything.

He looked at her, and she looked at him. Took in his exhausted eyes, the deep line between his drawn brows, the gray in his hair. He still looked like hell, and she was oddly glad. This wasn't the youthful Miles of the planetarium. This was the Miles she knew. The Miles who owed her.

He said, "You're wearing my dress."

And when she looked down, she saw that the stealth suit had indeed transformed back into the poppy-red confection she stole from his closet, and Harper burst into tears all over again.

EPISODE FIVE
TESSERACT

This week on Infinite Odyssey:

Now that the Argonaut remembers who he is, he must uncover the events of his past that made him who he is today. With First Mate Lucinda Freely at his side, the Argonaut visits all the moments in a past he gave up everything to forget.

15.

UPSTATE NEW YORK
WINTER, 1972

Miles pulled the stained motel curtains closed and plunged them into darkness. The room possessed the faint, bitter odor of mothballs and traces of lemon soap. He had used a tarnished brass key to get into the room—she didn't ask him where he'd gotten it; she was just glad he had.

She sat on the edge of one of two double beds and watched his silhouette shuffle around in the shadows, slamming into bed frames, groaning in annoyed pain as he continued his mysterious ministrations. Her thoughts were a whirlwind, too big to be contained or parsed. Names entered her mind and scattered as new ones came. Anthony. Angie. Indira. Dottie. Joseph. Sheila. Peggy.

She needed a list, dammit. What was known and unknown. What had worked and had not worked. Anything that could help her rationalize this situation. Anything that could help her figure out what to do next.

"Why didn't we go to your house?" she asked. "The one in Greenwich?"

Another groan as Miles banged his knee. "How on earth do you know about that?"

If the version of him she met at the planetarium had sent her the key, or even the harmonica she'd retrieved at the club, would he remember it now? Or was this an example of time travel enabling new choices, new timelines?

"I found you in the directory," she said.

"First that stupid television show and now a directory with my name in it?" he muttered to himself while he rifled through a duffle bag. "What's next?"

Her eyes adjusted a little, and she watched him put a small round object on the desk by the door. More alien tech. He hit what she assumed was a button on the side, and the device glowed softly in response. A virtually transparent bubble emerged, only visible due to its somewhat oily texture, the light smeared across its surface like a soapy bubble. The bubble expanded, coming alarmingly close to Harper and then encompassing her altogether, sending a brief, fuzzy wave of static through her ears as it swallowed her, the bed, and soon the entire room before passing through the ceiling. Harper went to the window and watched as it swallowed the motel whole. It shimmered against the starry night for a moment, then melted into the atmosphere and disappeared.

"What," she said breathlessly, "was that?"

Miles, job apparently done for a moment, closed his eyes and pinched the bridge of his nose, as if soothing a headache.

"Psychic disruptor," he said. "Argo needs time to recover; she got pretty banged up hopping through the universe to get here double-time, and there's too many damn frequencies emitting from the three of us—we're practically Times Square. This should buy us enough time to get her charged again."

"This is how you've been dodging them for so long," Harper realized. "The Incarnate can track psychic frequencies, so you get rid of yours."

"Yes, Harper, I am a coward who has relied for many years on psychic disruptors to stay alive. Sue me." He pulled something else from the duffel. "Now hold out your arm."

Harper did as she was told before realizing she should ask why.

As if he'd heard her thoughts, he said, "I'm going to give you a shot of something." He held up a syringe filled with a red viscous liquid.

Her body went taut. "The Paradox Serum."

He pressed the needle against the soft flesh of her arm. "I shouldn't have let you run wild across 1971 without making it impossible for you to muck it all up. I just . . . Well, I thought it was going to be a one-way trip and you'd settle down with a nice young man and forget all about this. God, if Jason knew he'd tear me a new one."

"You called me a causality bomb."

He tilted his head. "When did I do that?"

"At the museum. I found you at the planetarium when you were younger."

"Can't have been," he said. "I left after . . . well, I left before you and I arrived."

"It was you, Miles. I'm not an idiot."

He sighed. "Of course not. Are you ready?"

Her breath hitched. "No, I'm not ready. What are the side effects? How long does the serum last? How—"

"We don't have time for this, so I'm only going to say this once. Without this injection, you cannot leave 1971. Argo won't let you. Not again. So, take it or don't—but without it, you're stuck here."

Her jaw clenched involuntarily. "Fine. Do it."

The needle pierced her skin and her veins flooded with icy cold and then icy hot. She yelped in alarm as the freezing heat spread to her fingers and up her arm, across her chest, and finally into her heart like a bolt of lightning.

"This feeling," she panted, "is this . . . is this normal?" The act of forming words was suddenly excruciating.

"Yes." He put the syringe back in the duffel and watched her carefully. "It'll be over soon." He stood and put the duffel on the dresser.

She opened her mouth to respond, but then her mind exploded. Her body flung itself backward without any input from her brain. Her blood was boiling, killing her from the inside out, and her mind . . . her mind was on fire, the serum crossing the blood-brain barrier and igniting every pain receptor she possessed. Miles was at her side in two strides.

Apparently, not so normal.

"Starling? What's wrong; what do you feel?"

"Fire," she gasped. She was spontaneously combusting. Her brain was melting. And the door in the back of her mind was creaking slowly, slowly open.

Abruptly, she understood.

"Hive," she managed to rasp, pointing at her neck.

"Oh, fuck me."

Miles stumbled backward and disappeared out the front door, and despite everything she was feeling, Harper laughed. If he'd just bolted for the second time, she was going to revise her mission and hunt him down. But he was back a moment later with a jar of something that looked suspiciously like congealed blood. He turned her on her side and smeared the stuff against her perspiring neck. It cooled on impact, and the door in her mind creaked closed once again.

"This won't give us more than twenty-four hours," he said, "but it'll allow the serum to finish its job on your physiology. After that, we'll have to find a different solution."

"What . . . is it?" she ground out. The fire in her blood began to dissipate.

"Same shit that's in the psychic disruptor," he said. "Alien tech, I swear. All fluids and amorphous blobs. How's that feel?"

Her body went limp. She lay still, breathing hard, her skin tingling all over from an intense but fading neuropathy. She tasted ash.

Miles sat down beside her on the edge of the bed, his back to her. The silence was blessedly dense. It filled her recovering mind until the pain had faded and she was able to untangle her thoughts again.

"I feel different," she whispered hoarsely after a time. After all that, she was weirdly calm.

Miles didn't turn, preferring, apparently, to stare at the dirty wall. "Your body's changing. Soon you'll be like me."

"Like you?"

"A full-fledged time-and-space traveler. Capable of roaming the universe's myriad histories and locales without any limits at all."

The way he said it made it sound like such a drag.

"Will I still be . . . human?"

Miles shrugged. "What is human, really? You're still you. Everything that makes you who you are still exists, just in a slightly different package."

This should have bothered her, but she didn't have the heart to be mad about it. Even though she knew it would just make the hive want her that much more, there were other things she was saving her anger for.

"Miles," she said, "why 1971?"

Miles huffed a bitter laugh. "I don't know. Disco?"

He ran a hand through his disheveled hair. Reached behind his ear for a cigarette he soon realized wasn't there.

"You said that Argo had chosen it. Back at the Starlight. That you wouldn't have taken us there." She pulled herself into a sitting position and twisted the knob on the nightstand lamp. Grungy orange light illuminated the room, creating more shadows. "So why did she?"

"You'll have to ask her," Miles said, but Harper suspected she knew the answer. Miles had too many emotional ties to this era to willingly leave Harper in it. But it was becoming clear that Miles didn't command Argo. Not really. She knew the ins and outs of time better than he did—she knew where Harper needed to be and when, and she had acted upon that knowledge without Miles's input.

Miles cleared his throat. "You know when I . . . when I lost Peggy, I could have reached her in time to save her. I just . . . didn't. She told me she wanted to see her family for a few days, so I dropped her off in Colorado. I had sensed something off on that planet, but I thought we left in time to escape it. I promised to come get her when I was done drinking myself silly during an ancient Greek bacchanal. I brought a bottle of wine back with me so she could taste Grecian wine from thousands of years ago.

"When I arrived, they had already filed the missing person report. But I understood in that moment that what I'd seen on that planet was real. And that it had gotten hold of her. And I'd known, somewhere in the back of my mind. And I did . . . nothing." He turned to Harper, his face shrouded in shadow. "I thought I was saving you, you know. I thought if I took you somewhere safe and got you away from all this, you'd never have to go through what Peggy went through. But I was wrong."

"That's not why you did it." Her voice scraped against her raw throat. "You did it because you're afraid, not because you were doing me some big favor. And I was easy enough to sacrifice because you don't know me."

"Go on," Miles said, nodding. "Say it. Say all the things you've been waiting to say to my face. May as well."

"Fine." Harper crossed her arms. "You're a coward. But not for the reasons you think. And yeah, I'm furious you left me here. Beyond furious."

"You've adapted somewhat, at least."

"Adapted? Are you serious? Do you have any idea how afraid I've been these last three months? The terror of waking up, paralyzed, inside a body that isn't fully yours? It was New Year's Eve when I realized that whatever surgery you did to get the Incarnate out didn't work. And there was nothing I could do. Because you left me here."

She shook, her anger quiet and quick. A dull ache gaining heat, a new star forming, a wrathful sun. She hated this man, this coward whom she'd been foolish enough to believe was some kind of hero. She hated him more than the Incarnate, more than anything. She hated how pathetic he was, crouched helplessly over the bed, content to wallow in his own self-pity.

"Keep going," he said. "I deserve it."

"That self-loathing nonsense is not helping."

"You sound like Peggy."

Harper sucked in a sharp breath. The last thing she needed were more casual reminders that Peggy had chosen this pitiful wretch over her. "You know what? Don't talk about Peggy anymore."

"What do you want from me? An apology? Fine! I'm sorry I showed up that night. I'm sorry I even bothered to help you. I should have driven away."

"Fuck you."

"No, fuck *you*!"

The words dropped like a grenade and Miles shut his mouth. Too late.

"You know what? You're right," she said. "Fuck me. Fuck the life I lived before I met you. Fuck the best friend you took from me. Fuck the illusion I lived with all my life that there are heroes in this universe and that you might have been one of them. Fuck me for dreaming, for all of it."

She stood, weak and exhausted, her cells mutating, transforming her into something else. Her anger was going to suffocate her and she couldn't take it any longer. She marched to the door and slammed it open, January air rushing in to cool her heated face. Argo sat in the parking lot, as lifeless and still as the other vehicles that were not sentient spaceships.

Harper tried to feel her, to let Argo calm her erratic heartbeat, her troubled mind. But there was nothing, and somehow it made everything so much worse. She hated how vulnerable she felt and how angry she was. She hated that she had loved the Argonaut as a child, because if she hadn't, she would not have felt such deep, soul-crushing disappointment upon meeting him that night in Harlem, and every day after. But the man from the show was just a made-up person with a made-up mission. A mission Harper gave him when she agreed to write *Infinite Odyssey.*

He *ahem*ed behind her.

"As long as the disruptor is in your system, you won't be able to hear her." He sidled up next to her, hands in his pockets. "It was the only thing I could think to do in the moment."

"Quick thinking."

"It won't stop the Incarnate, of course, but it should keep it fairly dormant, for the time being. While the serum does its job."

Does its job. A euphemism for *changing her DNA*. Warping her genes, twisting her cells, altering her brain chemistry. What would she be at the end of this? In the TV show, the Argonaut was an alien with a third eye and a nearly infinite life span. Miles might not have had the obvious physical differences that the show's protagonist possessed, but that didn't mean they weren't there in some form or another.

She tucked her hands under her armpits to warm them. She missed her bomber jacket, that incongruous coat that had kept her warm all that time in 1971. She missed the heat of Anthony's apartment, where the radiators hissed and squealed all night as they pumped steam into the air. She missed the humid diner kitchen, ovens piping hot while they baked that day's pies in the wee hours of the morning. She missed Paul French's quiet town house, scattered with the remnants of a life well-lived.

Miles fidgeted with his pockets. "It all went sour again when I met Peggy." It sounded almost like an apology. "Not because of anything she did, of course, but because of the things I never told her. About my past.

"I met her one night in New York. Before I met Ron. I was probably wearing that dress," he said, pointing at Harper's borrowed outfit. "I was younger then, but I needed a change. I needed to be someone new. We had a wonderful night, and then I left, figuring I'd see the city a bit before I called on her again. But then . . . I met Ron. And when I found Peggy again, I'd lived an entire, happy life—until I lost him."

"I'm sorry," Harper said, meaning it. She'd seen the pictures of them on the wall in Greenwich. She had seen on their faces how happy they were together.

"After that, Peggy and I simply didn't discuss it. I was glad to have someone around who didn't seem to need that from me. She was content to have adventures and leave the past well enough alone. I'd already lost so much. That's the thing about this existence. The longer you're alive, the more you lose. And I thought I should spare her from my grief because it was so great.

"She could always tell there was something. But she let me have that, and I think, in that way, we were kindred spirits. Too kindred. I let things get out of hand. I wish, now, that I had told her because I think what I need, what I've always needed, is someone to help me understand when I'm being a colossal fool." There was a brightness in his gaze, a gleam she had never seen before. "And then, you. You, Harper . . . Where do I begin? You're brash and rude and you have a tendency to yell. You're incredibly stubborn and quite possibly the most frustrating person I've ever met."

"I—"

"But you're also courageous, observant, and resourceful. I abandoned you in 1971, and what did you do? You thrived. You don't beat around the bush. If you say you're going to do something, you do it. If you told me you planned to kill me, even in hyperbole, I would honestly believe you."

"What are you trying to say?"

"I . . . I guess I can't ignore that I don't know what's best for anyone. That I ruin things when I think I'm doing what is right. You're better than I am, Harper. Just better."

A charged silence fell heavily between them. Did he believe what he'd said? That she was better? She didn't. She couldn't. What did Harper have that was so much better than whatever Miles offered his companions? Nothing. Just a diner apron and a habit of letting her life slip by.

"So, look," he said, "I know we keep getting off on the wrong foot. I know I'm not great at expressing myself. But despite what you have every right to think of me, I don't want you to die. I'm an asshole, but I'm not heartless."

"Are you an asshole who's at least sorry?"

He sighed, chastised. "Yes. I am sorry. For all of it. Much as I might have trouble saying it."

"You need therapy, dude."

To her surprise, Miles laughed. "You know anyone who specializes in space-time travelers with healthy Catholic guilt and a generous helping of self-loathing?"

"Maybe you should get a degree in psychology," she said. "Fill the gap yourself."

When he didn't say anything, she turned and found him staring at her. "So," he said. "What now, Starling?"

She looked around the empty parking lot, as if there was any chance he was speaking to someone else. "You're asking me?"

"Did you not hear a word I just said?"

Harper tilted her head thoughtfully. "Now . . . we save Peggy. And we figure out how to get the Incarnate out of her and me."

"I was afraid you were going to say that."

For the first time, she noticed that her feet were bare—her pumps abandoned back at the club—and the winter chill was finally getting to her, so she walked back into the motel room. It wasn't much warmer in here, but it was better.

Miles followed and shut the door behind him. They faced one another, unsure how to converse now that they'd decided to stop yelling.

"Look," Harper said. "I need answers. I need to know why the Incarnate seems willing to destroy lives across the universe just to find Argo. I want to know what happened to you in 1971. I want to know who gave me the key to your house and the note at the *Star Trek* convention. Tell me everything. Because if you don't, I swear to god, I *will* kill you, and Argo and I will save Peggy without you." A watery smile cracked his exhausted face. "From the beginning, Miles."

He paced a little, fingers laced nervously together as he considered where to start. "The first thing you should understand is that the show gets a handful of things right, but a lot of things wrong."

"Okay . . ."

"And I won't apologize for not being the man in that program."

"You won't apologize for much."

"You're an excruciating audience, Harper, do you know that?"

It was the kind of thing Anthony would have said. Anthony, who was probably still shaking off the effects of Miles's sonic bomb, wondering where the hell Harper had gone.

"It's a gift," she said.

"I could kill for a cigarette right now." Miles ran a hand through his increasingly rumpled hair. "All right. Here it is then."

And he told her his story.

16.

IOWA
1969–1989

Miles Murphy was born in an Iowa farmhouse on a twilit mid-June morning, the same year a group of American astronauts walked on the moon. He was the third of six children born in an agricultural town two hours from anything, where children were known to disappear without much to do, and where he was often confused for his brother Thomas by his parents, whose declining farm required long hours of work that tired them to the bone.

He had a few friends at school, other weirdos and a girl named Willa O'Leary, but they lived far enough in all directions that they rarely saw one another outside of school. While his brothers were off at the lake with the neighborhood boys or terrorizing animals in the woods, his older sister monopolized the television in the den, playing MTV nonstop when she wasn't at school, and on the days when Miles did not have enough money from doing odd jobs to see an old western at the singleplex, he would sit with her while she groaned and sighed her way through that day's homework, watching the glamorous musicians lip-sync to their own music against foggy backgrounds. Soon, he began teaching himself guitar on his father's old untuned acoustic he found in the attic. He told his sister that he'd like to be a musician one day too. She'd just laughed and said, "Good luck getting out of Iowa."

He had his favorites, of course—Michael Jackson and the Cure and the Bee Gees—but no one topped Miles Moonraker. He was nothing like the other musicians Miles loved—besides his raw croon, he kept his face painted in every video, every concert, stripes of green and blue and purple and so much glitter it was a wonder the rock star didn't suffocate. The alien androgyny that would have gotten anyone beaten to shit out there in farm country seemed perfectly normal on the musician's made-up face, and it forced people to pay attention to the music, melodies about people adrift among the stars.

And on his way home from school one evening, he found himself daydreaming about what a person had to do to have a life like that. Where did one go? How did they dress? How did they pass the point of being bullied and enter the phase of being taken seriously? He wondered about Miles Moonraker, who was . . .

Standing in the road in front of him.

Miles blinked. No, not Miles Moonraker after all—there was no paint on his sun-loved brown skin, no glitter gracing his brow. But the man's bright eyes were framed with lines of smudged black, his Titian curls crisp with product, and the costume he wore was straight out of a Miles Moonraker video.

Something stirred in Miles's heart, in his stomach. A kind of ache, a kind of longing.

"Ah," said the man. He studied Miles curiously. "I see that someone has played a joke on me. You are wearing a more accurate representation of your planet's uniform?"

Miles looked down. He wore a pair of baggy, oft mended blue jeans that once belonged to his older brother and a pilling flannel that no longer fit Thomas. He was still too small to wear these things, but his parents insisted he would grow into them one day. He eagerly awaited the day God gave him a growth spurt and made that statement true.

"Maybe," he said with a shrug. Having not met many people outside his small town, he wasn't sure it was safe to consult him on the dress of the rest of the planet. "You all right, sir? You need some help?"

"I'm looking for something," the man said. His voice was deep and smooth but strangely accented, like he could not quite figure out how to move his tongue around the English language. "I can't leave until I know what it is." He licked his teeth. "You know, your words feel rather funny in my mouth."

"Oh," said Miles. He was woefully inexperienced with interacting with adults, and though he admired the man's outfit, he was less sure of his mental state. Should he run home? Should he call for help?

The man regarded him thoughtfully. He didn't seem to be in much of a hurry for a person who couldn't find what he was looking for. The sun was drifting lazily toward the cornfields; soon enough, the man would be searching in the deep, Iowa dark.

"It's all right," the man said with a smile. He had a strange, lovely smile. "But you'd tell me if you've seen one?"

"Seen . . . what?"

The man bent close to whisper, "An anomaly." He looked around them furtively. Miles stared at him in disbelief. This man was really messing with him.

"I don't think so," Miles said. "It's just corn for a while."

"Shame," the man said, straightening up. "I was certain there were readings coming from this spot." He held up a small, rectangular, translucent object and looked at Miles through it, then frowned. "Yes. Well. Perhaps the reading is a few years off. Move along, young person. Thank you for your assistance."

"Okay," Miles said. He did as he was told and resumed his path home, trying to ignore the strange flutter in his stomach as he kicked at the pebbled road. When Miles turned around to ask the man's name, he was already gone.

The next few years passed like hours in a dream. Miles grew up—and up and up and up—and stopped watching MTV with his sister—who moved to Chicago, much to the family's chagrin—and then stopped going to school, instead working on the farm full-time alongside his brothers, while their father slowly descended into a fog of hellacious back pain from which he would never recover.

Miles never forgot the man dressed like Miles Moonraker but attributed his existence to a sugar-induced hallucination and tucked the encounter away into the corner of his mind reserved for his desire to try on his mother's clothes and the way he'd felt watching Joseph Monahan thoughtfully chew his pencil across the room during history class.

He got a single earring he wore on those rare weekends when he drove the five hours to Chicago to visit his sister in the city, something to appease those desires lurking in that dim corner of his mind. He let her take him to bars and spray gobs of hairspray into his thick hair. Sometimes, when he was feeling daring, he'd ask her to swipe eyeliner under his sleepless eyes or let him borrow one of her glittery tops. His parents would have killed him if they saw him like this, but his sister always just smiled and dug something she thought might be flattering out of her dresser.

He kissed men and women and hated himself for it later, unsure whether one could still be considered gay if they liked women too, and hoping to God it would mean nothing in the long run. He bought records from Miles Moonraker and Fleetwood Mac and popular hair bands and saved up enough money over a year to purchase a flimsy turntable. He horrified his family with his music choices, but with the same managed to woo Willa O'Leary, who accepted his proposal of marriage two months before his nineteenth birthday, and two months after they lost their virginity to one another. She had an easy laugh and a way of looking at him that made him feel unique and interesting, like the people at the clubs in Chicago, rather than, well, strange. He loved her, which was both a relief and wildly confusing.

He did not expect to ever see the man dressed as Miles Moonraker again, that strange figment of his overactive imagination fueled by old movies and music videos. But, as he would later learn, when something from the unknowable expanse beyond Earth came knocking at your door, it rarely only knocked once.

His father helped him with his tie the sweaty September morning he and Willa were to wed at the courthouse downtown. Neither wanted a finicky affair, both being rather embarrassed by the entire idea. Still, he wore a powder-blue suit, and his mother fussed with his hair until she was satisfied. Thomas loaned him a tie, and Ian gave him less-than-savory marriage advice. As the day wore on, it began to feel like there was a stone growing in his gut, and the more his family talked and laughed and speculated about his future children, the heavier the stone became. But he loved Willa. It was supposed to be enough.

Just as his family members were gathering their hats and jackets, she called him from a pay phone at the train station. Her voice was nasally, like she'd been crying. But she was resolute too. She'd been having doubts, she told him. She didn't want to spend the next ten years having children. She didn't want to get stuck with a failing farm and a drinking husband. She wanted to travel. She wanted to live amongst the artists in New York, breathe the air in Switzerland, and visit every museum in Vienna. He didn't tell her that he wanted those things too. That the stone inside him turned into a bird with her words, caged by his ribs. He didn't tell her that he, too, longed to be free.

But she wasn't inviting him to go with her. It was clear that, however much she might love him, in the end, it wouldn't carry them any further than this.

"Why are you smiling?" his mother asked when he got off the phone.

"Willa's running away," he told her. He ignored the way all the color seemed to drain from her face. The way his father stomped around like he thought anger might patch what had just broken in that eternal five-minute phone call. The way his brothers jeered and laughed, as if to say they'd known all along that it was too good to be true.

"I'm going to Chicago," he said and left the house mid taunt. His car's engine had died a horrible death the spring before, so he borrowed his uncle's busted old Dodge Charger and sped out of Iowa as the sun set over the corn.

He spent six days moping on his sister's couch, ignoring the stares of her roommates and rudely eating all the Cheerios. He went to clubs with them, did their drugs, drank their alcohol, and generally overstayed his welcome. With his sister's help, he found new roommates in a new apartment and got a job at the Riviera Theatre box office. He introduced an earring into his everyday look. He ignored phone calls from his parents, to whom he'd barely said goodbye, and who were now threatening to throw away all his things if he didn't come back for them. *What things?* He could barely remember what any of his stuff looked like. An armload of hand-me-down clothes forgotten in a hand-me-down dresser in the corner of a hand-me-down room on a hand-me-down farm.

Chicago suited him. It just did. While he could wear black liner and call it punk rock, in Iowa it would have been a sign that he was one of those devil-worshipping teenagers, the ones snatching babies in the night all over the Midwest. Here he could borrow a swipe of his sister's lipstick before a shift at the box office, and while he couldn't deny that he got funny looks from time to time, in general his customers didn't pay much attention. They were there to see Iggy Pop, after all. Who cared about some too-skinny twenty-year-old clerk wearing a flattering fuchsia in the dark of the cashier's box? He often wondered about Willa, about where she was and what adventures she was having. If they looked anything like his.

Eight months after Miles from Iowa tumbled headfirst into Chicago, Miles Moonraker came to the Riviera. Miles didn't buy a ticket; usually, after his shift at the window ended, he would grab a watered-down drink from the bar and watch the shows from the back of the balcony. While it would have been nice to have a ticket, to be down in the audience with the rest of Miles Moonraker's adoring fans, he was low on cash, and, anyway, this method was more punk rock, he was pretty sure.

By the time he switched shifts with a coworker, the show was well underway, the wall of sound radiating from the stage loud enough to cocoon him in the familiar groove of Miles Moonraker's music. He was sad to have missed the first numbers, the slightly older songs the rock star often used to reel his crowds in. Miles loved them even more than the new stuff, which tended toward a higher tempo and more conventional themes. Clean sound, clean-cut. The older stuff was gritty, full of longing and galaxies and unsettlingly deep oceans—the stuff Miles had reared himself on through hours and days and years of TV and music videos in his parents' basement. Still, he was grateful for the chance to see his hero at all, and leaned into the euphonious thrum.

He acquired a Jack and Coke from the bartender, who complimented tonight's earring and intentionally unkempt hair, and wandered onto the balcony, cola fizzing in his nose as he sipped. The lack of ventilation in the venue meant that he was slicked with sticky sweat the moment he stepped inside, the odors of smoke and weed and bodies pressed together now clinging to his own skin.

On the stage, Miles Moonraker serenaded the crowd, and Miles's own stomach did a funny swoop. He thought he'd be able to play it cool, but seeing the artist now, his lacquered eyelids picking up the swiveling neon light and flaring like a disco ball, Miles wasn't sure he could stop himself from going full-on fanboy.

Even his drink didn't seem to quell his joy and nerves, which were quickly tripping over into nausea. His stomach squirmed, the sensation becoming more unpleasant the longer he watched. His heart worryingly skipped several beats. His knees went strangely wibbly and buckled. The room began to tilt and move, spinning like a carnival ride, which he was now pretty sure was not a symptom of enjoying oneself at a show. His excitement soured into fear as his body crashed to the floor without his consent, drink spilling against the sticky carpet. A few people watched him go down with boozy disinterest, and he lay still on the balcony for several long minutes, stomach tying itself into tighter and tighter knots—so tight that his lungs began to constrict—before someone leaned over him.

"Ah yes," said the shadowy figure, "I thought it might be you."

17.

CHICAGO
SPRING, 1989

Strong arms threaded under his armpits and hoisted him off the floor and out of the balcony area, guiding him through throngs of wasted people, clouds of pungent marijuana smoke, couples joined at the lips. They pushed him through the front doors of the venue and into the clammy May night. Miles gulped down lungsful of gritty Chicago air and felt strangely better.

"What just happened?" he gasped. He turned to his savior and blinked.

It was the strange man who had stopped him on his way home all those years ago—and he had not aged a single day. Now that Miles saw him with adult eyes, his childhood image of the man shifted and warped to accommodate the person standing before him. There were no grays to be found in the man's burnished waves, no wrinkles in his deep-olive skin besides the attractive crinkles at the corner of his laughing eyes. The only difference in his appearance was the new outfit: a much subtler tattered black T-shirt and worn jeans. Though he'd been at least two decades older than Miles that fateful evening, and perhaps more, they now looked to be much closer in age than before.

"You," Miles managed to stutter.

The man smiled. "Me."

"But . . . what . . . ?"

"Paradox," the man replied. "Or an almost-paradox." He turned neatly on his heel and began walking down the street. It took Miles a moment to realize that if he wanted more answers he should follow, and he skipped to catch up.

"Paradox?" he asked, jogging up to the man. "What does that mean?"

"It means you were in the wrong place at the wrong time," his companion replied. "Only question, of course, is which one of you."

The man was setting a brutal pace and Miles struggled to keep up.

"Which one . . . ?" he panted. "What are you talking about?"

The man turned promptly around another corner, causing Miles to bump into and become somewhat entangled with a stumbling couple as he attempted to follow. This street was not so crowded nor so well lit, and Miles began to feel uneasy. Beyond the theater's radius, Miles didn't know this area very well at all. Chicago as a whole was still a mostly uncharted map made up of neighborhoods he'd never seen and subway lines he'd never ridden. He was beginning to think it had been a mistake not exploring more.

"A paradox happens when one thing intersects at the same time and place twice," the man was saying. "And judging by the physical reaction you had back there, I'd say that thing is you. It does jog the innards, doesn't it?" He pulled an object from an invisible pocket, that same translucent item he'd held when Miles first met him years ago, and waved it vaguely around Miles's head, then clucked his tongue in confirmation. "Yep. It's you."

"But how were you even there? How did you know it was me? How have you not aged?"

"You're asking a lot of questions that I simply can't answer if you don't possess a basic understanding of the universe. Do you?"

"Do I . . . What the fuck are you talking about?"

The man sighed. "As I thought." He halted abruptly and Miles barely stopped himself from plowing into him. "Here's the situation, Miles Murphy."

"How do you—"

"I don't usually make it my business to interfere in these matters. My crew and I, we're searching for something specific, and Earth is of little consequence to that search. However, your planet is not capable of time travel, and a glance at your timeline tells me it never acquires this ability. So how, I ask you, does a young Earthman nearly cause a paradox in the middle of a rock concert on a planet with no ability to produce paradoxes?"

Miles stuttered as he realized the man expected him to answer. "Er, I don't know."

"Well, I don't either. Which leads me to believe that, in some way, it's my fault. There's no other explanation."

"There isn't?"

The man shook his head regretfully. "I'm afraid not. In taking a detour to investigate an anomaly in time, I believe I have inadvertently *created* said anomaly. Which means there's only one thing left to do. Given that it's already happened."

The man stepped closer to Miles, and even in the tenebrous night, his green irises caught the light of the streetlamps and managed, somehow, to twinkle.

Miles swallowed hard. "There is?"

"Miles, have you ever wanted to see beyond your tiny, inconsequential little world?"

"What, like . . . Europe?"

The man threw his head back and laughed, throaty and full. "Think bigger! Think further! Further than you've ever been, further than you've ever dreamed. Past the moon you Earth-dwellers so love to aim for. Past the stars you can count from your bedroom window."

His mind was a whirl of new questions and exclamations, frothing up like champagne bubbles and popping into obscurity just as quickly. There were too many possibilities to count. Perhaps this man was a murderer and Miles really shouldn't be talking to him. Or, this man had lost his mind and Miles really shouldn't be talking to him. This man was an alien and Miles . . .

Stepped back.

"You need help."

"Help?"

"Yeah. You're insane. And you need help."

The man seemed disappointed but not surprised by this response. "I see. Too much, too soon. I think your fiancée would have understood me, but it's understandable you'd be hesitant. A person can only live such a restrained life for so long before their worldview is permanently narrowed."

Miles went still. "What do you mean, my fiancée would have understood you?"

"Oh yes," the man replied breezily. "We had a wonderful conversation. Talked for hours. I don't know how she put up with that small place for so long."

The last time he'd thrown a punch, his brother beat him down so hard he never made the mistake of starting a fight with anyone ever again. But this man was taunting him, and without even meaning to, Miles curled his hands into fists. This stranger had been stalking him for years apparently, from Iowa to Chicago, and now here he was, throwing Willa in his face.

The man's eyes softened. "I've angered you. You feel some pride of ownership over her, then? How very strange. You Earth-dwellers have such odd modes of morality."

"You've been following me since I was a kid. You've talked to people I love. You pulled me out of that theater spouting nonsense about paradoxes and the universe and now you're leading me down some dingy street to god knows where. You have it out for me, and I don't even want to know why anymore. I just want you to leave me alone."

"I can't do that, Miles."

"And why not?"

"Here," the man said, narrowing the gap between them. "I'll show you."

Before Miles could protest, the man had placed both palms against his temples, those green eyes boring into his own, and the world spun away into a kaleidoscope of stars.

He'd been so wrong. Not just about Willa, and the world, and the man himself; he'd been wrong about everything. About the universe and his place in it, about what was important and what was of so little consequence that it was laughable he'd ever cared at all. He understood down to his DNA that the things happening in his life, on his world, didn't matter. Or perhaps they mattered intensely, but that mattering burned for one white-hot second on the vast spectrum of universal time. There were a hundred thousand Earth-like worlds with humanlike species and a hundred thousand worlds bearing alien life so intrinsically different from humanity it was practically impossible to recognize it as life at all. The yearning he'd felt his entire life exploded into something as vast as the universe he was seeing now, and it was ancient and raw and blinding. It didn't belong to him, not really—it never had. Another thing he understood as deeply as he understood how to breathe.

And through it all, he saw himself, the hunch of his shoulders as he slunk past that Iowa cornfield at ten years old, and then later on, head held a bit higher as he made his way to work at the Riviera, an earring dangling from one ear, a hack-job haircut he'd given himself the week before. He saw Willa through the stranger's eyes—a confused girl on the verge of tying her life to another's, sadness and fear in her gaze, not happiness. And he saw *himself* as Miles Moonraker on the very same stage at the very same time he'd almost lost consciousness just moments ago, and he understood something that seconds before had been utterly unknowable: he would follow this green-eyed stranger through the stars and through time and through any sea he traveled, and one day he would come back here, a decade older, and perform on that stage while his younger self looked on, songs and stars in both of their hearts.

He saw it all in that moment on a Chicago street, face clutched between hot humanlike palms, eyes reflecting a warming universe only he and the man could see.

He tried to speak but found that he'd quite completely forgotten how. His face was streaked with tears.

"Do you understand, now, why I'm here?" the man asked.

Miles shook, then nodded, then shook his head again. He understood that the universe was beyond the scope of human understanding, and that innumerable planets thrived with intelligent life while the most brilliant minds on Earth set their limited sights on trying and trying to reach their dead moon once again. He understood that he was insignificant, both precious and meaningless simultaneously. He still felt like he was falling through an edgeless black vacuum dusted with stars.

The man started walking. This time, he took Miles's hand, gently guiding him through the throngs of people as they stumbled out of bars or asked casually for spare cigarettes. "She's going to have a fit," he told Miles. They passed under a streetlight that limned them briefly in gold. "She would insist. It's much too late, unfortunately. The damage is done. I'll take my punishment for it, though I'll plead that I was only trying to do the right thing. The Waystation will have to decide what to do with you. You'll understand one day. But now, it's time to go."

Miles followed the man across the street, to an impossible old Ford Model A sitting in the shadow just outside the perimeter of lamplight. It looked just like the one his father had inherited and kept under a sheet in the barn, long before the debt collectors came calling and his father sold the car. It had to be at least fifty years old.

Painted across the side was a word that looked like . . .

"Argo," Miles read. The name tickled a dusty memory—Miles and his family watching *Infinite Odyssey* on Monday nights in the family room, the only thing they did together besides church on Sundays. Argo and her Argonaut traveling space and time. Miles barely remembered the show, but he remembered that much.

The man laughed. "She'll like that."

"I guess that makes you Jason," Miles said, remembering the names from his favorite unit on Greek myths in school. Jason and his Argonauts, traveling the world, in search of something precious that did not really exist.

"I guess it does," the man replied, and that was that. He was Jason. Miles would learn his real name in time, but it wouldn't matter; like Argo's real name, it was impossible for Earthen tongues to pronounce. It didn't suit him like Jason did, anyway.

Miles got into the car when the door was opened for him, falling into the deep, hard seat without protest. Why deny the universe?

As the engine stuttered to life, he wondered briefly if his sister would miss him. He didn't know where the man was taking him, but he knew that it would be far away, far past the limits of where she or the rest of his family might look for him. His roommates would rent the room to another bright-eyed farm boy new to the city, and no one would give him a second thought. His family would stop wondering where he'd gone sooner than the rest of his hometown, and Willa . . . he just hoped she was happy, wherever she'd gone. He doubted she ever planned to contact him again anyway. Somehow, he knew these things to be true, and he found that he wasn't sad about it.

The man kept muttering to himself as the Ford puttered out of Chicago and onto the highway, wind funneling between them, but Miles didn't hear him. He fell into a deep, contented sleep.

He awoke in a cloud of blankets on a bed that was most definitely not the lumpy futon he'd been sleeping on the last six months. The moment his eyes opened a sharp pain stabbed his ocular nerves and traveled through them like a lightning-fast electric current, fizzing outward into the rest of his neural network. He rolled out of the bed, palms to his suddenly sore eyes and temples, a pathetic attempt to wrangle the migraine that was slowly spilling into his entire body. When he simply couldn't take it anymore, he screamed, which did seem to provide a slight release, and the spiderwebs of agony in his brain dulled to a manageable throb. Calm enveloped him despite the pain, and he felt better.

Now that he could see again, it was obvious he was not in any room he recognized—not back at his parents' farm, not his sister's living room, and not any of the rooms in the apartment he was currently renting. This room was meditative and organic, all curves and earth tones and natural textures. He knew better than to confuse what had happened, where he was, with a dream. The truth was fused into his memory, impossible to scrub away.

He wandered out of the room. Outside, there was a long hallway of doors, presumably to other bedrooms. Everything felt a little cramped, like the belly of a ship. Which made sense, he supposed—he *was* in the belly of a ship. He knew this as innately as he knew his own name now, thanks to Jason's mind trick.

He heard dishes clinking and smelled something divine cooking somewhere down the hall, so he followed his nose to the end and turned, finding himself in a large kitchen where a massive wooden table hosted at least ten people, all talking and chatting in a language he didn't recognize. Jason was at the stove, cooking something that was definitely not of Earth.

Miles cleared his throat. Ten pairs of eyes swiveled to greet him.

"Friends," Jason said in English, "this is Miles. He will be staying with us for a few days until we reach the Waystation."

"Greetings, Miles," ten people said in that same guttural English Jason used, as if their tongues were too heavy to move around the letters. He wondered how they were able to understand him and speak his language at all.

"Good morning," he said, voice cracking. "Um, where are we?"

"We're on the good ship Argo," Jason replied with a wink. Miles felt another strange pressure against his brain, a feeling that didn't belong to him. Almost like . . . a hello. "And I apologize for the headache—a side effect of the medicine. But now you'll be able to travel with us without causing any more paradoxes."

"Medicine?"

"Changes your physiology a tad. You'll find you're a bit more psychic than you once were. An upgrade, if you ask me!"

Miles's mind reeled. "Psychic?"

But Jason's attention was already elsewhere. "All right, come get it!"

The ten crew members stood and rushed the stove area, filling their plates with the strange mash Jason had made.

Miles fully synthesized what Jason had said and looked at his surroundings with new understanding. This was the Ford. *This* was the *Ford*?

Jason stood by Miles and watched his companions argue over the pan. "She takes on shapes that make sense for the planets we visit," he explained. "Like the Earth vehicle. But this is her true form."

"She looks like a ship," Miles said.

"She is a ship," Jason said.

"What's the Waystation?"

Jason sighed. "About that. I'm sorry to leave you there, but we're on a quest, you see. And it wouldn't be fair to bring an ignorant Earth-dweller along."

"What if I want to go with you?"

"I don't think that's a good idea."

"But you . . . you changed me. It's not fair."

"I'm sorry about that too. Even so, we can't always get what we want, Miles."

And Miles had no basis of understanding with which to argue. He was not a traveler of the universe. It was no one's job to make sure he got it. As a brief guest of the Argo, all he could do was listen and glean what knowledge was passed between the Argonauts in his presence. Perhaps Jason had given him a gift.

With the Rolling Stones stuck in his head, Miles ate breakfast with the Argonauts. He learned their names, asked about their quest. They were seeking the kidnapped princess of one of their planet's richest nations. She'd been stolen by Gadsian smugglers, and as Pelegaea's greatest hero, Jason was tasked with finding her.

Miles couldn't believe it. This was what he'd wished for all his life, an adventure that took him out of those cornfields and put him on the road to something magnificent. He yearned for the stars Miles Moonraker sang about, and despite Jason's insistence that he could not join, this seemed to be his chance to see them.

"What will the Waystation do with me?" he asked.

"Put you to work, probably. There are good jobs there. You can live comfortably."

But living comfortably was not what Miles wanted.

So, he made himself useful. He learned to cook the strange mash the Argonauts ate for breakfast, and he cleaned up after them, and he tidied the ship. He learned Pelegaean fighting from Orleus, who reveled in having a student, and how to play an instrument suspiciously like a guitar from Penelope. After their tiring days of travel, the Argonauts sat in rapt attention as he played the stringed instrument and sang Miles Moonraker songs. They loved hearing about the man who journeyed across the stars, just like them. And on the seventh night, Jason came to Miles's room.

"The Argonauts," Jason said, because he enjoyed Miles's cheeky name for them, "like you very much."

"Well, I like them very much," Miles said.

"Listen. I know you feel it's unfair to be left at the Waystation. But it's for your own good."

"I know," Miles said, even though he didn't.

Jason could see it on his face. "You're young, Miles. You have your entire life ahead of you. I would not have you waste it chasing a princess across the universe."

"I don't think it's a waste."

Jason looked thoughtful at that. He played with an irregular curve on the wall. "No. I suppose you wouldn't."

When he didn't say anything else, Miles asked, "Is the ship . . . is Argo . . . sentient?"

"Of course."

"Oh." The strange pressure on his mind, the emotions that didn't seem to belong to him, the things he seemed to just know, despite never having traveled away from Earth before. It all made sense.

Jason sank down on the edge of Miles's bed. "I never told you. Damn."

"It's okay."

"This is why you cannot come with us. There's so much I don't have time to explain. I can't help you if we end up on a hostile planet and things go badly—I must look out for the quest."

"I know that," Miles said, a strange confidence filling him up. "But I can learn. I can handle it. You made me an Argonaut too. Even if you didn't mean to."

"I suppose I did."

They looked at one another silently, and for a moment Miles wondered if Jason would try to speak in his mind, put images there like he'd done back in Chicago. But the hero just stood and swept from the room.

When they landed on a small dusty planet a week later, Miles asked where they were. Jason told him a word that he could not pronounce.

"What happened to the Waystation?"

"We're nearly there," Jason replied. "But there's no harm in bringing you along just this once."

Miles and the Argonauts did not find the princess on this strange planet, but they did receive intel from locals who had seen her and explained that she was no longer there, so they moved on. The next world was not the Waystation either, and when asked, Jason replied, "Nearly there. Just making a quick stop."

This was how they traveled: Jason promising that Miles would be dropped off soon and that they were going to make a stop on this planet here or that space station there before completing the trip. The longer it took, the more time Miles and Jason spent together.

At first, Miles felt like a boy with a crush. Jason was traveled; Jason was worldly; Jason was older and therefore possessed a certain allure. He was a Pelegaean, a proud people from a planet many systems away from Earth, whose biology allowed him to psychically pilot his ship, to converse silently with his Argonauts, and to plant suggestions into the minds of malleable beings. Their ships, such as Argo, were born from the wood and tesseract crystals found in a forest on Pelegaea with psychic and quantum properties. They called it the Sight Wood. Should the forest burn, their ability to make those wondrous ships capable of traveling time and space would burn with it. Jason explained this to Miles over a particularly caustic glass of some backwater planet's excuse for rum, his eyes sad. He loved his planet. He loved his people. He loved his quest and his ship and his Argonauts.

But as time went on, Miles began to see the cracks. He learned that Jason sometimes mistook his pride for implicit wisdom. And that his confidence got all the Argonauts in trouble when he was wrong. He saw Jason's frustration with the length of the quest. How long it took to follow the scant leads they had.

And still, Miles loved him.

He wasn't sure when he realized it. It would have been an ordinary morning on Argo, the table overfilled with twelve chattering people, slurping and chewing their breakfast like always. Jason would have been sitting at the head of the table, smiling at his friends, his family, happiest when they were happy, when they were fed and sheltered and questing. And he would have smiled at Miles too, the piece that did not fit but who was there and trying, an accidental Argonaut. And it would have been enough for Miles to know.

They visited an Aepholian seer who had been exiled to Sekundos and followed her visions of the princess to Myzsst. The journey to Myzsst was long and arduous: Warp to Malderah. Avoid the asteroid belt at the warp-point by nosing up ten degrees. Stick to the dark side of the planet Sialista's rocky moons to escape notice. Jump again. Jump again. Jump again. For two weeks they leapfrogged through space, dodging debris or solar storms or hostile forces at their emergence points, until the arctic planet finally shook its snowy head at them through the haze of a particularly milky nebula. It clung to the gravitational tug of a dull star. Jason maintained his smile, his confidence, but the fervor of the crew waned as the objective of their mission grew murky. This was supposed to be a straightforward quest, but they were at the very edge of the universe, following a nearly baseless lead. And frigid, snow-packed Myzsst revealed little more than the word of a few locals—all of them wind-burned and stuffed into thick coats made from the pelts of arctic animals—who told them to try Aster, a two-week journey away.

Aster was a dead end too.

Months turned into years while the Argonauts hopped through the systems. They spent six months on a planet called Windfall while they waited for a dust storm in the next system to end. On another, Orleus cheated during an ill-advised game of risk with which none of them were familiar and lost a hand in the ensuing brawl. Eurystus married Penelope in a tasteful ceremony organized by Jason himself on a planet where mica snowed over the rocky peaks, blanketing everything in glittering silver. Cesarius died in quarantine deep within the bowels of Argo, shivering and hallucinating from a virus picked up on a dying world. After that, Aeon left the quest altogether, opting to stay on a planet named Persipiope, where the land was flat and green and fertile, and where the people had no words for *war* or *quest* or *hero*.

The princess became almost like a god in the minds of the Argonauts, the light of their belief in her guiding them across a vicious, storming ocean. But the crew only sometimes remembered her name and why they were looking for her. They forgot she was not only a will-o'-the-wisp, bobbing formless over a roiling sea, but a lighthouse, steadfast on the cliffs. They lost sight of land altogether. It was difficult to see just how they could ever bring glory back to their aureate city now. It seemed inevitable that they would return empty-handed, if they ever returned at all.

But in the end, the Argonauts could not delay the inevitable. The princess was gone, and their quest had come to an end. It was time to go home—and they could not bring Miles with them.

"We could take you to the Waystation," Jason told him one quiet evening. The mood was somber; Miles was now one of them. Pelegaea, though, would not see it that way. "But Earth is closer. It's your choice."

Miles had spent ten years living like a space-and-time traveler with the Argonauts. He'd known it would end—Jason had said so from day one—but he hadn't considered what his future might look like after that. Even at the Waystation, a sprawling space station in a galaxy hundreds of thousands of light-years from the planet of his birth, he would never again have adventures like the ones he'd had with the Argonauts.

And then he remembered the circumstances under which he met Jason—a concert in 1989, his favorite performer, a blip in causality. It seemed so long ago, a hazy dream.

"Take me back to Earth," he said. "To 1975." That gave him a year on Earth. A year to prepare, to get his act together, to perfect his face paint, to record his songs. Because they *were* his songs. Jason confirmed it that night when he rescued Miles from a near-paradox. After all, who better to write them, to perform them with the kind of longing Miles

Moonraker had always possessed, than a human who had been singularly privileged to travel the universe? He'd never taken a moment to understand, even these many years later. But now he saw his future, clear as day.

They gave him an antidote to the serum that had allowed him to be with them all this time, and they drove from the stars to Chicago, just as requested.

It was harder than he'd ever imagined to say goodbye. To turn away from his Argonauts, knowing it would be the last time he ever saw them. They were his family, chosen, more real than the one he was born to.

"That will never change," Jason assured him as they embraced for the last time. "And you will see us again. I promise."

He clung to that promise like a life raft. And then he got to work.

18.

LONDON
SUMMER, 2006

He looked good for sixty. Everyone said so. Thirty years of raucous music, of whirlwind international tours, of makeup and drugs and alcohol and one-night stands, had aged him, of course. But he was happy most of the time, and that seemed to do wonders for the skin.

When it happened, he was midway through his newest European tour and preparing for an early flight the following day with a moisturizing face mask and a glass of forty-year-old scotch in his pristine London hotel room. These days, he felt the burn going down more acutely than he used to, but it never stopped him from enjoying the finer things that came with money and fame. So, when a knock resounded softly from the door, he didn't think anything of it—he'd just ordered room service, after all—and got up to answer.

It was not room service in his doorway. It was a man he hadn't seen in decades, a man with burnished curls and deep-olive skin and bright, intelligent eyes. It was a man who had been older than Miles the last time they embraced; now, though gray streaked his hair and crow's-feet crinkled at the corners of his eyes when he smiled, he was markedly younger than Miles by at least ten, if not twenty, human years.

"Hello, Miles Moonraker," Jason the Argonaut said with a smile. "You're looking well."

"And so are you," Miles said, throat thick with emotion. "You're so young."

"There is no such thing as young or old when you are a traveler." Jason raised his hand toward Miles. "Would you like to take a trip?"

Miles loved his life; there was no question about that. Though he'd never settled down—who could ever compare to the man who showed him the stars?—he had made a name for himself. He was Miles Bloody Moonraker, beloved by the world. He had the privilege of making music for a living, the same music that had inspired him so ardently when he was a child, and he never tired of sharing it year after year. He rarely showed his bare face in public, though that was becoming harder and harder these days, with gossip rags and the internet, and he managed to maintain a comfortable semblance of anonymity in his day-to-day life as a result. It worked for him. It had worked for thirty years.

And still, when Jason asked, he said, "Yes." He had a flight in the morning, and he didn't care. He had dreamed of Jason from the moment Argo left him, once again, on the same Chicago street from which she had swept him all those years ago. He had dreamed of his Argonaut family, dreamed of the time-and-spacefaring ship who had taken care of him for a decade. Thirty years seemed like nothing, suddenly. Miles Moonraker felt strangely far away. A blip on his timeline.

"What changed?" he asked as they entered the elevator.

"I promised we would see each other again."

"A promise? As simple as that?"

Jason looked at him seriously. "A Pelegaean never breaks a promise."

"I missed you," Miles said.

"There's that too."

Argo was waiting for them around the corner outside, disguised as a taxi. He felt her psychic presence as soon as he saw her, the familiar touch of an old friend, and breathed deep as he clambered into the passenger's seat, her woody, warm scent unfolding the memories he had neatly tucked away. Those nights practicing swords with Orleus, learning about galactic navigation from Aeon—before he left the quest—or playing Eurystus's stringed instrument for the questers on lazy evenings.

Miles soon realized, though, that it was just the three of them.

"Where are they?" he asked as Argo drove away from the hotel toward Cromwell Road.

"It has been a long time since we went on a quest," Jason said with a sigh. "There has been war with Gad—everyone was needed. But once it was over, those who were left settled down with families or scholarships. They are doing well, Miles. We all are."

"Then . . . why now?" Miles asked as he felt that familiar tug at his navel, that feeling of being at the top of a roller coaster, of slowly falling, falling. The lights of Chelsea blipped out and became stars, billions of them, and he gasped as if seeing it all for the very first time.

"Because the laws have changed in Pelegaea," Jason said, "and I wanted to show you my home before . . ."

Miles laughed. "I thought you said there was no such thing as old or young."

"That is true for me," Jason replied. "We could make that true for you again too. If you wished."

He thought about his European tour, his forty-year-old scotch sitting, undrunk, on the side table in his swanky hotel room, his fans packed into the stadium, expecting to see their favorite musician.

"I could bring you back," Jason offered, "to the moment you left. If you'd like. Only stay with me for a little while. Visit with your old friends. I've thought about you every day for many years."

And what could Miles say to that but yes? And so, for the second time in his life, he was given the time-traveling serum that would protect him from time itself, and the three of them made their way to Pelegaea.

As they approached Jason's world, Miles expected to see a planet shining like a beacon in the dark of the void. The way the Argonauts had always described it, Pelegaea was a radiant world full of universities and bustling city centers, the capital of Aepholia its brightest star. Gilded marble columns supported massive, majestic halls made entirely of gold, intricate murals created by the most skilled painters Aepholia possessed brightened every exposed wall, and a domed building towered at the center of everything like an ancient Greek tholos. Even the Sight Wood, the sacred forest where tesseract crystals were mined and their famed time-and-spacefaring ships were grown, bore lustrous golden leaves.

He was somewhat disappointed to see that the gilded beauty he had been promised seemed tarnished somehow, the spires of Aepholia brushed with rusty black. The universities, too, looked dingy and unwashed, and something like oil or tar oozed down the stairs of the capitol building, whatever gold it once possessed now encrusted in dark muck. And where were the people? There should have been thousands of Pelegaeans rushing around the dense city center, but the city was apocalyptically empty.

"Did the war cause this?" Miles asked as Argo landed in the plaza in front of the capitol, but Jason stared at his city with wide, fearful eyes, and Miles guessed that this was not the Pelegaea Jason had left.

"Stay here," he told Miles, and Miles obliged, watching through the wide window of the flight deck as Jason approached the capitol steps.

None of it felt right, and after a moment he realized that Argo, too, felt uneasy. He thought about reaching out to Jason on the communication system they carried at all times—the same one that allowed them to converse with Miles in English—to suggest they leave and sort out what had happened from a safe distance. He didn't get the chance.

Jason walked up the tarnished steps of the capitol. He was greeted at the doors by men in billowing robes who pulled him close, as if in an embrace. It took Miles a moment to realize that Jason had not returned the embrace, that he was struggling against it, his body resisting a grip so firm he couldn't seem to break free. Then: Jason was in free fall, plummeting down the once-golden stairs.

For the first time in all their years together, Jason's voice was in his mind.

Run, Miles heard. The voice was weak, already fading. *We are invaded. Parasites. They have taken us, mind and body. They will use me to get to Argo. You are her captain now. You must protect her. Run.*

"No!" Miles said fiercely. But Jason said nothing. Jason was perfectly still on the ground by the stairs of the capitol.

The men who had killed Jason looked past their prey and saw, finally, the ship. Even from this distance, Miles could see that their eyes had gone black, the whites blotted out.

He ran to the doors as Argo rumbled to life. He pulled on them, banged on the keypads, demanded Argo free him. But she was going to get them out of there, no matter what Miles had to say about it. He could only watch helplessly at the window as Jason began to stir at the base of the steps and get up, his movements jerky and unnatural.

"We can't leave him here!" Miles screamed. "Look, he's waking up!"

He is no longer our friend, came Argo's voice, another he'd never heard in his mind. He hadn't known she could speak. But she was a space-and-time-traveling ship captained by psychics—he had known, deep down, that she, too, would have a voice, a mind of her own.

Argo's engine revved, and gravity tugged Miles's belly button down.

"But he's awake!" he said again, even as he realized that Argo was leaving no matter what. At the last moment, Jason turned his gaze on Miles, and his once-laughing green eyes were now dark glassy marbles in his strong face.

Argo plucked them from the surface of Pelegaea and warped past the atmosphere into the void beyond, where the planet was only a small blackening speck. Miles paced the deck, trying to understand what had happened. Quelling his anger against the ship who had saved him. Roiling in alternating waves of grief and shock. Then, he sat in the captain's chair—Jason's chair—and watched as Pelegaea, Jason, and his Argonauts disappeared from view, from Miles's life altogether.

"What happened?" he asked after a time, his voice crackling. "What happened down there?"

The wide window turned milky and became a vidscreen. Argo created a slideshow for him, a terrible series of videos and pictures from various now-dead worlds. The parasite had no name. Wantless, ambitionless, floating like spores from planet to planet, where it would burrow deep into the world and invade every corner. It fed on life, and until it found the Pelegaeans, it was satisfied with sucking those planets dry and moving on.

But Pelegaea changed that. The Pelegaeans' minds, so advanced, so ambitious, gave the parasite a new kind of life. Gave it thought. Gave it awareness. Gave it a psychic frequency across which each individual barnacle was connected—a hive mind. It was no longer a million pieces of space dust adrift through the void; it was alive. It had desires. And the Pelegaeans wanted everything—therefore so, too, did the parasite. The very basest of Pelegaean desires made one and made flesh. Made incarnate.

The Sight Wood is burning, Argo told him as they stared down at Jason's planet. *The place of my birth. All my brothers and sisters are screaming.* He felt her anguish, and yet, they both understood. The last of the Pelegaeans would see that sacred grove die before they allowed it to fall to such a parasite. *The Wood is dead,* Argo said after a time. *There will be no more ships like me.*

That brought another raw wave of grief.

We must run, Argo told him.

And though he desperately wanted to save Jason, he knew that if a sentient time machine was telling you to go, you went.

That day, Miles opened the golden door and became Argo's captain. Her engine, many-sided and incandescent as a star, greeted him. It was not to be touched unless he wanted to access his own timeline, which should only be used to reverse his age in the event he became too old to travel and had to make the choice. He learned that she did not make a habit of looking at the timelines either—the vastness of it was too overwhelming, even for a mind born to time travel. He came to understand that Jason had not told Argo where to go so much as he had collaborated with her, navigating a path they could both agree upon. They were friends, family. She was an Argonaut as much as she was the Argo. Forging a path across the stars.

Miles and Argo didn't get along like that. While he came to understand her needs, her whims, her emotions, and she his, at the end of each day she was still closed to him. They bickered like children, spending days at a time in huffy, silent moods. They were reluctant partners, the only one the other had left.

They went back, of course. Many times, many ways. Each time, the outcome was the same. Each time, the Incarnate was waiting for them. And even though Argo was flagging, barely escaping each time, because she could only retrace her own steps for so long before the wear and tear on the fabric of time became too great to mend, she loved Jason as much as Miles did. She loved him enough to keep trying.

But they were ghosts on the timeline. And that had seemed so rational before, when Jason turned him into an Argonaut. If you were a quantum ghost, then you could avoid ripping the fabric of time to shreds. Responsibility for every action you took would be accepted by someone else. But now, as they desperately tried to save the people they loved, their touch against the world-ending event was featherlight, meaningless. After decades of trying, they gave up, their agreement unspoken, and they did not look back.

He did not go back to his life as Miles Moonraker. He couldn't face it now. He had seen the other side of traveling across the stars, across time, and a bitter resentment toward his past self had crept in. How idealistic he'd been, how naive, to sing of the stars as if they would never burn him.

Instead, he had Argo turn back the clock on his life. And those times when his body felt like a betrayal, Argo helped him transform even further—the shape of his physiology was easy enough to change, for a vessel like Argo. He would spend this new life being the swashbuckler he'd been with the Argonauts, honoring their legacy, honoring Jason. But his help on other worlds was just as futile a gesture as it had been on Pelegaea. He got old once again, with nothing to show for it. No matter what he did, good or bad, the action was slowly picked apart by the universe like an unwanted seam. It never really mattered that much, in the end.

So, drink. Drink and gambling and sex and a companion for a few months here, a lover for a few months there. He lived as a woman and as a man at various points over his lifetimes, giving in to the deep, bodily pull of one until he felt the pull of the other once again. He became a connoisseur of various vices on various worlds (and most worlds did provide), and he fell into a deep, time-traveling stupor out of which no one could pull him. Not even Argo, who went along with him, he suspected, because he was her last remaining link to the Argonauts. He dreamed of Jason and Pelegaea engulfed in stygian tar, and he tried very hard to pass the years without allowing them to drift into his waking hours.

She was Flora when she met Peggy at Rockwood in 2019 New York. She bought Peggy a drink because Peggy seemed lonely, even though she was with friends, and Flora knew what it meant to feel that way. And though she only spent one night with Peggy, roaming the city, talking about nothing, everything, she felt a spark she hadn't felt in many, many years.

That spark carried her back into the past, her curiosity finally blooming anew, where she met Ron. Ron, whose tie was crooked and whose hair was perfectly slicked back, with the requisite wave at the front that was popular at the time. Ron, whose smile was assured and whose courage was rock-solid, even as he kissed Flora under the mistletoe at a holiday party to which she'd received a passing invitation and told her he thought she was beautiful. They lived comfortably for many years in their Greenwich Village town house, and though Flora insisted they could live their full truth in another time, on other planets, Ron didn't want to leave, and Flora could not, would not, leave Ron. Nothing else had felt so certain—not since Jason.

Flora had a heart attack at seventy-three and, after allowing Argo to turn back the clock, decided to live as Miles again. It was ten years before Ron had his turn, a debilitating stroke that pulled at the left side of his face and cursed him with tremors that made holding anything difficult. Looking at him broke Miles's heart. Still, Ron would not even think of touching Argo's engine, of rewinding his own clock, despite the begging and pleading of his partner. In the end, Ron wasn't afraid of death. He was afraid of eternal life.

It was somewhat unexpected that he met Peggy again. For her, it had only been months since their first meeting, but for Miles, it had been a lifetime. He had returned to 2019 for a concert, a flighty whim Argo had indulged, when he saw her in a coffee shop, and he finally revealed to her who he was and what had happened to Flora.

Peggy was a balm on Miles's wounded heart. She didn't ask him to explain himself or his past. She was content to go on adventures, to seek out and explore uncharted planets, to witness the birth and death of stars in galaxies far, far away. There was something triumphant about traveling with her, something in the way she experienced the universe, and it elevated his own grieving spirits.

He should have known better than to expect anything less than heartbreak from the companions he collected. His life was designed for danger and loss, and for the first time in many, many years, on an empty planet he had assumed was safe, he came face-to-face with the Incarnate once again. It had stolen Jason from him. Now, it was stealing from him again.

And then, Harper on a muggy night in August. The hive, come to collect. An altercation at a nightclub in 1972. And . . . well. You know the rest.

EPISODE SIX
ENTANGLEMENT

This week on Infinite Odyssey:

The Argonaut comes face-to-face with himself—from the future. He warns our intrepid Argonaut that war is coming, and if he doesn't act now to prevent it, the Argonaut's home world will be utterly lost. Can the Argonaut face his future—even if it means certain death?

19.

RIVERDALE
SUMMER, 1986

When she awoke, it was from dreams of twisting nebulae, striations of green and blue and yellow against a rippling darkness, hours and lifetimes zipping past her like semis on a lonely highway. They were ordinary things now, time and space, and looked like ordinary things in her dreams, in her peripheral vision, as much a part of her as blood cells and DNA and skin and teeth and fingernails.

Miles talked deep into the night, until his voice was hoarse and his eyelids drooped. She felt his heartbreak, for the home he made with the Argonauts and Jason, the home he made with Ron in Greenwich, and the home he made with Argo in their shared grief. She understood his pain at losing the part of himself who once strutted across stages around the world, his face painted, his vocals stretched thin after long international tours. And she felt his desperate love for people who no longer existed, whom he could not rescue from the clutches of time or the Incarnate. She shared that love, for one of them. It seemed like they finally understood one another.

And so, Harper told him her own story. About meeting Anthony and writing *Infinite Odyssey*. Receiving the notes and the letters passed through middlemen at the café, at the convention, at the row house. Passing out on New Year's Eve and realizing she was not free of the Incarnate after all. Seeing Peggy again at the club. Miles.

She hadn't really given herself time to process it, not in all the time she'd schemed how to reach him again. But now, her mind loaded with his stories and her own, she was overcome by the colossal truth of it. The man next to her was not a man and not a woman, and though he had been once—which was a surprise in and of itself—he was no longer a human at all. He was a space-and-time traveler who had seen centuries born and watched them die again, on dozens of planets across thousands of galaxies and a handful of lifetimes. He was nothing and everything like the alien spacefarer she'd grown up watching on television. The man she'd written about with Anthony Detweiler, a little buzzed on scotch and laughter. He was utterly impossible.

And now, with her own burgeoning psychic awareness and her neck smeared with psychic-frequency-disrupting alien goo and time-traveling serums coursing through her blood, so was she. Utterly impossible. Could she even call herself human anymore either?

It was wind, lapping against her skin like water on a shore, that brought her fully to awareness.

They were back in Argo, the windows down, air rolling in and out, frothy and warm. Summer air, somehow, even though, just last night, the January cold had bitten into her toes outside the motel. He must have carried her out of that place. She'd been utterly exhausted by the time they were done talking. Her body still changing, still becoming something . . . else. Something like Miles.

Now, he drove with eyes straight ahead, humming a song that was not playing on the radio. She could hear the disruptor whirring its almost imperceptible frequency from his jacket pocket. She looked down at the red dress, inexplicably unrumpled. Everything was bright, limned in faint rainbow light.

"Where are we?"

He jolted a little, so lost in his thoughts. He didn't look at her.

"Argo."

Harper rolled her eyes. "Obviously."

"We didn't go far. She still needs a little time to recharge. But I could hear your stomach growling even in your sleep."

"We're getting breakfast?" She didn't mean to sound so excited about the prospect of pancakes and bacon, but the moment he mentioned her growling stomach, it answered with another ferocious snarl.

"Almost there."

"How far did we go?" she asked, a small thrill at the idea that she had time traveled for the second time, and a small fear at what he might do when they reached their destination.

"Just far enough to hopefully throw Peggy off the scent and still give Argo time to recharge," Miles said. He turned the wheel and Argo slowed. Harper sat up straight so she could see properly out the window and was both dismayed and delighted to find that Argo was driving down familiar streets, toward a familiar destination.

"Are you serious?"

"Serious as a heart attack," Miles replied.

"Why?"

"Because it's always here," he said with a shrug. "And I thought we could use something familiar right now."

She watched a woman with exaggerated shoulder pads and a suspiciously mullet-like hairdo sashay down the street.

"What year is this?"

"It's 1986."

Her heart skipped a beat. Could Angie still be around? Indira? By this time, *Infinite Odyssey* had been on the air for over a decade. Probably Anthony had set his sister up with a summer house in the Hamptons and a main residence adjacent to Central Park. She wondered if they ever thought about her, if they thought about what happened to her that night when a sonic pulse laid the dancers in a midtown club out flat and disappeared Susan Feldman without a trace. And then she wondered if either of them would remember her at all, or if the Paradox Serum had ensured that they would forget.

Miles pulled into the parking lot, and the hot-pink neon of the chronically busted Starlight Diner sign, now haloed in that same pale rainbow she could see on everything, told them they had arrived.

Her legs wobbled precariously as she exited the disguised Tesseract Engine, but she managed to stay upright, the skirt of the red dress draping perfectly as she straightened, as if it had not been through hell and back. When she turned to give Argo a grateful pat, she was momentarily stunned to find the muscle car they had left in the motel parking lot was now a lime-green VW bus. Harper's dad had had a bus just like this when she was a kid, which her mother made him sell, much to Harper and Peggy's dismay. They used to sneak the key from her father's nightstand and play in it, pretending the bus was a vessel that could take them anywhere and anywhen. Argo must have re-created it from Harper's memories, down to the fuzzy peace sign dangling off the rearview mirror.

She appreciated the gesture.

Miles clambered out of the bus and approached her. She eyed his rumpled T-shirt and jeans and said, "We can't go in there like this."

"Agreed. Keep your wardrobe neutral. Denim and leather are good, but no insignia."

"What?"

He swept a hand vaguely in the area of her person. "The dress. You'll have to change it."

She looked around helplessly. "Change it where?"

Miles sighed. He closed his eyes and put a hand on her shoulder. The fabric rippled, and then it began to morph. She'd entirely forgotten about the transformations it had gone through of its own volition the night before. Now, the once-red fabric grew heavy and stiff against her skin, the comfortable satin transmuted into an oversized pink cotton T-shirt tucked into an obscenely high-waisted black skirt. She looked like a *Breakfast Club* reject, which, now that she thought about it, was probably Miles's historical reference.

"I didn't know I could do that," she said in astonishment. She rolled the new clothes between curious fingers, shocked to find they felt just like the stiff cotton and wool the nanotextile bots were imitating. "I just assumed they changed under duress."

"What use would they be if they could only be changed in emergencies?" Miles reached past her and through the passenger-side door, then banged on the glove box, which fell open and revealed a firm red flannel shirt and baggy jeans, confirming her theory about his references.

"You don't have . . . bots?" Harper asked as he removed the stack of clothing.

"You're wearing them," Miles said, before climbing through the passenger side and disappearing into the back of the bus.

He emerged a few minutes later in his new clothes, and they entered the diner. Miles looked oddly at home in the grungy '80s outfit; his five-day scruff and tired eyes sold what the ensemble didn't. Harper made less sense in her new clothes, the pink-and-black getup a little too suggestive with the fallen hairdo and smudged makeup from the night before. She hoped no one looked too hard.

The Starlight was, as expected, just the same inside. She looked for Angie and Indira out of habit, but the waitstaff was entirely unfamiliar to her. The booths maintained their dinginess, and the cracks Harper remembered from her time were just beginning to split, pale fluff poking through like sun-greedy sprouts. Tears for Fears warbled about being head over heels out of the same crackling speakers.

A haggard waitress approached their table without looking at them. Her voice was a fried wire. "What'll you have?"

Harper opened her mouth to ask for a minute, but Miles interrupted her. "We'll both have the number three with bacon. And coffee, black."

"Sure thing."

The waitress left, and Harper turned a reproachful eye on her companion. "I didn't ask you to order for me."

"We need to eat and go." He kept staring around the diner, as if he expected the early morning customers to spring out of their seats and attack.

Harper looked around too, but none of the faces belonged to Peggy, nor any of the other friends she'd hoped to find in this place. She fidgeted in her starched clothes.

"Should . . . should we talk about last night?"

Miles shrugged. "Hasn't it all been said?"

"Just . . . I guess I didn't realize . . . you're human."

"Can we please not talk about this?" He looked so much younger than his years, suddenly. She'd asked him to dredge a very old wound, and he'd done it. Now he looked different. Hunched in the booth, rounded shoulders mocking his age. "I'm sorry," he said, releasing the tension in his shoulders with a sigh. "I owed you that. I know. But I can't keep the party bag open. You've seen all my tricks now. You've seen everything."

"I suppose," she said, "that I'm looking for anything in it that might tell me the outcome of my story."

"I won't let what happened to Peggy happen to you."

The waitress reappeared and set down two cups of steaming coffee. Harper blew on hers.

"What do you think happened to her after the club?"

"If she's given up the chase, she'll go back to Pelegaea. Argo thinks it's their home base."

"How are they able to travel without a ship like Argo?"

"My best guess? They've got tesseract crystals like the ones Argo's engine grew from. The Sight Wood burned, but maybe some crystals remained. Rudimentary, because they're traveling without a vessel that protects from the effects of space and time. But it would get the job done, for a time."

She recalled Not-Peggy's wristwatch, the crystal in the place where a watch face should have been. A tesseract crystal. She should have known.

"Having Argo would be better," Harper said, finally understanding why Peggy was chasing the ship. "More precise. More horsepower." The hairs on the back of her neck prickled—Peggy wasn't here, not yet, but that didn't mean no one else was listening in, waiting for them to let down their guard. Just how many of these crystals did the Incarnate have in their possession? "How many Incarnate spies, or whatever, do you think there are?"

"What do you mean?"

"Do you think they could have sent anyone else besides Peggy?"

Miles looked around. "I suppose it's possible. But traveling that way . . . it isn't easy."

"How so?"

"Just jumping from Varlanos to Earth to rescue you required a full night of recharge for Argo, and she's built for that kind of travel. Pelegaea is at least twice that distance, and you're traveling across time as well. Peggy has no spacecraft—just her suit, which serves as its own kind of ship. Pressurized, with air. But it's been a long time since she re-upped her serum, and with the Sight Wood gone, I doubt the Incarnate has found a way to make more on Pelegaea. Her body won't be able to withstand the traveling much longer. One day, the void will simply tear her apart. I'm surprised she's lasted this long. But then, she's always been strong."

Harper thought back to the night before, when Peggy busted into the bathroom stall, black blood dripping from her nose.

"That's why you run," Harper realized. "You know if you travel far enough, fast enough, you'll outlive them."

Miles put down his cup. "That was before I knew that it was Peggy."

She sipped her coffee, taste buds scalding as it sloshed over her tongue. "You know, I've been wondering something."

"Not surprising."

"We could go back to the moment she was first taken," Harper said. "We could still go back."

"You think the Incarnate didn't think of that, back then? Even now, they'll be expecting us to be arrogant enough to believe we might undo what has been done, and we'll bring Argo right to them. It's too risky."

"So then, what's the plan?"

The front door opened. Another couple tottered in, eyes heavy-lidded and bloodshot. They glanced at Harper and Miles as they stumbled in, staring a second too long at the pair. Harper tried not to read anything into it; they were two unfamiliar faces in a local diner, stopping for a bite on their way to someplace else. Worth a second glance, but little more than that.

Miles leaned back in the booth. "We find the Off switch. We kill the hive."

"Just when I thought I'd heard everything," Harper said.

"Look, it won't be easy, but—"

"Won't be easy? Are you fucking serious? It won't be possible!"

"I'm sorry you didn't understand what you were asking for when you asked for it," Miles said savagely. "But you were never just asking to save Peggy, Harper. It's not a one-and-done kind of job. This is the kind of job where you have to find the big red button that nukes the whole facility. You understand?"

"I don't—"

"Peggy isn't Peggy anymore. The hive will see us through her eyes, wherever she goes. It's going to require a real plan, and the plan can't just be 'save Peggy.' We need time to strategize, time to implement. To gather supplies."

But Harper didn't want to take on an entire alien species. She wanted her friend back. That was it.

"You know what?" she said. "I'm having a serious case of déjà vu here." She realized only as she said the words that it was true. That it didn't matter what he said, what he did, what he promised. "The two of us, drinking coffee in a shitty diner after a very long night. I have this funny feeling that the minute I go to the restroom, you won't be here when I get back. Except it won't be because you think you're saving me; it'll be because now you've got a hero complex about this whole thing, and you'll think you're saving everyone else. Jason, Peggy, Pelegaea."

"Trust me, I've learned my lesson," Miles muttered.

"I still don't trust you," Harper snapped. "That's the problem."

"What do I have to do, Harper? I saved you, didn't I? I came all the way back here and I got you out of that club. I risked everything to come back for you. If we're going to do this, we need to trust each other."

"You think that fixing your mistake is the same thing as saving me?" Harper said incredulously.

Someone *ahem*ed; Harper looked up to see their waitress holding two plates of greasy eggs, toast, and bacon. She didn't even bother to hide her blue-shadowed eye roll.

They ate in tense silence. Harper wanted to stomp away, to let her anger carry her off. But she was still so fucking hungry, and her stomach growled even as she shoveled the mountain of congealed hash browns into her mouth. The lukewarm food—whoever 1986's cook was, they sucked—probably would have been more disgusting if she weren't ravenous and already buzzed on her blistering coffee. When she was done, she pushed the plate away and crossed her arms, not caring that she probably looked like a petulant child in her oversized clothes and grouchy expression.

Miles put his napkin on his empty plate. "Better?

"Fuck you."

"Fine. Believe what you'd like, Harper. I'm in this now. We both are. You can trust me or not. I understand that proving I deserve it takes time and we don't have much of that. But I'll do what I can."

"Fine. I'm going to use the ladies' room."

"Be my guest."

It was a test, and they both knew it. Could he resist leaving her behind? Could he sit still and wait for her? Part of her wanted him to go. Part of her wanted to have a reason to hate him forever and ever and ever.

She walked into the bathroom, reeling a bit at the smell and the flickering, sallow light, and relieved herself in the stall. A memory of the night before flashed behind her tired eyes—Peggy pacing in the bathroom, waiting for her prey.

Harper closed her eyes against the memory. She was running out of time.

She approached the scratched, cloudy mirror and assessed yesterday's damage. Under-eyes purple as a bruise. Curls nested on the top of her head. Makeup smeared. Eyes hard. Was there any point in trying to wipe at the dried trails of salty tears and mascara? At attempting to detangle her hair with water from this grungy bathroom sink? Maybe not; her outsides finally matched her insides, and there was some satisfaction in that.

Her reflection tilted her head. Which was odd because Harper hadn't done that. And when she lifted her hand to fix her crooked earring, the reflection didn't, well, reflect the movement. It just stood there, watching her.

And as she stared, certain that she was hallucinating after a long night with little sleep, the clothes she wore now morphed into something else in the reflection, crimson and black, fabric thick and tactical. A scarf covered her reflection's hair, but an inexplicably white curl had escaped and rested against her forehead. Bulky goggles perched atop the scarf. Mascara still tracked down her cheeks, though paired with this ensemble, it somehow looked intentional. Terrifying.

And then her reflection spoke.

20.

RIVERDALE
SUMMER, 1986

"Where is this?"

Harper required several tries to get the words out. "Th-the Starlight. With the . . . breakfast."

Mirror-Harper nodded. "Right. I remember. It feels so long ago, even though it was just . . ." As she spoke, she smiled wearily. "Oh. I remember this too. My reflection. I guess now I am the reflection."

"I . . . guess you are." She was glad at least one of them knew what was going on because out of all the time travelers and Tesseract Engines and brainwashed assassins she'd come into contact with, this was turning into the strangest thing she'd seen yet. "How are you . . . ? Won't we, I dunno, paradox?"

"I don't think so," Mirror-Harper said. "I'm not really there. I'm observing you from . . . somewhere else."

Harper just nodded. Uh-huh, sure, that makes perfect sense. Glad we figured out the deal. Mirror-Harper kept smiling that uncanny smile, as if this was all actually kind of funny. An adequate joke. She was different from Harper in a way she couldn't pinpoint, exuding something unnamable. Not confidence, not quite; and it wasn't just that she seemed older, weary, her eyes a little haunted. She seemed younger too, two negatives pressed on top of each other and exposed into a single image. Two versions, or multiple versions, of herself, all staring through one pair of fatigued eyes. Besides being on the other side of the mirror, her very presence just felt . . . wrong. Her edges fuzzy. And then Harper realized what it was—the rainbow halo she could see glinting off of everything thanks to the Paradox Serum was missing. Mirror-Harper had no aura.

"How are you doing this?" Harper asked.

Mirror-Harper winced and pressed a hand against her side—a wound? She looked like she had a secret, something she thought Harper should probably know. But she didn't share it. "I'm not sure I should answer that. How I got here might be different from how you get here, if you get here at all. I don't want to mess with things."

"Aren't you already doing that? Just by being here?"

Mirror-Harper shook her head. "I'm sorry, it's all just so jumbled. In here. In my head. I was going back, back to the door, when I looked up and there you were. And I remembered this, so I knew I had to stop."

Back to the door? What door?

"Where are you?"

Mirror-Harper gestured to the space around her, as if expecting Harper to see and know where she was. But she was surrounded by mirror things—the dim light of the narrow room, the scratched and graffitied stalls behind her.

"I'm . . . everywhere. And nowhere. It's super weird. And honestly, I'm having a hard time keeping it all straight." She winced again.

Harper didn't want to leave Miles alone at the table much longer, but she couldn't possibly tear herself away from her confused, wounded reflection. This seemed important, like she might actually learn something useful for the first time since her adventure began. And dammit, if Miles left again, she would just find a way to make his galactic life a living hell.

"Please, I have to know," she said. "Are you the one who sent me the note at the café and the convention? Or the key to the row house?"

Mirror-Harper shook her head. "I don't think so. That hasn't happened yet."

"Hasn't happened yet? But you don't even know when you are."

"Listen," her mirror self said. "I should tell you. You have to be careful not to get too angry or upset about things. The Incarnate is hungry. It wants your hate. Hate is fuel. And with enough fuel, it can do horrible things."

Harper's leg stopped jiggling. "Like what?"

"Use you to get to the thing it really wants."

"Argo."

"If she weren't inherently good, imagine how she could be used," Mirror-Harper said. "Whole galaxies, turned to dust. Entire civilizations, subjugated or obliterated."

Harper braced herself against the wall, the diner breakfast souring in her stomach. She knew what was coming.

"You have to kill the Incarnate," her mirror self said. "You have to end this."

"I just want to save my friend."

"You can't do that if you don't deal with the thing that took her."

Harper closed her eyes. Fine, Miles. You win. "How?" she asked. "How the hell am I supposed to kill it?"

The reflection flickered.

"Simple," Mirror-Harper said, as though she knew it was anything but. "You have to love what you hate. Love what you hate, before that hate destroys you."

The words imparted a kind of vertigo, shifting and distorting the bathroom around her. Harper knew those words. She'd heard them out of the Argonaut's mouth a million times—with Peggy at her side while they watched the pilot for the first time as kids, and then over and over again for years after. She'd heard them more recently than that too; months ago in that empty planetarium, the Argonaut had told Betty Fisk to do the very same thing. Love what you hate. Harper had written those words herself, typed them out on an old typewriter. Had written them for this. A message to herself.

"Hate is a parasite, Harper," her mirror self said. Her voice echoed distantly. "Starve it out."

Harper stepped closer to the mirror; her reflection did the same. "Did you find it?" she murmured, looking for the truth in the eyes of her other self. "Did you find the Off switch? Did you save Peggy?" But those eyes were cloudy and gave away nothing. Mirror-Harper flickered again. The edges of the reflection began to twist and fade into quantum mist.

"Wait." Harper put her hand on the mirror, disappointed when all she felt was glass. "What about Miles? Can I trust him? Can I trust him not to leave again?"

Mirror-Harper faltered. This she had heard. "Trust is earned," she said. "Has he earned it?"

"I don't . . . I'm asking if he will!"

"Only you can answer that question." Her mirror self looked up suddenly, beyond Harper's shoulder, into the bathroom itself. "I'm remembering something I forgot. This moment. Peggy is close. You have to go."

"Wait—"

"Go!"

Mirror-Harper blipped out of existence, leaving Harper alone with her own disheveled reflection and the misty edges of the space her future body had occupied only seconds before. A headache started up a steady drumbeat at the base of Harper's skull. Why did everyone insist on keeping her in the dark? In giving half-truths, lies still lurking at their edges. Even the reflection of her own self, finding her way to a dingy bathroom from some other time, didn't want to give Harper the real tools she needed to save her friend. A play-by-play of what was supposed to go down. A list of useful ways Harper could beat the Incarnate. Love what you hate? Even in 1972, clacking them out on Anthony's typewriter, the words had only made it to the page because she had already heard them first in the episode. But they'd always just been for show. Not actionable. Not a detailed instruction she could write down in a notebook for future use and experimentation. For the first time since the club, she felt that hot little sun inside her, radiating the anger her body remembered.

And then, the words of Mirror-Harper hit.

Peggy was close. And she was coming.

Harper spun around, half expecting to find Peggy lurking in one of the empty stalls, staring at her coolly. But Harper was alone. Still, the tingle of a headache where Peggy's fingernails had penetrated the skin said Harper wouldn't be for much longer.

Miles should have known better than to choose this place. And she should have known better than to let him.

Unless . . . unless that had been the entire point.

I have this funny feeling that the minute I go to the restroom, you won't be here when I get back. Except it won't be because you think you're saving me; it'll be because now you've got a hero complex about this whole thing, and you'll think you're saving everyone else.

For as smart as she prided herself on being, Harper was a real moron sometimes.

She jogged out of the restroom toward their table, not wanting to draw attention while still hurrying the fuck up. God, she was going to be sick. She rounded the corner and stopped dead, only a few feet from the table and still, somehow, an ocean away.

Miles was getting out of the booth. He didn't see her before dropping a wad of crumpled cash on the table and pushing through the diner doors. She watched him go with a strange detachedness.

And then—something snapped.

"Mother. Fucker."

She stomped toward the door, catching the wary attention of other diners as she burst through the entrance like one pissed-off bat out of hell.

"Oh, no you don't," she started to say, but the words disintegrated in her throat. Someone stood beside Argo's lime-green door in the parking lot, watching them. She smiled when Harper halted at Miles's side, teeth blackened by the gunge oozing from her raw mouth.

"How did you find us?" Harper asked, hating how small she sounded.

"Ask him," Peggy said, and for the first time since bursting through the diner doors, Harper noticed that the gentle whir that had emanated from the psychic disruptor in Miles's coat pocket was conspicuously quiet. The soap bubble of protection was gone.

She turned to her time-traveling companion. "Are you fucking insane?" She didn't like this new Miles, suddenly so desperate to right his wrongs that he was willing to lure a hostile alien entity straight to the very thing they desired in some fucked-up effort to pick a delusional fight. She'd thought the version who left her in 1971 was bad; the version who was about to get himself killed and Argo stolen was even worse. "Let's get out of here, Miles. Let's just get into Argo and go make that plan you convinced me we need."

"This is the plan, Harper," Miles said. "I'm sorry. You were right about me."

"Oh, see, I thought the plan was to deal with the entire hive. Whatever you're doing right now, it is the exact opposite of that plan!"

But Miles was walking to meet Peggy like a Viking accepting a warrior's death, his back straight and his scrawny chest as broad as he could make it.

"You can't take Argo," Harper said to Peggy. "Even if you have Miles, she won't let you in."

"I'm aware," Peggy said. "We will take this one as a new sibling, and he will help us acquire her."

"That's not going to happen," Miles said. "I won't let it."

"Miles, stop being such a colossal idiot," Harper said. "You're not going to kill them all on your own. Please."

But something was happening to him. The rage he'd suppressed when she first met him, the guilt, the grief of a dozen lives lost, seemed now to be vibrating out of him, brightening his rainbow aura. What had she done? What had she unleashed when she demanded his story, when she forced him to relive the horrors of his centuries as a Ping-Pong ball in the universe?

He stopped in front of Peggy and opened his arms wide. "Take me to him."

Him? she had time to think, before Peggy removed something from a pouch on her belt: a small black object, catching the light like . . . another crystal, which protruded from a smooth metal disc no bigger than Peggy's palm. "As you wish," she said and pressed the item to his shirt, where it clung to his *Breakfast Club* flannel. Miles didn't seem the least bit shocked by the action.

Harper was frozen in place by the fear her body remembered from the club. "This is a shitty plan!" she said, wishing she didn't sound so afraid.

"Peggy," she tried desperately, hoping to distract the assassin while she thought of some way to get them both out of there. "Please don't go. I know you're dying, and I know every time you travel, you die a little bit more."

Peggy's smile slipped. "It doesn't matter what happens to this body, Harper Starling. Once it can no longer be used, we will have his. And then we will have yours."

Harper had almost forgotten.

Still, she took a step forward. "Think about it," she said to Peggy. "We could get rid of the Incarnate. You could be free. We could see the universe together."

"What are you doing?" Miles hissed. "I have this totally under control."

Peggy's expression softened. "You speak of things you do not understand, Harper Starling. It's one of the things we love about you. But it is too late for this body. Do you not see that?"

She was close enough to see all of the assassin's scars, angry red hatches, wrathful little constellations. That face she once knew so well, ruined by years of fighting battles that didn't belong to her.

"I miss you," Harper said. "So much it hurts." She didn't know what made her say it. It was simply the truth. And if she was going to die—if Miles was going to let himself be taken—then to hell with the Incarnate. To hell with Miles, standing still as a rod in Peggy's grasp and doing nothing. To hell with all of it.

"Sometimes we look at you," Peggy murmured, so quietly Harper almost didn't hear her, "and think we could just scream and scream." For a moment, she sounded like herself, like Peggy, and Harper nearly forgot that she was afraid. "We could scream until the world shakes apart. Wouldn't that be something?"

The assassin felt something for her. The Incarnate felt something for her. More than hatred, more than a predatory desire. More than bloodlust.

Something like love.

Peggy was still in there, somewhere. And she was bleeding through.

Maybe it was enough. Maybe Harper could reach for her, hold her hand, remind her of the things Peggy had once loved.

Peggy smiled. "Time to go."

Harper turned to Miles, incredulous that he was just going to let the Incarnate take him, that he could ask for this, as if he stood a chance against them. What did he think he could do against an entire parasitic alien hive?

Peggy turned a dial on her sleek black wristwatch, the twin of the crystal device she'd pinned to Miles, and the disc on his shirt made an almost imperceptible *whir*. Nanobots released from the device and, with the efficiency of an ant colony, spread outward and solidified into something akin to neoprene, just as the textile bots of Harper's dress had, until this new material covered his face, his arms, everything.

What had Miles said? That Peggy's suit was its own kind of vessel.

So, it was too late. Already, Peggy's own suit was expanding up her neck, her ears, her face. In seconds her entire body would be covered, and the device on her wrist would whisk the two of them away, light-years from Earth.

When Harper spoke, she didn't recognize her own voice. "I'll find you."

Peggy stepped behind Miles—there was a click, as though she had snapped them together somehow—and smiled. "We are counting on it."

And just like that, no sound, no fanfare, no indication at all that they had ever been there, Peggy and Miles were gone.

If Harper wasn't careful, she would have a panic attack. But a panic attack wasn't useful, couldn't help her at all. She gulped as much air as her lungs could handle and willed her nerves into another shape—a razor-sharp blade, fine, focused. Anger anger anger anger. A brightly burning sun. Miles had left her before, and so much of that rage was for him, but this time everything was different.

I'll find you.

We are counting on it.

Argo still sat in her parking space, a livid lime green, the fuzzy peace sign vibrating in the window with the force of Argo's trembling anger. The ship watched. The ship knew.

Harper stalked to the driver's side and was pleased when the door swung easily open. This was insane—she had never flown a Tesseract Engine. She'd never flown anything. She'd barely driven a car since moving to New York.

But Argo didn't need her to know. Argo only needed a destination, and Harper had one, knowing it would be the end and asking for it anyway.

"We're going to Pel—"

A searing pain exploded from the back of her skull, eating her words and eclipsing her vision. She was falling, just like on New Year's, when the Incarnate had finally found a way in. Or, not quite like last time. Because she was aware of herself, of everything, of her own mind in Peggy's body, seeing through Peggy's eyes, the image hazy as if Harper were looking through a two-way mirror. A blurry Miles stepped into her vision, peering down from above, as though Harper herself was lying on the ground. He looked like he was going to be sick, his skin tinged a worrying pale green. Above him a canopy of monolithic red trees towered, obscuring a sunset sky.

He stared at Harper through Peggy's eyes. He knew, she realized. Somehow, he knew that Harper would be looking at him from across the universe. His words were distant, crackling as if he were speaking through a walkie-talkie. "She's weaker than she thought. I got hold of her crystal and diverted us, but not for long. Don't come after us—I'll finish this myself."

And then Harper was spinning out, arms and legs flailing wildly as she grasped for purchase, anything to grab onto in the lightless bridge between their minds. She heard Peggy's voice, *her* Peggy, the one she was trying so desperately to save, screaming in the dark.

She was thrust violently back into her own body, which still sat in the disguised ship, seat belt halfway clipped, hand hovering in midair.

I know that place, Harper heard, or felt, Argo say. *Sekundos.* So, the psychic disruptor Miles had smeared on her neck was fading. She didn't have the space to care. There was no question that neither of them planned to heed Miles's demand. She wasn't about to let that martyr shit slide, and neither was Argo.

The bus rumbled to life, engines galloping. Every organ in Harper's body compressed and was pulled toward her naval, her skin so heavy her bones threatened to break under the weight of it. Gravity contorted and warped her body until she was certain it would never be the same again. She tried to breathe and couldn't. Stars popped in her vision.

And then there was sweet, sweet relief, and she slipped out of the seat and onto the floor of the ship.

21.

ARGO
SEASON AND YEAR UNKNOWN

She'd been sucking in lungsful of air for a good two minutes before she realized several things: One, the VW bus was no longer a bus—it was double the width it had been only a moment ago. Two, it looked properly like a spaceship, though not like the Tesseract Engine of the television show.

She recognized it as a navigation deck of sorts, with a console at the center and several more lining the wall. And at the very front where the wide VW dashboard had once been, there was a massive window, dense as a cement wall. And through that window, an infinite ocean of stars and planets and the swirling, luminous nebulae of her dreams, clouds of celestial dust and gases ionizing the ultraviolet radiation cast from all the stars contained within. She could not have ever guessed that she would one day be able to stare into something so transcendent with her naked eyes, the universe laid out like a heavenly feast before her. No sky, no horizon, no ground. This was not only a different time; this was a galaxy far, far, far away. It was all of her far-flung hopes and dreams.

Harper turned and threw up the contents of her stomach into a conveniently placed wastebasket.

There was something else there too, something more sinister. An ache in the back of her mind, and in her heart—the Incarnate making sure she remembered it was there, stirring awake after a forced hibernation.

"Argo?" her voice crackled painfully. "Are you there?"

I am here, Harper Starling.

The voice, the feel of it brushing against her thoughts, sent a jolt of relief through her. It was just as Harper remembered it, the strange sensation of another mind against her own, soothing despite the chaos of the liftoff. Something was missing, though. Miles wasn't here. It was just Harper and Argo the Tesseract Engine, drifting alone in the aftermath of the events at the Starlight.

Love what you hate, before that hate destroys you.

And used her to get to Argo.

No. Harper wouldn't let that happen. Not to the only companion she had left.

She wiped her mouth and made a new list. First things first: "Where's Sekundos?"

In the Adama system, Argo sent. Harper felt the words the way she would have had a thought. *But our path is imperiled by a solar storm.*

A pulse at the back of her mind. A starburst of anger, white-hot. She wanted to be calm, to heed her mirror self's words, but there was nowhere for all this anger to go.

Keep your cool, Harper.

Second: "How long until we can get there?"

Ten hours, eight minutes, six seconds.

"That's not good enough," she said. "They might be gone by the time we arrive."

They won't, Argo replied. *She is too weak.*

Three: "How am I supposed to help them?" she asked. "To save them?"

You must have patience and faith.

Patience? Impossible. Faith? In what?

Rest, she felt Argo tell her. *You will need it.*

No, she wanted to say. She felt the pulse of the Incarnate seed probing her neural pathways, settling into her hormone receptors, making changes to her brain chemistry. It was impossible to fight it off. She was already so angry—she wanted to feel every ounce of her frustration, to use the fuel of it to end this. It was so tempting to give in to it. So tempting to let that little sun consume her.

Sleep, Argo sent again. The ship was meddling, trying to impose that artificial calm.

Let her show you the way, said another, more sinister voice at the back of her mind. It did not sound or feel like Argo, and she didn't think Argo could hear it. Let her show you how to find her heart.

Yes, she thought. That would be a sight to see.

"Okay, Argo," she said. "I'll sleep. Show me the way."

With Argo's psychic guidance, she plunged down the narrow ladder at the back of the deck into the bowels of the ship. She found herself in a long, cramped hallway lined with doors, probably to other bedrooms. This must have been where the Argonauts slept, once upon a time.

Infinite Odyssey depicted Argo as a sleek, futuristic vessel with shiny chrome interiors and mysterious lights and buttons and levers everywhere you looked. Fog billowed out from under doors whenever they opened, and a crackling intercom delivered updates and alerts to each of the ship's many rooms. In reality, Argo looked a lot like the old wooden vessels that predated the hulking steel ships of the Industrial Revolution. But instead of a damp, frigid interior infested with rats and seasick sailors, Argo was downright balmy, the air comfortably toasted, like a fire-warmed cabin in the woods.

A door at the end of the hall beckoned her. It was more honeyed in color than the rest of the doors, and a subtle glow emanated from the crack between the door and the jamb, warm and inviting. She started toward it, faltering a little when Argo's consciousness pulled at her, a sort of psychic slap on the wrist. *Not that door, Harper Starling. Never that door.*

But the door was a lure, and Harper's hijacked mind was a ravenous, razor-toothed eel. The temptation to see what was on the other side hooked into her stomach and reeled her forward.

A drumbeat kicked up at the back of her skull as she drifted dreamily toward it. She wanted to do as Argo asked and turn away from the golden door. She really wanted to. She almost managed it. But that drumbeat was in her mind, pulsing insistently as she made her way toward the end of the hall, toward that golden door.

No, Harper Starling, she felt, but Argo's presence was strangely distant suddenly, miles and miles away. She reached for the doorknob, certain that this was where she was supposed to be, that all the answers were in the room behind the door. Fuck everyone who had ever told her *no*—the contents of this room would be hers. They belonged to her. She was tired of giving and giving and never having anything for herself. That little sun inside her burned with the injustice of it all.

Get away from the door, she heard, but it didn't seem necessary to pay the voice any heed. The metal of the doorknob burned beneath her hand, but she didn't care; it was an annoyance, nothing more, nothing in comparison to what—

"Ow!"

She sprawled backward as if struck, reeling at the white-hot crack that had splintered through her mind, more savage than any migraine, and cradled the burned palm she could suddenly very much feel in painful shock.

The anger she'd felt toward Miles and Peggy only moments ago disintegrated and she was left reeling and breathless on the floor of the ship.

"What," she breathed, "the hell did you do to me?"

You were supposed to go to sleep, Argo sent. *Why did you not go?*

She sat up, head and palm throbbing. "I don't know." The whole event was hazy now. Like she'd had too much to drink. But she was a liar. She did know.

She got unsteadily to her feet and wandered to the end of the hall in search of a restroom so she could hold her singed flesh under a stream of cold water. She found the kitchen instead, the hallway blossoming open to a small but cozy galley that looked just like the kind of kitchen one might find on Earth. Stove, oven, sink, dining table. Drawers, cupboards, countertops. So normal, so human.

Her anger reignited.

"Argo," she murmured, "I need help. The Incarnate . . ."

You need a psychic partition, or the hive will take over your mind completely. We are too close to Pelegaea. It is getting stronger.

Harper went to the sink and turned it on.

The Incarnate knows the crystal that powers my engine lies behind the door.

Harper swore and yanked a drawer open, looking for a towel. She found one, wet it down, and pressed it to her palm, hissing in pain. Already a constellation of blisters bubbled under the skin. She looked at the towel in her hand, at the empty kitchen. Could feel the insistent pulse of the Incarnate in her mind.

She stared at the fabric in her hand, realizing how pointless it was against the damage done. Barely even a Band-Aid. The blisters were there, and they would swell and burst, regardless of her action.

The thought turned her stomach.

"Will . . . will it fix me? The partition?"

For a time. But like the disruptor, it is not a permanent solution. And I, too, will be shut out.

She dropped the towel on the counter. "This just gets better and better."

It must be done, Argo sent. *For Miles and for Peggy.*

Yes, Harper thought. Argo needed her captain. And so did Harper.

And if she needed to go on from here without Argo's help, then so be it.

"Argo," she said. "Before you do it, tell me about Sekundos. Just in case there are things I should know."

That would take too long, Harper Starling.

She gestured helplessly. "Is there a way to . . . I don't know . . . fast-track the process, then?"

The ship hesitated. *It would be painful. I am not even certain if a human mind could survive it.*

"And the partition?"

More painful still.

"Good. Cool. Yeah."

The ominous promise of pain made her hesitate. But they were running out of time, and she couldn't afford not to know things, to be stuck on a planet alone with a psychic partition and no knowledge of what to touch or eat or avoid like the plague. Besides, Harper was no longer a stranger to pain. Mental or otherwise.

"Okay," she said. "Let's do it."

You should sit.

She pulled a chair away from the family-style table, wondering which Argonaut once ate their dinner there, and sat.

If I sense that you are dying, I will cease the process.

"Great," Harper replied. "I appreciate that."

For a moment, she was worried it wouldn't work. The ship went deathly quiet, the whir of mechanics Harper hadn't even noticed now silenced. But she didn't feel anything. She looked around, waiting, her anticipation a cresting wave in her gut, until the wave broke, and nothing was different.

"Ar—"

Her mind flowered open, and she screamed.

Images and information that had not existed moments before now materialized in all corners of her brain. The intricate history of an alien world; social customs, costume, religions; an encyclopedia of words in a language she had never learned but now somehow understood. The information had to be stored and it had to be done quickly, which meant cramming it in like too many socks in a crowded drawer.

If she thought the whipcrack of Argo's psychic slap earlier was painful, she was a fool. This was agony, a psychic encephalitis, pressure and pain in places she couldn't touch, couldn't relieve. It was almost more than she could bear—her brain was still only human, modest in size, incapable of retaining too much lest the levies break and spill brain matter everywhere. Pelegaeans, she thought, must use so much more of that mushy pink organ between their ears than humans would ever dream.

One day, Argo told her as the flood ebbed and the words, the images, the histories, slowed to a trickle, *I will tell you the truth about Pelegaeans.*

And then it was over. Despite already being seated, Harper fell out of the chair. She lay on the floor of the kitchen, chest heaving like she'd just run a marathon. Her brain felt tender, smashed inside the cage of her skull.

"How long will this last?" she panted.

Your mind cannot hold it for long, Argo replied. *It will fade quickly. You have no more than two days.*

"So, there's no time to waste."

But as she pushed herself back into a sitting position, she found with a thrill that she knew everything there was to know about Sekundos. It was a world whose indigenous peoples had left for the stars centuries before the arrival of new settlers. Sekundos as it existed now was a kind of Island of Misfit Toys, a formerly empty, forested planet dotted with ruins, now colonized by exiles and criminals from neighboring worlds and galaxies. The people she would find here were just that—people. Life forms that required the same basic necessities she did, that looked similar to or were descended from the humans she had left behind on Earth. Thousands of years of exploration had brought them here, the Earth she knew long gone.

She tested a few sentences in Sekundian, an apparent mishmash of several other languages spoken by those who first arrived, and found that her tongue was ill-equipped to roll the words through her teeth. Even those words descended from English were now spoken with such a bizarre accent that they were unrecognizable to her. Her pronunciation was good enough, but her tongue would soon be sore if she talked too much. She would be understood, if barely. She reminded herself, too, to avoid the poisonous shrubs with heart-shaped leaves that grew all over the place, knowing that even if she accidentally cut herself on one, the antidote could be made from the bitter sap inside the stalk. It was important, as well, that she make no eye contact. She found that she knew, suddenly, thrillingly, how to use a blade. A lot of different ones.

"Holy shit," she breathed. She wished she'd known Argo when she was going to school.

Was this what their life had been like, Miles and Peggy? Jumping across galaxies, dumping entire cultures and languages into their minds before plunging into dangerous adventures, alien wildernesses, long sabbaticals on foreign worlds?

No, Argo answered, startling her. *Miles has never asked to know so much about the planets he visits. He may not even realize it is possible.*

"Why am I not surprised," she muttered. What a fucking waste of an amazing power. That little sun gave a sputter.

No. She would not feed her anger.

"We'd better do the partition thingy," Harper said, her good mood degrading again. The idea of not having Argo's voice in her mind, ready to answer a question at a moment's notice, right when she was diving into the arms of the beast, was enough to stir up an anxiety attack.

Do not panic, Argo said, her voice inducing calm instead. *Even if you cannot hear me, I will hear you.*

"You're right," Harper said, as much for herself as for Argo. "Nothing to fear."

Trust yourself. You know what to do.

Harper nodded like she actually agreed. "Okay then. I'm ready."

She closed her eyes, expecting a similar experience to the one she'd just endured. Instead, there was a rush in her ears, like the inevitable surge of the ocean, followed by an almost unbearable ringing, and then, just as quickly, utter silence. She'd gotten used to Argo's psychic presence quickly and easily. But the lack of the ship's voice, or the open channel between her mind and the Incarnate awakening there, was unmistakable. She felt . . . barren.

And how had she not noticed before just how quiet the ship was? No voices, no laughter, no others besides herself. Only the faintest whir and stutter of machinery, and the oceanic rush of an impossible, far-off tide, like listening into the hollow of a conch shell.

"Argo?" she said, just in case. But the ship did not respond, and Harper could not feel her, the comforting heaviness of another mind against her own gone. She was alone, truly alone, in a way she had not been in three months. It felt like grief.

She wandered up to the navigation deck, where a countdown was slowly ticking across the sleek center console. Nine hours, fifty minutes, nine seconds.

Suddenly, she was exquisitely tired.

She went back downstairs to the hall of doors, pointedly avoiding the one at the end of the hall, and began shaking the door handles. Many were locked, so she entered the first door that opened when she turned the knob. The room was pitch-black, and she found no light switches, no lamps, no candles to light her way, so she gave up, inching forward until she stumbled into the edge of a bed, and crashed instantly into sleep. Had dreams that felt more like abstract paintings. Photographs of space.

There was no Peggy here. No Incarnate. Nothing.

22.

ARGO
SEASON AND YEAR UNKNOWN

Wake up, Harper.

It came back to her in pieces. She was not in the motel. She was not in her shared apartment, nor in Anthony's comfortable bed, nor in the room she'd claimed as her own in Paul M. French's secret Greenwich town house. No, she was much, much farther from home.

Hazy sunlight filled the room. But it couldn't have been sunlight, actually, because the window on the wall displayed a dark, starry void, and the illumination had no discernible source. It allowed her to see whose room she'd stumbled into: Peggy's. She could tell it was Peggy's because Peggy's things were here, the biggest giveaway being the poster tacked to the wall opposite the bed. It was an *Infinite Odyssey* poster, the one Harper had given her before they started high school. She could tell Peggy was nervous to leave middle school, though she would never have admitted it, and Harper knew that if there was anything that could have cheered Peggy up, it was the kindly, determined face of the fourth-season Argonaut (when he was in his ugly Christmas sweater phase) gazing down from the wall. After Peggy met Flora, it disappeared from her dorm room wall, and Harper had taken it to be a sign that she was growing tired of the show, and tired of Harper.

Yet here it was, curled edges straining against the thumbtacks holding it tight to the walls.

Dust had collected on the rest of her scattered things. A framed photo of Peggy and Harper on the nightstand. A pair of scuffed boots that once belonged to Harper before they'd mysteriously disappeared from her closet. A sweater Harper recognized from Peggy's Argonaut cosplay for InfiniCon the second to last year they attended. A bottle of Peggy's favorite cologne, with notes of cedar and vanilla. It was all over the pillow Harper had slept on; probably it was what had lured her into this room in the first place.

This was what Peggy had chosen, all those years ago, when she left Harper behind. A warm room near the beating heart of a sentient time-and-spaceship, and a man with the universe at his fingertips. Except, she hadn't left Harper behind. Not really. Harper was here, in this room, her presence as ubiquitous as Peggy's, even though she had never seen it before today.

"You didn't really get tired of me," she whispered to the room. "I should have let you explain that day. I shouldn't have chased you away."

Harper thought about her mom and dad back in Colorado. About Anthony and Angie, Dottie and Indira. All of Harper's own left behinds. Well and truly left, now. She was their very own Peggy, and she was gone, gone, gone.

She went to the window. She expected to see the void once again, the limitless expanse of black and the distant light of dying stars. But instead, a planet greeted her, swathed in vibrant blue and red and green and the wispy white swirl of clouds, a habitable Earth-like planet NASA would have lost their shit over. But they weren't here; it was just Peggy and Miles and soon, Harper, and myriad future human races who had colonized its surface millennia beyond the era she had left on Earth.

Argo? she thought, before remembering that Argo had installed a psychic wall in her mind, a way to keep the Incarnate, and the Tesseract Engine, out. Harper was on her own.

She put a hand to the shoulder of her pink T-shirt from breakfast and imagined herself a version of the Sekundian uniform with which she was now intimately familiar—a hodgepodge of clothing items in dark colors, mostly crimson and black, designed to protect the skin from Sekundos's bright sun and provide camouflage amongst its red-leafed trees. She was delighted when the clothes transformed beneath her touch, the fibers loosening, spinning themselves into something more like linen and canvas, sturdy enough to protect her from errant branches and stones but lightweight enough to move without restriction. A scarf formed itself around her neck and head, covering her hair, and the look topped itself off with a pair of thick, sturdy goggles. Mad Max would have been proud.

She remembered her mirror self's reflection back at the diner. Remembered she had been dressed like this. Whatever had happened to her in that mirror, it was happening soon.

She went upstairs.

Where before the wide navigation window had exposed an ocean of stars, that planet now loomed, verdant and bright. Sekundos was a sight to behold from here.

Are you ready, Harper Starling? she imagined Argo saying.

"I'm ready." She closed her eyes.

And then, unexpectedly, wind. A cool breeze against her cheeks, tousling the loose edges of the scarf. She opened her eyes again.

She was standing in a forest, and Argo was gone.

She was alone.

The monolithic forest was alive with a cacophony of animal and insect sounds. The trees around her possessed smooth crimson bark and humongous, fan-shaped leaves the color of old blood, trunks so wide in circumference they must have been centuries old, bigger than any tree one might find in North America. Even the protected redwoods of California were no match for the beastly size of these trees. And god, the scent! It reminded her of the Ponderosa pines back in Colorado, the creamy hug of butterscotch and vanilla beneath the more ubiquitous tang of pine and resin.

She took a step and almost took another before realizing that this, *this* was her very first step on an alien planet. The wind and the air and the sounds all warped and bent and melted into a kind of sensory overload, the truth of this place, of Argo, of herself almost too overwhelming to contemplate. It was one thing to have the whole history of an alien planet downloaded into your mind; it was quite another to set foot on that planet as a human who had, days before, never imagined such a thing might be possible in her lifetime. And who the hell was Harper Starling to be taking this on, really? She had no special skills, nothing that made her so different from any other human who could have been chosen for this. She was a waitress in a diner, a failed would-be scientist, a girl mired in grief.

And yet, the ground underfoot felt like, well, earth. Spongy soil littered with leaves and the mulch of seasons past. The air resembled the atmosphere she knew. So, alien, yes. Momentous, yes. But the people on this planet were like her. They had the same basic needs, if not the same basic language. Water to drink, air to breathe, fire to cook, solid ground from which to grow food. It helped, to think of it that way. Otherwise, she might be in danger of floating away, her emotions carrying her off into the Sekundian sun. It should have been too much for her to handle. It should have been too much.

And yet.

A gentle vibration hummed at her back, and she reached around to feel for the item thrumming there—a backpack. She pulled it off and looked at it, searching for a tell.

The pack vibrated again. "You have got to be kidding me," she said, barely suppressing her astonished laugh. "Now you're a fucking backpack?"

A moment ago, Argo had been the size of a spaceship large enough to house a dozen Argonauts, a kitchen, a navigation deck, an engine room, and who knew what else. Now, all her mass was comfortably compressed into this new disguise.

The pack shivered again.

Harper was finally beginning to understand what should have been obvious from the start, what the Incarnate had been trying to tell her: Miles was not the impossible one. It was Argo. A spaceship with a brain, a voice, a heart, an entirely separate dimension within. She was a friend, family even. And without this ship, this impossible machine, Miles was, at heart, just another human with dreams of the stars.

"Okay." She turned a circle, psyching herself up for the task of finding Miles and Peggy. "How do we find them?"

"Who," said a voice in clumsy Sekundian, "are you talking to?"

Harper spun around, now spotting the man she hadn't seen before among the trees. He was ridiculously tall, in a bulky flannel that did not fit him in the slightest. A halo of sunlight glanced off the top of his disheveled graying hair. She could not have explained the way her heart filled up at the sight of him, even though she knew better. Traitor, she admonished her own heart. But with the absence of Argo's voice, he was dry land after days on an unfriendly sea.

He smiled, and it was, for perhaps the first time, a real, honest-to-god smile.

"Hello, Starling," Miles the Argonaut said.

She pushed her goggles to the top of her head. Heat pulsed in her cheeks. He had never looked at her like that. Now that she thought about it, he'd barely looked at her at all. Now he couldn't seem to look at anything else.

"In case you weren't already aware," she said, "you're a fucking idiot."

He rubbed the back of his head sheepishly. "Yes. I . . . I understand that now."

She chewed her lip to keep the sudden and unbidden tears from falling. "So, we're agreed. No more pseudoheroic martyr bullshit."

He laughed. Something was different in him. Lighter. "We're agreed." He started to turn. "Come on. We're this way."

"Wait," she said. "Wait."

He did. But when she tried to think of something, anything, to say, it wouldn't come. Frustration killed all the words that couldn't seem to push through her new encyclopedic knowledge of Sekundos.

His expression changed, and before she knew what was happening, he had crossed the distance between them and pulled her into a hug. A fucking hug.

They had never hugged before. They had never been friends before. Were they friends now? No, she thought as those unbidden tears came, hot and unfair. They were not friends. The word did not encompass whatever the hell they had become to each other. So, she reached her arms around him, his lanky body enveloped in too much denim and plaid, and she hugged him in the middle of a crimson forest on an alien world.

"I'm glad you could join us," he said to the top of her head. Cheeky bastard.

Gross snot dripped from her nose, and she sniffed loudly. "Yes, well, the invitation was so last-minute."

He pulled away. "I'm sorry about that," he said seriously.

Argo the Backpack vibrated, and Harper didn't need to hear her to understand. It's easy enough to let hate take over your heart. It is much harder to lead with love.

She looked up at him. "I got here in the end."

EPISODE SEVEN
FUNDAMENTAL FORCES

This week on Infinite Odyssey:

The Argonaut has been kidnapped by a warrior seeking vengeance for atrocities he insists the Argonaut committed. With no first mate on board, it's up to the Argonaut to rescue himself and determine if the warrior is telling the truth about his own dark past!

23.

SEKUNDOS
SPRING, YEAR UNKNOWN

The moment Peggy hit the dial on her device, Miles regretted his decision to ditch Harper and face the Incarnate alone. Not only because spinning shipless through the void was arguably one of the worst things he'd ever put himself through, but because he could see, now, the mess he was making. He just so badly wanted to fix this, and it was his fight, after all. But what heroics had he expected to employ? He didn't have one iota of the plan he'd insisted to Harper they needed. He didn't even have a weapon. And now here he was, tumbling end over end through space and time, attached to another person like an amateur skydiver.

Despite the quantum serum in his veins, the void confused his insides, stretched and squashed his organs, and squeezed his body until it felt like it might simply cave in. He could not see the space-time around him; everything was moving too quickly; everything was too bright. Peggy was a buoy and burden both.

And she was dying. He felt it almost as soon as she hit the dial on her wrist, the way her body grew heavy against his, like she could not even be bothered to hold herself up. Consciousness left her—she would be dead by the time they reached Pelegaea. He couldn't save Peggy if she was dead, and he would never forgive himself for losing her twice. Worse, Harper would never forgive him. He had barely known her a cumulative total of twenty-four hours. But every time she looked at him with those burning, incredulous eyes, he couldn't help it. Something in him wanted to fix what he'd broken. He was, as it turned out, very bad at fixing things.

The force of the void around them had him quite well pinned in one position. But with a little maneuvering and more muscle than he'd ever exerted in this lifetime, he was able to get his hand on the dial. Jason would have been proud of him. Using his wits to maneuver a bad situation into something better, like an Argonaut would. He had no idea what to do with the device once it was in his grasp, but somehow, perhaps while thinking about Jason and wishing for his presence, the pair ended up on a small outlaw planet called Sekundos, a world Miles remembered well from his travels with the Argonauts.

The journey was over almost as quickly as it had begun.

For the first time, he looked at Peggy. Truly looked at her. It had been years since he last saw her, and god, it showed. Her face was scarred and bent in the places it had broken and never healed right, her mouth set in a tight line, a hard expression she never used to make, not even in sleep. The stories these scars could tell. Each one a match strike in the dark he'd left her in all this time.

"Peggy," he said gently, though he didn't know what made him say it. The way her half-lidded eyes seemed to stare up at the canopy made him think maybe she was awake, maybe she was listening. Maybe things had been jostled just enough that there was a chance she'd hear him. "I'm getting us out of here. Just hold on a little longer. Please."

He wondered if she'd even believe it, coming from him. If she even remembered the adventures they once had, or if the Incarnate was in there, whispering insidious thoughts into what was left of her mind. That's when he remembered: Harper, too, was connected to the hive. Maybe there was a chance the psychic disruptor had faded enough to reach her. It would mean giving the hive his message too, but he didn't care anymore. He just wanted Harper to know that they were still alive. That he was going to take care of things.

While Peggy's eyes were still half open, he delivered his message, praying to some god, any god, that it had any chance of reaching Harper at all. He wanted to believe it could, but he knew he couldn't count on it, especially once Peggy shut her eyes, consciousness lost. When he felt for a pulse, he found one, though it was faint. She was alive, and they were on their own.

He cut himself free of her, pocketed her device, and spent the next hour pacing restlessly between two colossal trees while she lay nestled between roots, breathing uneasily in sleep. He'd returned to Sekundos once after the tragedy on Pelegaea, many years before he met Ron, and got stuck in the middle of a shoot-out. He left the planet with a festering bullet in his leg. It was not his favorite place to visit.

But Peggy wasn't waking up. Iridescent black ooze dripped from her nose, her ears, a glimmer of it at her tear ducts. She would not be able to hold on much longer. But if Harper was right, trapped somewhere in that mind was the girl who had traveled with him for years, their riotous friendship the stuff of legends on some planets. He owed it to her to see this through. To make sure she didn't die before he had a chance.

Besides. Harper would be unhappy, and he was tired of being yelled at.

She would not even bother to yell at you, he imagined Argo saying. *You would simply be dead to her.*

He'd forgotten how terrible it felt to disappoint someone. Even someone he didn't like all that much and would probably never see again.

Now that he'd gotten his bearings a bit, he recognized their position. These trees, with their fan-shaped crimson leaves, were unique to the forest surrounding Shinloya, a small trading post far from any major cities. Trading posts on Sekundos were neutral ground—all gangs, warbands, and loners with an agenda could break bread and parlay with one another without risk of being betrayed. The punishment for those who broke the unspoken trading post rule was greater than whatever price those unlucky enough to trade with a traitor would pay. There would be a healer there, too, and food.

But Peggy was heavy, all dense muscle and bone, a fact he learned when he tried to gather her up and carry her over his narrow shoulder like a limp sack of potatoes. He'd only managed to trudge a quarter of a mile before he was too tired to continue and set her down again.

What to do, what to do? Could he tie her to one of these old trees and walk the rest of the way without her? He had a vague sense of the direction, and her device seemed equipped with a complicated map feature. Did he dare leave her alone, even in this state? *Especially* in this state?

In the end, he didn't have to. The aggressive hum of hoverbikes, a ubiquitous form of transportation on this planet, alerted him to the approach of two strangers. Friend or foe, one never did know on this planet. Not until it was too late.

They appeared as small beige dots at first, zigzagging expertly through the dense crimson thicket. They were far enough that they might never notice him at all, positioned as he was in the shadow of a massive tree. So, he did the intelligent thing and began to wave his arms.

"Hey!" he shouted, hoping his voice would carry above the roar of their bikes. "Over here!"

The strangers saw him and slowed their raucous vehicles. As they neared, he saw the glint of a knife in one of their hands, and a strange joy surged in his heart. It had been so long since he'd had the desire to fight. To use what Orleus, his gruff and stubborn teacher, had taught him.

These would not have been worthy opponents in Orleus's estimation, but they were useful; expecting a helpless traveler, they were sloppy in their offensive and easily disarmed, the outstretched knife of the first clutched tight in Miles's hand before either understood that it was *they* who were under attack and not the man without a hoverbike. That one crashed soundly into the trunk of a nearby tree and was out cold; the second managed to inflict a few surface wounds before Miles gained the upper hand. He knocked this one out too, feeling more than generous for leaving them with one hoverbike.

The second bike he took, slinging Peggy on in front of him so she leaned over the handlebars, and he clambered onto the vehicle behind her. He stepped on the gas and the bike rocketed creakily forward, engines vibrating hard beneath them. It was fast, considering just how busted it looked. And the longer the bike maintained its speed, the faster it seemed to be able to go. The forest turned into a blurry tunnel of red, and he was thankful for the lack of wheels—in a moment they were going so fast that even the tiniest twig or rock might have sent them careening into the immense trees.

The forest gave way suddenly to a wide sandy beach and a clear, vivid ocean, or perhaps a lake so large the other side could not be seen, rocking and rolling beneath the shocking cerulean sky. He kept close to the water for a long time. They skirted the edge of the land and sea for another fifteen minutes, just long enough to lull him, the oxygen-rich atmosphere making him giddy and tired all at once. Beyond the water the Sekundian sun began to set, bringing violent reds and purples into the sky.

He couldn't believe how long he'd let himself hide from this. Not just the truth about Peggy or facing the person he had left behind on Pelegaea, but adventure. It had been a very long time since he sparred with strange people on a strange planet, or breathed in the sharp scent of an alien ocean, or felt the brisk wind on his face. Already his arms were cramping from fighting for the first time in decades. The last few years he'd tried to hold himself still, suspend himself like a mosquito in amber. Drinking alone on Varlanos or Kipthee or One Tree Twice Fallen, where the liquor was strongest and the wars minimal, until his memory was shot and all the traumas of recent awareness were swept into the comforting cloud of inebriation.

They lost the light just as they veered off the beach and back into the woods. He checked Peggy's pulse to make sure she was still breathing as he slowed the bike. The wind died. Peggy's map showed Shinloya beyond the trees.

The woods were different at night. Something glowed in here: long, interconnecting threads of a bioluminescent fungus, not bulbous like the clustered mushrooms you were sure to find in the forests of Earth or fan-shaped like the ones Jason told him about on Pelegaea, but delicate and fine, threaded across the surface of the arboreal giants in an intricate weave. He'd forgotten about the beauty of Sekundos at night. They called this particular fungus Exa's Lace, named after a god whose mythology was brought to Sekundos from a small planet called Exatarr. Its glow reminded him of Appalachian foxfire.

He could tell by the way the fungus seemed to gather along the edges but not into the space below the hovering craft that he was following an oft trampled path. No lace grew where feet and hooves had stamped the earth down. It crowded greedily along the edges and up the trunks of trees instead. As he drifted forward, admiring the light, he heard the susurrus of chatter and laughter. And if he looked hard enough, he could make out the flickering shadows of firelight and, incongruously, neon blues and greens. Shinloya.

Everything caught up to him in a rush. He hovered uncertainly in the shadows at the edge of the wood, the adrenaline that had gotten him this far souring into panic, sadness, hesitation. What would the healer, if he found one, tell him? Had he come all this way only to learn that Peggy could not be saved? Days ago, if he had not wanted to face this, he would have turned around and left. Waited for the situation to sort itself out.

But that was learned behavior, not innate. He had not learned cowardice as a young man when he'd braved Chicago's clubs with lined eyes and his sister's clothes or when traveling alongside his fellow Argonauts. He learned in the aftermath of loss, of grief thrice inflicted.

The hoverbike drifted out of the woods and into the neon glow of Shinloya.

The market was Shinloya's beating heart, a thoroughfare lined with corrugated metal stalls coated in chipped paint and lined up neatly, like shipping containers. Neon signs brightened the smudgy night, boasting wares and vendor names. Behind them, dirty container-shaped shacks and huts sat unlit, spaces where one might find more mercenary offerings. People haggled over necklaces and fruit and tech, bathed in the glow of bright-blue, hot-pink, and livid-green light. The smell of something spicy wafted from a few stalls down, the herbs pungent and unfamiliar and delicious. The firelight was brighter in the market, where torches lit the way alongside tall lanterns shining like neon suns.

"Excuse me," he said to a burly man passing leisurely by. "Can you tell me, is there a healer here?" He gestured to Peggy's slumped form in front of him. "My friend took a fall."

The man grunted—Miles presumed that was a yes—and pointed down the street, where the market was ill lit. Miles thanked him and urged the bike forward.

It was an inconspicuous little hut, no hints that this might be a healer's house except for the heady smoke filtering through the moth-eaten holes in the loose-weave curtain that served as a door. They'd used a similar smoke in Argo's med bay; the Argonauts brought it from Pelegaea, where it was used to sterilize the air in hospitals and sick rooms. It had a sharp, herbal scent that reminded him of them.

He parked the bike in the shadow of the hut; gathered Peggy over his shoulder, grunting with the effort; and pulled the curtain aside.

There was a long table at the center of the hazy room, where patients presumably were treated. A bowl at each corner of the room emitted the pungent incense, the smoke burning blue and then dulling to gray as it dispersed into the air. The healer stood with her back to the door on the other side of the room, grinding something against the hollow of a stone bowl with a sturdy pestle. Next to the mortar sat an array of murky glass bottles in green and amber and blue. She looked up as the smoky air was disturbed by his entrance.

"May I help you?" she asked. His Sekundian was rusty—the translators the Argonauts used were all back on Argo—but it shared several words whose roots were the same as Pelegaean, which he'd picked up quite a bit of in those early days, and he was confident he could at least ask for what he needed.

"Help," he said. "Please."

The healer's gaze flicked to the limp figure on his drooping shoulder, and she gestured for him to lay Peggy out on the table at the center of the room. He tried to be gentle, dipping low to settle her against the slab. The healer caught Peggy's head before it could hit the table and laid it gently down.

"What happened?" she asked. Her voice was gruff, no-nonsense.

"A . . . disease," he said. He wasn't sure how one could explain the parasitic spread of the Incarnate in any language. "A mind disease."

The healer just nodded. "What do you expect me to do?"

"Whatever you can. To make her comfortable."

The healer turned and busied herself with the mortar and pestle. "This should help," she said. "But you already know that there is much more to be done."

It took him a moment to realize that she had spoken in fluid Pelegaean. When he did, he couldn't believe he'd been so obtuse.

"I know you," he said. "You're the seer who sent us to Myzsst."

The seer spared him an indulgent smile. This time, she spoke in English: "The one and only." She must have had a translator somewhere on her person.

She turned back to her mortar and pestle.

Now that she'd revealed herself, he saw the clue he'd initially missed. There was something otherworldly about her, a soft aura around her person that sometimes flickered the way an old light might. He saw it with Argo too—a sort of double-image effect whenever he looked at her. It was the result of being born in the Sight Wood, Jason once explained, a forest that existed both in and out of time.

He glanced around the hut, as if expecting to see other clues he remembered from his first visit—divination tools and frothy silks and an altar stacked high with blessings and tokens for her chosen goddess—but there were none to be found. Just the spare, clean room of a medic.

"So, you're a healer now? What happened to being a seer?"

"Things change," she replied. "These days on Sekundos, they do not like anything that even smells of magic." Sweat broke on her brow as she ground the substance in the bowl. "And seers seem to be high on that list."

"Then why stay here?"

Miles traced his hands along the edge of the surface where Peggy lay. The smoke was making him dizzy.

"And why don't *you* go home?"

He looked away. He'd become used to not needing to explain himself when it came to the world he'd left behind, the world that reminded him too much of Ron and the person Miles once was, the person who had also died. Least of all to someone who could, it seemed, stare into the very heart of him. "It hasn't been my home in a long time."

The seer let out a long sigh. "I don't have the choice you do," she said pointedly, "you and that ship. But if I did . . . I crave the days of heroes in Aepholia's golden streets. The university filled with brilliant scholars. I miss my sisters at the temple. And I'll tell you, I'd do just about anything for a glass of real ambrosia, the severely alcoholic kind."

But Pelegaea was gone. Ruined. The temples destroyed, the sisterhoods crumbled, the gilded streets tarnished to sinister onyx.

"So, it seems we understand each other."

She added a splash of an orange liquid from one of her myriad vials. "It seems we do." She scraped the mixture from the sides of the bowl. It was piceous and thick, like mud. He watched as she scraped the concoction into a small glass and mixed it with water until it became a murky tonic.

"Lift her up. We must get her to take this."

Miles obliged, reaching beneath Peggy's head and grasping her matted hair. She looked more like his old friend than ever, now that the assassin was sleeping, and her face had softened.

The seer managed to pry Peggy's mouth open, and Miles held her, her unconscious body fidgeting as the healer drained the medicine down her throat. She sputtered and coughed but did not wake. The seer dabbed at the corners of her mouth with a cloth, clearing both the medicine and the black dribbles of the Incarnate from her face.

"That should help," she said. "For a time."

"What will it do?"

"Slow the spread of that hideous parasite, though I fear she is already too far gone."

"Will she wake?"

The seer hesitated. "It's possible she might wake, for a time. But I would not expect it. The most I can do is ease her suffering." She turned back to her table and busied herself with disinfecting her hands with some kind of oil. "Now, for the other reason you are here."

He let out a laugh at that. He'd almost forgotten that, naturally, she was expecting him. "You know the rest of the story, I assume."

"I know a little," she replied. "But I don't have the answers you're looking for."

"And what answers are those?"

"You want to know how this ends. How *you* might end it." She turned to face him, expression grave. "And I can't tell you because I don't know."

His stomach turned to mud and devoured the hope he'd so desperately tried to hold on to. He just wanted someone to tell him what to do. Because, if the events of the last few years were any indication, he'd been doing it wrong for a very long time. And now the one person with any hope of guiding him had no light to shine on his path after all.

"It's because of the Incarnate, isn't it?" He knew that he sounded like a pouting child. Ron would have been appalled. He would have looked into Miles's eyes and said, "Flora, you're better than this." Peggy would have rolled her eyes and told him to come get her when he was done sulking.

Well. Ron wasn't here, and neither was Peggy. Not really.

"I know that there is another of your party due to arrive soon, but my ability to see much further ended when you brought the Incarnate with you." She gave an apologetic shrug.

"How?" Miles asked. "How is it so strong?"

"Something about it changed when you and Argo left Pelegaea. Beyond that, I'm not certain. You would be wise not to let it near your ship."

"I have no ship," he said. "Not anymore." He thought of Harper, her own mind contaminated because of his bad decisions, just like Peggy's, and wondered what would greet him; if Harper, too, would be replaced by whatever personality the Incarnate saw fit to give her. If he ever saw her again.

The seer's expression softened. "Argo is not yet lost, Miles. Take care that she is well protected when she arrives. Tonight is Exa's Awakening, a sacred day celebrated with bonfires and revelry and much drink. If the rest of your party lands too close to Shinloya, you'll certainly be set upon by scavengers before she can disguise herself." She produced a pair of magcuffs from a basket beneath her worktable, fastened them around Peggy's wrists, switched them on, and watched, satisfied, as the magnetic charges in each cuff grabbed onto each other and pulled Peggy's wrists together.

"Thank you," Miles said. "For everything."

"I'm afraid it would have been worse not to help you."

The story of his life, these days. "What do I owe you?"

The seer closed her eyes. "A story," she said softly. "One Jason might have told you. Tell me about home."

24.

SEKUNDOS
SPRING, YEAR UNKNOWN

It was late afternoon, the sun setting on Miles's second day on Sekundos. The vivid blue sky was slowly morphing to violet through the canopy. They weren't too far outside Shinloya, Miles had explained, certainly not as far as they had been when he and Peggy arrived. But far enough that the lights of the market he had described were not even sparks in the distance.

"That's quite the tale," Harper said. She was chewing on beef jerky Miles had fished out of Argo's pantry. They sat across from one another, a small fire between them.

When they arrived at the campsite, Argo had gleefully expanded out of backpack form, joints popping in relief. She took on the shape of what Miles called "a rusted space junker": a cramped vessel that reminded Harper of the compact Viper ships on *Battlestar Galactica*, whose dented exteriors spent much of their time on screen weathering explosions and lasers and the impact of space debris.

The point, of course, was to make Argo as unappealing as possible to any passersby. Sekundos had a habit of attracting murderers, thieves, and scavengers—unscrupulous exiles who wouldn't blink twice at slitting their throats and stealing their things. She knew this as deeply as she knew a million other impossible things. If anyone came upon them, it would be clear that Argo was not a space-worthy vessel. To those passing by, Miles and Harper had nothing of value at all.

"Your turn," Miles said. He took the jerky from her and bit into it.

"My turn for what?"

"For your story. What happened on Argo?"

Harper shrugged. "Nothing much." She looked across their small clearing, where Peggy now slumped, magcuffed to a tall, willowy tree. She had not regained consciousness at all since Harper arrived, and Harper both feared and hoped she would. Miles had suggested keeping her locked in one of the rooms on board, but Harper had vetoed it before the words had left his mouth. She knew what the Incarnate would be whispering to Peggy, conscious or not, once inside. What it would see and want.

"Oh, come on," Miles said. "There has to be more to it than that."

"I slept like the dead."

She wasn't sure why she didn't tell him. About the engine room, about taking in all Argo could give her about Sekundos, about the psychic partition. Perhaps it was what Argo had said before—that Miles had never asked Argo to do the same for him, and might not even realize it was possible. Maybe she wanted something about all of this that was hers, and hers alone.

Please, Argo, she thought, *don't tell him yet.*

Miles threw his hands up. "Fine. Don't tell me. I'll find out sooner or later."

He said it playfully, so Harper obliged him with a smile. "I'm sure you will."

Somewhere between locking Peggy to the tree and starting the fire, Miles had produced a murky bottle of something Harper assumed by its general appearance to be alcoholic. Sure enough, it was a local liquor he'd picked up on his way out of the market, remembering fondly the last time he'd had it here, just before finding himself in the middle of a shoot-out. He'd sloshed it into two tin glasses from Argo's kitchen and passed one to her. She almost didn't take it—each time she'd allowed herself to imbibe, the Incarnate managed to open the door in her mind a little more. But there was a partition now; the door was nailed shut. For now.

"Was it strange?" Harper said now, the buzz settling in. The drink had a jagged swallow.

"Was what strange?"

"Seeing a Pelegaean again."

Miles shifted uncomfortably. "Of course."

"That's it?" She ate another strip of jerky to quell the bite of the liquor.

"What do you want me to say?"

"I don't know. What do you think about what she said? About going home?"

"I think that ship has sailed."

Harper considered him. Thought about the version of him she'd encountered that first night. Miles Moonraker T-shirt, shitty attitude, bitter apologies across a weathered menu in a '70s diner. Compared him to the youthful man in a nice suit she'd found in the planetarium, the one who had seemed legitimately sorry but still unwilling to do anything about her predicament. He'd lived a life on Earth, back then.

"Sounds like she disagrees," she said.

"None of that will matter if the Incarnate destroys everything."

She drained her glass and winced. "I have to tell you something."

"All right."

"Back at the Starlight, I saw my future self."

Miles looked at her sharply. "I don't think I heard you right. It sounded like you said you'd met—"

"My future self. No need to be so dramatic, Miles."

"Well, I beg to differ."

"It was the mirror in the restroom. My reflection."

"Your reflection? That's very odd."

"But she seemed legit. Not like . . . a trick." She didn't even know if such a trick was possible. Had she imagined the whole thing? Had the Incarnate caused her to hallucinate? But that made no sense either. Why would it warn her about Argo? Why would it tell her to keep the ship away? Why would it warn her to run?

"I'm sure she seemed that way. But we don't know the motives of your future self," Miles said. "And that's the problem."

"I think I can trust me."

Miles rolled his eyes, though the gesture didn't seem to contain its usual disdain. "You would think that."

"I'm here, aren't I?" *I came all the way to Sekundos for you,* she didn't have to say. "Pretty sure I'm a better authority on trust than you are."

He opened his mouth huffily then closed it again, bait left on the table. "She's not you, Harper," he said, a bit more diplomatically than he clearly wanted to. "You have to remember that. Whatever she's been through, she's trying to influence you depending on what she experienced. She might be trying to change the outcome of a bad circumstance or maintain the outcome of one that may or may not be what you, Harper Starling of the here and now, actually want."

"You don't even want to know what she said?"

He scraped a handful of twigs off the ground and started breaking them. "Let me guess. You're in danger; don't trust anyone, especially that Miles. He's a tricky one—"

"She said, 'Love what you hate.'"

Miles paused. "What does that mean?"

"The Argonaut says it too, in *Infinite Odyssey.* I think it's a message I left for myself."

"I still don't understand."

"I think it means . . . maybe we have to try to understand the Incarnate. Maybe we have to see things from its perspective."

"That's ridiculous."

"Is it?"

"As directives go, it's pretty fucking vague, Harper."

"Maybe not," she grumbled, though it was hard to disagree.

"I like my theory," he said. His body relaxed, the liquor doing its work. "Future you is fucking with you for some reason you don't know yet. Well, I say fuck that. Do what you want. Hate who you like." He chuckled to himself.

"And what if that's you?"

He just shrugged. "I haven't done much to deserve more than that."

"You did save me once," Harper allowed, just to be nice. "That's not nothing."

"You wouldn't need saving if I wasn't such an asshole. Same for Peggy. I do get it now, Starling."

He took the jerky again and finished it off, then licked his fingers.

"Which is why you tried to play the hero back at the Starlight."

"Yes, I see how that, too, was a flawed plan."

"Face it: you can't ditch me, Miles," Harper said. "I'm the partner you've got. We have to work together."

His mouth quirked. "Love what you hate?"

She leaned back and didn't say anything, contemplating what remained of the daylit sky, and the stars as they emerged through the veil of violet-turning-midnight blue. All around them, the massive trees were beginning to glow, Exa's Lace waking up, and she was reminded of the glow-in-the-dark galaxy she and Peggy had decorated her bedroom ceiling with as kids.

She wished Peggy could see this with her too. But instead, she was stuck with Peggy's slowly dying husk, the form of her an ever-present reminder of everything they would never do. Thankfully there was alcohol, Sekundos, and Miles, and she could do the work of pretending for a little while longer.

"You should rest," Miles said softly, interrupting her meditation. "You're probably exhausted."

Harper shook her head.

She was wide awake. Breathing in highly oxygenated air, surrounded by a vast network of bioluminescent fungus, staring into the shadows of the flora on a planet several galaxies away from the only one she'd ever known . . . she was incandescent. She would never sleep again. And Miles seemed just as restless. She wondered how long it had been since he'd done something other than hide out on some backwater planet, waiting around for signs he'd been found, just so he could shove off again.

How long had it been since either of them had felt this truly alive?

"I'm not tired either," Miles confessed, confirming her suspicion. "I should be falling asleep where I sit, and yet." He looked around. "Ron would have loved this place."

"Yeah?"

"He loved nature. We camped a lot. On several different planets, before he decided he didn't want to travel anymore. He loved the small ones, with ruins and rusty spaceships reclaimed by the forests. We never came to this one, though. Too violent."

"He must have loved *Star Wars*. All those planets and dusty old tech."

Miles's mouth quirked. "He never got a chance to see them."

"I forgot. *A New Hope* was 1977."

Time was such a funny, fickle thing.

"He would have, though," Miles said. "Knowing him, we would have gone back to see it several times. I should have thought to take him. He was happier to stay home toward the end, but it would have been a short trip."

"You can't beat yourself up about the things you didn't think to do," Harper said. "That's not how life works."

"You're right, of course."

A breeze stole through the clearing, bringing with it a generous waft of terpenes scenting the clear air like butterscotch.

"I spent a lot of time waiting for Peggy to come home," Harper said. "A lot of years not going after my dreams because I thought they were only worth chasing if I was chasing them with her. When we got to New York and she started pulling away, I couldn't see it. Our friendship, it was going to carry us through all four years, that was what I thought. Then she met you at that club in Rockwood, back when you were Flora, and I knew something had changed—she pined over you for weeks—but I didn't want to believe it." She chanced a look at Miles, whose gaunt cheeks had flushed. "But deep down, I knew. And I was jealous and angry and hurt. Which is why I said the things I did that night."

"You loved her. It's understandable."

"So did you. Clearly, our love is dangerous. Guess we have that in common." She huffed a laugh and drank again. "I've been chasing her because I want to save her, yes, but also because . . . because I want the chance to make things right. And I can't go back to the Starlight after this, I just can't."

"I wouldn't let that happen." He waved off her shocked expression. "Don't look at me like that. I owe you a lot more than that. I could apologize for the rest of my life, and I don't think it would be enough."

"It would be a start."

"I'm sorry, Harper. And I'll say it every day for however long it takes."

"Just . . . don't leave me here," Harper said quietly. "Let's just finish this. Like you said before, at the diner. Kill the hive. Push that big red Destruct button, I don't care. Whatever it takes."

His eyes glittered in the firelight. "Is that really what you want? You would go, knowing you might not make it out?"

She thought about her future self, the white curl escaping her scarf, the look in her eyes. The evasive answers and half-truths. Miles wasn't wrong. Harper didn't trust herself as much as she wanted him to think. But she couldn't tell him the whole truth either. The things Mirror-Harper had asked her to do. The massive consequences to the galaxy, the universe, if she failed. The real reason that, no matter how much Mirror-Harper had left out, Harper believed she was telling truth.

It wasn't just about Peggy anymore. It was about everyone. And Harper hadn't planned to go out like a big damn hero, but it appeared that was the plan on the table. And she found, as she sat there drinking Sekundian liquor and conversing with Miles more amiably than she'd ever thought possible, that she didn't mind the idea as much as she first thought when it was presented to her back at the diner. There were worse ways to go. Worse ways to be remembered.

25.

SEKUNDOS
SPRING, YEAR UNKNOWN

She stood, swaying a little. Night had fallen on the forest around them. A quick peek through the canopy above provided an eyeful of Sekundos's three moons in all their silver glory.

She left her seat and walked toward the tree where Peggy slept some feet away, her heart pounding suddenly. Miles didn't protest as she left.

She walked slowly, avoiding the forest detritus as best she could, but there was no need to worry about making too much noise. Peggy was fast asleep, only a sliver of moonlight through the vast canopy providing the light by which to tell. Harper crept closer, noticing that Miles's cuffs had replaced the time-and-space-traveling device on Peggy's wrist.

She knelt on the grass. Even from here she could see there was dried black blood beneath Peggy's nose, around the inner corners of her eyes—it caught the light and glimmered. Her skin was pale, the faint sheen of a fever slick above her brow. Her body was giving up.

Harper hated seeing her this way. She wanted to look at her and think only of the good times. If neither of them came out of this, Harper wanted to be sure that Peggy was Peggy and that, even though there had been bad times, she had the chance to remember the rest. The things that were good.

And there were so many things. Playing dress-up in the basement—Harper the first mate and Peggy the Argonaut; the pair of them huddled together in class, passing notes back and forth; studying the stars from their sleeping bags in the yard, vowing one day to travel there together; the girls on their bikes in the neighborhood, Harper on Peggy's handlebars, Peggy speeding down Cottonwood Avenue with wild abandon, thick hair streaming behind her, giving her wings—no, a cape. She looked radiant in those days, those summer evenings, angelic sunset haloing her hair. She looked like she belonged to another world, another life. It was always like that. Peggy had always glowed brighter than the stars they both so desperately yearned to visit, and Harper had admired her so ardently she wondered now if she'd come closer to pure worship than love.

But no, that was the booze talking. Because Peggy had her hateful moments too, her cruel moments. Those times when she and Harper could not stop fighting—about stupid board games and who ignored whom in the hallway and who had been a bitch when all the other one wanted was to make nice. Peggy could be such an asshole when she wanted to be. She could be secretive and mean; and didn't that explain that last year, after all? Didn't that explain how she could travel across time and space with a man shaped like an alien they both loved and never breathe a word of her mind-bending adventures to Harper?

An urge to be angry flared and died in Harper's heart. This wasn't the time. Peggy was not Peggy anymore, could not answer for her faults, the hurts she'd caused. She looked so young like this. Wrathless.

There was a world out there, somewhere, in which Harper saved her. Where Peggy never became a monster at all, the ghost haunting Harper across time and space. Where she was never swept away to see the universe by a time-traveling mystery man, and she and Harper became experts in their fields, moved somewhere near Cape Canaveral, and cooked dinner together every night. Where they lay side by side on the beach in the summer, marveling at the full moon as the late-night tide brought water up the sand to baptize their heated skin.

She cleared her throat. "I met my future self today," she started, knowing Peggy would enjoy the opening line. "You would have hated her." Cue laughter, if Peggy could even hear. "Anyway. I'm going to fix this. You deserve that much."

Peggy was silent. Beyond their clearing, she heard the faint chime of music. Wondered, briefly, where it was coming from.

Harper got to her feet. "This is ridiculous. You can't hear me. You're stuck in a place I can't reach. I guess I just wanted to say . . . I hope you know I'm trying."

"You miss her."

She startled and stumbled backward, clutching her chest uselessly as her heart nearly beat right out of it. "Holy shit," she said. "Don't do that."

Peggy opened her crusty eyes. "You miss your friend."

Harper stood up straight. She hadn't expected to have a conversation; that wasn't the plan. She'd wanted to be with her friend without interruption. "Of course I miss her."

"She misses you too. We can feel her in here, missing you."

It was not Peggy saying these things in that rocky imitation of her voice. Harper had to remember that, no matter how difficult it was. Something else was using Peggy's mouth, moving her lips, saying words designed to taunt, to hurt.

"Yes," Not-Peggy said with a heavy sigh, as if Harper had responded. "It's burdensome. We never used to feel her in here. We were only the Incarnate. Until you." Her skin glistened with sweat, even in the blue half-light of the Exa's Lace.

"Do you want me to apologize?" Harper felt her face twist when she said it, ugly with anger.

"We want you to stop this futile game."

"I'm going to save her."

"She will be dead by then."

"I'll save everyone."

Peggy's mouth wobbled into a smile. "We understand what she sees in you."

Harper knelt into the brush again. Maybe if she got down to Peggy's level, if she took up the beggar's stance, she would appeal to something in her, something past the reach of the Incarnate, something that was still good. "Let me talk to her."

But Not-Peggy just shook her head. "We can't do that, Harper Starling. This body is weak; she might take it from us."

"She will anyway. I'm going to make sure of it."

"We do not think so. We have hope. A newer emotion for us; a gift from your friend, we think. She has the loveliest dreams."

Harper swallowed hard. Resisted the urge to touch Peggy's pale cheek. "She always was a dreamer."

The moonlight was shifting across the clearing, dragging from Peggy's face to rest as a barrier between them.

"You are here too," Peggy said. "In her dreams you are a beautiful regret. She wishes she had done things differently."

Pressure built in Harper's chest, all that unsung grief boiling over.

"I've forgiven her," she lied.

"She was young and foolish. She wanted the stars all to herself. She knows you longed for them too. She's glad, now, that she denied them to you."

She couldn't hear this. It wasn't helping. She wished she'd never come over here.

She stood, preparing to leave. She didn't want the Incarnate to see that she was shaking.

"She can hear you, Harper Starling. Say what you would like to say." Harper paused. "Will you not speak to her?"

She wanted to, god, she wanted to. *I miss you. I love you. I hate you. All this time I thought I couldn't do this without you. That you took part of me with you when you left. Now I'm realizing that all the good things you gave me—they were never gone. I wish I had seen it sooner.*

But it was too much to say, and in the end, it was not for sharing, not with the assassin who wore her friend's face. Harper had hoped to extricate the Incarnate from this body like an unwelcome leech, but she wondered now if it would be harder than that. If their personalities were becoming entwined, the dam between them breaking, as this body was breaking. Would some of this parasite remain, even once they destroyed the Incarnate? Was there even a chance Peggy could ever be the same again?

Harper turned. “Peggy knows everything I would have said anyway.”

“Wait.” Peggy struggled into a sitting position. A dribble of black trickled from her eye down her cheek, an oil-slick tear. “I believe in you, Harper.”

Harper almost ignored her, but the quality of her voice was different. Softer, suddenly, the flatness gone. *I* instead of *we.*

She spun to face her in disbelief. “What did you say?”

“I believe you can do this.” Peggy smiled with an earnestness Harper truly did not believe the Incarnate could replicate. “I believe you can save me.”

Harper watched, horror-struck, as Peggy’s scarred face finally, finally wore an expression only her lost friend had ever made. Just as quickly, that expression melted away, retreating into the dour blankness the assassin favored.

There were no words Harper could have mustered. She backed up slowly until Peggy’s face was once again obscured by shadow, afraid to turn away, to miss the moment Peggy became herself again. But Harper watched and waited, and waited, and waited, and the moment did not come.

She stumbled back to the fire. That was, quite possibly, the last time she would ever see Peggy Mara, and she had said nothing to her, nothing. She ran away like the coward she accused Miles of being. But she couldn’t go back there. Her stomach roiled, threatening to upend everything she’d just eaten and imbibed, every emotion she’d stirred into the pot. She needed somewhere to put it all, all this feeling, before it brought Argo’s partition tumbling down and let the sinister thing in.

The music was getting louder.

“Harper?” Miles said. She approached but didn’t sit, pacing the width of the rest area they had made.

“So, what is it? What’s the plan?”

“The plan is to rest. To take a breath and start again tomorrow.”

"That's not good enough!"

His brows knit together. "What did she say to you?"

"Nothing," Harper said, and in a way it was true. She'd just allowed the Incarnate to torment her, imparting nothing of value, nothing Harper could use, nothing at all. "I just can't keep doing this. I can't keep looking at her and not seeing her."

Miles leaned back, watching her. "Try another century of it," he said quietly, "and then we'll have a chat."

Harper made an aggrieved sound in her throat. "Then why do it? Why not choose to die with Ron, or any of the other times you could have just lived out and ended your life like a normal person?"

"Because I'm a coward," he said with a phony indifference. "Wouldn't you agree?"

"You're not a coward. You're just a busted human being, and now I am too. What's the point of me, Miles? What's the point of us?"

Miles just laughed. "I'm not sure. And a couple of centuries doesn't change that. Can you live with that, Harper? At the end of all things, can you live with never having an answer to that question?"

"No," she said, and god, it stung like a motherfucker. "I've wasted the last three years of my life, and for what? For what?"

He stood and placed two firm hands on her shoulders. It was strangely reassuring. Very slowly, he turned Harper to face the darkness where Peggy sat, dying. "For her. So, let's make it count, Starling."

She was about to respond when the shriek of a fiddle pierced the air.

She spun around to face him. "Where's it coming from?"

"There's another clearing just through these trees," he said. "They've set up a bonfire."

"Why would—" But then it hit her. Exa's Awakening. A celebration of the end of Exa's annual hibernation and rebirth as a young man. It was celebrated with spirited music and dancing around a bonfire and fruit so ripe it burst against teeth and lips, juices dribbling down chins. Miles pointed through the trees and she saw them: a handful of musicians surrounded by giddy revelers and a growing bonfire gorging itself greedily on the pure, clean air.

"Guess we didn't get far enough from Shinloya," she said, but she wasn't afraid. The Sekundians looked buoyant as they worshipped their god through dance. She knew how it felt to worship something so ardently.

She smiled at Miles, and before he could stop her, she was running toward the fire. The people spinning around the blaze let her in without question, their own troubles melting in the heat of the flames and communal frenzy. Shinloya's boundary would guard them all from violence. Tonight was about rebirth.

She laughed a little crazily when she realized that she, too, knew the moves—it was a common jig on Sekundos, more exuberant than skilled. The goal was not to do it perfectly; the goal was to move. To use their bodies in celebration of Exa and the fertile world that greeted him once his winter slumber ended. And Harper knew this because Argo had jammed the whole history of this place into her little skull, nestled it alongside the latent Incarnate and the Paradox Serum and her psychic partition, a myriad of incongruous invaders, each one with a shorter shelf life than the last.

Where moments before she'd been heavy as an anchor in a furious sea, now she was buoyant, afraid of floating away. Jubilant in her grief, the cementing of it into her fragile bones, the memory of her friend, of herself and of who she had never been now laid to rest in the grave she made in her mind. She had never felt her sorrow so deeply. She was light as air and nearly gone, nearly gone. Even the Peggy-shaped mirage drifting in the dark of the trees around the clearing couldn't distract her, couldn't draw her away.

And then, he was there. Dancing next to her, taller than he had any right to be, eyes shadowed with that same grief, that same heartbreak. The twin of hers. Had it always been that way?

Miles took her hand and they spun, colors and sounds turning into shreds of confetti around them, every person indistinguishable from the rest. Closer and closer, the heartbeat of their sorrow turning into one song, plucked along their twinned heartstrings, tuned to each other. It was strange to be so close to him. There were freckles and flaws she hadn't noticed before—a small scar above his lip, a pockmark below his eye.

At some point, the music slowed, and the dancers swayed together languidly, taking a break from the jig. It was quiet enough to talk. There was Peggy again, drifting at her periphery. An illusion. A wish.

"Are you okay?" Miles asked. His hand lay lightly against her back.

"I . . ." she trailed off, leaning her face against his chest so that she didn't have to keep looking at him, this person who was finally asking her a question he should have asked months ago. "I don't know," she admitted. "I just feel wrung out. Empty. And at the same time, I'm feeling . . . everything. And I'm trying to have hope, because Peggy would have, but it's so hard. I just need something to make me stop thinking for one damn minute. Maybe then I could answer your question."

She pulled back a little. They looked at one another. He saw what she was holding back, keeping in. The destruction, the heartache—she watched him see it. It was in him too.

"If you ask me to," he said, "I will."

He meant it. She could see that he meant it. She thought about what he insinuated, about kissing him, about pouring the rest of it, this blackening celestial debris, into him. Letting him bear the burden of it, at least for a time.

Several things happened then.

A face appeared behind him, that impossible mirage. She smiled, lurid black ooze on her teeth, and Harper belatedly understood through the haze of her euphoria and unthinkable proposals that the Peggy mirage was just the Peggy assassin after all, free, somehow, of the magcuffs. Black blood dribbled from her nose, her eyes, her ears. She looked like some kind of hellspawn, a ferocious creature straight out of an '80s horror flick.

The creature slipped a hand into Miles's pocket and produced two things: a knife, the one the scavenger had brandished at Miles hours earlier, and . . . her confiscated time-traveling device.

"We will wait for you, on Pelegaea," Peggy told her, her voice broken gravel.

She lunged past Miles and buried the knife in Harper's gut. Harper looked down. Saw the hilt of the blade protruding from her stomach.

Looked up. Miles's hands hovered over the handle, but he didn't touch her. She'd heard you weren't supposed to pull knives out, if you could help it. That leaving it in would keep her from bleeding out. But she still felt ripped open, her skin and muscle wrapped around a foreign invader, unsure what to do with it. Now that she had seen the knife, she could also feel the knife, all of its sharp, minuscule movements inside her, ripping through threads of muscle and fat and delicate tissue.

She was having a hard time getting the words up her throat, past her teeth.

Miles looked at her with a strange mixture of anguish and resignation, but before Harper could investigate that expression, the assassin threw an arm around his waist, turned the dial on her device, and smiled that beastly, blackened smile as the pair of them disappeared.

And all around, the music continued, and so did the dancing, and so did the celebration. And Harper, shocked and infuriated and in pain, made her way back to Argo.

She left the warmth of the fire and stumbled back to her clearing, Argo's rusted outline coming back into sharp focus.

Argo did not deny her entry. The door squealed with manufactured age as it swung open for her, anticipating her, and she clambered into the lightless cockpit with extreme effort. She could feel Argo's adrenaline as a shiver underfoot and knew that the ship was aware of what had just happened. Knew Argo was going to do something stupid too, just like her captain. She was going to go after Miles and Peggy, and without any way of communicating, or of overriding Argo's functions, or stopping this ridiculous wound from bleeding out, Harper was only a passenger, helpless to stop her.

Gravity pulled her naval downward—Argo was booting up.

Just as with the VW bus, Argo's rusty interior reflected her new disguise. But when Harper pushed through a small door behind the tattered captain's chair, she found herself at the top of a familiar ladder that led down into the belly of the ship. A guiding light blinked at her from the floor.

"Don't do this, Argo!" she shouted, holding the knife as steady as possible as she descended the ladder from the navigation deck. "Please, please think about this." She staggered through the narrow hall, gasping in pain as the knife jostled with each step. "I know you love him, but this is what the Incarnate wants. If you go to Pelegaea, we're all dead—including Miles, Peggy, and the rest of the goddamn universe."

But Argo didn't hear her.

No one ever fucking heard her. Harper Starling, doomed to be forgotten, left behind, ignored, aching, used. Forget that she'd traveled across time and space to end this nonsense and get her friend back. Forget that she'd been left in an era she didn't know, chased by an assassin in her best friend's skin, infected by an alien parasite; Harper just wanted someone, anyone, to listen to her.

But maybe that didn't matter now. Maybe Harper would simply bleed out inside this ship, and no one would ever know. Miles would die on Pelegaea because he was alone and outnumbered, and she would never see him again. Her parents would mourn her the way she had mourned Peggy—as a shadow. As a dream.

She needed to focus. She was losing too much blood, and with it, her tenuous grip on consciousness. How silly, come to think of it, that something as intricate as the human body required something so easily lost to properly function.

She reached the end of the hall and fell painfully to her knees. She wanted so badly to find the energy to seek some kind of answer. But she didn't have it. She didn't have it anymore. All this time, she'd fought. And now, she simply no longer could. The world went fuzzy, darkening at the edges. She was going to black out in three, two, one—

26.

ARGO
SEASON AND YEAR UNKNOWN

A sound. No, a song. A song she recognized, tinny with age, a classic. Miles Moonraker, warbling from a vintage stereo system. When she opened her eyes, she expected to find herself in the front seat of Argo the muscle car, Miles fiddling with the volume dials as they breezed through the desert.

But she was still at the end of the hallway, and the music was coming from all around.

"Harper Starling!" Miles Moonraker sang from somewhere above, "Harper Starling, listen to me! I can fix you for a time, but it will be temporary, who-oah!"

Harper shook her head deliriously. *That doesn't even rhyme, Miles Moonraker.*

"I will have to remove the partition, do you understand?" Miles's voice crooned with the sweeping music. "You must keep the Incarnate at bay or all will be lost!"

All is already lost, she wanted to say. *I'm not the one who jumped the gun. I'm not the one walking into a trap.*

She rasped, "How long until we reach Pelegaea?"

"Hours, Harper Starling, hours! Can you do it? Who-oah!"

What was left of her awareness understood that this was Argo communicating through Miles Moonraker's classic melody "Stars in the Dark." That she had found a way to circumvent the psychic partition and speak to Harper in this desperate hour. Now it was Harper's turn to convey that she understood.

"Okay," she rasped. "I hear you."

"Get to the engine room, Harper Starling! Get to that golden door!"

"You can't go to Pelegaea," Harper said as she forced herself into a sitting position. Stars crackled in her vision. She urged her agonized body to its feet.

But the ship didn't answer.

Harper grabbed a rung and pulled herself into an approximation of a standing position, biting back a scream as the knife jerked under her skin. She wished she could hear Argo, encouraging Harper along, telling her it would all be okay. She wished Argo could take away some of her pain. But Harper understood why she couldn't; Argo would keep the partition up as long as possible. Harper was compromised. Just like everything else.

And she was moving too slowly.

Little by little, one hand holding the knife as still as possible and the other keeping herself steady against the wall, she walked toward that golden door.

In the flash and the bang of that moment, the knife sliding into her gut, the realities of the situation had melted away. But now, everything was coming back to her: dancing with Miles French/Murphy/Moonraker. Dancers circling a bonfire. A knife in her gut. The look on Miles's face before Peggy grabbed him and turned that little dial. The two of them in Pelegaea, where everything was about to fall apart.

The hallway was just too long, as it turned out. Her energy was all but sapped. She didn't remember the distance feeling like a football stadium the first time, but magical Tesseract Engines were probably funny that way. Probably. It reminded her of a later episode of *Infinite Odyssey*, when one of Argo's settings became stuck and the ship was caught in a perpetual state of expansion and contraction, a universe unto herself, stuck in the moments between the big bang and the inevitable collapse.

Inside the ship, it meant hallways went on forever and ever, until suddenly they were the length of a fingernail, and so were her inhabitants, their matter all squished and bendy. In the end, they realized that if they timed the distance between contractions and expansions, they could get to the engine room and do a hard reset. Time was of the essence, as the Argonaut explained, because at some point Argo would go nova, and in an instant they would all cease to exist.

Come on, Harper Starling, she thought she heard. *They need you.*

She lumbered toward the engine room door, the last two steps feeling like miles and miles, and grasped the golden handle in her slick palm, anticipating the same blistering pain as before. This time, though, the door opened and Harper was bathed in honeyed light, which emanated from the blinding star at the center of the room, the tesseract crystal that powered Argo, which was cradled in a kind of chassis, where it spun slowly like the turning of a world.

"I'm here," she panted. "I'm here. I made it."

For a moment, all she heard was the turn of the engine.

And then, with no warning at all, the psychic partition was gone. A million thoughts that didn't belong to her flooded her mind. Look at that beautiful, beautiful heart . . . Take it, take it for yourself, take it all—*Harper Starling, don't listen to the Incarnate, listen to me!*—It's so lovely, it belongs with someone who can appreciate it, it belongs to you . . . just reach out and—

"Argo!" she screamed through the noise, the need, the pull. "Tell me what to do!"

There is something you must know, Argo said.

"Tell me!"

This will not save you.

Harper screamed again. The voices of the hive were becoming harder to block out. The heat of the crystal engine was too hot against her clammy skin.

It will seal your wound, for a time, Argo continued. *But not forever.*

"How long will it give me?"

Hours, Argo said. *Any more and you would experience a hard reset.*

Hours. Only hours to save her friend. Only hours to save the planet, the galaxy, the universe. She stared into the blinding heart of the Tesseract Engine and tried to summon any regret, any sadness about it. But she was too tired, and the longer the knife was nestled in the hollow it had carved through muscle and skin, the more tissue it found to cut—*snip, snip, snip*—and soon it would slice through one too many things that could not be repaired. And there were more important things, after all, than Harper Starling.

"Then I'll do it," she said. "But you have to promise me something."

Tell me, Harper Starling.

"You have to promise that the minute we reach that fucking planet you will get the fuck out of Dodge. Do you understand me?"

There was a pause. God, this ship was so like a person, sometimes. Like Miles. Charging into danger like a complete idiot. Knowing the consequences and doing it anyway.

I am not an idiot.

Harper laughed. It hurt. "It's you the Incarnate wants, not Miles, not Peggy, not me. You. You have to leave us there."

She felt the ship's grief like a tidal wave.

Then . . . I will leave you there.

"Thank you," Harper said, holding back tears.

Touch the engine, Harper Starling.

It was Argo's voice commanding her, not the Incarnate's. Argo's voice telling her to place a hand against the heart of the most dangerous machine in the universe.

So she did.

Go back and find the you you were before, she heard Argo say as the light blasted so bright she was forced to shield her eyes. *Do not go any further back or—*

She doesn't know where she is, at first. Or she didn't know, or she won't know. It's loud, very loud, like a crowded café where the music is blasting and every conversation being had thinks it is the most important. She's standing on a flat plane, or she was, or she will, which is strange because there is so much activity around her, things moving too fast to see, only the colorful, blurred light trails they leave in their wake. She's worried that sooner or later one of these ghostly light trails is going to crash right into her, but they never do—instead, they seem to race right through, as if she's simply an apparition. She is still bleeding, or she was, or she will be. But the knife is nowhere to be found.

One thing is for sure: she doesn't want to stay here. She's supposed to be looking for something—the her she was before, whatever that means. But she's oddly alert now, despite the bleeding, and she's running out of time, so she takes a step forward, or did, or will, and immediately doubles over in pain. To her horror, the wound begins to congeal. When she touches her skin, it's ice-cold. Death cold.

She goes backward, instead, and to her gasping relief, the wound reopens, the skin warms. She takes another step back, and another, watching in astonishment as the wounded skin begins to knit itself together.

As she crosses the plane, the trails of light around her begin to slow and take shape. Or perhaps she has been here long enough that she can simply see it better. The trails are people, figures traveling at various speeds across the plane. She can see the details on their faces, the expressions they wear, or rather, the details on her *face,* her *expressions. Because they're all her, rushing around, trying to get somewhere. This—this is Harper's timeline.*

She walks through them as they fade and flow from one location into the next—the diner, the row house, the nightclub, Argo, the forest—awed by their complete oblivion, like she's watching them through a two-way mirror. And as she moves, the wound heals further. But, no, healing *is the wrong word; as she crosses her timeline, the wound rewinds like a tape, undoing itself, going back to the beginning. She knows that once it is gone, Argo will want her to leave this place, and no later.*

One more step and the wound is gone, a miracle, and awareness has returned, the haze of her impending mortality lifted. She should go back. She should find the exit and return to the engine room. She should go to Pelegaea and finish what she came to do.

But . . . all the answers are here. All of time is splayed out before her,

her past and her future unfolding, flowering like a rose. To her left, her childhood. Two girls sit in front of the television, watching their favorite show. One with unruly curls her mother never could tame, the other with dark hair high in a ponytail. Just beyond them, their teenage selves ride bikes down Cottonwood Avenue, that same hair flying behind them like capes. Even further, both girls run around in the basement of Harper's childhood house, wearing too-big costumes and imagining that they are the Argonaut and his friend. Young Harper watches Peggy with shining eyes. And further than that, Harper is alone in an apartment bedroom late at night, watching old reruns of that same show, when she gets a phone call . . .

Here, she doesn't need a seer; now, she is the seer.

Harper, *comes a warning voice, but it's her own, and she ignores it.*

To her right, another Past-Harper dances around a bonfire. She looks wild from this perspective, her hair unbound, coils reaching for the sky. Closer to manic than happy, soaking up the firelight and the music and the laughter like a thirsting sponge removed too long from the ocean. It hurts to look at her. To remember.

She moves on, passing herself and Miles as they reunite in the forest, surprised by how bitter the scene makes her feel. Harper, so desperate for love and validation; Miles, finally admitting that he should have been offering it this whole time.

Rapid movement beyond the forest distracts her. It's far away, but something catches the light there, like the glint of sunlight off the glassy surface of the ocean. It's not so far, not really. Alarm bells ring somewhere off in the distance, but the allure of that glistening moment in time is louder. She walks with purpose toward it.

Because this is Pelegaea. And it isn't just any moment—it's the final moment, the last one that matters, the last one, she's pretty sure, on Harper's timeline, period, because her wound peels open, and the pain she remembers so keenly pokes its head out of the dirt, heralding an early spring. Beyond the tarred and ruined city she has only imagined during Miles's stories, there is only a dark eclipse along the flat plane of her life.

The scene before her is chaos. The movements of its key players are frantic, barely discernible, much more like the light trails of her arrival. But through the commotion, she makes out herself, Miles, and Argo presided over by the Incarnate, who orchestrates the wreckage from many different bodies all at once. There is no glee, only stoic concentration. For all their talk of anger and love and hope, the Incarnate is not a person—the Incarnate is only hungry. It's going to subsume them.

Argo isn't supposed to be here. Harper was assured—but she knew better, knows better, will know better. She heard the warning from the mouth of her future self.

It hits her like a bolt of lightning. She is a time traveler now, well and truly, and she knows something important about time travelers. That none of the moments on their timelines are guaranteed. None of the things she sees here, now, are irrefutable. And that she has an imperative message to give.

The Incarnate in her own mind begins to wake up. It's a prickle in her brain, the spark of anger that brought her so very far before. She's running out of time, or she already has. If not now, then when? This is it; it has to be. She remembers her reflection looking both old and young simultaneously, a sloppy double exposure, two incongruous images laid on top of one another by some careless photographer who had not even bothered to line the images up properly in the darkroom. It all makes sense now.

Harper turns from the scene in her future and runs. She knows she is fucking with time, that she is defying the laws that Argo lives by, but she also knows that this happened. Harper has already been here once and would be here again, many times. It was always going to be like this.

She finds Past-Harper in the Starlight restroom, pulls her scarf over her hair, which has gone inexplicably white, and steps into the moment. It's agony. She's both in the diner with her past self—the reek of the bathroom and medicinal hand soap cueing up her own sense memory of this moment—and not in the restroom at all. She is divided, in both places simultaneously, and therefore in neither. She is only in the mirror, watching the past unfold.

Her past self looks at her, startled, with tired, mascara-streaked eyes. She can see how she looks now through the memory of this moment—makeup-streaked face looking somehow intentional with her Sekundian uniform, like war paint. Past-Harper fixes her earring and Harper just watches, transfixed by her former self.

"Where is this?" Harper says. She asks even though she already knows. Her heart pricks. This is the script. She remembers it, somehow, even though she only lived it once.

Past-Harper opens her mouth to respond and requires several tries to get the words out. "Th-the Starlight. With the . . . breakfast."

Harper nods. "It feels so long ago, even though it was just . . ." She smiles, because it's kind of funny, when you think about it. "It's so strange, to be on this side of it. I guess now I am the reflection."

"I guess you . . . are." Past-Harper looks around, baffled. "How are you . . . ? Won't we, I dunno, paradox?"

"No," she says. "I'm not really there. I'm observing you from . . . somewhere else."

The conversation unfolds as she remembers. A few changes here and there, of course—a time traveler's timeline is a tricky, ever-changing thing. She is beginning to understand this too well.

Past-Harper just nods as if to say, Uh-huh, sure, that makes perfect sense. Glad we figured out the deal.

"How are you doing this?" she says aloud.

Pain shoots through Harper's abdomen and she presses her hand against it. Her wound hasn't reopened—this feels more like a warning. Time will not allow her to stay here much longer. "I'm not sure I should answer that. How I got here might be different from how you get here, if you get here at all. I don't want to mess with things."

"Aren't you already doing that? Just by being here?"

Harper shakes her head. She can feel the rest of her timeline pushing in, chaos outside this moment, just at her periphery. "I had to tell you. To deliver a message."

"Where are you?"

Harper gestures around her, until she remembers that her past self can't see anything beyond the mirror.

"I'm . . . everywhere. And nowhere. It's super weird. And honestly, I'm having a hard time keeping it all straight.

"Listen," she says, because this is the crux of it, the real thing she needs, needed, to know. "You have to be careful not to get too angry or upset about

things. The Incarnate is hungry. It wants your hate. Hate is fuel. And with enough fuel, it can do horrible things. It will."

"Like what?"

"Use you to get to the things it really wants."

"Like Argo." Her past self turns a sickly pale green and Harper feels the nausea by proxy. "Argo is powerful."

"If she weren't inherently good, imagine how she could be used," Harper says. "Whole galaxies, turned to dust. Entire civilizations, subjugated or obliterated.

"You have to kill the Incarnate. You have to end this."

Her past self looks queasy. "I just want to save my friend."

"You can't do that if you don't deal with the thing that took her," Harper says.

Harper blinks. The scene around her flickers, like the guttering flame of a candle about to go out.

"How?" Past-Harper says. She looks terrified. "How the hell am I supposed to kill it?"

How do you break the heart of a parasite?

"Simple," Harper says, remembering this part, remembering the answer and still not sure whether it's the right one but hoping, hoping. "You have to love what you hate."

"You want me to love the Incarnate?"

"Hate is a parasite. Starve it out."

God, it sounds so cliché coming out of her own mouth. It sounded mysterious, even wise, before. Now she can see that even her future self, the one she thought she could trust, had no idea what she was talking about.

"Will I, though?" Past-Harper asks. "Starve it out, I mean."

Harper falters. This is not in the script. "What do you mean?"

"You just . . . aren't acting like someone who won."

"I . . ."

The power in the conversation is shifting. If she isn't careful, she'll say something that could alter her past for the worse, not the better.

A twinge at the back of her mind, of seething desire, trying to distract her—to pull her attention back to the engine room. She's been here too long.

Her past self steps closer to the mirror. "Did you find the Off switch? Did you save Peggy?" The scene around them flickers again. The edges of the reflection begin to fade. Past-Harper's voice echoes, far away. Harper is out of time.

"Wait." Past-Harper puts her hand on the mirror. Harper remembers watching her reflection fade out, questions unanswered. "What about Miles? Can I trust him? Can I trust him not to leave me again?"

At this, Harper feels a spasm of anger in her mind. Part of her still hates him for trying to be the hero. For leaving. For not even bothering to hear her.

"Trust is earned," Harper said, the words a bitter memory. "Has he earned it?"

"I don't . . . I'm asking if he will!"

"Tell him," she says to Past-Harper before she can think it through. "Tell him what Peggy told you, and don't let him be a fucking martyr. Tell him it'll just end badly, that your future self knows." She looks up, beyond Harper's shoulder, into the bathroom itself, remembering the other, more pressing problem at hand. "Peggy is close. You have to go."

"Wait—"

"Go!"

"Wait!"

But she doesn't. She steps out of the moment and back onto her time-plane, her whole body sagging with the relief of being whole.

There are so many things she wants to change, so many things that would be better if she could just fix them here, now. But she can't, she knows she can't. The Incarnate will ruin everything if she isn't careful. And she hasn't been careful. She has to get out of here.

"Argo!" she calls. "Argo, how do I get out?"

But Argo can't hear her here.

Harper closes her eyes. She wills herself away from this place, back into reality, to her time, to the shining heart, to the engine room.

EPISODE EIGHT
OMEGA POINT

This week on Infinite Odyssey:

The Argonaut and First Mate Sheena Washington are on the adventure of a lifetime when they're hit with a psychic blast from an enemy ship—and Argo loses her memory! Can they remind Argo who she is before the jungle on Planet Zip eats them alive?

27.

PELEGAEA
SEASON AND YEAR UNKNOWN

Harper gasped awake like someone drowning. She felt like she'd just gone three rounds with a professional wrestler, even though she knew, without having to look, that her wound was gone, and she was sprawled across the floor of the engine room, bloody knife in her hands. But the room looked different than it had before, the light of Argo's heart so dim that Harper might have mistaken it for a regular old machine if she didn't know better. That was probably strange, but she didn't have enough experience to know for certain. Maybe the intensity of Argo's light came in cycles, like sleep.

But that was not the only thing that was strange. It was also quite cool in the room, despite the choking heat that the machine put out when she first entered, bleeding all over the floor. The spinning tesseract had stopped glowing, stopped spinning, and was now still and silent as the dead.

"Argo?" Her voice was cracked and impotent. "Argo, you there?"

Only silence answered her.

She struggled to her feet, gasping at the remnant pain that stung her, a reminder that the time she had acquired was borrowed.

She looked around the room. "Argo? Are you . . . here?"

But the room just felt . . . empty. Empty of Argo's presence, which, until now, could always be felt, even peripherally, a welcome presence at the back of your mind, a comfortable, perfect warmth.

Did something happen while Harper was inside? Had she done something that broke the ship entirely? Maybe that was what Argo's warning was going to be. *Don't go too far, or I'll die.* And Harper, selfish and oblivious, had pranced up and down her timeplane like she owned the place, completely disregarding Argo's fear.

She looked at the incomprehensible engine, wondering if she might be able to make head or tail of how it worked, of what went wrong. Maybe it was a jam. Maybe it was a simple fix.

But when she saw it, she went cold.

It was not a jam. It was not a simple fix. A thin thread of onyx, a seam of what could be mistaken for precious gemstone by someone who didn't know better, winked at her from the surface of the dead tesseract. The Incarnate had hitched a ride into Argo's engine while Harper distracted herself with a conversation with her past. Argo the Tesseract Engine, last of her kind, was taken. It was over.

And it was Harper's fault.

This was what the Incarnate had wanted. When it took Miles's knife, when it hurt her, this was what it had hoped for. And she had delivered it straight into Argo's shining heart.

She picked up the bloodied knife, the only weapon she had with which to protect herself, and fled the engine room, barreling through the belly of the ship to the navigation deck, where, looking out the massive window through which she had once seen beautiful stars, she saw what she feared.

She was already on Pelegaea, and Argo was dead.

While Harper fucked around on her timeline, Argo had taken them inside the once-golden city of Aepholia. She didn't know how she knew, she just . . . knew. But now, the sky above was a burnt smear of polluted brown. And just ahead, the towering capitol building stood quiet and haunted amidst the crumbling buildings and streets that once bustled with life, its columns corroded and dull. Inside, Miles and Peggy waited. She felt them there, their energies muted and cold through the hive mind. The Incarnate had what it wanted. It was over.

Harper felt it too. The finality. The Incarnate inside her, the pull of it, the hate of it. Her psychic partition truly gone now, just like Argo. It would be so easy now to say fuck it and let it win.

And as she stood there, staring at the fallen jewel of a once-shining city, she felt a tug at the center of her being. Let it pull her like a leash toward the door of the ship. Allowed it to press her palm to a crystal device on the wall. Watched with only mild interest as the crystal turned an unnatural prismatic black and the door swung up and out, the release of pressure creating a squeal that echoed painfully in the silent metropolis. She planted her feet on the cold ground and a strange vibration quivered through her, her body an unwilling tuning fork, recalibrating to match the planet's frequency. The invisible string tugged her again, toward the stairs of the capitol. She took one last look at Argo and wished she hadn't; the ship still looked like the rusted Sekundos junker. There were no lights on inside, no engine gently humming. Already, the windows began to smear with black.

Harper tightened her grip on the knife and went inside the capitol.

There was light here, but only just, and she couldn't see the source of it—only the way it refracted off of the hundreds of thousands of black mirrorlike facets the Incarnate had crystallized into over the centuries. A memory; she'd been here before. She recognized these speleothems, these anthodite formations, from a moment in a dream on a frigid New Year's Eve. They had formed inside what Harper imagined was formerly an entry hall, where citizens might have gathered as they awaited an audience with their government.

She pressed a palm to a smooth black plane and yanked it away again—the crystals were alive. They were part of the hive.

The Incarnate tugged again. Time to walk.

What did it matter to her, anyway? What had it ever mattered? She'd already lost everything. But even her everything hadn't been worth very much; Harper Starling led a stagnant, ambitionless life. What had she truly lost? A shitty job at an even shittier diner? A half-finished degree? Even creating *Infinite Odyssey*, a thing she had finally, truly loved even in the absence of Peggy, had been taken from her by the very nature of what time travel was and how it had changed her. How Miles had changed her.

She wondered what her family was doing now. Would they look for her? Would they think she'd been kidnapped, or would they do what Greg Mara had done and convince themselves, for the sake of being able to live their lives, that she'd been in a terrible accident somewhere and that they would likely never find her? Maybe they would chalk it all up to a case of burnout, a young woman snapping, unable to move past the grief of her perpetually broken heart. Probably there would be some relief for her parents in that. No more dealing with the daughter who couldn't get her shit together.

Part of her knew the Incarnate had something to do with the onset of this melancholy, overtaking the determination to save Peggy that had fueled her all this time, and part of her wondered if it even really needed to. If she'd survived on the zealous conviction of her mission for so long that it was finally dying out, swallowed up by her inner, hateful sun. Still, came another small distant voice. If it has to be over, then the least you could do for yourself, the least you've ever done, is go out with a bang.

The sun inside her flared. Adrenaline surged. Rage made a home in her gut. She wanted to see the Incarnate's true face.

She wanted to carve it off.

Something inside her laughed. Images flickered behind her eyes—a cavernous onyx room, hardened, iridescent tar coating the monumental columns that would have shone with gold, once upon a time. Three people standing utterly still at the center of it. Waiting for her.

By now she had circled the capitol and was being led through its mazelike corridors to the towering great hall at the center, where dignitaries and heroes greeted each other beneath the windowed dome overhead through which so much light once poured that it was like standing on a sun. She understood, now, why she knew such things—she knew because the Incarnate knew. Because Jason would have known.

We are here, Harper Starling, came a thought, unbidden. Not Argo. A voice she knew, somehow, though she couldn't place it. We are waiting for you. It was Miles's voice in her mind, and it was not his too.

I know, she thought, because now that she was here, now that she was calibrated, she felt him yearning. And for a moment, it was like the night before, when they were dancing around a fire, wanted and wanting.

We could hear you screaming, Not-Miles said now, even without access to your mind.

You know nothing about me.

It was in the way you moved. In every breath. In every counterfeit smile. How lonely you are. How deeply you wish for the love and hate that you do. It blinds you.

Humiliation burned in her throat at that, and she couldn't explain why. Because it was true. Because Miles had finally seen her, by the light of the fire. And now they were both here, and he had succumbed to the psychic embrace of the hive, and Harper was falling, falling, falling. Because they were not worthy, after all. They were never going to save Peggy. Not when they couldn't even save themselves.

It all comes full circle, in the end.

The corridor flowered open as she made her way toward the grand hall, and the towering ceilings, the columns of glittering black, where kings once met and decided the fate of a world, greeted her.

Three people turned when she entered the cavernous room, all in a line.

"Hello, Harper Starling," they said together. "Welcome home."

28.

RIVERDALE
SPRING, 2020

It was May, and the sweet pink magnolias that dotted the city's parks were in full, fragrant bloom. The sun had burned off the gloom of last night's rain, finals were finally over, and Harper Starling was sitting in her customary booth at the Starlight Diner, nervously twisting a frosty Coke between her sweating palms while she waited for Peggy to arrive. Nervous, because she wasn't sure if Peggy would actually show up—she'd missed their last two standing dates, and both times Harper had made the expensive mistake of ordering the burger her friend always asked for here, only to watch it slowly deflate as it cooled in front of Peggy's empty seat.

Things had been strange between them this year. They'd had a handful of good weeks in their new city, discovering it together in the days before classes started, and then on the weekends after classes started. If asked to pinpoint when the change occurred, Harper would have said it happened the night Peggy met Flora downtown, but she knew, deep down, that it had started even before that. She knew Peggy wasn't enjoying school, and Harper knew it bothered Peggy that she didn't want to go out with her on weeknights, favoring long hours of homework.

But Harper was learning about the framework of the universe; it was everything she'd ever wanted, everything she'd dreamed. This was why she was here at all.

So, Peggy went out on her own and had an amazing time, the most amazing time she'd had so far in New York, and Harper felt a nasty spike of jealousy drive the first splinters of a wedge between them.

Nine months later, here Harper sat, wishing things could go back to the way they were. Before New York, before Flora, before Peggy started disappearing for days, weeks, at a time.

The waitress came by and asked Harper if she wanted to order some food. She opened her mouth to politely decline when Peggy's voice answered. "She'll have the pancakes with bacon on the side, extra crispy. I'd like a cheeseburger, please. Well-done, no onions." The waitress scribbled the order and walked away, and Peggy sat down in the empty side of the booth.

"Hi," she said. She smiled, but it didn't reach her eyes. "Sorry I'm late."

"It's okay," Harper said. She sipped her Coke. "How were finals?"

Peggy looked pained. "They were . . . fine."

"Are you ready for summer? We could do some camping, maybe." Even as she said it, so casual, so nonchalant, a lump built up in her throat. Something about the look on Peggy's face, the way she hadn't taken off her jacket even though it was too warm for layers, gave Harper the strangest feeling.

"Well, look," Peggy said, "there's something I want to tell you."

"Okay."

"Yeah, it's just . . . I'm not coming home this summer, Harper."

"Oh. Well, maybe I could do a short-term rental here or something, and we can go upstate or—"

"No, I mean, I'm going to travel. With someone."

Harper tried to sip her Coke, but her throat was tight and it hurt to swallow. "Who? Do I know them?"

"Just a guy I met. You won't know him. Paul French?" Harper shook her head. It didn't ring a bell. "I know I should have told you sooner; I just got nervous, I guess."

"Nervous?"

"About what you were going to say. How you would react." She pulled her long hair out of its ponytail, and it cascaded over her shoulders. Harper wanted to tangle her fingers in it. To forget what Peggy was saying entirely. "I was afraid you'd be upset."

"I'm not upset," Harper said. In fact, she felt weirdly numb, distant from herself, from this table, from Peggy. "I just didn't think you were into guys."

Peggy looked stricken. They'd never talked so openly about it, though Harper wasn't sure it had ever been a secret. Harper had wished over and over again during their friendship that they *would* talk about it, that they could clear the air and leave room for other confessions. But neither of them had ever mustered the courage. Harper wasn't sure her friend Peggy had ever guessed her truth, the way she'd guessed Peggy's.

"Well, there's a lot you don't know," Peggy mumbled.

"I'm sure there is. My calls only go through a quarter of the time anymore. You don't answer my texts. If you don't want to hang out with me anymore, you can just say that, you know."

"I never meant to disappear. I guess I just needed to figure out what I wanted, you know?"

"What does that mean?"

Peggy laughed bitterly. "Harper, New York was your dream. Columbia was your dream. Becoming an astronaut? *Your* dream. What am I even doing out here? Going to a local school on a track scholarship, failing all of my basic classes? I don't have any other friends, and you're busy preparing to take off into space. Where do I fit in the plan according to Harper?"

"You fit," Harper protested. "We belong . . ."

"What? Together?" Harper was quiet, and Peggy laughed again. Harper didn't like the way it felt like a weapon. "You can't even say it! All these years and you can't just fucking say it. So, that's why I'm going. And I don't know how long I'll be gone. Maybe I just won't come home."

"Fine," Harper lashed out. "You're right. If you're going to be so fucking careless with your life, then I *don't* know where you fit. Go off with that guy, do whatever it is you're going to do, and when you run out of money and you decide to hate him, you'll go home and get married to someone else you hate and have kids you don't want, and that'll be that."

"Wow, Harper."

Harper gathered her jacket. "Yeah, well, why do I want to waste my time with someone who has no future, anyway?"

She scooted out of the booth and left the diner before Peggy could come back with something as shitty as what Harper had just said, overcome by a feral spite at the thought that Peggy would now be left with the bill.

That night she got the first text from Peggy she'd received in months:

> I'm sorry that everything got so fucked up. And I'm saying it now because I'm blocking your number so there won't be another chance. Don't look for me, Harper. I'm never coming home.

This was where it started. The Incarnate wanted her to know it. To remind her that everything that had occurred beyond that day was launched from the dock of this moment. Peggy would be Peggy right now if Harper had not chased her away. Harper deserved to be here—she *wanted* to be here. It was time to embrace her fate.

She looked up, startled out of the memory.

"Stop it," she said, her eyes refocusing. Peggy and Miles stood stock-still next to one another, watching her impassively. But the man beside them was a man she should not have recognized because she had never met him. Only in the stories Miles told, only in the way she imagined him, like something out of a Greek myth. He looked nothing and everything like she'd expected. Olive skin, burnished curls, laughing spring-green eyes.

"But this doesn't make sense," she said to Jason, and her voice was trembling. "You should be dead by now. I mean, look at Peggy, look at . . ." She gestured to her deteriorating friend beside him, the one she had come so far to save—even if it meant death. She tried to meet Miles's eyes, but he couldn't seem to see her.

"This body's circumstances are different," Jason said with a shrug. "That body is sharing a mind with another, the original inhabitant. Though it has been useful for our purposes, that body is rejecting us like an incompatible organ. This body was stronger. Pelegaean. A more appropriate vessel. It is not the same."

"Well, it doesn't matter anyway." She raised her voice, trying to quell her tremors with bravado, but the resounding echo of her words caught her off guard. Quieter, she said, "I'm here to end this."

Pathetic.

His responding laughter shared that grating, rocky sound Peggy's voice had developed. How much of the man before her resembled the Pelegaean hero Miles once knew? How much of it was a show for her benefit, and hers alone?

"How do you plan to end this?" he asked, and he seemed genuinely curious.

"You're a parasite," she told him. "I'm going to starve you out."

He took a step forward, his gait lazy and assured. "You may try," he told her earnestly. He was too close. She gripped the knife harder, but it gave her less comfort than it had before. Could she even use it, if she wanted to? She was frozen in place, the Incarnate lulling her, poking at her mind with deft psychic fingers, keeping her still. "But we already have nearly everything we want."

"Nearly everything?" she said. "But not all of it?" How could that be true? She had hand-delivered the final piece of the Incarnate's puzzle, the one thing she'd vowed not to give him. She'd ensured his victory with her own two hands. What else could there possibly be?

Is it not obvious? He was in arm's reach now. "What is dominion without companions? Without family? We want the thing whose hate screamed so loud we could hear it from across the universe. We want the anguished mind whose pain has fed us so well these last months. Whose love for a disintegrating body has made us yearn for a love like that of our own."

"My hate?" Harper said in disbelief. "I never hated anything. I . . . I was lonely and grieving. I was sad. I was angry. But I never hated anyone."

"You hated me," Miles said, his voice startling and empty. She searched his face over Jason's shoulder, looking for any indication he was himself. But it was all the Incarnate in his eyes.

"Yes," she said, "I hated Miles, but it wasn't . . . I never . . ."

"He was not the only thing," Jason said. "You have near bottomless reserves of it. You are like us; you feed on it too."

"That isn't true."

"That is what we love about you, Harper. We love your hate. It makes us strong. We can make you strong too. Whole."

And then his palms were braced gently against her face, his green gaze searching hers, searching for the thing that made them kindred, made them the same. And his eyes were so . . . so human. Just as alive as they had been when he was just Jason, just an Argonaut, staring down into Miles's eyes, searching for the same thing. The knife slipped from her grip and clattered to the ground. Her stomach fluttered, betraying her. It felt like all the times she'd allowed someone this close, like that night with Anthony after the convention, those moments of urgent want, wishing for connection, for another heartbeat drumming in time with hers, lasting only a few hours before she rebuilt that wall and was alone with herself again.

When Jason looked into her, when the Incarnate looked into her, was that all they saw? When they told her they loved her, was that what was meant? She couldn't help but wonder if he was right after all. If she belonged here, in the gloom, in the dark. If she was resisting a truth too powerful to contest. Harper couldn't love, not really. Not since Peggy. And neither could the Incarnate. In that way, they were the same. They might as well be the same.

As if he could hear her thoughts, the war of her mind, Jason smiled, triumphant. He leaned forward and brushed a curl from her dirty face, the gesture oddly lovely, as if he wanted to get it right. This strange seduction.

"Okay," she murmured, imagining that it was Anthony there, or even Miles. Someone like her.

And then he was kissing her, the Incarnate that had consumed him communing with hers. Feeding it, nurturing it, fueling it.

Everything inside her was wrath and fire, that hateful little sun about to go nova. He was here; he was everywhere; he was winning; and through their linked minds she saw the beginning, the first days of the Incarnate, and she understood.

The parasite had not experienced Life before the Pelegaeans. It did not know what Alive was until it was inside a Pelegaean body, a strong Pelegaean mind, admiring all those delicate nerve endings and synapses, the way they sparkled with electricity and, somehow, created complex thought, reasoning, language, emotions. Fear, rage, sadness, hate. These electrical impulses in the Pelegaean mind and the resultant emotions were Life-giving. Those impulses sparkled through the parasite's own primitive brain, and the parasite, in turn, replaced the Pelegaeans with itself. Before, it was akin to mindless, interstellar anemones. Nothing more than spores, drifting on solar winds. Once inside the whole of Pelegaea, they were born. Made Incarnate.

And she would be too, if she let them in. If she was willing then she would be youthful forever, unlike Peggy, who had been fighting since that day in an alien ocean when they invaded her mind. Harper would be something new. Her fire made crystal, hardened into strength. And everything she had felt since Peggy's disappearance, all that poisonous sorrow, would become something new as well. It would be a relief to feel it, rather than a burden. Part of her forever. It would make her impervious, loved. No one would forget her, or use her, or betray her. No one could.

Not ever again.

Yes, Jason's voice resonated in her mind. We will love you forever.

Love. She remembered something about that, someone's urgent words, a long, long time ago.

Let us show you what we will do.

And then she was not in Pelegaea anymore. She was falling through a starless void, cold and alone. No, not falling—she commanded it, commanded the emptiness, and she was not alone—Jason was with her, his hand firmly in hers. A planet came into view—Sekundos. So lush and fertile from this distance; she remembered the heady air, the sparkling ocean, the crimson forest, the bioluminescent glow of Exa's Lace.

As she watched, the whole planet turned black.

She wanted to be terrified. The right feeling in this moment would be outrage, a horrible sadness. She had known Sekundos. Had breathed the salt of its oceans, relished its air on her skin. But she couldn't summon the grief. Because Sekundos was not dead; it was part of her. Every chlorophyll-seeking vein in every shivering leaf. Every blade of grass. Every drop of blood. It was all hers. Sekundos would one day die, as planets were wont to do. But the Incarnate was life. Now Sekundos would never die.

And the Incarnate, already so much closer to perfect than the day they were Born, would be made better with each new planet, each new species she helped them consume.

It was a vision of things to come; its purity was a rare, shining thing.

You have been so alone, Jason told her. *Abandoned. You have hated yourself. Now you will be full of life. Never alone. Never again.*

Harper ceded control to the Incarnate. And as it spread, little tendrils spider-webbing through the intricate networks of her mind, memories popped like little bubbles and fizzled out, no more room for such luxuries. If she was going to be like Jason, then she had to be empty like him, the way he had allowed the Incarnate to make him when the parasite first found that shining planet. Distantly, she heard shouting, someone screaming a name, but she couldn't tell where the sound was coming from. A memory? That seemed right. She watched several go with only distant curiosity. Felt them leave her without much worry at all. Bad memories, good memories, memories she hadn't thought about in years. Out of business, warehouse clearance, all sales final. Everything must go. Everything must go.

When Harper was eight, she learned how to ride a bike. Her parents worked too much to teach her, so someone else had. A girl her age, a girl she knew. A girl with dark hair and dark eyes and a gap in her toothy grin. The other girls gave her shit for hanging out with Harper at first, but she didn't seem to care. *Sometimes it helps to start by pushing down with the pedal on top*, she told Harper, and so Harper did. She whooped and hollered as she raced down the street, her first successful sprint on a two-wheeled bike. The girl had raced after her, laughing and clapping and cheering.

What was her name?

When Harper was fifteen, she went to homecoming. She danced until she was perspiring, her coiffed hair melting in the heat of the gym, though she didn't mind. She wore a dress that was too tight around the ribs and glimmered with a million sequins, but it wasn't Harper who picked it—it was someone else, a girl with long limbs and laughter like a song.

But what was her name?

When she was seventeen, she lost her virginity to an older boy, a boy who left for college and never called her again. She told the girl in a phone call late one night, whispering so as not to wake her parents. They spent the weekend watching bad rom-coms until those started to make her cry and they switched to reruns of an old show they both loved instead.

When she was nineteen, she was watching that very same show when she ignored a phone call from the girl and learned only later that she was gone, just gone, and that Harper would never see her again.

When she was twenty, she decided to defer school for a year, and then another, and another. And there were no more dreams, the sleeping kind or the ambition kind, for Harper Starling.

Everything must go. Don't you want to be beautiful? Don't you want to be loved? Just like you were when the girl was your friend and everything was easy. Everything is expendable. Everything here is worthless.

Or not quite everything.

Because there it was. Dangling like bait on a hook, incandescent amidst the swirl of fading memories, guttering lights on the marquee of a theater going permanently out of business.

The name. She reached out and held it between her fingers. It warmed her palms. It warmed everything. Something about love. Something about hate.

Peggy.

The bubbles stopped rising. They changed direction, diving down, diving into her, soaking back into her mind, into the skin of her, thought after thought after thought subsumed back into her brain. Peggy and Harper watching *Infinite Odyssey* for hours on end, discussing and dissecting each plot and character thread in exhaustive detail; Peggy and Harper in the science lab after school, chatting with the physics teacher about black holes; Harper alone in her room, watching the Argonaut zip across the universe, year after year on the anniversary of Peggy's disappearance. Peggy's favorite candy bar ("Baby Ruth is for sociopaths," she told Peggy once, to which Peggy'd replied, "At least I'm a gorgeous sociopath."); the name of Peggy's crush in fifth grade, the one she wouldn't admit but Harper guessed all the same. She was no longer a rapidly emptying vessel. She was solid as stone.

For the first time in months, Harper's mind was glass-clear, bright as a star. It was an incorruptible assuredness, fishhooked into her latent desires and pulling her into full awareness, picking up the pieces of her that had scattered across her subconscious. It went deeper than the places that missed her best friend, deeper than the ones that had hated and hated and hated. It plugged her directly into the darkly beating heart of the planet that had once been Pelegaea. If the Incarnate could invade her, then it could go both ways—she could invade it too.

She saw the Incarnate's heart in her mind's eye, pulsing at the hot core of the world. She wrapped her psychic fingers around the shivering nerve that connected the heart of the hive, breathing hate into the world and beyond, to the bodies the Incarnate had stolen scattered across the galaxies, and she didn't let go. Emotions kicked in left and right, exploding inside her like fireworks, and memories, too, small dumb memories. Big important memories. And Peggy. And Peggy. And Peggy.

Love what you hate.

You have hated yourself.

She opened her eyes and realized that Jason was no longer kissing her. He had stumbled backward, his stolen face a mask of shock, his fingers twisted against his mouth. Something black and iridescent leaked from his lips.

Love what you hate.

She hadn't understood when she heard the words out of her future self's mouth. When she watched the Argonaut explain to his new friend how he planned to defeat the Kixorians on that curved planetarium screen. She hadn't understood when she said them to the reflection of her past in that bathroom mirror. But she understood them now. It wasn't hatred for Miles or the world or Peggy.

You have hated yourself, the Incarnate had said.

It was time to fix that.

And then: pain in her gut. Such horrible agony that she was ripped from the beautiful dream and spat out onto the stone floor of the capitol. She opened her eyes but couldn't get her bearings straight, nausea crawling up her throat as the room tilted around her. She looked down at her stomach and willed the nanotextile bots in her Sekundian garb to clear away from the skin so she could see the wound that had sealed shut begin to unknit itself, stitch by horrifying stitch.

Time had caught up. She was almost out of it—but it would have to be enough. She was linked with the center of the world now, from where the energy of the hive radiated. She held the Incarnate's mind between her psychic hands. It was so clear now how she was going to end this.

Because it was Argo who had loved Miles enough to risk her life, to risk being exposed to the Incarnate just to save the person who'd spent so much of his life with her. Argo who had saved Harper when the Incarnate left her for dead. It was Peggy whose love had kept her fighting all these years, denying the Incarnate, rejecting and rejecting and rejecting. And it was Miles who had saved her, and then tried and tried to save her again. And when she looked at Miles now, recalling too easily how she had felt all the times he had let her down, she did her best to see the space-and-time traveler she had loved so ardently as a child—only a man, after all, who had lost his way.

Love what you hate.

She stumbled to her feet. Jason was on his knees now, still in the aftershock of being ripped from the illusion, of Harper's mind kicking him out, kicking the whole hive out. Black oozed from his eyes and his mouth. She felt something wet against her cheek. Her fingers came away slick with Incarnate—dripping from her eyes like tears. There was a grim satisfaction in that—finally, she and the Incarnate shared something real.

But it was the figures behind Jason, the ones who had, only moments ago, been steady under the hive's thrall, that caught her attention. They were both on their knees now, hands to their aching heads, warring with what was left of the parasite in their minds. She felt the hive wrestle in her psychic grasp, but she did not let go.

Starve it out.

"Harper!" Miles coughed flecks of black. "What did you do?"

She closed the space between them, got down on her knees, and stared him in the face, knowing she probably looked monstrous.

"I love you," she said. "You are such an asshole, Miles, but then, so am I, and I think it's for the same fucking reasons. I think we're both under the impression that we don't deserve to be loved."

"You're bleeding." He reached for the wound but again stopped short of touching it. Harper watched as the nanotextile bots there reformed into a thick pack of gauze. She turned to Peggy, hoping to find her friend awakening after three years of sleep. But Peggy just stared into the middle distance, and Harper worried she was already dead, her mind finally torn apart by the Incarnate. She gripped Peggy's cold hand anyway. At the back of her mind, she felt the hive clench tight in pain, her emotions tunneling into their core, starving them of hateful fuel.

"I love you," she told her companions, relishing the way the Incarnate resisted and fought back against the love with which she now held them firm. She could feel their agony, both in her own mind and at the center of the planet they had become. But she held firm.

Peggy blinked, and Harper's heart ramped up. "I love you," she said again, rewarded with another twitch of Peggy's Incarnate-leaking eye, a tremble of her blackened lip. "Even when you can't love yourself, I love you." Peggy made a small strangled sound.

It wasn't enough. The Incarnate's grip on her was still too strong, too spiteful. They would hold onto her until they were both dead, long after Harper crushed the heart of the world with her metaphysical hands. Harper was a telepathic being now, but she didn't know what to do.

I need help, she thought desperately.

And was heard. Miles's hand on hers, the other against Peggy's perspiring temple. Of course—the Paradox Serum in their veins gave them access to many psychic frequencies, not just the loudest ones. If anyone could find Peggy, it was them.

Harper mirrored his action, closed her eyes, and stepped into Peggy's mind.

29.

PELEGAEA
SEASON AND YEAR UNKNOWN

Into Peggy's mind they dove, pushing past the spongy cobwebs the Incarnate had left in every corner, every intelligent fold. She felt the pulse of the Incarnate's heart in another realm of her mind, and she kept one psychic hand there, wrestling it into submission. When she looked at Miles, Harper found he was already watching her, waiting. Absolute trust, an almost alien thing to behold in his eyes. He wanted her to tell him what to do.

So, she listened. And in the bone-deep cold, in the anger that pulsed here, a gentle, wrathful Incarnate hum, still clinging to Peggy's brain matter like the parasite they were despite the loss of connection to the hive, Harper heard her. Screaming into the void the parasite had created.

Ahead, Harper said, and Miles followed her lead. The farther in they went, the brighter it became. Scattered memories seemed to have eroded more slowly closer to the core of Peggy's mind, pieces of who she was still untouched—dying, but free of the darkness that had hardened into crystal everywhere else. There was Harper's face, hazy but real, and a stuttering clip of an episode of *Infinite Odyssey*. There was Flora in the club at Rockwood that night in New York, smiling at Peggy like she was the sun, and there was Miles months later, his face gaunt but happy as he approached Peggy in a coffee shop and told her who he was. And there, there was the Starlight Diner, a memory that glowed like a star all its own—a happy place, a safe place. Harper had never known Peggy felt that way, until now.

They went inside.

Peggy sat in their booth, head in her hands. All around them, the same two stanzas of "Galaxy Man" looped through the jukebox's shitty speakers, as if the rest of the song had been cut out. Full plates of food sat steaming on the tables—pancakes and bacon, burgers with fries, the diner's dubious cherry pie, and globs of vanilla ice cream. Otherwise, the Starlight was empty. Peggy muttered to herself, unaware of their entry.

"Peggy," Harper murmured. "Peggy, it's me."

Peggy did not hear her. Harper stepped closer.

"Peggy, I'm here. I came all this way. I came for you. Please—try to hear me."

Peggy rocked back and forth, muttering to herself, oblivious to Harper's presence. Harper looked to Miles, asking for advice without saying anything at all, and he nudged her forward, as if to say, *You know what to do.*

Harper knelt at Peggy's side and reached for her hand. Peggy gave it but continued her unintelligible chant.

"Where are you right now?" Harper asked her.

"I am nowhere," Peggy said automatically, and there it was. The spark.

"Peggy," Harper tried again, and this time she did not say the words with fear. "When I told you that you were careless . . . when I said you had no future . . . it was horrible to say those things. I didn't even believe them; I just wanted to hurt your feelings, like mine were hurt." Peggy's gaze was on her now, unfocused but listening, the words piercing through the haze, just a little. "The truth was, I never felt good enough for you. Everyone loved you, Peggy, but no one loved you like I did, and I never knew how to tell you that. I never knew how to make you see. So, I just didn't. I was a coward. But I didn't come all this way not to tell you." She wiped her tears away. "I love you. Everything else doesn't matter. I love you."

And Peggy blinked slowly. Once, twice, as if emerging from the grip of an all-encompassing dream.

"Oh god, Harper," she said, "you're really here." And it was Peggy's voice, strangled and raw. Peggy's voice that was hoarse from crying. It was Peggy reaching to hold Harper, to wrap her tight in strong arms that belonged to no one but herself. Not the Incarnate, not the hive, not Jason. Not anymore. And even in this dreamscape Peggy had built to protect herself, she felt solid and real and whole.

Harper gasped in sudden pain, and Peggy gave a feral cry as she noticed the blood-soaked gauze against Harper's stomach.

"Harper, what happened?"

"Get out of here," Harper gritted out. "We'll meet you on the other side."

The pain of the wound yanked her screaming out of Peggy's mind and back into the capitol.

Now back in her own body, Harper watched over Peggy's shoulder as Jason got back to his feet, panting like a wild animal caught in a trap.

She should have been scared, but she barely felt it now. She was electrified. Peggy was here. Peggy was real. Peggy was free. When she looked at Jason, she could see everything inside of him was breaking. Just like her. Just like all of them. But she was different in the most important way: She was capable of big, terrifying love and she deserved, finally, to give some of that to herself. If no one else was going to, then by god, Harper had to be the one to do it.

You've fed on my hate, she told the Incarnate. *My self-loathing and my bitterness.* The parasite writhed, still trapped in her psychic grip, their fuel source waning. She was flooding their engine with bad gas.

Her strength was bleeding out of her, but she thought she might have just enough to finish this. She pushed herself unsteadily to her feet. It hurt. But she had the upper hand, now. It was time to cast the Incarnate out—out of her mind, out of her friends, out of this planet. "But what happens," she said with a grunt, "when all you've got is love?"

She watched Jason fall motionless to the floor. It was like watching someone yawn—the minute he hit the ground, her own body swayed, the room spinning until her legs buckled in solidarity.

"Oh my god," she heard Peggy say, and it was like music—Peggy was there, her arm nudging under Harper's, holding her up, holding her steady. "Honestly, could you be any cheesier?" Peggy smiled at her, and then she was crying too, black tears streaking across her beautiful, scarred face, and it was enough simply to look at her—in that moment, Harper's pain was gone.

"Yes, I bet I could be," Harper laughed. "Should I try?"

Music echoed through the cavern before Peggy could respond.

Harper looked at Miles. "What is that?"

But she didn't need his answer; in the next moment, a vintage muscle car burst through the cavern entrance, blaring Miles Moonraker songs from its tinny, retro speakers, headlights catching every dark mirror face and refracting like a disco ball.

"Holy fucking shit," Harper said.

Argo's tires squealed across the black floor, and she screeched to a halt in front of them. She had driven up the capitol steps, straight through to the great hall.

Harper laughed incredulously. "I thought I killed you!"

The Incarnate is breaking, Argo sent, *but you are weak. We need to amplify your signal to get rid of them for good.*

"How do I do that?"

Pop the hood.

Harper did as she was told.

There, glowing up at her, was Argo's shining engine, as bright as she remembered, no Incarnate left.

"Will it take me back to the timeplane?"

I will send you where you need to go. You will know what to do.

Harper was finding more and more that she trusted that to be true.

She took Peggy's hand in hers. To her right, Miles watched the scene with an unreadable expression.

"Miles. I need you to take Peggy's hand."

"What?"

"Take it, so I can navigate us."

"Navigate . . . Harper, what are you talking about?"

He really had no idea what Argo was capable of. All those years he'd traveled with her, and he'd never bothered to see just how far her power went. Well, that ended now.

"It must suck to not know," Harper said with a grin and was pleased when he seemed to understand the gentle chastisement and took Peggy's outstretched hand.

Then, her hand was on Argo's crystal engine for the second time that day and the world around them spun out.

Down, down, down they went. Incorporeal, inconsequential, they moved through the Incarnate, through the stone and rock and membranes of ancient sediment that had compacted in the aftermath of the big bang and formed this doomed little rock that had once been a glowing beacon of ambition and war and heroes, that innate Pelegaean sensibility distilled and perverted by the parasite down to the essence of what once drove the people of this world: Wrath. Ambition. Manifest Destiny. Hate. Harper could not see her friends, but she felt them there, hands still clasped by the car back in the cavern, and the deeper their minds went, the more deeply she felt them. They burned bright inside that grim place; even Miles, uncertain as he was, seemed finally to understand what needed to be done.

Doubt rose up out of the shadows but died against their fire. She thought about the planetarium, the feeling that burst inside her each time she was enveloped in the starry twilight of the dome theater. She thought about the sensation of typing out a screenplay for the very first time, the clink of fresh ice in the glass of scotch Anthony brought her after a job well done each night. She thought about the fullness in her heart when Peggy used to look at her, much like she'd looked at her only moments ago, the Incarnate's hold on her mind shattered. She carried the three of them through the aphotic darkness toward the core of the world.

And there they were. Their black crystalline heart shivering, afraid. A wave of hatred hit them, slowed them, obscured the planet's core from sight—fear and bitterness and anger, the livid components of the awful sun that had once burned inside her. All at once, she remembered how it felt to be abandoned. She remembered how it felt to be alone. And, god, it hurt but it was familiar too, a comforting kind of misery. It would be so easy to let it press down on her like a blanket, retiring her from the fight.

For a moment, they were stalled in the gloaming.

Fight them! Harper screamed, as much for herself as for them. *Remember what you love! Keep going!*

And then they lost one of their number. Suddenly, painfully, like an arm being ripped away, and the fear invaded their light, and they were shoved back.

Miles! Miles, come back! We need you!

There was no answer. The shadows around them were thick as molasses, swift as spilled ink bleeding across a blank page. The Incarnate was coming for them. They would consume them, as they nearly had so many times these last months.

But then, someone was singing. Someone was singing, and for a moment, Harper just stopped and listened. It was a memory, one of hers, or several, or maybe none of them at all. Maybe the voice was here and now, or maybe it was the girl at her side, pushing back against the overwhelming desire to sit down and give in.

If you wanna know, I'm a galaxy man, Peggy sang, like it was taking everything she had to get the words out, to push the melody through her clenched teeth. But she was doing it. *It's dark out here, but I do the best I can.*

The syrupy darkness slowed its advance. Harper smiled without meaning to.

And when I say I love you, I know you understand!

Leave it to Peggy to sing at just the worst, stupidest, best times. A thing Harper would never have thought to do. Leave it to Peggy to make her laugh in the face of giving up.

Without you I'm alone in the wide universe, Peggy sang, luciform unto herself, free for the first time in three years. *I'll never let you leave me, baby; nothing could be worse!*

And it was working. The light around them flared again, chasing the swiftly retreating darkness.

Could you be any cheesier? Harper said.

Peggy was a force of light at her side. *I can try.*

And then they were through. They were reaching with incorporeal hands and hearts and minds, with all the love in their hearts, toward the center of the world, until they were inside of it. Filling it with warmth, with hope, with love. Wiping out the fierce bitterness that festered there, obliterating the hatred that had rotted for centuries, a seeping, mortal wound.

Time to go, Argo sent, and ripped them out of that place.

They slammed back into their bodies and hit the floor hard.

"Are they dead?" Harper managed to ask. She pressed a hand to the nanobot gauze over her stomach—it squelched, thick with blood. "Did it work?"

Peggy pushed herself to her feet and helped Harper stand. Her own face was slick with feverish sweat and remnants of the Incarnate. How long could she last in this place? Only last night she'd been near death, battling with the hive, rejecting them, as Jason said, like an incompatible organ. What was going on inside that Harper couldn't see?

"I'm not sure," Peggy said. "I still feel it."

"Me too." Harper looked around. "Where's Miles? What happened to him?"

"He's there." Peggy pointed.

Harper turned.

In the beam of the headlights, a dance was unfolding. The Incarnate, inhabiting the body of a man once named Jason, circled Miles, neither figure advancing nor retreating. In Miles's hand, the scavenger's knife, gooey with Harper's congealed blood. In Jason's, a wicked shard of onyx.

The planet trembled again. She didn't want to call his name, to distract him, but they needed to get out of there. Pelegaea was shaking apart; it wouldn't wait for them to escape. They would be flung out into space like so much celestial debris. Harper wasn't so worried for herself—she was pretty sure half of the room's violent spinning was her own blood-loss-induced vertigo and that soon enough it wasn't going to matter what she did. But she'd come here to save her best friend, and that was what she planned to do.

"Hey, Jason!" she said. She hadn't thought this through, but there was no taking it back now.

He didn't turn. "Incarnate, then," she tried, but still his focus remained on Miles.

"Not helping, Harper," Miles muttered.

"Hey, parasite," she tried, and this time, he did turn. What faced her now bore little resemblance to his former youthful appearance. Now his skin was sickly gray and cracked, his muscle rot-black beneath it, it too peeling away, revealing glittering black bone under it all. There was nothing of the real Jason left in this crumbling body. It was just a disintegrating piece of the Incarnate, disconnected from the hive, hopeless.

"You," he said, and it was like the rumble of an earthquake. Inhuman, no longer trying. "We offered you everything."

He stumbled toward her, his movements stilted and wrong.

"Nothing I didn't already have," Harper said. She felt strangely brave as she watched him stagger toward her. Maybe it was exhaustion, or the wound slowly leaking her last reserves of self-preservation, or Peggy, who was leaning on Argo, breathing hard. Maybe it was this full heart, refusing, even now, to give the Incarnate anything at all to feed on.

Jason put a hand on her throat, but he didn't squeeze. This close to him, she saw that even though the rest of him was falling apart, his eyes, his eyes were still an unearthly green. Still capable of anguish, of heartbreak.

"Even if we kill you," Jason said, and she thought that was sadness she detected in his gravelly voice, "nothing will change. We are dead already."

"You had a beautiful vision for the universe," Harper told him. "You just didn't know how to make that happen. Now it can."

"Now it can," Jason repeated, as if he'd never considered this before.

Over his shoulder, she met Miles's eyes.

A stalactite dislodged from the ceiling and fell, crashing with the deafening shatter of a mirror against stone. Jason, as if he could sense him, turned to face Miles head-on as Miles lunged. The knife met skin. Jason's eyes went wide. And Miles, using all his strength, pushed the knife through. But Jason was not human, not even Pelegaean anymore, and his body had hardened into black diamond. He lifted a hand and Miles dodged backward, expecting a swift strike or a continuation of the fight. But Jason only grabbed the hilt of the knife and drove it home. His mouth fell open in a soundless scream. Miles caught him, and together they slid to the floor.

She felt the moment the planet died. A quiet gasp, an inconspicuous exhale, a final breath. The Incarnate, and Pelegaea, were dead.

The tremors intensified.

"This place is going to blast apart," Peggy said. "We have to go."

"Miles!" Harper yelled. He did not look up from his place on the ground, bent over the ruined man he had once loved. "Miles, we have to go!"

"Leave me," he muttered.

That was it. The nanogauze against her stomach was soaked through. Her legs could barely hold her upright. The world was shaking apart. This was the last straw.

Harper used her remaining strength to march toward him.

"Fuck you," she said. "I did not come all this way just for you to be a selfish, insufferable rescuee. End of discussion. Now get up."

It was easier to let some anger rush back in than to look at the body on the floor.

Miles did as he was told and stood. The movement was too quick; her mind couldn't parse it. She saw him in doubles. The adrenaline of holding the Incarnate fast in her psychic grip, of flooding the hive with love, had worn off. The reality was, Not-Peggy had killed her back on Sekundos. She was living, quite literally, on borrowed time.

Another spear of Incarnate crystal fell and shattered.

"We have to move!" Peggy shouted at them over the din. The world was fuzzing out, but Harper wasn't scared. In fact, she felt pretty damn good about everything she had done. About the things she had accomplished. About the things she now knew about herself.

"It's okay," she told them. "I'm okay."

She couldn't hold back anymore. She was ready. She looked at Peggy one last time and smiled, hoping she understood. Miles said nothing, but he didn't need to. For once, she could see it in his face.

The world spun away and became an ocean of stars, and Harper Starling dove in.

AFTER

NEW YORK CITY
WINTER, 2023

She felt like she'd been dropped in front of a truck. Her mouth tasted like cotton and pennies. There was a gross, spitty film on her tongue that made her want to vomit. She had to pry her heavy eyelids open, flecks of sleep flaking off into her eyelashes as she blinked. She couldn't remember anything but static. She groaned. It felt good to groan.

"Oh, hey, steady," a voice said, the sound garbled and strange in her half-awake ears, and she whipped her head in surprise, causing another spasm of pain.

"Peggy?" Her own voice was mangled and raw.

The person sighed. Not Peggy. No, now that she really heard it, that familiar voice, her mind rebooting too slowly for comfort, she knew. It didn't belong to her best friend.

It belonged to Miles.

She opened her eyes.

His blurry form stood by the hospital bed, holding her hand lightly, like even the barest touch might break it. There was a blanket and pillow tossed carelessly onto the armchair beside her, and a few books on the side table she would never have picked up. He must have been sleeping there, next to this hospital bed. That was strange. Then again, maybe not. She was confused. Things were confusing. Words were coming back to her in the wrong order. Her mouth didn't want to pry itself open to say them.

"What happened?" she managed.

His mouth quirked. "How far back shall I go?"

How far back? A good question. Just how much could she puzzle together? Everything was fragmented. Bits and pieces floating around in the void, the debris of some obliterated planet drifting in the vacuum of her mind.

"Am I on drugs?" This would answer her question, of course. The question of why nothing made sense.

"Of course you are, Harper. You were badly hurt. We thought . . . Well, it doesn't matter."

"Hurt. Right. Yes. Good."

"Good?"

"Not good. Just good that I know."

Miles tilted his head. "Do you remember?"

"Yes. And no." It didn't matter, anyway. None of it mattered. How she got hurt. Why they were here. The only thing she wanted to know, the most important thing, was—

"Where's Peggy?"

She reached for that psychic connection at the back of her mind before remembering that it was really, truly gone.

His face fell. Perhaps he'd hoped they wouldn't get to this part so soon. Perhaps he'd hoped they never would. Well, Harper had never been very good at doing what was expected. Ask her mother. Hell, ask Miles.

"She left," Miles told her. "She made sure you were taken care of, and she left."

Ah, yes. Not too drugged to cry.

"So, she's alive."

Miles nodded. "She's alive. She was here a few days too. They wanted her to stay longer—wanted to run a battery of tests, couldn't believe what they were seeing—but she slipped out in the night. No one knows how."

Harper swallowed hard. She wanted these damn tears to stop. "That's an assassin for you."

"I suppose it is."

"Did she say where she was going?"

Miles shook his head. "Just that she was sorry. And that . . . that she loved you."

It should have felt like losing her all over again. But it was, strangely, a relief. She'd chased Peggy for so long, desperate to free her from that mental prison, that now she'd done it, Harper mostly just felt deflated. Maybe that was the morphine talking, but she didn't think so.

"I'm sorry," she said, squeezing his hand. "I know you loved her too."

The words were a kind of permission Miles had never given himself, and they wept together in that sterile hospital room. It felt nothing like the other times she'd cried over her friend. It felt final. And once the tears had mostly dried, they talked. They talked about Pelegaea, and the Incarnate, and Jason, and Peggy. They reminisced about Sekundos, what almost was and wasn't, teased each other about the club, and the diner, and their pigheadedness. They talked about 1971, and the still-unanswered questions about the note passed to her at the café and the convention and the house key sent to her from some mysterious observer. She told him again about watching the pilot of *Infinite Odyssey* on the planetarium screen and the riddles it left her with. She told him about the people she had grown to love there, the people she now missed.

She was not the same person she had been when Miles arrived on her street over three months ago. Which was terrifying, because it meant all the ways she'd allowed herself to be complacent in her own life were no longer acceptable. She wanted to be someone. She wanted to pursue her passions and discover new ones. She wanted to travel for selfish reasons; no more mad dash rescues across the galaxies.

"Your parents were here earlier," he said after a time. "They'll be back tonight. They're worried about you. There's an investigation, of course."

"Oh." She couldn't help the small laugh. "Because I was stabbed." It was such a small piece of the entire fractured puzzle.

"And because you disappeared for several months," Miles said guiltily.

"Well, that's perfect then," Harper replied. "We'll say I was kidnapped or something. That I got away."

"They'll be looking for the perpetrator, Harper. What if they arrest someone? Someone innocent?"

"Well then, you'd better get going," Harper said brightly. "Because it's your description I'm going to give them."

"You're lucky I've grown to like you." He stood. "And so am I."

A spike of panic sat her upright, and she gripped his hand. "Where are you going?"

"I'm just getting something to drink, Harper. I'll be back."

The tea he brought her soon after was hot and bitter. When the sun set outside, he read his book at her bedside, and when he asked if she wanted music, she told him to play Miles Moonraker. Even though it clearly pained him to hear it, and she mostly asked to tease him, they listened to that long-lost version of the Argonaut as he crooned about a man adrift across the galaxies. When she awoke the next morning, there he was, snoring softly in the chair beside her bed.

It was a start.

DENVER
SUMMER, 2024

Harper Starling sat in the dining room drinking a cup of coffee. It was late; only the light above the table illuminated the dusty gloom of her parents' house.

She paid the night no mind as she typed out the last few lines of a new episode of *Infinite Odyssey*, for which inspiration had struck just as she was preparing for bed. Anthony had been the writer of the two of them, but while lying in her hospital cot, the ideas came to her unbidden, born from the fluorescent boredom of the sterile room and the seemingly endless time she had to ruminate on the things that happened. Once released, she'd ended her lease on the Harlem apartment and, though it felt unexpectedly bittersweet, quit the Starlight Diner.

All of this, of course, was more ceremonial for her than anything—after four months of no rent and no-shows while she was stuck in the '70s, her things had been dumped on the curb and taken away and she'd been removed from the diner schedule without fanfare.

Though she had insisted it was temporary (there was a much more comfortable bed waiting for her in a town house in 1972 Greenwich), she moved back into her parents' house in Denver and had been sleeping in her old bedroom upstairs for the past six months. Her mother seemed to need to dote on her, and Harper couldn't dispute that healing from her wounds, both mental and physical, had taken longer than expected.

Next to her computer and her mug sat a tarnished old harmonica, the same one she'd dropped while running from Not-Peggy all those months ago. She'd found it under the radiator in the foyer of her old apartment building, exactly where it had fallen months before, just with a fine new coat of dust. She'd brought it back with her to Colorado and cleaned it thoroughly and scrubbed it with an old toothbrush, much to her mother's somewhat alarmed confusion. What did Harper need with an old harmonica? Wasn't she concerned that it had been sitting under that radiator for so long, gathering dirt and bugs and who knew what else? But Harper had simply kissed her mother's cheek and continued with her ministrations.

She didn't go anywhere without it, and when she'd finally put it to her lips several days before, the sound was just as unearthly as she remembered: strangely pitched, decidedly unmusical.

Miles the Argonaut had not delayed in answering the call.

A tap on the sliding door pulled her attention away from the computer. Outside, his familiar lanky figure was silhouetted in the moonlit glass.

"Stop being dramatic," she called, "and come inside."

He opened the door and walked into the dining room. He was wearing the same suit he'd worn all those months ago at the planetarium—the same suit, in fact, that she'd picked out for him just a few days before from the closet of the Greenwich row house in 1971. Once she'd figured it out, a lightbulb moment in the hospital, it was easy to put everything into motion. She should have known, after everything, that Harper Starling had saved herself.

His face was now a decade younger, if not more, thanks to Argo. It had been a startling change, at first, but she was getting used to it. She liked that the transformation had not only wiped away the exacerbated age he'd brought on himself thanks to alcohol and spite, but the gaunt exhaustion he'd carried around for so long seemed to have diminished as well. This was the same youthful face he'd worn when she approached him at the planetarium on New Year's Day.

"I could never figure it out before," she said when she first told him the plan. They had gone back to the row house in Greenwich, where she fit him with a bow tie for his suit, the same one he would be wearing at the planetarium when her past self found him there. "I didn't understand why you couldn't seem to remember that your younger self had met me at the planetarium."

"You don't think it's kind of cruel, playing games with your past self?" he had asked.

Harper shook her head. "It happened, and I needed it to. I needed to hear you say that the universe could fall apart if I didn't do the show. And if you'd still been the version of you that left me there, I would have been too angry to hear it. This is how it needs to go."

"So, I'll go the planetarium, pretend to be the me I was before Peggy, and let you berate me relentlessly, all so I can tell you that I have no idea what's going on and that if you don't work on the show you might destroy the universe?"

"Precisely."

"Well. It's been a minute since I did any theater, but I'm sure I can muster up my old talent."

"I'm sure you can."

"And the notes?"

Harper had pulled the envelopes out of her pocket and pressed them into his outstretched palm. "The top one goes to the café, the next one is the one you give me at the convention, and the bottom one is the key to the house. I tried to disguise my handwriting so I don't know they're coming from me. Which is an odd thing to say out loud, now that I think about it. Oh!" With a wistful sigh, she had retrieved the harmonica from her pocket and put it on top of the pile. "This goes to the guy at the club with the bushy mustache. Got it?"

"Got it," he'd muttered while she fixed his hair. "And remind me why this is even necessary?"

"I went back and looked at the credits of *Infinite Odyssey*," she told him, "and Susan Feldman was all over them. She wrote fifteen episodes."

"So?"

"So, the point of going back was never to save me from you or from Peggy," she said as she straightened his tie. "And Argo knew it, even if you didn't. Now, if you'll excuse me, I have a sleepy projectionist to visit."

Miles had not questioned the plan again.

Now, in her parents' dining room in Denver, he pulled the bow tie free of his collar and set it on the table. "Is there coffee?"

"Just a little."

Miles retrieved a mug for himself and filled it, then leaned his newly young form against the counter and watched her. Though he'd only met her parents a handful of times, he often stopped by late at night and now knew the layout of the kitchen like the back of his hand.

"So?" she said. "Is it done?"

"It's done."

"The key too? And the harmonica?"

He nodded impatiently. "Yes, yes, it's all done. You should have warned me you'd be yelling on the street, though."

"I thought the surprise would be more fun." She put her mug in the sink, then picked up a completely full duffel bag from the foot of the chair and set it on the table. "I've packed this time so I won't have to buy all new clothes when we get there."

He feigned disinterest, but Harper didn't mistake the glint of curiosity in his eye. "Oh, I see," he said. "You have a trip planned, do you?"

"An extended holiday, even," Harper replied. "If you will."

"I might. Where is this extended holiday taking place?"

Harper grinned. "New York. June 1972."

Miles tried so hard not to smile, the prick. But he couldn't seem to help himself.

Harper tucked her computer into her backpack. "I've been writing."

"Go on."

"About you." She started for the back door. "I assume you parked out back?"

"I didn't know there was parking anywhere else. Here, let me."

He opened the door and pulled it shut once they were both through. The air was crisp, that mountain cool of Colorado summer. In the alley, a vintage muscle car sat idling, the music she knew was blasting inside inaudible from out here.

"Your parents know, then? That you're going?"

"Oh, yeah. They think I'm going to spend the summer catching up on work so I can start school again in the fall."

"You will go back, won't you?"

"One day," Harper said. "But there's plenty of time for that."

She crossed the fence that bordered the yard, leaving the grass and hitting pavement. She reached for the door handle. She could hear Miles Moonraker warbling on the tinny old speakers inside. A familiar feeling warmed her as she opened the door, the presence of another mind, another being she knew and loved, saying hello.

Miles got in on the driver's side and turned toward her.

"Well then, Harper Starling." He smiled at her. "Where to first?"

"The Starlight," she said, "1972. I'm craving pancakes. Then, the planetarium, November 1971. I owe a projectionist a visit."

Argo hummed her agreement, and Harper felt that familiar pull at her naval. The alley dissolved around her in a sea of falling sparks, and the world blinked out for a split second before blinking in again. A moment before, they'd been in a Denver alley at the beginning of summer; now they found themselves in a more familiar place, the wintry air of late January greeting them as they exited the car. The neon sign above the diner still flickered, hot pink and dirty and perfect.

"I'll just be a minute," she told Miles and Argo. "Wait here."

She entered the diner. Indira was taking a trucker's order at a far booth. A youthful couple drank coffee and smiled shyly at each other near the bar. The crooning of Neil Young warbled out of the jukebox. It was exactly as she'd left it. It was perfect.

"Harper?" She turned and saw Anthony Detweiler in their booth, disheveled and surrounded by a plate of half-eaten fries, a dozen napkins he had nervously shredded into confetti, and three empty coffee mugs. "Where have you been?" he sputtered. "I thought . . . I thought you'd been kidnapped! Or killed! Or disappeared by the goddamn Mafia, for Chrissakes!"

She couldn't help but grin as she sat down. "Anthony Detweiler," she said, "have I got a story for you."

CREDITS

BLACKSTONE PUBLISHING

Chief Executive Officer	JOSH STANTON
Chief Operations Officer	MEGAN BIXLER
Editorial Director	JOSIE WOODBRIDGE
Acquiring Editor	DANIEL EHRENHAFT
Development Editor	DIANA GILL
Managing Editor	ANANDA FINWALL
Print Editor	KATHRYN ZENTGRAF
Cover Designer	ALEX CRUZ
Compositor	AMY CRAIG
Publicist	REBECCA MALZAHN
Marketing	FRANCIE CRAWFORD

BLACKSTONE AUDIO

Narrator	SARAH BETH GOER
Producer	BRYAN BARNEY
Producer	JESSE BRICKFORD

IRENE GOODMAN LITERARY AGENCY

Representation by	VICTORIA MARINI

SPECIAL THANKS
(IN NO PARTICULAR ORDER):

VICTORIA AND DAN:

While you are both of course credited above, I would be remiss in not thanking you more personally for loving and championing this book. Your enthusiasm for this story has meant the difference between *The Infinite Miles* finding a home and not. Thank you from the bottom of my heart.

LAUREN SPIELLER:

I have been chattering at you about this novel for years now, and it was your early encouragement when I was just starting this weird little story that helped push me to finish. Thank you for always being my rock.

BESS MCCALLISTER:

You are always there when I need your very good brain. Thank you for lending an ear and your wisdom when I need it.

BROOKS SHERMAN:

I will forever be indebted to you for your keen eyes and your genuine enthusiasm for this story. This book would not be what it is now without you.

ROMA PANGANIBAN:

You got this book in the way I always hoped someone would. I can't tell you how important that has continually been throughout this process. It made all the difference.

JESSE SUTANTO:

I can always count on you to cheerlead me when I'm uncertain of my own skill. Thank you for being such a wonderful hype man—it meant the difference between an abandoned first act and a finished book.

KT LITERARY:

My KT Literary family have continually cheered on my wins and supported me through the rougher parts of my publishing journey. I'm forever grateful for your guidance and love.

TRACEY BARSKI AND CHELSEA FOUGHT:

Thank you both for being supportive and thoughtful readers and for the generous feedback you provided.

BENJAMIN GARST:

You have always encouraged me, challenged me, and brainstormed with me, and I am forever grateful for your love and support.

MY DEAREST MAMA:

As always, you are my constant. Thank you for reminding me as often as you could that my craft was worth advancing and that my dreams were worth pursuing.

HISTORICAL FIGURES WHOSE STORIES WERE REFERENCED:

ETHEL WINANT:

It's worth mentioning that while in *The Infinite Miles* Sheila is named as one of the first female TV executives, in the real world that honor went to Ethel Winant in 1973, whose stories about working her way up with odd jobs on set and putting her shoes outside the restroom door once she was an executive were used in this book.

THE COMMITTEE:

The Committee was a real committee made up of *Star Trek* fans who organized the very first *Star Trek* convention at the Statler Hilton in 1972, comprised of superfans Joan Winston, Allan Asherman, Eileen Becker, Elyse Pines, Steve Rosenstein, and Al Schuster.